Forest Folk

For Ann,

Best wishes

Alec D'Arcy.

27/6/23

JAMES PRIOR

THE JAMES PRIOR MEMORIAL COMMITTEE,
Hon. Sec., Mr. H. Betts, 1, Middle Pavement, Nottingham.

Forest Folk

By
James Prior

Leen Editions
Nottingham

Published by Leen Editions
Spokesman Books
Russell House
Bulwell Lane
Nottingham, NG6 0BT
England

Phone 0115 9708318
Email elfeuro@compuserve.com

www.spokesmanbooks.com

First published in 1901
This edition published in 2017

Introduction copyright Rowena Edlin-White
Cover copyright Paul Fillingham
Cover designed by Thinkamigo

ISBN 978 1 99973 961 4

Distributed by Central Books
www.centralbooks.com

Printed and bound in Nottingham by Russell Press
www.russellpress.com
0115 9784505

CONTENTS

Chapter		Page

FOREWORD

Rowena Edlin-White

Although not widely read today, the best of Prior's regional fiction anticipates D. H. Lawrence by at least a decade. Lawrence read him and admired him, as did one-time Nottingham journalist, J. M. Barrie. In some respects he represents the next generation of the Sherwood Forest Group of writers and deserves our attention.

Prior was born on Mapperley Road, Nottingham, son of James Kirk, hat-maker, and his wife Sarah. He had the advantage of a private education but was to reject both the law (his father's choice) and millenary. Instead, he aspired to become a writer, cutting his teeth on short stories and plays. After his father's death in 1880, he was obliged to support his sisters in the family business for a while, but escaped as soon as he could, trying his hand at teaching and farming without success.

Eventually, he married his cousin Lily in 1886, and they settled at Lushai Cottage in Bingham, where he gave up trying to get a 'real' job and resumed writing, this time going to the Nottinghamshire countryside and villages for inspiration. At last he had found his genre and several successful novels followed.

Not the first, but best known of Prior's works is the historic novel, *Forest Folk* (1901), set in and around the village of Blidworth by Sherwood Forest during the volatile era of the Luddites in the early 1800s. Southerner Arthur Skrene, travelling to claim an inherited farm, witnesses an episode of violent machine-breaking on the Rufford Road by a group of local activists. One of these is Anthony 'Tant' Rideout, a young farmer whom Skrene will have reason to recognise again. Within the hour, Skrene has also made acquaintance with Rideout's feisty sister, Nell, ploughing the fields of Low Farm in men's clothing. She treats him with some hostility and threatens to smash his gates if she finds them locked – a reference to the infamous enclosures of a few years before.

Bemused, Skrene surveys his inheritance, decides to stay, and sends for his sister Lois to keep house for him. Gradually, Arthur's admiration for Nell's spirited defiance develops into love, and Lois finds herself unaccountably attracted to the rough-and-ready Tant, who saves her from serious assault when a group of local malcontents attack High Farm.

Machine-breaking carried the death penalty after 1812, but Lois saves Tant's neck by testifying in court, only for him to be betrayed by a former mate. Local enmities run high and another embittered local accuses Nell of witchcraft. In a horrific attack, he and his drunken mates try to drown her in a bog, from which she is saved in the nick of time by Arthur Skrene. The plot has all the ingredients of a rollicking historical adventure, but Prior transcends the merely sensational by two supreme gifts: his sense of place and his ear for dialect.

All the places in *Forest Folk* are real, from Blidworth Bottoms to Nottingham Assizes. The local hunt, in which Nell's beloved old horse dies, can be accurately followed across country on an early one-inch map of the area. Blidworth Methodist Chapel and the Parish Church are the backdrops of two untypical love scenes between Lois and Tant (church) and Nell and Arthur (chapel). The local dialect spoken by the Rideouts and their neighbours, strongly contrasted with the Skrene gentry, is a real joy and perfectly intelligible once the reader gets 'their eye in'.

Forest Folk is probably the only Nottingham novel to have had a pub named after it. (I await contradiction on this point.) Built at Blidworth in 1926, four years after Prior's death, the hostelry is now, sadly, demolished, that generous tribute gone forever.

Other titles by Prior include *Renie* (1895), *Ripple and Flood* (1897), *Hyssop* (1904), *A Walking Gentleman* (1907) and *Fortuna Chance* (1910).

Prior died at Banks Cottage, Bingham in 1922 and is buried (as James Prior Kirk, along with his wife Lily and their sons) in Bingham Cemetery, near the railings alongside the Grantham Road.

Places to visit

Blidworth Take the A60 Mansfield Road to Ravenshead and turn right at Larch Farm, following Main Road to Blidworth Bottoms near where 'Low Farmhouse' (home of the Rideouts) and 'High Farm' (the Skrenes' farm) are placed. High Farm is supposed to be Heywood Oaks Farm, which may be admired from the road. Prior mentions the 'primeval oaks', the remains of the ancient forest, on the adjoining land.

Fishpool (the original name for Ravenshead), the Druid Stones and Rainworth, all mentioned in *Forest Folk*, are close by.

Bingham Lushai Cottage is on Fisher Lane, Bingham. It no longer bears the name, but a Bingham Heritage Trail leaflet is available free from the local Library, which shows where it is. Banks Cottage was round the corner on The Banks.

Nottingham Stand on the corner of Forest Road and Mansfield Road, opposite Saint Andrew's Church – this was Gallows Hill. Lois, Nell and her sister Tish rode this way to the assizes and shuddered at the thought that Tant's body might soon be hanging there.

Dr Tony Shaw has written at some length about Prior on his excellent blog and I am grateful for his help (see http://tonyshaw3.blogspot.co.uk).

Discover more 'forgotten' local authors in Exploring Nottinghamshire Writers *by Rowena Edlin-White, published by Five Leaves.*

Dawn of the UNREAD

When the dead go unread...

There's gonna be trouble!

- WINNER -

theguardian University Awards 2015

Nottingham City of Literature Illustration: Andy Tozer

JAMES
WALKER
PRODUCER/EDITOR

PAUL
FILLINGHAM
ART/DIGITAL PRODUCER

ADRIAN REYNOLDS - PANEL BEATER

WAYNE BURROWS - RESEARCH

CHAPTER I

FROM SOMEWHERE UP'ARDS

IT was on a day in the early years of the just defunct century. A horseman with some marks of travel upon him was riding northwards from the county town of Nottinghamshire, after a leisurely fashion which seemed to show that his journey was either of no pressing importance or was nearing its end. His way lay through the southern portion of Sherwood Forest, which nominally was almost as extensive as in the reckoning of the Doomsday Book and still had its full staff of officers, the Lord Warden with his bow-bearer, ranger and steward, his verdurers, keepers and woodwards; but in reality had been sadly despoiled at the hand both of enclosure and of illiberal waste. The noble trees which a hundred years ago had made a thick unintermittent shade from Mansfield to Nottingham had gone and left no trace save here and there a clump of scrubby oak, here and there a solitary veteran naked to every wind. Arnold and Calverton were being fast brought under cultivation, and though much of Bestwood and Papplewick was still barren moor, it was not until the traveller left the Mansfield road just after the fifth milestone that he came upon a scene of unreclaimed wildness.

It was a day of an ever-varying greyness, as the days are grey in November under a brisk south-west wind, when the sun is never quite successful in breaking through the clouds, never completely in prison behind them. Snow had fallen the day before, rain in the night; there were reminders of both in the dull glimmer of the wayside puddles, in the narrow strips of white by hedge and bank, under furrow and bush, or occasionally in larger patches on the sunless side of a hill. The afternoon of such a day did not show such a country to the best advantage; an undulating expanse covered as far as the eye could reach with green gorse, brown bracken, grey ling. A horseman's cursory glance would hardly be caught by the scanty gleam of yellow amid the gorse, which true to the proverb that it goes out of bloom only when kissing goes out of fashion, showed here and there the peep of a warmer colour between its sombre spikes. There was no shelter anywhere from the keenness of the wind. The fallow deer, which when the then old men were young had browsed the sward in large herds, were gone, as the trees under which they had harboured were gone. But there were plenty of rabbits.

The occasional little movements of the traveller's shoulders under the cape of his great-coat may have been shiver as much as shrug, but there could be no mistaking the disapprobation of the quick critical glances which he cast about him. Probably he was comparing the outlook with more genial scenery which he had lately quitted; a country possibly of better roads for one thing. The road he was then following was much like a sheep-trail, being nothing more than a trodden track, sometimes sandy, sometimes grassy, winding between gorse and gorse. He began to fear that he had missed his way. There was no house in sight, no wayfarer on the road, no shepherd on the hills, no sound of labour; only the whistle of the wind and the wail of the never-resting peewheep. He was the better pleased therefore, when he had ridden thus some three or four miles, to see before him a carrier's van travelling in the same direction as himself. He put his horse to a quicker motion in order that he might overtake it and make inquiry of the driver. But when he was yet some thirty yards distant, suddenly half a dozen fellows rudely masked with black, two or three of them having pistols in their hands and one a blacksmith's sledge-hammer, jumped out of the bushes and surrounded the van. The horseman hastily pulled up, astonished at what had every appearance of being an act of highway robbery. There was no loss of time. One pair of hands stopped the carrier's horse, another pair dragged the carrier himself down from his seat, while two or three of the ruffians jumped in back and front and forthwith began to pitch the contents of the cart out into the road; some heavy sort of hardware they appeared to be, parts of machinery or the like. But the men's purpose, it seemed, was destructive rather than thievish, for as each article fell with steely glitter to the ground, the man with the sledge-hammer smote it to shivers. The rider particularly noticed that man, the man indeed was particularly noticeable; a tall lithe fellow with hair red or reddish, of a frame magnificently proportioned and to judge by the ease with which he did his destructive work of remarkable strength. The driver stood by, apparently more chagrined than surprised. So far as could be heard not a word was uttered either by him or his despoilers.

But presently the latter appeared to remark and resent the presence of an on-looker. A couple of them made towards him armed with pistols; townsmen they looked like, of the artisan sort, in ragged cloth coats and greasy breeches. Evidently the horseman thought it more prudent not to await their coming, for he turned about and galloped off. But as soon as he was fairly out of pistol-shot he again reined in and looked back. The two men stood watching him, and with threatening wafts of the hand seemed to be bidding him continue his retreat. He did so, and soon a dip in the road hid them completely from his view.

What should he do? The day was on the wane, the country was unknown to him, there was nobody to question. He did the best he could, he continued his backward course until the road divided, and then turned off down a sandy trail, on his right hand as it happened. Again and again he

turned – tracks were plentiful, of sheep or men – hoping by
so doing to recover his former direction; but there was still
the gorse upon every hand and never a sign of a house.
Many a time he spoke ill of a country which had neither
road nor inhabitant, nor anywhere a friendly finger-post for
the information of belated travellers.

At length he came where a rain-swollen brook crossed
his path. On his right its waters were held up by a dam, and
widened out into a marshy pool bordered by willows and
overgrown with rush, sedge and persicaria, the haunt of
water-fowl. The opposite bank was for a short distance at
any rate impracticable, being the almost precipitous
termination of a low spur from the more considerable hills
beyond. His way being thus indicated for him he pulled his
left rein, gave his back to what there was of the sun and
followed the stream's course. After a while he saw straight
before him a curl of smoke and a roof; the roof low and
humbly thatched, the smoke issuing from a single
dilapidated chimney, but both a welcome sight in such a
wilderness. At his approach he found it to be a wayside
alehouse of the meanest, a one-storied "mud and stud"
erection, situated at the crossing of two ways somewhat
better marked than those he had for the last hour been
finding and losing.

A man was coming out of the door as he drew up to it, a
man of the town artisan sort, in clothes much worn and
begrimed with swarth. He did not carry a pistol nor wear
crape on his nose, yet the rider immediately bethought
himself of the lawless gang who had driven him from the
road. But the man seeing him had at once drawn back into
the house. The stranger did not like the look of the house
any the better for the sample offered him of the company it
held; but while he hesitated between calling for the host and
passing on, another man came to the door, a sturdy thick-
necked low-browed burglarious-looking fellow. If he were
the host, he had nothing of the host about him but his dirty

white jacket and his red nose.

"How far am I from Blidworth, pray?" asked the horseman.

The man seemed disinclined to answer at all, but after a look and a pause said surlily:

"I'm i' Blid'orth, yo're i' Cauverton; an' if yo want ayther Farnsfield or Oxton, they're the tother side the road."

"Thank you. And which is the way to the village of Blidworth? I presume there is more village than this."

The man uncrooked a surly grimy reluctant finger and pointed; the horseman again thanked him and rode away. But he had not gone twenty yards before he heard a loud voice behind him, another voice:

"Tek the first turn to the raight."

He looked quickly round, and even as he looked what he saw in the doorway of the inn vanished from it; the tall youthful figure of a man finely formed and crowned with long red or reddish hair. He was almost sure he had seen it before; there wanted but a sledge-hammer and a bit of crape to complete his recognition. He put his horse to the quick trot, willing to change his neighbourhood as soon as might be. In five minutes he came where an ill-defined track crossed that which he was pursuing. He doubted whether he should go by the inn-keeper's finger or the correction of the younger man; but the view to his right on the top of a straight-chined hill, perhaps two or three miles away, of a church and a mill standing out with grey indistinctness from the cloudy horizon determined him; he turned to the right up a sandy rise. On either side of him the gorse and heather had recently been fired. Their charred remains and grey sodden ashes made a sorry contrast with the snow that glimmered in the hollows. After that there was a stretch of land from which the gorse-roots had been grubbed and part of it brought under the plough. Then where the descent began there were fences, crops of turnips, winter tares, potatoes and peeping wheat; and down in the hollow a farmhouse, or it might be two adjacent cottages of different altitudes, the higher thatched, the lower tiled. The horseman rode down towards the house, but as he was about to pass through a field-gate leading thereto, he saw on the other side of the way a plough-boy turning his team of three near the hedge. He was partly obscured by the smoke which issued from a row of burning heaps in the adjacent enclosure, and swept over ridge and furrow at the wildly capricious pleasure of the wind; sometimes like a thick scudding mist barely a man's height above the ground, or rarefied to a diaphanous veil ever shifting, every varying. As the horseman was about to address the plough-boy there was a momentary lull, the smoke rose straight into the air, the field was clear before him. He could see the scarlet glow of some of the heaps, the brown smouldering of others, and the labourer plodding to and fro tending them. Beyond which there was an inconsiderable breadth of plough-land, then moor until it touched the November sky persistently, varyingly grey. The plough-boy had turned his team on the headland, and now stood resting on the hales and looking at him; the stripling who acted as driver but just indicated by the projection of a long whip over the back of the leader.

"Is that Blidworth yonder?" asked the horseman.

"Eh? Blid'orth? Ah, yon's Blid'orth," answered the plough-boy.

"Thank Heaven for that!" said the horseman heartily.

The lull was brief, the wind boisterously renewed its sport, the fires crackled and roared or smoked and smouldered; the air was filled with the puther. The plough-boy, leaving his plough, came to the hedge-side and fixed a pair of remarkable grey eyes upon his questioner.

"Yo're from somewheer up'ards, I reckon?" he shouted in shrill competition with the wind.

The rider did not understand or did not choose to answer, but pointing to the building on the other side of the road said:

"What may the name of that house be?"

"My question's as good as yourn, *I* reckon," said the plough-boy.

There was a certain shrill unusualness in the plough-boy's style of address; the rider did not ride on, as one might have expected; he was pleased for the moment to amuse himself.

"Somewhere upwards? I don't quite know – I know what 'uppishness' means. Perhaps ..."

"Let it stan' at that," said the plough-boy with unexpected promptitude. Apparently he was willing to take his own question as answered, for he continued:

"It's the Low Farmhouse, that is."

"The Low Farmhouse? And I am in search of the High Farm. Can you direct me?"

The plough-boy pointed out a conspicuous white house about half a mile off, on the crown of a slope which rose behind the Low Farmhouse.

"And how shall I best get there?"

"Turn to the raight when yo get to the Bottoms." The plough-boy pointed to a little cluster of houses at the foot of Blidworth Hill. "From theer yo may cross the fields; as straight as yo like; it's their own land. Mebbe yo're the new man at High Farm?"

But the horseman's complaisance was exhausted; he made no answer; with a jerk of the reins he put his steed to a walk. Just at that moment – his careless eyes were still on the plough-boy – a sudden gust blew the boy's hat off; boy's hat or man's, but immediately there fell about its wearer's shoulders such a mass of fine long hair as only women are permitted to display, lustrous waves of that eloquent hue which is nearest to red but not red. Whereupon the rider also saw through the smoke and the hedge what had escaped him before, a short breadth womanish skirt between the hem of the old blue smock-frock and the drab cloth gaiters. Whether it were out of curiosity or a larger courtesy, he again reined his horse in and made answer: "I have come to walk over the farm." The woman in plough-boy's guise let her hat lie, and holding back her wind-blown hair with both hands looked him over as though she began to take an interest in him. She saw a quick-eyed well-dressed young man, rather slightly made but remarkably vigorous and alert-looking. He was clean-shaven but for the small close whiskers half down the cheek, and his dark brown hair was neatly tied up in a club that hung below the nape of his neck. He appeared to be about twenty-five years of age, and was mounted on an excellent roadster. His broad-brimmed hat, his long-skirted riding-coat and cape, his top-boots and chamois-leather gloves, his silver-mounted whip and spurs, all in good unpretentious style, gave him the appearance of a man of considerable taste and means; if a farmer, certainly one of the bettermost, fit to rank next to the squire himself. Did her scrutiny take in so small a feature as his nose, she would perceive it to be slightly finely aquiline.

He returned her direct gaze so candidly resolute with a glance which was amused rather than interested, of which indeed the most noticeable quality was perhaps an air of careless superiority. And yet even to criticism so negligent as his it seemed strange that such a face should be associated with a labourer's threadbare frock, none too clean, a labourer's shoes and gaiters all patched and mired, a labourer's old leathern gloves. The labourer's hat lay under the hedge whither the wind had blown it. He noticed the broad brow with a scattering of freckles about the temples, the healthy weather-tanned cheeks, the lips of glowing red, the largish mouth, the straight nose, the stature above the mean, and with equal accuracy and coolness how the wind brought the smell of the burning heaps and a few flakes of whitey ash.

"That's a middling hoss of yourn; what price do yer put upon him?"

She spoke as self-collectedly as though she had been all the time examining the animal and not his master.

"He is not for sale," answered the latter rather stiffly.

"Well, he's nobbut a hack when all's said and done."

The sun must have forced a rift in the clouds, for over her head he distinctly saw the under-wings of a flock of peewheeps flash white as they wheeled and wheeled again in elaborate manoeuvre, flash like a thousand little mirrors set to catch the sun. But its rays did not directly strike the ground; the disconsolate snow by the hedge showed bluely grey in the waning light. Again he was starting as she called shrilly after him:

"Well, I hope yo'll be easier to get on wee nor he was."

The rider again stayed his horse, though there seemed little or no reason for his so doing, and fixed his dark eyes keenly upon her.

"Why," he asked, "do you express such a hope?"

"Becos we're none so easy to get on wee oursens, so we look to hae extry good neighbours."

"In what respect did you find the late tenant not easy to get on with?"

"In respect of a gate, first and foremost."

"In respect of gates probably I shall do as he did."

"Then probably we shall do as we did."

"What was that?"

"Smash 'em."

His dark fiery eye threw a menace forth.

"Madam, I beg leave to hope you won't."

He raised his hat, but when he seemed to be going for the fifth or sixth time, yet he did not go. Perhaps there was the not unmanly dislike to leaving a woman with a threat upon his face. He pointed with his whip to the springing wheat on the other side of the road, among which intrusive beans were thickly showing.

"If that's your wheat, I see your beans shelled a good deal this year."

Which apparently she resented more than cause was.

"Mebbe yourn don't on light land i' dry seasons."

There seemed nothing then to stay his going in reality; but on the sudden as it appeared to him, for his perception of it was sudden, the part of the sky farthest from the sun was lit up with a glare which loaded the atmosphere with an eye-troubling ruddiness. The smouldering heaps of rubbish on the headland smoked purple; the restless peewheeps still circling in the sky flashed red instead of white; the wan snow in the furrows put on a blush. But even while he looked on this and that a flood of crimson glory poured through the break in the clouds, growing and growing, as overflows do once the little rift is made, until the whole west was ablaze with orange, purple and violet. Clouds might have been inflammable, and the torch of the sun a near danger. The slant splendour slid down to the cold earth and rested on it.

The woman had stepped aside to where her hat lay in the ditch, and there she stood gathering the abundance of her hair into a loose coil. The smoke was round and about her like a cloud, but a rose-tinted luminous cloud, sky-born, ever-changing into new beauty. Where it was thicker there was the more colour, and where rarer the more light. And she herself had suffered equal transmutation. The smock frock no longer looked sordid, the leathern gloves uncouth; but the face! Surely it was not the same face which he had examined a moment before with the coolest negligence. The freckles and the tan had disappeared. A carmine radiance seemed to issue from the fine curves of her thin cheeks; but it burned among her hair, which was now red of reds; flames ran along the silky threads of its twisted tangles. Either ear was a hanging transparency, flame-tinctured; and behind her surged, ever lessening and increasing, the billows of smoke, from palest rose to darkest purple. Out of such a sea perhaps, Tyrian-dyed but with the effulgence of her own body, Aphrodite first uprose between Cyprus and Cythera; the air shuddered with a red gladness. But this was no Aphrodite. Her eyes were unchanged, grey and grave.

From her different point of view she evidently did not see in the man the miraculous alteration which he saw in her. His wondering gaze amused her for a little while, then perplexed her, incensed her. At last she cried out:

"Yo mean to know me when yo see me again."

He awoke; but as a man awakes suddenly; the sleep has left his eyes but not his brain. He muttered a confused word of apology, turned his horse and rode slowly away.

As he rode, the short-lived magnificence died out. The wind dropped. Grey became the sky again, grey the air; the earth and the snow were mere differences in greyness. The smoke rose straight up, merely brown. He was ashamed of his late enchantment; he was minded to ride back and disabuse his mind, make sure of the freckles about the temples, the wind-beaten skin, the sordid apparel. He had pulled the off-rein and half turned before he was fully aware of his folly. Besides her eyes would have been unchanged, gravely greyly fixed upon him. Across the field her voice was blown shrilly to him as she shouted to her driver and her horses:

"Auve, auve a bit! Steady, Tidy! Whitefoot, yo sloomy!"

He put spurs to his horse and galloped off in his proper direction. Only for a minute however, for as he reached the turn in the road and the little cluster of houses which she had called the Bottoms, a child ran across before him and obliged him to rein up hard. The child, a sturdy boy, did not seem in the least concerned either about his danger or his escape; he had been calling an old woman who stood at the door of one of the cottages, and he continued to call her.

"Witch!" he cried with the insolence of a safe distance. "Witch! Wheer's yer broom-stick? Len's it; I should like a ride on't."

He approached her and chucked a stone after his words. But when she turned her almost sightless eyes upon him he fled back; only however to renew his verbal insults.

"Witch! Witch! Len's yer broom-stick, witch! Do, witch!"

An old, old woman leaning palsy-shaken on a crutched stick, with snow-white hair, snow-white eyebrows and lashes, snow-white moustache and a crop of snow-white bristles on her chin. Of a strange whiteness too was the wrinkled skin, both of cheek and of the trembling hand which she held up to shield her eyes, as though even that grey waning light were too much for them. She looked towards the horseman, wagging her head, but whether her attention were directed by sight or hearing was doubtful.

"Witch, witch!" cried the urchin. "Who killed Morley's blue cow? Gie's yer mop-stale, I want a ride on't."

But a sickly-looking woman issuing from a cottage on his own side of the road came round the corner, took him by the shoulders and soundly berated and cuffed him.

"Yo little rascad!" she said. "I'll gie yer a bensaling the next time, see if I don't. If she be a witch, yer soft sawny, the more reason to speak 'er fair. What's other folks's cows an' coughs to huz? On'y do't again, on'y do!"

Amid which confusion of blows, abuse and promise both disappeared within-doors. The old woman dropped her quaking hand and tottered into her own house. The horseman rode through the fields towards the High Farm, as he had been directed. Dimmer grew the light; the patches of grey snow looked colder than the white had done. Down across the valley, three-quarters of a mile off, he could still descry the burning heaps, the smoke, the plough and its team, she who directed them appearing just such a crawling earthy animal as they. But in his thought there would needs be yet some ray of that fugitive glory about her rude semblance.

CHAPTER II

BY THE FIRESIDE

MEANWHILE the young woman continued following the plough until she had turned a couple of furrows more; then she left the driver to unhook Tidy, Whitefoot and their unnamed comrade from the clivvers, and herself strode before them to the small irregular building which we have already heard named as the Low Farmhouse. She entered by the gate, stood in the yard and holloaed, "Tant, Tant!" As soon as she raised her voice dogs began to bark, pigs to squeal, calves to blawt, horses to whinny; but there was no other answer. It was dusk and the promised rain had begun to fall. Thrice she holloaed, "Tant, Tant!" but as it seemed without any heart in her calling; then a woman opened the housedoor and answered her with loud harsh voice:

"Yo nedn't call *him*. And Lambert's gone home wi' his gethered hand bad. And Spettigew hain't coom back yet from the ship. I've milked the cows an' suppered the fat beast mysen."

Again the door was shut; the only cheerful thing to be seen was the glimmer of a candle through the window next the door. The plough-horses came in before their driver and with heavy clumsy foot blundered into their proper stalls. The young woman went into the house, brought thence a lighted lantern, set the boy Dick to look after the pigs and herself proceeded to the stable. From the farthest end of the long dark shed came a gentle whinnying.

"Bide a bit, sweetheart," she said with a glance thitherwards and a remarkable softening of the voice.

"Labouring folk moot be sarved; the quallity can wait."

At those words a greyhound came dancing delicately down out of the greater into the less obscurity and offered herself to attention, a beautiful fawn-coloured bitch. She received a kindly smoothing of the silk-clad skin between her ears, and then a "There, lass, there!"

The hound with cold nose uplifted to warm hand seemed to protest against the brevity of the caress.

"Down, Treasure, down! I'm throng to-night."

There was something of sternness in the tone. The bitch immediately desisted, and with dainty deliberation tripped back over the rough stones into the dark. The woman set before each of her roughhaired thick-steaming fellow-labourers two or three carrots and a moderate allowance of chaff, which they munched while she carefully rubbed them down. That done she went up to the innermost partition, where an old hunter was stalled. The greyhound lay under his manger.

"Yo were a good oad Hasty," she said stroking the horse's fine glossy brown coat, "to let me tend to the commoners first. I mun hae come, yo know, if yo'd stood on your raights."

The old horse twisted his lithe thin neck, put his fine muzzle over her shoulder, and with a low deep quavering from the bottom of his chest grunted his contentment.

She had given the calves their hay and carrots when Spettigew came from the sheep; two of the hogs had been missing from his count and he had been long in finding them. She left the watering and suppering-up of the horses to him and went into the house. The blazing coal fire and the light were a pleasant change from the wet and darkness of without, though the light was but from one home-made tallow dip on the round central table.

"It's raining," she said, and that seemed to express her satisfaction at the change.

"*He's* none getting wet," said crustily enough the woman

who had spoken to her from the door.

The latter was perhaps some thirty years old, stout and tall and sufficiently like the other in feature and complexion to suggest sisterhood. Her red hair was partly hidden by a white cap with a purple ribbon; she had a blue kerchief pinned about her ample breast, but her neck was bare. Bare too were her strong red arms from where the sleeves of her dark-brown linsey-woolsey gown ceased at the elbow. She was bustling to and fro, white-aproned, laying the table for supper, like a woman who has much upon her hands. Not another word was said. The new-comer put off her damp soiled outer garments and then in her new slimness appeared much younger than before, being evidently but on the threshold of womanhood. Above her short light-red petticoat she wore in place of bodice a long-sleeved snuff-coloured jacket, gathered at her waist with a leathern belt. She changed her miry foot-gear for shoes of a more feminine fashion, and then went straight to the fire which burnt in a huge outstanding chimney-nook, which took up nearly the whole of that side of the room. She sat down on the floor, stretched her legs across the hearth in front of the generous blaze, and leant her head back against the petticoats of an old woman who sat in an ancient arm-chair in the warmest corner.

Hitherto the old woman had sat stroking her knees with her eyes fixed on the opposite wall of the chimney, and apparently giving little heed to what was going on. Now however she passed an age-blemished hand gently over the girl's locks, and said in an old woman's croak:

"How comes tha hair to be so wet, child?"

"I've been to the Bottoms to see gret-granmam."

"Are ta wetchud[1] too?"

"No, granmam; I've shifted my shoes."

"That's raight. Let foot be warm an' heäd cool."

"I will, granmam."

1. Wet-shod the grandmother's hands lingered among the

girl's tresses, with the other she renewed the stroking of the knee nearer the fire. She kept her eyes fixed on the opposite wall of the chimney and said no more. At her elbow stood an ancient spinning-wheel. The girl lay in the languor of weariness along the hearth, and let the fire do as it would with her. One of her legs was so near to it that the heat stung her through the blue worsted stocking, but she was too inert to withdraw it ever so little. The blaze shone full on her face until it was scorched to the colour of a peony; she blinked her eyes lazily and let it scorch. The dim candle had no influence within the chimney, where the colours taken, the shadows cast with varying differences were of the fire's gift. It lighted with its capricious illumination what it would of the beldame's long skinny neck and rigid head, stiffly outstanding from the skimpy black gown, of the eyes ever fixed on the opposite wall and of the hand that stroked the knee. It flamed in the girl's hair turning the part most exposed to it to the reddest gold; what lay in the shade was the obscurest of autumnal browns. It deepened, if it did not create, the languorous lustre of her large grey eyes. It lavished of its own warm colouring on the many folds, creases and crinkles of her old red petticoat. One of her knees was slightly bent, and the long deep furrow thus made adown the skirt was as a narrow pool filled almost to the brim with a dusky fluid, uncertain, gleamless, like dead blood. Far up the chimney a sooty cavity was displayed, whence issued strange roarings and rumblings, soamings and meanings as the wind came and went.

But beyond the fitful fringes of the fire's red predominance the colder, hardly more certain light of the tallow dip shared a wavering victory with the shadows, whose flitting unranked troops, routed though they were from the white extent of the table-cloth, still disputed every inch of the well-sanded red-brick floor and of the white-washed walls which bounded it; while all the nooks and corners and especially the timbers of the open ceiling they possessed undisturbed. Still the light, such as it was, served here to reveal, there to suggest the homely details of an apartment which was living-room, kitchen and scullery of farming folk of the humbler sort; many-doored, draughty, sparely furnished, but scrupulously clean. The heaped fire and the table spread with coarse plenty upon a clean cloth gave the whole an air of rude comfort. An open staircase set against the wall opposite to the chimney led to the sleeping chambers. The elder of the sisters went to and fro amid the unstable lights and shadows preparing the meal, fetching and taking away, straining potatoes, frugally mashing the tea, liberally carving the cold boiled pork garnished with carrots and the quartern loaf of wheat and barley mixed.

The old woman by the fire woke up from a brief doze, during which her hand had ceased to smooth her knee, and said:

"I doubt yo forgot to goo an' see how mother is to-day."

"No, granmam, I've been," answered the girl, "I telled yer so."

"Telled me? Well, tell me again. A oad tale forgotten's as good as a fresh un new gotten."

"She's middling, granmam. Her head's a little better and her feet's a little worser. She telled me to tell yer there's noat like horehound and Robin-run-i'-th'-hedge for a cough."

"One on's mun hae a cough," said the old woman; "or she'll be offended."

So far the girl had spoken in a slightly raised key, which suggested that the person whom she addressed was a little hard of hearing; now she dropped her voice to its ordinary pitch. What she said seemed rather meant for the fire than for her sister who was just then busy at a side-table out of sight.

"I catched Spettigew's Tommy calling her and pelting her door wi' stones, the gallous young Turk. I gied him a jacketing, not hafe what he desarved though, and I telled him I was going to be a witch some day mysen, if I'd the luck to live long enough, and if he didn't behave hissen different the first person I witched suld be him."

"The bigger fool yo, our Nell," was the curt answer from the side-table.

When presently the last speaker came to the centre-table and within sight she added:

"A crack-pot's speech like thatn may be remembered agen yer long after yo've clean forgot it yoursen."

"Let it," said the girl carelessly.

"Yo talk!" answered the other scornfully. "As if bad reports curcheyed an' axed leave afore settling on yer back!"

The girl straightened her bent knee and lolled yet more luxuriously against her grandmother in the full blaze of the fire.

"Tish, I've seed the new man at High Farm," she said.

"What's he like?" said Tish, pausing in the act of removing a saucepan from the fire.

"He's a little un, and he's a dark un, and he wears Lunnon clo'es, and he looks at a body as if he were head Sir Rag. I've spoken to him."

"Is he civil spoken?"

"He een't mealy-mouthed. He rides a good hoss."

"Who's that yo're talkin' on?" said the old woman, apparently just waking up.

"Oad Bagshaw's nephew, granmam, him he's willed the farm to, yo know. The moment I glegged him I reckoned him up. I axed him if he warn't from somewheer up'ards. He axed me what I meant, if I meant as he looked uppish. I *might* ha' said 'yes.'"

"Why didn't yer then?" asked the elder sister.

"I believe the smoke were in my eyes and I were minding that."

"Pugh! I believe i' saying what yer think. Specially to strangers; they might get a wrong impression on's."

Dick the plough-driver slipt in, not opening the door an

inch wider than necessary; a pale stunted lad ill-clothed. His look was towards Tish and apologetic of the weather; he took the place at the table farthest from her and the fire; whereupon he was sharply bidden draw up and warm himself. Nell's eyes were still on the blaze and her thoughts languorously persistent.

"He looks keen an' all, but not just our sort o' keen."

"I don't like other sorts o' folk," said Tish decidedly.

"I don't ower much, but –" Nell mused with her eyes languorously searching the fire, "but – he rode a good hoss. And there een't a good hoss that een't my sort."

Spettigew came in from the yard dropping wet, and was ordered out again by Tish to cleanse his clarty shoes by the application of scraper to sole and besom to upper.

"I'm not a-gooing to hae my clean floor mucked up wi' yo men paddling in an' out."

That done he hung up his frock and limp hat to drip by the door, and sat down to the table at the place vacated by Dick with the heavy satisfaction of a tired man. He was a heavy man altogether, slow-motioned, unexpectant, such a one as would make no calculation as to the supper presently to be set before him; at the most there would perhaps be a dim hope hardly stirring the salivary glands, that it might be hot, succulent and abundant.

"Say grace, Nell," said Tish in the voice of command, standing over the ready table.

The girl raised herself to her knees, put her hands together, closed her eyes and said grace, as she had probably done in childhood, the first few words distinctly enough, the rest in an undivided gabble.

"For what we are about to receive thLordelpstbetrool-thankflamen."

Then she reclined back against the aged knees; she looked as though a feather might sway her.

"Ain't yo cooming to the table?" said Tish.

"I'm as well here," said Nell lazily.

"I don't ho'd wi' bein' so nesh," said Tish.

However, she brought Nell's plate of meat, vegetables and bread, set it on her knee and put a cup of tea by her side. That was the women's fare; there was a mug of home-brewed ale for the man and a hornful for the boy. As they ate, the few needful words about the food before them were but thinly interspersed with remarks about to-day's and to-morrow's weather and its influence on flock and crop. At every hush of the wind the perpendicular rain hissed in the chimney, and forthwith was again driven aslant upon the window-panes. They felt it if they did not hear, and their sense of it coloured their indoor comfort. Spettigew was the last to finish eating, but at length even he pushed back his chair along the sanded floor and rose. Nell also rose and said:

"I mun hae yo here and agate by six to-morrer, Bill Spettigew. Put your clock on hafe an hour. To begin wi' yo can do an hour's thrashing wi' Lambert. Yo nedn't reckon on Tant seeing to the hosses; for he wain't. When yo fother the beäst don't gie 'em so much hay, they nubbut traddle and waste it. Remember the sauve for the gilt's ears."

The alert authoritative way in which she stood and spoke was in singular contrast to the lackadaisical attitude of the moment before. Spettigew had been donning his moist frock and hat, and now with no more answer than a gruff "Good-night" went forth into the rain.

Dick was sidling out after him as though willing to be covered by his departure, but was recalled by Tish.

"What are yer gooing to do as soon as yo get home?" she asked with the severity of a magisterial inquisition.

"Help mother wi' the children," the lad faltered.

"Noat o' th' sort; yo're gooing to hull them wet things off and skelter off to bed. I shall ax yer to-morrer if yo did. How's mother?"

"She's no wuss."

"That such a poor cratur suld hae so many children's one

o' the mysteries o' Providence. One's tempted to think they're scattered about as random as pepper drizzles out'n a brucken caster. I doubt she'll mek noat out on yer all. And now be off wi' yer."

But as she so rudely bundled him out, she pushed into his hands a paper containing the remains of the cold pork from the table. Nell having risen did not return to her couch; she set briskly to work helping her sister to clear the supper-table and wash up. The grandmother had sat silent a long while with her eyes fixed on the opposite wall of the chimney.

"Now, granmam," said Tish, "it's past eight o'clock time."

"I heerd it strike," said the old woman.

But still she sat.

"He'll none coom. He's bin to the door two or three times a'ready an' said, 'Dal, how it rains!' and then turned again to the fire."

The grandmother said no more; she rose to her feet; Nell took her by the hand and led her up-stairs. From her manner of doing so it was evident the old woman was blind. Half an hour later the household was abed; save one.

About midnight there were heavy unsteady steps outside, a rude opening of the door, an unregulated trampling over the bricks. If Nell were asleep she was a light sleeper, for almost immediately she came down-stairs hastily draped with no mark of sleep about her eyes. The candle she carried showed the new-comer to be a tall young man, finely formed, completely drunk. His clothes – dark-green coat, pink waistcoat, drab breeches, brown boots – were as though sodden, and were besides as plentifully bedaubed from top to toe as if he had fallen in the road and wallowed there. His face, his tangled hair, of the same hue as Nell's, under a damaged felt hat, bore similar disorderly marks of the weather and rough usage. A white terrier which had come in with him had suffered equally from the rain and the roads, but was apparently sober. The man glanced at

Nell with a stupefied blink, so different from the gaze of her own clear grey.

"Well, Nell!" he said thickly. "It's rainin'. Drot it, how it does rain! Wheer'sh Tish? I tho't yo'd all be abed."

"Tek your boots off," said Nell.

She helped him to find a chair, she brought the bootjack, she held the candle. He tugged awkwardly at his miry top-boots, tugged and desisted and tugged again. The terrier had coiled himself up under the grandmother's chair out of the way of men's feet or other notice.

"There'sh to be a ratting at Gill's next week. I've put a sovereign on Mosley's Patty. For yo, Nell. Dang it, how it does rain! Hark at it! Yo're a good wench, Nell, an' g-good-looking."

"Be sharp wi' your boots," said Nell.

"Tom Bradley bauges 'bout his Polly. Damn Tom Bradley's Polly!" He brought his large fist down mightily upon the table, so that it resounded hollowly and seemed to try to hop on its stiff-kneed legs. The terrier looked up, but seeing it was all about nothing coiled himself again tighter than ever. "Tha'sh all I care for Tom B – Bradley. Or Tom'sh Polly ayther."

"Yo'll wakken Tish," said Nell. "What a fool yo are!"

"So am, so am. Bu' not such a fool ash" – here he looked at her with sudden sodden gravity – "ash by my actions m-might be sh'posed."

Nell did not say whether she saw any difference between his own wisdom and that of his actions; she said nothing. The boot-drawing made little progress; she knelt down and with hand to filthy heel dragged them off herself.

"Now coom to bed," she said.

But he settled himself on his chair; the scattered embers of a filmed red still in the grate did not even suggest warmth.

"Coom to bed wi' yer!"

"'M all raight 'ere; 'm not gooin' nowheer."

His eyes were already shut,

"By guy, but yo are!"

She set down the candle, and with a burst of astonishing energy in so girlish a frame lifted him to his feet. He showed no surprise at his change of posture; his obstinacy seemed to have been left in the slumber from which he had been awakened; he suffered himself to be led to the foot of the stairs. There his obstinacy also awoke, tardily; he turned again towards the sullen hearth. But she stood in his way.

"No, Tant, yo don't!"

Thrice he returned, and thrice she turned him back, as a shepherd withstands the wilfulness of a solitary sheep. Then he seemed to abandon his obstinacy, as the sheep seems; he stumbled up some half-dozen of the stairs. But there he sat down, lay down, sank down, and was immediately submerged in a deep sleep. Nell took him roughly by the legs and dragged him, bump, bump, bump! – three several jolts had his head – to the bottom of the stairs. Even for that he did not wake; he lay at the bottom like a log. The dog under the chair whined uneasily, as though feeling for his master's insensibility. In vain Nell strove to set him on his legs again; the dead resistance of his large frame was too much for her.

For a minute or two she stood looking down on him. What her thoughts were could only be got at by the unintimate process of conjecture. She uttered no word. Her face was turned from the candle's dim scrutiny. The bowing of the head is the natural posture of one who looks down; a shiver which runs through the body may be the physical effect of cold. But whether she felt the night chill or no upon her scantily clad person, she did not stand long. She went hastily and reached down a heavy hunting crop which hung on the outside of the chimney wall; then taking the candle as though to light her to its exact application, she smote him several times smartly about his legs and body. The first stroke or two he did not seem to feel; at succeeding ones he stirred uneasily as though a dream of blows troubled him;

but at last one must have lighted on a feeling part, for up he sprang with an oath, suddenly awake, white wrath on his face, his fist back drawn for the return. Terribly strong he looked and terribly angry. The dog came just out from under the chair and looked on whimpering a little, as in a deprecation that expected nothing. Nell made no effort to escape or ward off the threatened blow; she stood straight up, pale but dauntless, and held the candle high as if to light its aim. But the blow did not fall; or not visibly.

"Damn it, was it yo, Nell?"

"It was, Tant."

He laughed; she did not, or not outwardly.

"Yo did lay on, damn yer."

"Don't say so, Tant!" she said with pale sternness. "It's a fearful thing to say unless yo mean it. If yo mean it I've noat again it."

"Mean it? Bless yer, lass, I meant no more nor if I'd said, 'Bless yer.' I' my opinion this here damnation's like the French invasion; plenty o' talk, but no sign. Every mouth's as full on't as a pedlar's budget, but nubbudy's seen the colour of a French cooät."

"Yo fool! There's hunderds o' thousands o' cooäts and Frenchmen in 'em the tother side the watter."

"So they say at th'ale'us." A present smart fetched him out of those abstrusenesses. "Yo did lam me devilish free an' all. That last were clinker; it'll tek some rubbing off. However" – he spoke with a sudden drop to deeper feeling – "bless yer, Nell. And now let's goo to bed."

They mounted the stairs. The dog having with an unenthusiastic wag of the tail approved the recurrence of his betters to a temporary reasonableness, went back to his couch by the fire. On the landing the young man said:

"That sovereign I put on Mosley's terrier – I'll mek it two; and it's for yo, Nell."

"Shut up! Yo'll wakken Tish."

She entered his bare bedroom with him, set the candle

safely on a shelf and left him.

"Good-night, Nell," said Tant.

But she made him no answer.

In a while she returned to his room and looked in. He was abed and snoring; his dishevelled hair was about his handsome flushed face like an alehouse aureole; his wet soiled raiment lay in a heap on the plaster floor. Taking the candle she carried them down-stairs, and hung them on a clotheshorse before the fire. As she arranged them a mask roughly fashioned of some black stuff dropped out of one of the pockets. Hitherto her face had been palely impassionate, but that sight broke its phlegm suddenly, as though it had been the first blow. An upsurging of emotion troubled its surface. She sank down in her grandmother's chair and sobbed outright. And there were low cries between the tears, the purport of which seemed to be something like this:

"That an' all! that an' all! Oh the fool, the fool of a lad! Welladay, welladay! Oh, father! Oh, mother! Oh the gret soft fool of a lad."

The dog sat up, as one who thinks that something must be done; the dog lay down again in the impossibility of sympathy with the excesses that afflict superior intellects. But it was not for long; Nell soon stayed her moans and dried her tears; and as she put her handkerchief back in her pocket she seemed in a strangely complete manner to put her grief off from her face. She returned to her cold bed.

CHAPTER III

AN EXCHANGE OF PRESENTS

NELL got hold of Tant next morning before the headache
and repentance had worn off. He rose none too early, and
when she entered his room he had not quite finished
dressing. She had the black mask in her hand.

"What's this?" she said.

Tant shrugged his shoulders as men do at yesterday's
follies, and turned away to take up his neckcloth.

"Nubbut a bit o' tomfoolery," he answered.

"I don't like any-coloured tomfoolery mysen, but what
am I to think to black tomfoolery?"

"Was I drunk last night?"

"Drunk? Some! If yo don't know yo may be sure on't.
But that warn't the worst; there were some machines
brucken on Rufford road."

"Ay? War there?"

"Yo know; yo were theer."

"How d'yer know? War yo?"

Nell still had the black mask in her hand; she again held
it under his eyes.

"Yo may duck and dodge and twizzle, but yo'll never
deny it, our Tant, I know that."

"Well, and if I war?"

"Well? Much well! If yo get hanged or transported."

"We tek good care o' that. We clear the ground o'
witnesses aforehand."

"Yo don't clear it o' yoursens. There's a fifty-pound
reward; one on yer's doomed to addle it."

"We've took the oath, we're sworn to be true."

"Yo may talk o' sweering blackamoors to be white, yo may talk."

"We're a band o' true honest-hearted mates, 'sociated together for our common weal."

"At least yo get drunk together."

"But nubbudy durst; it'd be all his life was worth; we're sworn to be revenged on him. A man wouldn't sell his life for fifty pound."

"I dunno that; but I know he'll sometimes sell his life for his life. Fear's a very venturesome thing."

Tant had at last got his coat on; he had no resource but to stand and answer.

"I mun tek my chance. It don't matter a hop to me whether they mek their rotten laces on wide frames or narrer uns, but I wain't hae town machinery and town smells bro't to Blid'orth. It's bad enough to hae the country cut up into mouthfuls wi' these damned fences, it shan't be turned into town. Blid'orth law provides agen it."

"Blid'orth law's a knife wi'out a handle; yo can't cut wee't wi'out being cut. An ep'n tool, sure-lye!"

"It's better nor no tool."

"Ay? When? Just when a far-fetched damage is better nor biding still."

"I dunno but what 'tis allus. Anyhow the country's for country folk. Folk as don't care whether they breathe air or poison mun goo to Sheffield. I mean to keep a place for the ling and the larks."

"Rammel! Yo men as stan' gos-hawking at the corners tek into your mouths what others 'ud hardly care to set foot on. Is it yo, think yer, as grows the ling and breeds the larks? If it een't, what consarn is it o' yourn to provide the soil they grow on or the air they sing in? M'appen yo've planned to be God A'mighty at Blid'orth? I let yer to know God A'mighty don't slive about with a black bluft on; that's more liker another sort o' person."

"Let *him* list; we'll accept him. We've noat agen nubbudy, good or bad, heder or sheder, if they'll on'y sweer to be staunch and stayable."

"He'll sweer."

"There's lanes at Nottingham chockful o' these cursed machines, and ower every one on 'em a little white-faced monkey scrooching as if he dussn't for his life tek his eyes off'n it. Whirr-irr-irr, they goo, all the day and hafe the night. I'd as lieve hear the death-ruttle. Blid'orth's clean at present; there's noat in't to offend a kingfisher, and that's the daintiest o' birds. I were born here, and here it behoves me to die."

"Yo'll not, lad, yo'll die on Callers Hill."

"Yo'll be rid on me."

"And the disgrace, lad? That's not so easy gotten rid on. There's no market for't; it can't be gien away."

"There wain't be no disgrace; for yo at any rate."

"There'll be your last dying speech to be bought for a penny. M'appen yo think that's glory?"

"I wain't mek no speech; I'll die like a man."

"Yo'd better live like a man. Yo moot, afore yo can die like one. And this"- again she held forth the black rag – "don't show much promise o' that. There's some harrering wants doing to Award Cluss; it strikes me that's as much man's work as smashing other folks's hardware, or e'en as much as hanging by the neck wi'out a speech. But if a man wain't do it a woman mun."

"I'll do't."

"And put this i' th' fire."

She handed him back the shred of black.

"Nell!"

It was Tish's voice from below the stairs.

"Ay?"

"Come down and gie Mason's lass a pennorth of oad milk; I'm fast."

Low Farmhouse and the few neighbouring closes of

sandy soil were the freehold property of the Rideouts, that is to say of the young man and woman whose acquaintance we have made under the names of Tant and Nell, and of their married sister Letitia, commonly called Tish; the remainder of their inconsiderable holding being upon a yearly lease. The freehold portion included a piece of land recently awarded them by the enclosure commissioners in commutation of their right of pasturage upon the wide common; but the greater part had been first won from the gorse and ling of the forest by John Rideout the grandfather. It had been the common boast of the family that no hand but theirs had ever turned a furrow there "sin man was first invented." "And none never suld" old John was wont to add, flattered into prophecy by the possession of six stalwart sons to succeed him.

But the grandfather went the way of all flesh, one of his sons pre-deceased him, two took to soldiering, one emigrated to America, another preferred a town life, only John, his youngest, remained upon the farm, and the secondary boast was no longer heard. John the second married, but while he was yet in the prime of life his wife died, leaving him with three children – a boy and girl quite young, and a recently married daughter, the intermediate issue having been carried off in one visitation of small-pox. John's mother said:

"Tek another wife, lad, out o' respect for the dead;" and again, "out o' pity for the living."

His grandmother in that spirit of promise which had made her so unpopular with her neighbours, said:

"If yo wain't marry stannin' yo shan't lyin'; if yo wain't i' your chair yo shan't i' your bed."

But he did not marry again; in less than two years he was killed by the fall of his horse out hunting. Of which all persons considered the beldame's threat and finger to have been premonitory; not a few, comprising all those at Blidworth who loved to get to the bottom of a thing (especially when that thing was a neighbour's character) held it to have been causatory.

Meanwhile Tish Gillott, the married daughter, had left her husband upon some disagreement and returned home. She after the father's death took upon herself the direction of the house and farm, being a person of a strong hand, a strong will and a quick temper.

To the son Anthony, commonly called Tant, the early removal of a father's restraint had been detrimental. He had resented his elder sister's interference, sometimes defying, sometimes eluding it. He had developed into a young man of a superb physique, a keen sportsman, the best boxer in all the Forest district. He could sing a song, dance a hornpipe, mimic a pig; was a careless acquirer and spender, and in the main of an easy temper, though it was not safe to presume on it; but such merits as those only gave him the readier access to the cock-fighters, poachers and beer-boys, whose society he chiefly frequented. Sometimes he worked, it is true, and at a pinch would put forth his energies with a vehemence which was too fierce to be called industry; but the larger share of his time was divided between his more active pastimes and mere idling at the pot-house or in the open air.

All the greater burden fell upon his sisters, who had not only to take his place in the direction of the labourers, but often at the plough-tail and with the reaping-hook. But as Nell the youngest grew up there came to be a tacit division of occupation between her and her sister Tish; the latter ruled house and dairy, Nell the fields, the yard being debatable land between the two. The younger sister became known in the neighbouring markets as a fair judge of a beast, a good one of a horse. She mixed little with the young of either sex. Her amusements were those of the male farmer, she coursed hares with her greyhound bitch, she shot rabbits for the pot, as often as she might she rode to hounds on her old hunter Hasty. Tish who had become somewhat less active as she grew stouter got sufficient bodily exercise from her household duties, her daily outbreaks of temper and the form of religious service in use at the Methodist chapel.

The household was completed by the blind grandmother. But at the detached hamlet half a mile off, which as it was situated at the foot of Blidworth Hill was called Blidworth Bottoms, lived her mother in a little cottage alone, a beldame who it was currently believed had turned her hundredth year. She had resisted with the fewest of words all persuasions to permit an attendant to reside with her and minister to her comfort.

"I've bin married once," she said, "to a man; I ain't a-gooin' to be married again, to a woman."

Neither would she let herself be removed to the farmhouse. She had been born in that cottage, she had promised that she would die there; and it was commonly expected at Blidworth that her promises would hold good.

"My next flitting shall be my last," she said, with an oracular wag of the head towards the churchyard on the hill.

In those days a rural community was as little complete without a witch as without a parson or a doctor, and at Blidworth many more persons were convinced of old Mary Fiddys's illicit powers than attended the Rev. Mr. Clay's ministrations on Sunday, or showed half-a-crown's worth of confidence in one of Dr Fletcher's bottles, though he lived so far off as Mansfield. She was an albino, and no doubt the singularity of her appearance, together with the nocturnal habits which her infirmity occasioned, had much to do with her supernatural reputation. Besides she had been a woman of much eccentricity of character, of a sharp temper and an edged tongue, given to express unusual opinions in rude epigram, though now a mere mumbler of forgotten matters. And if more reasons yet be required, the parish had felt the immediate need as soon as old Nan Tagg died of fixing upon her successor in witchcraft. The younger members of her family did what they could for her in paying a woman to give her by day such assistance in the house as she needed and would accept, and to keep an unobtrusive watch over her by night. The old woman was superacute in her likes and dislikes; some half-dozen attendants had already been tried and rejected, and latterly the office had been undertaken by the wife of their labourer Spettigew, who lived over the way. Hannah Spettigew, perhaps through the lassitude of chronic ill-health, was dull to the difference between frequenting a witch's society out of neighbourship and as a paid helper; but her husband only gave his surly consent upon the promise of a shilling a week more than she would have received for the nursing of a mere old woman like Liza Beeley.

The Low Farmhouse was a humble erection, made up firstly of an original two-storied thatched portion, comprising house-place and dairy on the ground with three bedrooms above; and secondly of a tiled lean-to which was added by grandfather John when his family of six sons and three daughters grew too large for the old dwelling. This became then the common living-room, which has already been described, while the former house-place, papered over the whitewash and with a new fire-grate, went by the name of "the room." At a right angle to the older part of the house a range of stabling extended along one side of the crew-yard; opposite to that stood the barn and hovels, beyond was the stack-yard facing the back of the house.

High House upon the hill was as different in itself and its surroundings as in the circumstances of its inmates. Its size and appearance were such as almost entitled it to be called a mansion; the farmbuildings at the rear were ample and of the best construction; its situation commanded noble prospects, particularly to the south, the direction in which its principal front looked. That dim grey appearance behind so many ridges of hills mounting one above the other in decreasing distinctness was said to be the sky-line of the Leicestershire Wolds. On the lawn in front of the house and scattered over the adjoining land were some three or four score primeval oaks, the sole remains in the neighbourhood of the ancient forest; gnarled and twisted trunks of unknown age, they gave the place an air of unusual dignity. A colony of rooks nested in them.

Mr. Bagshaw, the former tenant of this house and of the seven hundred acres attached thereto, had died shortly before the time at which our story opens, and had bequeathed his valuable furniture, stock and goodwill to his nephew Arthur Skrene, upon condition that he resided in the house and personally worked the farm for a period of not less than seven years from the date of the testator's decease. The said Arthur we have already observed on his way thither to ascertain whether it would be worth his while to accept the legacy and its proviso. He spent the following week, with professional assistance from Mansfield, in taking an inventory of crop and stock. He lifted his shoulders a little at the wild waste scenery, which seemed to him a bad exchange for the pleasant fruitful county of Kent, where his father was a substantial yeoman. He found the soil of half the farm to be of the lightest, but it was in admirable order; the stock, both live and dead, was the best of the most suitable, the farm-buildings and the house were convenient and in perfect repair; all had evidently been in the hands of a man who was the master of his trade and had besides sufficient means to back his judgment. And there were no restrictions on the shooting. It was undoubtedly a highly valuable gift, and Arthur Skrene, notwithstanding that lift of his shoulders, did not hesitate to accept it. He immediately took the concern under his own management, and wrote for his sister Lois who had promised in the event of his acceptance to keep house for him.

But before she arrived he had seen Nell Rideout again, and again had not quite hit it with her. He was making the circuit of the farm, gun on shoulder, partly bent on sport and partly on a business-like oversight of his labourers' operations.

Before him went his uncle's well-bred setter, and behind him a lad with a bag over his shoulders. It was a still and hazy morning; the sun shone but always with a sort of film between it and the eye. Still it gave warmth, and the slight hoar-frost which had settled in the night had melted before it, except on the cold side of some coarse upstanding tussock of the pastures or under the clods of muck freely scattered over the yet unploughed stubble. The turf, short-cropped by sheep and horse, was bedewed with countless tiny shining beads, on which his foot at each step left a destructive mark. The plough horses were half hidden in the breath of their mouths and the steam of their bodies. Distance was measurable by the gradations of the few trees visible. This ash close at hand showed (yet did not show) the merging of its brown and grey and green as in the clearest light; that thorn rising out of the opposite hedge was blurred as by a considerable interval; the old oak-stump two fields off on the top of the slope was a mere semblance of grey, but one degree more opaque than the atmosphere which surrounded it.

The young farmer had not long set out and was skirting the hedge and the dribbling brook which formed the common boundary of his own and the Rideouts' holdings, when he heard a shout some distance in front of him, feminine but loud:

"So ho! so ho!"

"Theer goos Nell Rideout's grew, mester!" said the lad.

But Arthur had already seen a beautiful fallow hound start a hare in the next field. He stood and watched her pursue the poor animal's doublings with inevitable speed. Its last resource was to dart through the intervening hedge, but the dog fenced in gallant style, bustled it out of the ditch and killed within thirty yards of them.

"She's got 'im, she's got 'im!" cried the lad with sportsmanlike enthusiasm.

"I see that she has," said his master dryly, and called his setter to heel.

"Theer's Nell hersen!"

"So I perceive."

She approached from the other side of the boundary which as the ground fell away rapidly was much lower. Just under them she stopped, and picked up the hare which the hound dropped at her feet.

"Beautifully done, my beauty!" she said.

Then she lifted her clear grey eyes upon Arthur. She was dressed much as when first he saw her, except that in place of the smock-frock she wore a man's fustian jacket, loosely buttoned. Her red blood stimulated by the pleasant prick of the keen air shone through the transparent skin. Arthur raised his hat.

"It was started on our land," she said somewhat defiantly.

She had had many a wrangle with old Bagshaw over fur and feather.

"I hope it's a fat one," said Arthur suavely.

"It warn't, mester," said the lad at his elbow, "'twar on our side the beck. It's ronk poaching."

"Permit me," said Arthur, "to prefer Miss Rideout's excellent eyesight." Then to Nell: "I hope you've had good sport."

"Middling."

"It's a beautiful morning."

"The morning's never better nor what the sport is."

Perhaps she was disappointed of a quarrel. Perhaps she disliked having been caught trespassing. Perhaps, obscurely, unwittingly, she felt that her own exterior was in sorry contrast to the young man's neat dress and handsome equipment. Certainly she stood on the lower ground, in itself a perceptible disadvantage. Anyhow she was in no very sweet temper, which his serenely superior good-humour only made the sourer.

"That's a good bitch of yours," he said.

"If yo think yo've a better I'll match mine to run again yourn for five pounds, where and when yo like."

"Unfortunately I haven't one. Or not unfortunately, for doubtless it would be a worse."

"We don't think much to setters hereabouts for shooting; we fancy pointers where there's so much goss."

"Quite right, quite right." Again he raised his hat. "I wish you good-morning, Miss Rideout."

"Ho'd a bit. Treasure didn't start the hare on our ground; 'twere on yourn."

"Really? Then I appear to have the more right to hope it is a fat one."

She was surprised herself that she was so much stung by the hardly perceptible tone of banter there was in his civility.

"It seems to me," she said, "yo don't think us worth a quarrel."

With the smile only a little more apparent he answered, "I trust I may never have to make up my mind as to that. But I am quite sure a trifle like a hare isn't."

"P'raps i' the wonderful country yo come from yo've cows to quarrel about every day. Here i' these parts if yo can't brangle about a' hare yo wain't about noat."

"All the better; I'm a peaceable man; I never – that is hardly ever – quarrel about anything."

"That 'hardly ever's 'a bit stret for what's in't."

"I beg your pardon," said Arthur, not quite under-standing her dialect.

"Yo know yo don't owe me no 'beg pardons'; if yo did I suldn't be back'ard to ax for 'em. If yo don't think it worth while to try an' mek *me* beg *your* pardon, that's your consarn."

With his eyes on the hare, not her, and the slightest additional drawl, he began, "I hope –"

"It's a fat un?"

"Most heartily."

She held the animal by the hind legs.

"Handle it yoursen."

She swung it round her head and hurled it at him over the hedge; it struck him smartly in the wind. Before he had fully recovered his breath he picked it up and thanked her.

"I – ugh – thank you – ugh – thank you. It is as I hoped," he added urbanely as his wind improved; "it is a fat one. My best thanks; it shall be for my Sunday dinner."

He handed the hare to the lad and resumed his walk, after bidding her good-morning in the tones of an obliged person. She amused him; and even without the sunset at her back she made a picturesque figure.

"I'll roil him yet," vowed Nell to herself. She needed the comfort of the prophecy; she felt that at every point her ill-humour had been worsted by his complacency.

In the course of his stroll Arthur Skrene shot a leash of partridges, which he bade his lad take to Miss Rideout with his compliments.

"To Rideouts' Nell?" exclaimed the lad, agape with astonishment.

"To Miss Rideout, if you please. It displeases a tenant farmer's sense of propriety that a labouring lad should know a tenant farmer's Christian name. Miss Rideout with Mr. Skrene's compliments. Kindly reduce the gape of your mouth and get that by heart."

So when Nell went in she was taken by Tish to see the birds hanging up in the dairy.

"'Miss Rideout with Mr. Skrene's compliments.' Mebbe yo know what it means, for I don't."

"I met him this morning and gied him a hare. I suppose it's to mek him level wi' me."

"What i' th' world did yo gie him a hare for?"

"For his Sunday dinner."

"Yo seem to be strange and in wee 'm all at once. Well hae *them* for Sunday. It don't seem as there'll be much lumber ower that theer gate wi' him."

"I'm none so sure on't."

CHAPTER IV

WITH MR. PEPPER'S HOUNDS

SOON after Christmas Miss Skrene came down by the Nottingham and Mansfield coach. Her brother was in waiting for her in the latter town with a gentle-mannered pony specially procured by him for her riding; upon which she trotted beside him by wood, moor and farm to High House. Her luggage came on more slowly, slung over a pack-horse's back. She was muffled in the many wraps necessary for a long coach journey in winter, which left little of her to be seen beyond this: that she was small and girlish, that she had dark hair in close curls and hazel eyes like her brother's, with that paler olive complexion which can be as quick and eloquent in its changes as the most obvious carmine and white, and that even in travelling she did not wear one of last year's hats. On the way she gave her brother in her young lady's manner a lively opinion of the exceeding dreariness of the country.

"It isn't much to look at," said Arthur, "but the natives are picturesque – some of them."

"Oh then, it is quite a foreign country?"

"And a capital hunting country too."

"In that case I've not one word more to say against it; I understand that it's just a prickly paradise."

Arthur's first practical proof of it as a hunting country was about a week later, when he attended the meet at Oxton of the nearest pack of hounds, the master of which, Squire Pepper, is still remembered for his hard swearing and (if possible) harder riding. Well mounted on a roan mare, white-breeched, scarlet-coated, black-velvet-capped, he cut a very good figure and was well received by those of the gentlemen and superior farmers who had already made his acquaintance. Nell came up a little later on her old horse Hasty, a big brown which had once carried her father's nineteen stone. He was a halfbred plain-looking animal, perhaps overlong in the back, with a sensible head however, but nothing remarkable about him save his mighty shoulders. Out of consideration for his age Nell only rode to hounds when the appointment was near home and never more than once a week.

The field met, as was the custom of our ancestors, in ample time to have seen the sun rise, had there been anything of it to see beyond a gradual chilly whitening of the general grey. It was a raw misty morning; every tree dripped like a rain cloud, every bush was covered with water drops, the herbage was sodden; it seemed as though the dank still air might be squeezable between the palms like a full sponge. Between every man's eyes was set a purple nose, and application to the brandy flask was frequent. Upon Nell's complexion and spirits however the weather seemed to have no more influence than on her horse's. She wore the high-crowned cross-ribboned hat much curved at the brim, which had been fashionable twenty years before, and a habit of country cut and weather-beaten fabric, which might once have been a homogeneous grey or blue or green, but was then a special moor-side blending of all three; it was girded at the waist with a plain broad leathern belt. She was the only woman present and kept herself to a decent reserve, neither avoiding those of her own degree who were mustered there nor making free with any, but giving and receiving salutations with the same business-like brevity as at Mansfield market. The only person with whom she exchanged a few sentences of conversation was the huntsman, and that all about the morning's sport. About anything else indeed old Joe Passon

would hardly have conversed with anybody. Dog was the
centre of his universe; horse was the animal that rode to
hounds, man being the animal created to ride him to
hounds. He was a wonderfully lean and bent old man, but
still rode with as firm a seat as any one in that gathering. It
was while Nell stood by that with his usual dry civility to a
title he said to Lord Mutch:

"Fine mornin' for the scent, my lord."

"And for nothing else," grumbled the shivering peer.

The huntsman instantly wheeled about, uncivilly
presenting his horse's quarters to his lordship, and growled
between his snappish gums:

"What the devil else does the man *want* it good for?"

But the master, who had been detained a short while by
the urgent hospitality of the hall, came up, and the hounds
were entered in a piece of heathery moor-land north-west
of the village. The first fox, after a zig-zagging run of no
great length, was killed in the open between the Grange and
Robin Hood Hill. Arthur's style, which trusted more to
horse's speed and man's courage than to knowledge of the
country and the fox's ways, was freely criticised by heavy-
sterned riders of the old school. One of them, a jolly rotund
old farmer of the name of Machin, said:

"Yon yoongster's got a good commencin' notion o' ridin'
to hounds; he nubbut wants to brek 'is neck once; that'll
larn 'im all 'e don't know."

While a neighbouring spinney was being drawn, Arthur,
happily unconscious of the unfavourable appreciation, got
into conversation with the speaker of it by remarking
slightly upon the singularity of two conical excrescences on
the hill-side hard by.

"Ah," said Mr Machin, "them's the tombs o' two o' the
oad ancient original Red Indian chiefs, long afore the days
o' Robin Hood an' Guy Fawkes. Major Rook dug 'em out.
He's fun' a many on 'em about 'ere; 'e's a sort o' gentleman-
resurrectionist. They say 'e's such a gift 'e could smell a oad

corp if 'twere buried a mile deep. Pride's a damned bad quallity in dead men. If them two chaps had been satisfied to be buried wheer their families buried, wi'out all their sidebord silver an' race cups about 'em an' so much splauge, they might a ligged i' peace while the day o' judgment."

But the fox was holloaed off from the far-side of the covert. As they put their horses in motion Nell cantered past. The exercise and excitement had warmed her blood and set her eyes on fire. She sat her horse as though she lived there, with perfect security and grace. A fallen tress hid the ear that they might else have seen.

"Een't she a picture?" said Mr. Machin. "Drot it, it's ommost as gret a pity a handsome wench should ever grow oad as a good hoss should."

"She's not bad-looking," said Arthur; and neither the terms nor the tone of his assent pleased the old farmer.

"Wheer yo coom from sich uns m'appen are as common as 'not bad' turnips? I were born an' bred i' th' forest, and lay mysen to die here; it's a fairish ordinary sort o' soil to live on an' be buried in. M'appen I shall goo theer when I'm dead; if I'm passed. Well!"

A sounding thwack of whipstock on solid horse-flesh emphasized his uncertainty about his future prospects, and he and Arthur parted company, the one preferring the gate, the other the direct line of the fence. They left the heath and entered an enclosed country of high hedges. The mist began to turn to rain, the clay stuck like glue; but the hounds went at a merry pace round Wolfeley Hill and straight for Halam. There the fox had doubled, and his too-eager pursuers over-ran their scent, but after a brief check found it again and tracked him along Halam Valley and up Oxton Hill. Old Hasty's stiff joints seemed to have been loosened by the former run, and Nell had ridden among the first few. Arthur consciously set himself to outpace her; yet hitherto her tact and knowledge of every yard of the country had held the advantage over his well-mounted impetuosity. But during that ensuing plunge into the Dumble, where the ground was rugged and beset with gorse, he passed her and lost sight of her horsewomanship. That was both loss and gain; but there was no time to balance their differences. The hounds were before their eyes, beautifully together, traversing the grassy expanse in which Oxton is situated. The scent was good; their encouraging music pervaded the thick air. But hard by the hall they turned sharp for Windmill Hill. Up the slope they swept, all together through the rain their white and tan had a filmy softness and soon disappeared behind the ridge. On the hill-side there was nothing to be seen but here and there a rain-blurred dab of moving scarlet or less conspicuous green or blue. The huntsman's horn seemed miles away. To the left there was a crowd of horsemen on the road.

Arthur happened on the roughest portion of the ascent, Nell took it inevitably at the easiest, and when they drew together again had gained considerably upon him. She was not more than ten yards behind – he did not look but he knew – when suddenly, there rose up out of the uneven ground before him a formidable fence, a quick-set hedge which had been newly "chubbed" or lopped, stiff, spiky, forbidding, with a yawning ditch on the take-off side and beyond it an unnecessary ox-rail set a yard and a half back. He had touched his mare's flanks with the spurs to let her know there was work for her, when like a flash the old horse behind crossed his thoughts, troubling them. He was fully persuaded that come what might Nell would follow his lead, and he misdoubted the old horse's powers; he felt as though he were carrying double weight. The rider's hesitation was sped to the ridden-on down the conductive reins, and by where his knees gripped her; she too hesitated, refused what was hardly offered her. Arthur looked down the fence for an easier place.

"There's a nice gap hafe a furlong off; it's out o' my road or I'd show yer; that-away."

That from Nell as she gave her old horse a kindly
encouraging tap of the whip; he rose mightily, spread
himself grandly, and cleared the oxer just, to a quarter of
an inch, like an old horse who knows himself. Arthur was
furious, with himself for his miscalculated generosity, with
her for her taunt. He went back a few paces; his spurs were
red; the mare bounded over like an undisciplined young
thing that disdains to count inches. For hot-blooded steed
and rider in such a mood the oldster and his considerate
mistress were no match; they parted company. The hounds
were running with the wind, if there were a wind, straight
for Loath Hill and the covert from which the fox had first
been ousted; but as Arthur rapidly descended he again lost
sight of them. He pressed after them as straight as the
rugged ground would allow him. There was a big man on a
big bay, a military exquisite on a light chestnut; he could
not shake them off. Nell kept wide of them and apparently
fell more and more behind.

Again Arthur rose to higher ground and again his view
was extensive. His quick glance recognized the tumuli close
at hand which had before attracted his attention. But no
time for that. Following the vagaries of the scent the hounds
had almost made the circuit of Loath Hill, and now came
round its shoulder just in front of him, and full in view
careered over the undulating gorsy expanse of Oxton forest.
Their tan and white ran through the vegetation like a bright
weft through a sombre warp. The field was scattered over
the country, here, there and everywhere, from Southwell
road to Edingley lane. The master had got on deep ground,
and was swearing and tearing round the other side of Horse-
pasture Wood. Nell was at the back of the hill but she had
not yet called upon her horse for what he was worth. Only
the huntsman had stuck to the hounds. A little to their right-
rear he rode on his great gaunt black. Arthur and the two
who kept him company dashed down in mad pursuit.

For two miles they galloped and the pace was fast. The

rain beat in the riders' faces; they set their teeth and looked
before them. The hounds' music, the toot of the horn, the
holloas of the men had ceased. No sound was in their ears
but the thud of iron-shod hooves and the thump of their own
hearts. The big bay that carried the big man fell behind; the
captain's light chestnut put his foot in a rabbit-hole and down
he went a cropper. Arthur did not look back, and if he had
done he would not have seen Nell who was hidden by the
long low abrupt ridge which was always on his right hand.
Old Hasty was going mightily, for his mistress's thought was
his own, and he knew he had ground to make up. But Arthur
saw only the hounds and the old huntsman. The old
huntsman rode a little to the rear of them on his great gaunt
black, not like mortal rider, rather like Death out a-hunting,
lean, bent, imperturbable, not to be shaken off.

Suddenly the huntsman was gone from before him –
Arthur with his coat cuff wiped the rain from his eyes –
gone as though he had sunk into the ground. A minute later
the hounds themselves swerved as quick as a swallow's
change; all together they wheeled, all together they
disappeared, every head and every stern of them, down-
hill. Arthur with difficulty reined in his own and his mare's
impetuosity, but thinking to follow found himself on the
brow of a low but impracticable declivity, cliff more than
hillock, the termination of the long ridge which had always
been on his right hand; and with savage disappointment he
saw hunted animal and hunting animals racing away from
him on the level ground below. Every hound had a voice.

"Tally-ho!"

Nell's shrill holloa came to him from beneath. He saw
her not above a furlong off, and just behind her the old
huntsman and his black. He was looking about for a safe
way of descent, when lo! the desperate fox again doubled,
and scampered for dear life back along the banks of the
streamlet which skirts the base of the cliff, and hard by is
broadened out by a dam. The manoeuvre brought him

considerably nearer to Arthur; in a straight line. But the
straight line led down a breakneck steep which hardly
promised safe footing to a hasty pedestrian. But Nell was
yonder lessening the distance, Nell and behind her the
huntsman on his gaunt black. He saw and did not hesitate;
he would not go looking for a gap this time. His spur was
remorseless, the mare had to obey though her discretion
was so much greater than her master's. Hopping, popping,
skipping, slipping, stumbling, recovering, sluthering,
puthering, hunge-plunge, down to the bottom she went, by
mere force of gravity as it seemed; stopped there a moment
as though assuring herself that she was there, and then
bounded forward. Again and yet again poor Reynard
twisted and turned, desperate to choose his place of death,
and got it at last in the clump of willows on the other side
of the dam. Only Arthur was in at it.

Nell came next, then the old huntsman. There was no
congratulation on her face or his. But soon the master
galloped up and stopped swearing complaint to swear
admiration. By ones and twos others of the company
straggled in, and their wonder was fervently expressed.
They went in a body to view the spot, and one of them
blazed a willow tree to mark it. Arthur remembered having
ridden by the dam and the cliff on the day of his first arrival.
But amid all that applausive babble Mr. Machin, who had
trotted round by Bawford steps, said to another cautious
oldster:

"I were mista'en; once een't enough."

"Eh?"

"I lay 'im to brek 'is neck *twice* afore his eddication's
complete."

Joe Passon was silent; perhaps not more silent than usual,
that was scarcely possible, but more determinedly, more
expressively silent. Until the master, noticing it, said to him:

"Well, Joe, what do you think of this devilish
extraordinary feat?"

"I warn't bro't up to circus ridin'," answered the huntsman; "I've no opinion on't at all."

"No opinion?"

"Mebbe the mare hes. Ax her."

The rain thickened, the wet dripped from the brims of the men's caps, from their noses, from their horses' manes. The hounds were taken to Sansom Wood, but it was empty. The moor-land to the south of it, already traversed by Arthur on his first coming to Blidworth, was next drawn, but they did not see the colour of a fox until they got to some marshy ground in the neighbourhood of Calverton. It was a vixen, and she led them through Grimesmoor wet with the waters of the Dover Beck, up Brockwood Hill, down Gonalston Hagg, by Thurgarton Park and finally contrived to get lost on or near High Cross Hill above Goverton. That was the end of the day's hunting.

Arthur Skrene overtook Nell as she rode out of Gonalston. He slackened the pace of his horse to hers and entered into chat with her; but her responses were brief.

"Quite alone, Miss Rideout?"

"No."

The monosyllable was eked out by a friendly drop of the whip on old Hasty's poll.

"Oh yes," Arthur replied lightly, "he's a remarkably clever old horse, but considered as company he leaves something to be desired."

"I hain't fun' it out."

"For instance he can't talk."

"He don't feel obliged to talk."

Arthur laughed.

"That's one for his two-legged inferior. Well – accepting the inferiority and with it the compensatory licence – have you enjoyed the day's sport?"

"I allus do, that's what I coom out for."

"That last was a pretty good run too, though it's disappointing not to have killed."

"Ay."

"This wet has made the clay fearfully sticky."

"Don't it allus?"

She never once looked at him; she plainly was not in a talkative mood. Yet he would have been ashamed to set it down to jealousy of his success. There were no signs of ill-temper about her, and the weather seemed hardly to have touched her person, not at all her spirits; only the moistness of her disorderly locks had deepened their hue to red and rainy beads glittered among their twists and tangles. Her face was still glowing with exercise, her eyes still shone, her lips were crimson. They rode in silence until they reached Epperstone then she turned her grey eyes full on him, which being unexpected its effect was the greater.

"A rider like yo, Mr. Skrene," she said seriously, "ought to hae a very witty hoss."

He knew what she was at, and answered jestingly:

"It would be useless his having the wit, so long as I kept the whip."

She gave him another glance of her grey eyes and no more.

"So I doubt," she said; and that seemed to be all.

They rode on.

"I believe yon village on the left is Woodborough?" said Arthur.

She pushed his question aside.

"I don't unnerstan' such riding as yourn, that's the truth. Yo refuse what yo might easily tek and tek what yo're in duty bound to refuse."

"Probably, Miss Rideout, there's something in every man's horsemanship to which you take exception."

"Allus; summat; but when the helping's so big I'm stawed afore I begin. Yo may vally your own neck raight, but a hoss has a neck too. M'appen yo owerlooked that i' your hurry? Yo've a raight to tek his opinion."

"Possibly he would advise me to stick to the highway."

"Sell him; he's none for hunting."

"Or I might have a difficulty in ascertaining his opinion."

"Sell him again; *yo're* none for hunting. And buy an arm-chair."

He felt so firm in his seat he was scarcely disturbed in his self-opinion; his amused urbanity was almost wholly sincere.

"You appear to have studied the subject most learnedly."

"I know noat but what I can't help knowing."

Where the hill begins to rise she leapt from her horse and began to walk beside him. So doing, she lifted the whip and pointed up-road.

"I'm obliged," she said, "to save oad Hasty on the road all I can, but yo've no call to accommodate your pace to hisn."

But Arthur dismounted also, and civilly hoped he might be allowed to keep her company so far as their roads were one.

"I'm no company for yo," she answered; "no more nor my oad hoss is for your young mare."

Still Arthur was for lingering, urbanely persistent.

"But indeed, Miss Rideout, I shall take it unkindly of you if you dismiss me before my time."

She turned her eyes on him once more, and they were strangely hot with anger.

"Yo may. I'll hae no man goo out of his road for me no furder nor I'll goo out o' my road for him. And that's not much."

He remounted, lifted his hat and trotted off in a very vile temper with the weather. Under which his main comfort, oddly enough, was a recollective conviction that the huzzy's hair was red after all; when it was wet.

CHAPTER V

'DON'T LAUGH'

THOSE were ill days for the handicraftsmen and especially for the machine-workers of the towns. Napoleon's decrees had fenced the continent off from English commerce. Food was dear and wages scanty. The ill-taught operative turned his hunger and his anger into arms against his unhappy employer, especially against such as sought to keep level with the times by making goods either better or worse than the old patterns. About the time of the opening of our story the breaking of machinery by the so-called Luddites began at Nottingham, and had quickly spread to the neighbouring counties. In that town more soldiers were quartered than had ever before been found necessary to keep order in an English borough. Large rewards were offered both by the corporation and the government for testimony against the malefactors, but no check was put to their proceedings. Many of the affrighted manufacturers began to remove their machines to out-of-the-way villages, to Blidworth among others; but the spoiler followed them thither.

At Blidworth, to the common dislike of new things and the imported hatred of the condemned machinery was added a local dissatisfaction with the parochial enclosure act, which was even then giving to the plough more than two thousand acres of common land. The restricted sportsman and loafer, the village politician so easily displeased, the small freeholder who put a higher value on his rights of common than the commissioners' award did, joined voices, sometimes touched hands and exchanged

drinks at the ale-house with the more dangerous schemer
from Mansfield, Sutton-in-Ashfield or Arnold. No doubt in
almost every case it was but a midnight sympathy repented
of or forgotten next morning, but with Tant Rideout it was
otherwise. An ill-satisfied commoner, somewhat of a
politician, more of a poacher and loafer, he touched
discontent at so many points. The voice of battle was in the
air filling it with its far-off nearness, and he was a born
fighter. It was hardly likely when throughout the land men
were either throwing up their caps for victory after victory
over-seas, or else hatching intestine broils, that he should
remain content with dancing jigs and snaring rabbits, or
even with an occasional victory in the ring over some
ignoble competitor. He often regretted, aloud of course, the
not distant days when many a herd of deer, fallow or red,
roamed the forest and the price of a man's life was set upon
their illicit destruction. He was hooked too, strange as it may
seem, by his sentimental side. Though he disliked the
drudgery of the farm he loved the brown and green and
grey of the country, the smell of gorse, broom and ling, the
play and the contention of the weather, while he contemned
the town and the prison clank of its new-fangled iron
labourer. All these smouldering combustibles needed but
the waft of chance to bring them to a blazing activity; and
it was hardly likely they would want it.

One or two acts of machine-breaking had already been
committed in the neighbourhood of Blidworth, one or two
had been frustrated by a timely garrisoning of the
threatened workshops, more were apprehended. There was
a general feeling of expectation, which was for the most part
fear. A number of special constables were sworn in to assist
Tom White, constable and baker, in maintaining the
authority of the law. The newly enrolled members of the
Mansfield troop of Yeomanry Cavalry and the Oxton
Volunteers were ordered to be in readiness for immediate
service. What more could be done? The Bow-street

detective, then stationed at Nottingham, came and went away.

To Arthur Skrene, who like most well-to-do persons had a fine sense of legality and property, violence so destructive was abhorrent. He had joined the Yeomanry soon after his arrival, and as he had already gained some experience in a similar capacity in Kent, he was promoted to be sergeant. He set himself zealously to organize and drill the troopers of his own neighbourhood, and devised an effective system of intelligence, whereby on alarm given by night or day they might be summoned from their scattered dwellings and speedily mustered at a convenient rendezvous. He had the more leisure for this because about the beginning of February after a season of open weather a four weeks' frost set in; the black earth was shut to the plough and there was no hunting.

After their first hunt together he did not meet Nell Rideout again until towards the end of the frost. He was out walking with his sister. Lois was not much of a walker, especially in the fields, the women of her day rarely were, but the hardness of the ground – no snow had fallen, and it was as dry and clean as any road – had permitted her to cross a few closes in her brother's company, in order that she might enjoy the fine prospects to be viewed from different points. For only a few yards their path touched the bounds of Low Farm; but in those few yards they met Nell coming from milking.

"Don't laugh," said Arthur hastily.

Of herself Lois would never have thought of laughing. What she saw over the black leafless hedge with a background of lowering sky was a superb head in a blue calico hood, poising a large kit of milk. It was like a glowing picture hung all by itself against a dim dull wall. But what most affected her at the moment was the wonder and curiosity raised by her brother's strange injunction. She saw nothing whatever to laugh at; but of course she looked for something and meant to find it. She was titter-ripe when a few yards further a sudden dip of the hedge and rise of the ground displayed Nell to her from head to foot; the old blue smock-frock; the thick boots, the clumsy gaiters, the wooden piggin ledged on her hip. The unexpected expectedness of it gave her an irresistible inclination to laugh, in spite of, or perhaps – so whimsical a thing is laughter – all the more because of the woman's eyes which were upon her, grave and grey. She had to turn away her head.

"Good-day, Miss Rideout," said Arthur. "The frost holds."

"There'll be a downfall afore long," said Nell, and passed on.

As soon as her back was turned Lois's laughter spurted out; not noisily but with dainty gush and gurgle, as of a tiny water-course battling with sportive fury against obstructive pebbles; smooth white pebbles, crystalline water. For his life Arthur could not help accompanying it with a slight manly guffaw, almost wholly inward; the back view especially of that conglomerate milkmaid, plough-boy and nymph was delightfully incongruous. But as they stood thus looking and laughing, suddenly she gave them face instead of back. Immediately they were as grave as might be. She walked on. Hoping and believing she had not seen everything, they still stood looking after her, each secretly admiring the springiness of her gait under the heavy burden, the robust ease, the natural grace of her carriage, the effect of which her ridiculous costume did not lessen; or if it lessened it to the eye it rather accentuated it to the understanding. At the same time Miss Skrene was a little jealous of her own admiration, and especially of the more or less conjecturable admiration of her brother; so what she said was neither the topmost or the undermost of her feelings.

"What a comical figure!"

She followed the exclamation up with a feminine click of tongue to palate; and she laughed a second laugh, which was neither so natural nor irresistible as the former.

"But – in justice – what a grand head!" said Arthur.

"Grand tapioca!" exclaimed Lois, both her little furry gloves uplifted. "She has red hair!"

Arthur answered with that under-emphasis which so well expresses the unbiassed rebuke of the unjust by the just:

"I do not quite think, Lois – in fairness – that it is to be called red. Perhaps the light –"

"The light? Oh yes! Of course it's the light. In the dark it's a perfect black, isn't it? So are carrots. What a charitable way of disliking unusual colours. It's the light! How much you've learnt, dear Arthur, in the article of Christian charity since you travelled North! I never heard you utter so kind an apology for Maria Simpson's conspicuous tresses."

"Miss Simpson's hair is of a quite different hue, if I remember rightly."

"A shade *blacker* perhaps."

"How strange the sun looks!"

Arthur's reference to the luminary, which redly overhung the murky horizon like a ball of fire, was unfortunate.

"Strange indeed!" exclaimed Lois. "I don't remember ever seeing it look so black."

"I think we had better be turning towards home," said Arthur.

After supper Nell sat on a cricket by the hearth roasting her knees. She leant back against the chimney wall, but with less of languor in her expression and attitude than she commonly showed after the out-door fatigues of the day. The grandmother sat opposite in her accustomed corner spinning. As the wheel hummed the twist of wool fashioned itself between her tremulous fingers. Tish sat a little withdrawn from the fire carding. The labourers were at the table prolonging their meal; instead of conversation the gritty grating of their heavy boots on the sanded floor kept company with the sounds of eating, the clatter of knife and fork, the champ of jaws, the smacking of lips, the gulping of liquid and solid.

"I seed Mr. Skrene's sister this afternoon," said Nell after a long interval.

"What's she like?" said Tish resting from her carding. "They say she's summat more nor ordinary nice-looking."

"She's a little gallous dark-eyed thing heaped up wi' clo'es."

"Ay?"

"But they're nice clo'es."

"What had she got on?"

"I dunno."

"It's about time yo began to tek some notice o' summat," said Tish disappointed. "Yo're oad enough. Any more meat, Bill?"

"A little bit," said Spettigew thickly, with his mouth full.

"Yo hain't no clo'es now-a-days," croaked the grandmother; "yo've nubbut foldidols."

Tish liberally replenished Dick's trencher.

"I don't want no more," said the boy.

"Yo mun eat it, to keep want away."

"I don't want so much."

"Yo eat it, iv'ry bit."

"She'd a fur cap on and a lot o' fur all round her cloak," said Nell, with much pains recollective. "Her cloak were crimson red."

"I'm thinking," said Tish, "of haeing a fur trimming to my Sunday mantle next back-end. But I want to know first what's the fashionable style. A bit more bread, Lambert, or some taters?"

"Some more taters, please," said Lambert, "an' a bite o' bread an' all."

"I could ha' holled her ower the hedge," said Nell.

"So little as that comes to?" said Tish. "Well! But then her brother's a little un."

"He's not a big un, but he's well set up; he looks well enough of hoss-back. But she *is* a little un."

"What did she say to yer?"

"Noat"

"What did yo say to her?"

"Noat."

"Yo couldn't have said much less. But I don't call it manners to pass a neighbour wi'out ayther a good word or a bad un; nayther manners nor Christian fellership. Yo remember oad Hollins, as used to swear at dad ivery time he seed him? We allus considered him a friendlier sort o' person nor that young Snooks as niver said noat."

The men had finished eating, as the simultaneous pushing back of their chairs announced. Nell came from the chimney, her face hot with the fire. She took down from the wall a man's jacket and hat and put them on.

"Where are yer gooing?" said Tish.

"To look round a bit. I shall want yo, Spettigew, to carry the lantern for me."

Spettigew made an inarticulate grunt, such as a tired animal might at an unexpected demand upon him. He nevertheless reached down the heavy horn lantern from its shelf and lighted the candle therein. Lambert made clumsy speed to sidle through the door in the midst of a hasty "Goodnight, all." Dick followed with his last unwilling mouthful in his mouth.

Nell took down her hunting-crop from its nail.

"What do yer want that for?" asked Tish.

"I dunno. I'm tekking it against I want it."

With the crop she unhooked her old blue smock-frock which hung beside it, and let it fall to the ground.

"I shan't wear that no more," she said. "Yo may gie't to oad Teddy Cliff."

"An' why?" asked Tish.

"It's too oad for oat."

"Yo're getting strange an' partic'lar all of a sudden."

"I'm no more partic'lar nor other folk; yo can't say I am. Yo may wear it yoursen, if yo like. And I mean to get my next bonnet at Mansfield; Betsy Porter gies us noat new."

Before Tish had gathered herself to answer she went out, followed heavily by Spettigew with the lantern.

CHAPTER VI

THE RIGHT OF WAY

THREE quarters of an hour later Arthur Skrene sat reading what the *Nottingham Journal* had to say of the introduction into the House of Lords of 'A Bill for the more exemplary punishment of persons found guilty of destroying stocking and lace frames' (by death to wit, without benefit of clergy). He had not done pishing at his lordship of Newstead's humane expostulation, when he was called forth from his snug parlour into the chill hall to speak to Selby, his foreman.

"Theer's summat, sir," he said, "which it behooves me to dror yer attention to."

"Where, Selby?"

"Outside," said Selby, with his oracular thumb north-west by west.

He was a large-built man, painstakingly slow.

"Will it take my attention long?"

"Can't undertek to say, sir. I seed it from my door."

Arthur put his hat on and followed his man out into the crew-yard. It was a dark night. The wind had got up a little and blew fluttering flakes of snow into his fire-warm face; which made him think of Nell Rideout, who had foretold it.

"In Hither Cluss, sir," said Selby.

Instantly he forgot Nell Rideout, for across the neighbouring field, and not above a hundred yards off, he saw a light; and from the same quarter came the sound of blows dully falling, as of iron upon wood.

"What's that?" he asked.

"I can't say, sir."

"We must go and see."

"Unless it's somebody interfairin' wi' the gate."

"Who should that be?"

"I can't undertek to say."

"Fetch Harris and Wells and come after me. Tell Charley to saddle Vixen."

"Unless it's them drotted Rideouts."

But Selby brought this out with his usual deliberation, so that it was lost upon his more impetuous master who was already twenty yards off.

There was undoubtedly a way of a sort by means of a gate from Low Farm through High Farm to the Oxton road; but whether there was a right of way by it had always been in dispute. Why that gate should break the continuity of the hedge if it were not meant to open as well as shut, had never been satisfactorily explained by owner or tenant of High Farm. Likewise the Rideouts, if right of way they had, were unable to show how they became entitled to it, and above all could not point to a time when they enjoyed undisturbed use of it. Altogether it was a very pretty quarrel, which it is not my intention to spoil by settling. The passage was guarded by two or three intermediate gates, which were usually kept locked; when there was anything of them to lock. In the lambing season, during the long harvest time, or when the shorn land was asking for the plough, the Rideouts had generally been too busy to trouble themselves about the enforcement of an easement which was of little or no practical value to them; but in the intervals when there was some slackening of toil, when the last lamb had been dropped, when the harvest cart had been led home in triumph, and especially when the plough was frost-bound, the wild youngsters of the last generation had looked on a little gate-smashing as a profitable and enjoyable way of filling the vacancy. Many a fight had there been, many a rail broken, and many a head, but when all was over, the bits of the gate were put together again, and a new lock bought.

The neighbours, whose only interest was in the discrimination of right from wrong, were continually advising both parties with contradictory encouragement to go to law. But they never did; I cannot say for certain why; there were not then by a hundred to one so many largely promising investments for spare cash as there are now-a-days. Only there had been a law-suit at Blidworth a little time before about a similar easement; both plaintiff and defendant were then on the parish and their property, including the still disputed right of light, was in other hands; a striking example of the impartial thoroughness of English justice.

After the death of Nell's father the Rideouts had shown a lessened zeal in the maintenance of their claim; Nell was at first too young and then too busy, Tant too indolent and negligent. But there had been some tussles, and how Tish Gillott had horse-whipped a couple of stalwart labourers from end to end of Nether Field was still talked of. Arthur Skrene however knew nothing of all that; he gave not a thought to the half-understood hint which Nell had dropped on the day of his arrival; his mind was full of machine-breaking; he had no doubt it was some attempt of the same lawless ruffians whom he had routed out of Calverton the night before.

It was dark; the wind blew the ever-increasing snowflakes into his eyes. He saw nothing on either hand of him, as he hastened across the field, but the shapes dimly apparent of two or three giant oaks. Before him was ever the small clear shine as of a lantern, and about it two moving shadows without form, one however larger than the other. The sound of blows and of the splintering of wood had ceased before he came up.

"Who are you," he cried; "and what are you doing here?"

There was no answer. He made straight for the light. The shadow which seemed connected with it fell back.

"I demand to know what you want here?" said Arthur again.

"*I* want noat," answered a man's rough sullen obstinate voice from over the lantern.

Arthur was then near enough to see distinctly the dirty old gaiters and coarse stockings of the man who held it. Some scatterings of light fell also on a shattered gate and on the stout forequarters, white below the knees, of a horse which was stepping through the gate-stead, but barely indicated his nodding head and the masculine appearance of his rider. Arthur sprang forward, seized the horse by what harnessed its head, and careless of his own danger began to back it. The somebody in the saddle urged it forward with strokes of the whip, but Arthur, who had now gathered the reins into his hands, hung all his weight upon the bit and held the advantage. The lantern by a chanced or purposed deflection was turned from them, and only illuminated an unimportant bit of hedge, and the glistening snowflakes which began to rest upon it. So they struggled in the dark and the silence, for no word was uttered on either side. The animal, which was evidently of no high temper, plunged a little under its rider's urgency, but was being steadily pushed back; until Arthur, who was afraid the other man might come to the rescue, let go the bridle and seized its rider by the leg. But almost before he knew whether he had laid hold of leather or prunella, he felt a smart blow on the arm. He was furious; he made a spring to seize his assailant's whip-hand. It was withdrawn from him by a quick upward movement; then came down again, whip and all. The blow glanced off his uplifted arm and alighted on his head. He was half-stunned by it, and what he did next must have been a piece of undirected animal savagery. The horse moved on leaving something in his grip; but the first things he was fully conscious of were the rider dragged to the ground and a heavy hunting crop in his own hands, but how done and gotten he hardly knew. His blood was up, his fury mixed with his strength like a terrible momentary drug, doubling it. He kept his antagonist at arm's length and made free use of the weapon. The man with the lantern hung back and gave his associate neither help nor encouragement. The latter made a resistance, fierce and brief, but taken at a disadvantage, disarmed, as it would seem disconcerted, and somehow hampered, suddenly ceased to struggle, stood stock-still as though resolved to take the punishment passively.

It must be confessed that Arthur's temper just then was next to cruelty; only let it be remembered that a blow which deadens the more intellectual activities of a brain can hardly do so without lessening the moral restraints also. All at once the silent butt of his indignation uttered a cry, a woman's cry, of angry pain, and fled away like a swift black shadow. Just then Selby came up with Harris and Wells, armed with shadowy forks and sticks. It will never be exactly known how much her flight was on their account, how much through the unbearableness of the whip and the shame.

For the moment Arthur was numbed, as though he had received another weightier blow in the same place; he dropped the crop. When he recovered himself he was sick at heart, as after a physical shock. He turned to his men and said:

"You may go back; you are not wanted."

His manner was imperious; they obeyed without a word. Then he hastened after the lantern-holder who was making a heavy-footed retreat towards Low Farm, and overtook him half-way down the close.

"Stay!" he cried.

And the man stayed after a step or two; not so much like a man who does not fear as like one who knows that he is outpaced.

"Who was it?" said Arthur.

"Who was what?" asked the man stolidly.

The light of the lantern wandered about his botched foot-gear, over the frost-bitten wheat and the gathering snow that flecked it.

"On that horse. What person was it?"

"If yer don't know –"

"I do not," said Arthur.

But he denied as men deny on affidavit, which the lawyer draws and they only sign. His shame was his lawyer.

"Then 'twere their Nell," said the man with a half-seen jerk of the hand towards Low Farm.

Arthur was shocked again, and doubly, as men are at the hearing of what they know.

"Why came she here? What was she doing here?"

But babbling why and what he did not wait for the answer; he now remembered perfectly what Nell had promised about the gates at their first meeting; he chose rather to put himself at a distance by fiercely grappling the man.

"Why didn't you defend her?"

"I'm not paid for that."

"You coward! She's your mistress; you ought to have let yourself been killed first."

"Sixpence a day," said the man with the sobriety of indisputable argument," sixpence a day an' what the parish 'lows me wain't pay for all that. Besides she een't my missis now; she gied me the sack a month agoo for comin' five minutes late – by her danged clock, an' now I'm on the parish. I've nubbut coom to her by houze-row for two or three days; I shall come to yo a Monday."

' You coward! you miserable slave!"

"Coward I don't think noat to, there's a many o' the same sex at Blid'orth; but I've no raight to be called a slave, not by nubbudy, it's again the law, I'm a Englishman."

"You stood by and looked on!"

"She's noat to me."

"You wouldn't lift a finger to help her!"

"Not I; not my least little finger."

' You didn't even speak a word for her."

"Why suld I? She's got a tongue of her own."

"'You ought to have shouted out, 'Shame on you; it's a woman!'"

"I tho't a tanning 'ud improve 'er; there's main few women but what it does."

"Since you wouldn't fight for her you shall for yourself. Up with your hands!"

Arthur set upon him with as hearty an appetite as though he were battling against his own self-condemnation. Spettigew dropped the lantern but hardly got his mind and his fists squared for combat; on the instant he was cuffed out of all thought of self-defence, if he had any, by the fury of the onset. He turned tail and fled laboriously across the wheat at a lumpish jog that was almost a trot. Arthur pursued, pommelling him.

"Lemme goo, mester," said the man; "I'm suppered up."

"Why couldn't you say as much for her, you mean-spirited wretch? Begone with you!"

The labourer made no sort of answer but turned and went on his lumpish way. Arthur took up the swaling lantern and returned to the place where he and she – terrible pronouns! – had encountered. He looked the shattered gate over, noted the trampling of the crops round and about with the reckoning mien of a man taking an inventory; but his thoughts were elsewhere. He picked the whip up, first looking round involuntarily to see if he were alone. He walked towards the Oxton road as if with the intention of examining the condition of the gate there, stopped half-way and looked upwind, as if interested in the weather. Faster and faster fell the snow. She had promised it. He turned his back on it as though he felt it, and struck straight across towards the lights of his house. On the way he heard a horse's champing and the jingling of steel. He turned aside and found it was Nell's horse which had strayed thither, and was grazing as unconcerned about her misadventure as her man had been. He took it by the bridle and led it towards Low Farm. He found the second gate also broken.

"The Devil take the man!" he ejaculated "Why couldn't he let me be?"

He must have meant Selby.

The snow fell faster and faster; the night grew darker and darker. When he had crossed the little brook which divided the farms and was nearing the house, it would seem he needed to have doubts. He uplifted the lantern so that it made a flickering patch of light on the horse's back. It was indeed a side-saddle. He walked on leading the horse, none too fast. But it would seem he had another thought, which just then meant another doubt. A half-light deceives men's eyes; especially on a winter's night when the candle swales and its rays tremble like a crowd of liars. He set down the lantern for a moment and put forth the hand which held it. Two stirrups on the near side. He walked on slower than ever.

A little further and the light of the lantern feebly travelling before him showed him Nell leaning on the gate of the croft with her back to him. She was sobbing, sobbing as those only do who sob in the night and think themselves alone. He stopped, he would have gone softly back, but she was speedily aware of the light behind her and sprang into erectness. He then came forward leading the horse. Her face glistened wet, her dress was disordered, her attitude proud. She had lost her hat and the snow speckled her hair, which showed black, as Lois had foretold it would. He recollected that she had. So men mix trivialities with untrivial moments.

"Miss Rideout," he began, "I'm exceedingly sorry –"

"Yo nedn't be, *yo've* lost noat."

There was a sniff; then the tears were gone from the voice, if not from the eyes.

"That's our lantern, I believe."

She took it from him and immediately extinguished it. Then we may believe if we will that her composure was complete.

"I think I can own that hoss too."

She received the reins from Arthur.

"If I'd bro't Hasty i'stead o' this lump o' lead ..."

But she did not pursue the supposition; and Arthur without a word put the whip too into her hand. He had to get rid of it."

"What's this? Oh, ay! I ought to know the feel on't."

Arthur was compelled to speak.

"Miss Rideout, I beg your pardon."

"Yo nedn't; I don't yo for that clinker I gied yer. It *was* a clinker."

As though the recollection of it somewhat consoled her.

"It certainly was, if that means something hard and heavy. But I beg you to believe I hadn't the least suspicion whose hand it came from."

"I reckon yo moot be strange furriners i' th' parts yo come from. We allus hae suspicions, at Blid'orth, about gates; as many suspicions as the gate has rails. I should like to know –"

"What is it?"

"What yo'd ha' done if yo'd knowed?"

"Nothing."

"I'm main glad yo' didn't know."

"I shan't lock them any more."

"Please yoursen; I shall goo by the lane; it's better road, and gainer if oat. Come up!"

That to the horse, whom she began immediately to lead away. But she stopped as soon as she was no more than a flat shadow to Arthur, and added:

"I'm sorry – no, I ain't sorry. All the same I didn't *mean* to rap yer ower the head."

"Thank you," said Arthur; "it certainly had me at my weakest."

He thought he heard a little sniff; which might have been either the weaker recurrence of a sob or the uncertain beginning of a laugh. She disappeared into the dark.

CHAPTER VII

A TWO-HEADED VICTORY

"Where hae yer been all this gret while?"

So said Tish to Nell on her re-entry, and she looked up from the man's grey stocking that she was darning by the candle. Tant was there too; he sat on a cricket putting a new thornwood swipple to a flail.

"I telled yer; looking round."

"Feeling round, I suld think yer mean; it's as dark as pitch."

"Feeling round then. I lay that brucken-mouthed oad yowe to lamb to-morrer,"

"Why, yer clo'es is all torn to jim-rags! Yo might ha' been dragged through and through a haythorn hedge."

"It's a rough night."

"Rough? Yo've soon dallicked that frock up. They might be easy come by."

"Tek care o' your own frocks, our Tish, and I'll tek care o' mine."

With that Nell went across to her favourite lounge against her grandmother's knee. Tant looked at her with stealthy curiosity but said nothing.

Next morning Nell felt sore and stiff but drove herself to her work. After she returned from milking she got Spettigew in a quiet corner of the barn, where he was tying wheat straw into bats, and spoke seriously to him.

"Mind yo don't tell nobody about last night; Tish nor your wife nor nobody."

"All raight," said Spettigew with that sulky down-looking

way of his to her; "I'm no talker. Whitefoot's dropped a shoe."

"If yo do I'll be even wi' yer. How did yer happen by that black eye? Drunk and faighting, I suppose."

Spettigew eyed her askance.

"No, I warn't."

"How then?"

"Same road as yo got what yo got."

A clumsy sidelong jerk of his head seemed to be directed up-hill towards High Farm. Nell got the next words out with difficulty.

"Mr. Skrene?"

"Ah."

"Why?"

"For a crackpot's reason; becos I didn't shove my shou'ders atween your back an' his whip. Would he a laid on any lighter, I wunner? I reckon not. An' what thanks would yo a gien me for interfairin'?"

"The same most likely as he gied yer for not interfairing."

"Then I were safe of a black oy any'ow. But 'twere a faight; I didn't stan' an' be smulled; I gied 'im a sour thump or two. Am I to tek 'er to the smith?"

Nell did not allow him to hang about the house; as soon as he had breakfasted and taken Whitefoot to be shoed, she sent him off to the sheep on the snow-covered turnips. But it was not in her nature to maintain a close supervision over him, or to resort to petty scheming to keep him at a distance. In the afternoon when she was away milking, he was in the cow-hovel with Tant tending the broken-mouthed old ewe and her new-born lambs. Tish came round in pattens with a Paisley shawl on her head and spoke to him over the half-door. He was getting one lamb to suck while Tant rubbed the bleating latest-born down with straw.

"What were yo an' Nell doin' last night, Spettigew?"

"Just lookin' round; she said so hersen."

"Listen to me, my man; when I ax yo a question, I don't

want somebody else's answer."

"Dang the little varmin; I don't believe it iver will soock."

"Leave it be a minute and attend to me."

"She told me not to tell."

"I tell yer to tell. Weigh that again the tother."

He sulkily hung his head over the ewe's back.

"It's no consarn o' mine, I've got a black oy a'ready ower it."

Tish opened the half-door and came in; that was for rejoinder.

"Now, out wee't; wi'out any more arley-parleying."

"We went to oppen them gates," he answered with sulky reluctance, bending obstinately over the trembling new-born thing.

"If I didn't think! And did yer oppen 'em?

"Three on 'em."

"And why not all fower on 'em?"

"Becos we got stopped."

"Who stopped yer?"

"He did."

"By hissen?"

"Not likely; there were five men at the back on 'im. He gied me this black oy, the –"

"William Spettigew, if yo dare to use such language afore me, I'll bang your back wi' the shaft o' this fork." She took the hay-fork up in readiness. "I let yer to know this een't the Lay Cross."

"I didn't say it to yo, I said it to him."

Tant laughed.

"I'll lay a tanner yo didn't, Bill. Yo said 'sir' to him and – to huz."

Tish brought down the shaft a sounding thwack upon Tant's broad shoulders.

"If you wain't be said!"

Tant moved neither muscle nor feature.

"I think this'n 'll do," he said. "Stan' 'im up t'other side the yowe, Bill."

"Yo've telled uz all about your black eye," said Tish; "yo hain't telled uz what happened Nell."

"He dragged her off 'n the hoss an' lammed into 'er wi' a gret long whip; while she screeted out; then 'e stopped."

Tant swore a loud oath; Tish forgot the promised punishment.

"Which on 'em?" he roared.

"The mester; the tothers didn't do noat but ho'd me off."

"That warn't much of a sweater, Bill, for five men," said Tant.

His hands lapsed into his breeches-pockets and himself into his usual careless demeanour.

"I nubbut wish I'd been there," said Tish, still grasping the fork.

"I'm thinkin' o' bein' there," said Tant.

And he began sweetly to whistle "Cherry Ripe."

I fancy it was some sort of consolation to Nell that Spettigew had a black eye against her sore back and shoulders; but it had not prevented her getting stiffer and still stiffer as the day advanced, until she could hardly lift hand to head or set one foot before the other. When she came home from milking she strove with painful courage to put an air of briskness on, but she did not deceive Tish's instructed eye.

"What meks yer drawl yer feet so?" she said.

"I'm a bit stiff."

"What's that wi'?"

"I may ha' ta'en co'd."

"Yo've ta'en co'd afore now, but it niver made yer walk so hotchelling. Yo seem as lissom as a cow-crib. What's done that gret bruise on yer arm?"

"I must ha' joled it again summat."

"Yo must ha' joled it hard."

"I did."

Tant and Tish exchanged glances.

"Get yer to the fire," said the latter, "and warm some o' that co'd out on yer. Tant 'll carry the kit and help me sile it."

"There's no occasion," said Nell, "for Tant to be doing dairy work, whilst hay wants cutting and all them beast wants fothering."

"They mun wait on me," said Tant; "as they've waited many a time afore."

So saying, with his irresistible hands he took the milk from her and carried it before Tish into the dairy. Nell made no vain resistance; she walked to the chimney and lay down on the hearth.

"What ails ta, child?" said the grandmother, who blind and hard of hearing was all the more finely alive to other differences. "It moot be the rheumatics for sartain-lye. Dear-a-dear! Thee mun drink milk hot from the cow i' th' mornin', wi' nubbut a little bawm in't."

Tant stopped at home that evening and worked with a will. Nell consequently was relieved of many an out-door task which generally fell to her share. After the men were gone he even condescended to housework, carried the remains of the bread and meat into the dairy, and showed unexpected talent in removing and folding up a table-cloth. Tish was scornful though she let him do.

"Yo nubbut want petticoats and napern, lad, to be as gret a wench as any trolly i' Blid'orth."

Tant laughed and continued to wipe knife and platter.

"If yo can find me petticoats," he said, "long enough to hide my ankles decently, I unnertake to wear 'em. I shan't be the fowest wench i' th' family nayther."

As for Nell in spite of the aching of her sides it was the pleasantest evening she had spent for many a day; for when the work was done they all drew to the fire, which Tant had heaped up with coal and wood. The hum of the grandmother's wheel was like drowsy distant music, to which the bassoon-like roaring of the chimney sang bass.

Tant, seeming to be doing nothing, quickly toused out with his strong dexterous fingers the sheep's tangled beltings, which Tish was carding and the grandmother spinning them into yarn, which presently he would take and plait into thick twists for mops. And as he picked, hardly looking at his fingers, he talked with that lively tongue of his of the doings and sayings of the parish, of Tom Cribb, of a wonderful pointer of Colonel Thornton's and of the army in the Peninsula. Nell sat and listened. Tish's harsher voice rating him and her at intervals was like the proper dash of pepper in a savoury dish.

Only once he spoke with a passing seriousness, only once he roused Nell, but not to speak. It was when he was describing with considerable knowledge and power the storming of Ciudad Rodrigo. All at once he stopped in the midst; he was speaking of the fall of Captain Hardyman of the 45th; leant back, he ceased picking and said moodily:

"Why ain't I hacking Frenchmen i'stead o' tunnips? doing the work of a Johnny Whop-straw and doing it badly?"

He cast the wool from him across the room.

"Yourn's a safer employment anyhow," said Tish.

"Safer? Much o' that!"

He got up and stretched his legs. He looked very tall standing over the fire. The red blaze stained his hands but did not reach his face.

"I tell yer a man's never so safe as when he's faighting i' th' oppen; and he's never so dangerous as when he's idling at home."

"Your Uncle George," said the grandmother's tremulous voice, "died o' th' yaller fever i' th' West Indies; your Uncle Jim were reported missing – that were in Americay – an's niver bin heerd on sin; your Uncle Ben died faighting black men wi' Colonel Sherbrooke at – I forget the name on't; there were a many queer outlandish marks on the letter as bro't the news. Home's a safer place a deal, lad."

"Dad died theer."

"'Twere God's will. And his mother laid 'im out."

The grandmother said no more; her wheel did not hum while she sat remembering and forgetting. Tant sat down again, picked up more beltings from the floor, and returned to his rustic tales of little import.

"Josh Jowers were i' th' stocks again a Monday."

"Drunk of coorse," said Tish.

"Ay, he's too oad to find a new road to 'em; if there were any partic'lar need. Hosspool seed 'im in 'em an' gied 'im the time o' day. Two or three hours later Hosspool passes again and says, 'Why, yo're still here!' 'Ay,' says Josh, ' I'm no starter.'"

So his talk flitted from sense to nonsense, and presently the spinning-wheel began to hum again.

Tant remained at home the next morning too, though it was Sunday, and took his full share and more in the indispensable labour of the farm. But about ten o'clock he strolled off. Ordinarily he was particular how he appeared outside the gate upon Sundays and other holidays, but on that day he was satisfied to go forth in the roughest of his work-a-day wear, an old low-crowned hat, botched half-boots, grey knitted stockings, leathern breeches and an old sleeved waistcoat of dark brown fustian, but no coat. The frost had given, the wet snow coldly and brokenly reflected the uncertain sun, but the air was of a damp despondent chilliness. Famished blackbirds flew late from under the hedges at his approach and made no outcry. At his heels followed his white terrier and he carried a longlashed whip.

The way he took was across his neighbour's land through the gates which Spettigew's hatchet had broken. There had been no attempt to repair them or otherwise fence the way. His going was leisurely; it almost seemed as though he hoped to be intercepted. His hands were in his pockets, his whip tucked under his arm, he whistled blithely all the way, and stopped every now and then to consider a hare's track

in the snow or in the air a kestrel's pounce and hover, hover
and pounce. But intercepted he was not though he thus
lounged along in the most leisurely manner, and though
Selby crossed the adjoining enclosure in front of him and
might have seen him had he wished. He espied the haft of
Spettigew's hatchet sticking up out of the slushy snow with
the Rideout brand upon it. He laid it under the hedge and
went on. He found the gate on to the road whole but
unlocked; whereat he seemed to be much surprised,
perhaps a little disappointed. However he walked down the
road keeping his eyes upon the house and its precincts;
nobody came out of it, nobody was about; he heard not a
voice, no sound but the jealous bark of the watch-dog.
There was a large wooden gate at the head of the short
carriage-drive which curved round to the front door; he
perched himself on its top rail, rested his feet on the second
rail, which brought his knees up next his nose, and waited.

At least he did nothing else; though it was not a pleasant
morning either for sitting or standing out of doors. The wet
dripped on him from the twisted limbs of an ancient oak
which towered over the entrance; the brightness of day,
such as it was, seemed rather to come from the ground than
the sky. Yet for an hour he sat there and did not seem to feel
either cold or damp or tedium. The terrier kept going a little
way down the road and returning; he sniffed at the snow
and looked wistfully at his master.

Tant was still there when Arthur Skrene, who was to dine
with his sister at a neighbour's, came out of the house. He
walked up and down the well-swept drive two or three times
without appearing to see Tant. But Tant saw him and got
what enjoyment he might out of the elegant figure he made.
He was freshly shaven, and had his dark hair brushed back
and notted into the neatest of clubs, which was properly
crowned with a glossy beaver. At the other extremity of his
town-made over-coat he wore highly-polished top-boots,
glistening rivals of the snow. His hands were handsomely

gloved and carried between them the burden of a
silverheaded rattan.

But at his third turn Arthur lounged quite up to the gate;
where we may suppose that he first became conscious of
Tant's presence; whom probably he knew by sight though
he had never had the slightest intercourse with him.

"A fine morning," said Arthur, just civil.

"That's as it turns out," said Tant, hardly that.

Arthur put his hand upon the sneck, but Tant's twelve
stones and a half had so weighed the gate-head to the
ground that it was scotched.

"Be good enough to descend," said Arthur.

Tant neither moved nor spoke.

"Get down," said Arthur less civilly; "I want to pass
through."

"It hardly follers yo'll pass if I do get down," said Tant.

Arthur took him by the leg and pulled him off. The
change was instantaneous, immense, from the loutish loose-
strung lounger to the superb fighting-man, coolly alert, with
a wary but a fiery eye and tremendous reach of arm. He
presented the handle of the long-lashed whip, saying:

"I've bro't yer a whip."

"I don't fight with whips."

"On'y again lasses?"

Arthur wasted no more words; undismayed, perhaps at
bottom not sorry to let the blood of his hurt pride, he pulled
off his gloves, threw under- and over-coat across the gate,
carelessly cast his trim beaver aside on the snow, and stood
prepared.

"We halve the sun," said Tant.

But he seemed to be struck by the smaller man's fearless
demeanour.

"M'appen yo think," he said, "as it's no fair match?"

"I've expressed no dissatisfaction," answered Arthur stiffly.

"If yo feel any yo've nubbut to say 'a fine mornin' for a
walk,' and I see a rabbit i' th' next cluss as needs my

partic'lar attention. Here, Pitcher!" The terrier sprang up all alert from his apprehensive ears to his up-curled tail. "What d'yer think to him for a tarrier? He's second in descent from Colonel Thornton's Pitch."

"You've no right," said Arthur haughtily, "to find a rabbit either in the next close or the next close but one or the next close but two."

"True! But afore yo stan' so strong on your raight, mek sure as yo can stan' on your feet."

He put himself to his guard with his right hand but hid his left behind his back, as though to make his opponent a contemptuous gift of half his skill and strength. Arthur perceiving it did the like.

"I see," said Tant with a little more respect in his tone, "yo're one o' them as would sooner loase an even set-to than win a handicap. I would mysen. Well, I've no raight to insult yer as well as lick yer."

He brought his left hand again to the front, and the fight proceeded on equal conditions. The sole spectator was a robin, which from the high vantage of the ancient oak with head on one side studied the peculiar ways of men.

Arthur as we have seen possessed considerably more strength than his bulk promised, and he fought with a fierce impetuous courage, dashing in blow after blow, which however were easily warded off by his skilled antagonist. Tant played his game, for a game it seemed to be to him, with scientific coolness, only hitting out every now and then; but when he did it was a knock-down blow. Thrice Arthur was floored, thrice he rose to continue the combat with unbroken spirit though diminished vigour; but the fourth time he lay awhile winded, blinded, spent. And as he lay Miss Skrene came forth buttoning the last button of her second glove. The little slim dainty creature, trimly velveted and furred, not a hair out of place under the wide brim of her bonnet, came along so intent on that last button that she mistook Tant for her brother.

"We'll take your lecture on feminine unpunctuality for granted," so she prattled "unless you can honestly say the time has been wasted."

Then she looked up and saw. The immediate brown fierceness of her eye was the girlish miniature of her brother's. Tant trembled before it, as he had not trembled before her brother's; he shrank again as at the touch of magic from the fighting man into the mere lout. Lois shook her little gloved fist in his face and cried:

"What have you done to my brother, you dreadful man?"

Tant was as if fascinated. He would not have looked, but could not help looking; he would have fled helter-skelter, as the routed fly, but stirred not a foot. Her anger was terrible to him, but more terrible her maidenhood. His knees knocked together, he saw no way of escape; he knew his enemies would pursue him fly where he might; he wished he might die by them there and then.

"I'll have you punished!" she cried and stamped her foot. "You shall go to prison!"

He could not speak; he could not say: "Order me to prison and I will go of myself; I am in prison already." His voice was locked up, behind stronger bars than his teeth. Lois turned and bent over her brother, who was beginning to raise himself a little in the slushy snow.

"Are you much hurt, dear?" she said, and her voice dropped at once the whole octave from defiance to a caress. Tant had never before heard a voice so bitterly sweet, so awfully tender.

"Not much. I think I feel a bit sickish; but there's nothing the matter, Loie. This man has been giving me a lesson."

"A lesson?" She almost thought he was out of his senses. "What sort of a lesson? What do you mean?"

"In boxing, among other things."

He stood up, a sorry object, with bruised face and soiled dress, highly different from the dapper personage of but five minutes before.

"Oh, you look – oh, it's abominable!" she cried, and turned again to confront the author of it; but he was gone, he had fled, he was out of sight. She and her brother returned to the house. She could not get him to say what had been the cause of the encounter, nor even to give the name of his assailant; her dissatisfaction whereat was a salutary counter-irritant to the distress she felt for his injuries.

As for Tant, he hardly deserves a paragraph to himself. His strange case might have been signalized by some new discovery in help or helplessness; but nothing of the kind; he just went and got drunk like any ordinary Englishman ordinarily-disturbed.

CHAPTER VIII

AS OTHERS SEE US

AT a quarter past two in the afternoon Tant was too drunk to stand, not yet too drunk to sit or walk. Why he should not have stopped in the Will Scarlett and there have achieved perfect drunkenness is what I cannot say. Man's mind is not one room built four-square, either hall or garret, it would seem, but an agglomeration of nooks, recesses, cupboards, closets, crinkum-crankums, blind passages with dead lights, doors that open not or open on nothing, stairs that lead up and down and no whither. So even in the process of getting drunk it would seem that the mere getting drunk is not all in all; there may yet be yearnings, whims, crazes; as to the modus of getting drunk, for instance. Perhaps Tant had become drunkenly weary of seeing the picture of "Poor Trust is dead; Bad Pay killed him" over the chimney-shelf of the Will Scarlett, and was taken with a desire to see how it looked over the chimney-shelf of the Barley Mow or the Marquis of Granby. Anyhow forth he staggered through the inn's wide door.

The Will Scarlett is built at a meeting of ways; Tant pulled himself up outside, perhaps in order to deliberate whether he should turn to the right for the Bottoms and the Barley Mow, or to the left for the Unicorn, or keep straight on as straight as might be – for the Marquis of Granby, or even return with a saving of thought and labour to the snug tap-room and home-brewed ales he had just left. But as soon as he stopped he was done; he lost his balance and sank down on his haunches. In front of the house there is a patch of stony ground two or three feet above the level of the road;

thereon he sat or crouched, a sample of the trade done within, a spectacle to passers-by, the plaything of the children who collected round him. He looked none the better for a raw red scratch across his face, gotten from an overhanging briar in his tumultuous flight from Lois Skrene.

The tinkle of the three bells of the church hard-by came thinly down the street. Thinly by ones and twos and threes demure worshippers went up towards it, all sober, all in their best clothes, on their best behaviour; and each as they passed cast an eye on Tant. Little innocents shrank behind their parents, nice damsels averted their disgusted faces, young men laughed, their elders shook their grey heads and prophesied. Tant saw them each after a fashion, as it were through fumes, dimmed and distorted; sometimes he laughed at the funny figures they made, sometimes turning to graver thoughts he pitied them.

All by herself, almost the last, came Lois Skrene, her brother being too disfigured to accompany her. She looked perhaps a little paler for her recent agitation, but the sabbath peace had re-descended on face. Tant saw her too; but clearly, with terrible clearness, in all her innocent youth and beauty. Drunkenly incapable of self-guidance he got up; the ring of children was broken before him; staggered towards what terrified him. Not till was close to her did she see him. She started away in horror. She laid hold of the arm of the first man and cried:

"Send him away! Send that dreadful man away!"

It was old Josh Jowers whom she held by, the roughest customer perhaps in all Blidworth, the completest drunkard and blackguard. He was not drunk just then only because it took so long and so much to make him drunk. Indeed it was a good day's work.

"Nay, ma lass," he said, as gently as his hoarse phlegmy voice would let him, "don't be scarred; he wain't hutt thee; he shan't hutt thee. It's on'y Tant Roideout. Theer, he's took off!"

So it was. Tant had been sobered instantly, completely, by that look of disgusted horror which she flung at him; he had disappeared round the corner with the speed of a flight. The day went back to Sunday, and she heard the tinkle of the bells again.

"Thank you!" she said to old Josh heartily, "thank you ever so much!"

"There warn't no 'casion to be fritted, not a bit on't, for sartain-lye, ma lass – miss. Tant's a good-natur'd lad; I niver heerd on 'im hutting nubbudy."

"He was drunk!"

"Ah? Well, mebbe 'e war a bit meller. It's Sunday, yo see, an' huz working-men hae to mek the best on't."

"Well, thank you once more for your kind assistance," said Lois, but shrinking a little from him.

"Y'ar welcome, ma lass – miss, 'eartily welcome."

They were turning from one another, she with her face set for the church, he with his for the Will Scarlett; at which moment she had a completer view of him than before; of his long loose coat, blue and rent and stained, of his ill-buttoned red waistcoat, of the shred of neckerchief scantly covering a swollen neck, of the ancient cocked hat, limp and greasy, long a castaway from respectability. A dirty fleabitten cur slouched at his heels. She was taken by a sudden pity for the poor pink-eyed beer-sodden wretch who had befriended her. She put her hand on his arm and said:

"Will you take me to church? My brother wasn't well enough to come, and I don't know many people here."

Josh Jowers could not answer, his answer stuck in the rude phlegmy passage of his throat. He could not answer, but he walked by her side up the street churchwards, with steps unsteady, but less from beer than surprise. The mongrel dog followed dubiously at a little distance. The three gloved fingers that Lois had laid upon Josh's ragged sleeve she kept there; in appearance it was much as though she went arm-in-arm with him. He felt their sweet compulsion, on his feet, in his brain; the sign of the Unicorn with its twisted thrusting horn stirred him not; he passed through the church gates. Then the dog which had followed him thus far fled with a howl back to the Will Scarlett.

The blackguard sat beside the lady in the cushioned pew; her dainty out-spreading skirts touched his tattered coat; the preparatory hush settled upon him and in him. When they uprose there was but one prayer-book between them; the lady's spotless glove held one corner, the blackguard's grimy thumb the other. He hardly heard the purchased mumble of the reader; he heard the young fresh ladylike voice beside him singing and saying, and listened to it as a man on the ground listens to a lark in the sky. He would have liked to say "Amen" to her "world without end," but his throat was stopped up. Yet by the time they were half through the Psalms he had managed, with much underbreath hemming and hawking, partially to clear a way for his voice; he was proud to be able to show her that he also could read.

"If thou, Lord, wilt be extreme to mark what is done amiss: O Lord, who may abide it?"

He stumbled at every hard word like extreme and plenteous, and was generally half a sentence behind, but she helped him along; and so his thick uncertain tremulous utterance mingled with her clear sweet tones, going the same way, heavenward,

I cannot say that Josh got much direct good from the dry sermon of the non-resident vicar, his hearing was not so good as it had been; but he ventured near the beginning to take a peep at the fair face beside him; he saw that she was listening for both of them, and he sat through the rest of the service with much satisfaction.

At the church gates she said to him: "My name is Lois Skrene. May I ask what yours is?"

At his first coming out from what was so strange to him, what was familiar had seemed strange, the trees and the graves, the clatter of the children, the eyes of men, even the chilly outside air with more daylight in it than he had expected; the very street with the thrusting Unicorn opposite. He had felt shy and uncomfortable, but her pleasant friendly voice comforted him.

"Josh Jowers, miss." A dirty hand went up to his old cocked hat; to his own surprise he made a clumsy bow of it. "At yer sarvice."

"Well, Mr. Jowers, we've got too large a pew, as you saw, for only two persons; the maids prefer chapel. There will always be a seat for you; and I shall be disappointed if you don't occupy it. Good-bye; till next Sunday."

Of the first person he met Josh asked the time of day.

"Gettin' on for fower o'clock time. Wheer's yer dog? Wheer's Posh?"

He did not answer the question, he was so struck by the thought that he had lost an hour and a half. He seemed to give up hope of getting drunk that day; he went home almost sober; that he might perhaps find dog Posh there was but a sub-motive.

Meanwhile as Lois re-passed the door of the Will Scarlett, what had befallen her there recurred with repulsive distinctness. "Tant Rideout!" she remembered the name; it seemed of the proper unusual sort for such a fellow. Of course she would have liked to know what the quarrel was between him and her brother, and she lost a good deal of pains in vain surmises; nothing she knew of her brother and his nice tastes gave her any clue to it.

She knew enough however not to ask him. But she mentioned her second meeting with Mr. Tant Rideout. How did she know it was Mr. Tant Rideout? She told him, and of her fright, and how she had been rescued from it by a funny pimply old man with a bent nose. Being safely by her own fireside she could venture to laugh a little at her fears.

"And he smelt of beer, Arthur."

"Better and better!"

"Not table-beer either."

"'Pon my word, Loie, you didn't choose your champion very sweetly."

"I didn't choose him at all; I should have chosen a churchwarden. It was fate, and nothing but fate. He was going afterwards into a public-house – perhaps to drink my health – so I – what do you think?"

"Gave him the money for it?"

"Begged him – you might say compelled him to – accompany me to church."

"You never did!"

"And I invited him to make use of our pew next Sunday."

"You can't be serious!"

"And every Sunday."

"Well, you've made it impossible for us to ask any decent people."

"If you mean Miss Perkins –"

"Miss Perkins and others."

"Ask her without the others, she'll like it all the better, and there'll still be plenty of room. I'll see that he sits next to me and looks over my prayerbook."

"I own I'm surprised, Lois."

"So am I, Arthur; I felt sure we should look at it in the same light. And look here! I've told you at once and given you a whole week to get over it before you offer him the welcome of a gentleman as you know you've got to do, and will do – next Sunday. Now I call that considerate. Don't you?"

Tant Rideout had seen the Sunday in her face transformed at sight of him into horror and disgust. Her horror horrified him. The narcotic influence was driven out by another form of stupefaction, more inward, more disabling. He rushed from her presence. Everything looked changed to him – surely he was gone mad! – the sky, the ground, the houses, the folk. Only her face, first with the Sunday in it, and then the horror; that never changed. What sort of monster must he be, who could so instantaneously confound a maiden's calm? He would have liked to take counsel with the men, with the women, with the little children; to ask them: "What manner of man am I? Wherein am I different from you, from your next neighbour, from Josh Jowers, whom she did not fear?" He found however that it was impossible to put such an inquiry into words. But he looked into faces as he hurried by, and out of the looks that were returned him of doubt or surprise he made an answer to it. It seemed to him that everybody was of the lady's opinion.

How long had it been so with him? Surely he had not been born so? When had the change come upon him? During his late drunkenness? or at the moment of his sudden awakening from it? No, for he remembered having seen the same disgust in her at their morning meeting, though the horror was nothing like so great or at least so apparent, being confused with her anger. How far back then went the change? Could it be that yesterday he was a man like other men, negligent, manly, selfish, well enough liked? Or had he been deluding himself for years? Surely he had been mad all the time; surely he had been grossly wrapping up the contempt or fear of men's faces in the happy delusions of a fool! But now that the deceit was rent away, how should he live among them? How could he live among them?

His thoughts drove him straight home, as though the sum of them had amounted to hunger. The tea-table was laid in the kitchen, but Nell was not there; he did not see who was there; he strode through and up-stairs. He rapped at Nell's door; she was within and answered him.

"Len' me a looking-glass a minute."

"A looking-glass? What d'yer want that for?"

"To get summat out of my eye."

"Shall I do it for yer?"

"I'll do it mysen."

And so he went to his own chamber with the square foot of hanging glass by which Nell tied her bonnetstrings. He took it to the window, peered eagerly into it, and saw a pair of wild eyes staring back at his own; saw a visage unshorn, unkempt, unwashed, with a great scratch across it and strange even to himself. He gazed at it for a minute with a disgust and horror like the lady's, then he opened the casement and flung the glass out into the yard. Plump into the miry midst it fell and disappeared; but took nothing with it.

He did not go down to the afternoon meal and made no reply to Nell's repeated call, so she went up to him. He seized her by the arm and anticipated her question with his own.

"What sort of looking man am I?"

She looked at him and said nothing, dumbfoundered by the strangeness of his question and his manner.

"For God's sake tell me, Nell! What is there in me that frightens ladies?"

"A good deal, lad, if yo look at 'em like that."

"Why didn't yo tell me afore?"

"' I never seed yer look like that afore."

"What did I look like? yesterday – the day afore yesterday – last Sunday?"

"Why, when yo were weshed and combed and shorn and your best clo'es on –"

"Ay?"

"Your blue coat wi' silver buttons an' all –"

"Ay, ay?"

"And quite sober –"

"I am now, Nell, terrible sober."

"The handsomest lad in all the forest. And now come down to your tea. There's pikelets."

CHAPTER IX

THE OLD HORSE

In the morning Selby informed Mr. Skrene that William Spettigew had come to him "by house-row" demanding employment. This was in accordance with the method of giving relief to the distressed labourer then in vogue in Nottinghamshire and other parts. In order to avoid his being thrown entirely upon the rates he was sent round by the overseer successively to the farmers of his place of settlement; who each in his turn were required to find him work for a number of days proportionate to the amount of their assessments at the rate of sixpence a day and his food; to which pittance the parish added another sixpence. Arthur bade Selby set the man to help the thrasher, but did not himself see him until the third day. Indeed he went out but little during that time, for his face had not yet recovered from the damage it had received in the fight. However at the end of the third day he crossed the crew-yard and looked into the great dim barn. The thrashing was done for the day; about the barn door a number of sleek stall-fed beasts jostled one another and munched the shorts which had been tossed out to them. Thick on the oaken floor lay thrashed-out grain, which Spettigew was pushing together with the back of a chaving-rake, while Coy, the thrasher, with a wooden shovel threw it up into a great white heap. The thrasher, a lean old man, lean and bent, gave a glance at his master and kept on shovelling. Spettigew touched his hat, rested on his rake and said:

"Weather's very slack, mester."

"It is so."

"The snow's thoein' nicely."

"Yes."

"This barley's a-thrashin' out uncommon well."

Arthur had been going, but the man's apparent interest in another man's barley had something in it which caused him to turn again and speak. But first he went out of the daylight, which still made a ragged circle about the door, into the inner dimness. Through one or two loop-holes that faced the setting sun jets of light entered horizontally, flickered on for a short distance, then were dispersed and lost. Still by them might be somewhat more than imagined the lessening mow of unthrashed corn at the one murky end of the building and the increasing heap of straw at the other. On the floor wanly gleamed the piles of grain. Spettigew still rested on his rake; in the dark background, little more than a flitting shadow, the bent thrasher shovelled and shovelled. Arthur knew he was deaf to anything under a shout.

"So you don't bear me a grudge for what happened on Saturday?" he said.

"Why suld I?" said the man. "Why suld I? Besides I gied yo a dab or two back. To the best o' my power. That theer eye o' yourn looks a bit mauled. I'd sooner be fisted by a man any day nor tongue-battled by a woman."

"Ah? You get more of the latter?"

"The women? They non reckons *theirsens* latter; i' their own estimation they're fust an' foremost at iv'ry turn. I'm main glad yer tantoozled 'er as yer did."

He touched a sore place; Arthur winced and turned away. Spettigew followed him to the door.

"She's a bad un an' cooms of a bad stock. It's well knowed as her gret-grannie's a witch. She lives facing uz at the Bottoms." Arthur showed interest to the extent of looking back a little but not of answering. "An' hersen's little or noat better. I don't like them fraunfreckles about 'er eyes.

It behooves yer to tek care, mester, or she'll be doin' yer a mischief."

"You're a fool!" said Arthur shortly over his shoulder.

He went, and Spettigew stood a minute or two resting on the rake and pondering his final speech; for the master's proven muscular superiority enforced on him a certain respect for his reasoning powers. Coy ceased to shovel, and began to lay the floor for the next day's thrashing. Spettigew went and helped him by forking down the unthrashed barley from the mow, but absent-mindedly, without zeal. After a while he seized the thrasher by the arm to bespeak his attention. The arm he seized was about the thickness of the sneath of a scythe, but of incredible hardness, almost like contractile bone. The man looked up. Spettigew shouted in his ear:

"I'm non sich a big fool as some is."

"Ah?" ejaculated the thrasher.

"I'm sure on't."

And the self-assertion comforted him, as it ever does. They finished the floor in silence. Then Coy raised his bowed head and in a strange high-pitched squeak said:

"I've knowed 'em bigger this-away, an' I've knowed 'em bigger this-away."

While with lateral and vertical extension of his two lean paws he by turns signified breadth and height; and never a word more he spoke that night.

Josh Jowers attended church for three successive Sundays after Miss Skrene's invitation, then was seen there no more. It was all Posh's doing; he refused to countenance the change of habit. He did not argue, he did not scold or tease; his contemptuous silence, his avoidance as soon as Sunday came round, the indifference with which he went off ratting and poaching by himself were more than Josh could bear. He tried as a last compromise to get extra drunk on Saturday; but he could not do it, it was impossible; the best-spent day has but twenty-four hours for sleep and duty. And even if he could have crowded two drunks into one industrious day, he had a heart-sick presentiment that Posh would have disdained the sop. The fourth Sunday night he passed insensible to discomfort in a ditch; Posh lay beside him, sensible but perfectly happy.

"I'm disappointed," said Lois to her brother on their way home from church on the fifth Sunday.

"Did you expect anything else?" said Arthur, who bore his own disappointment well.

"Expect? To be disappointed? I should think not indeed."

"Ah, Loie, you think you can tyrannize over men's appetites as you do over your own home."

"I tyrannize? Oh! When you know, you know, you have your own way in everything. Now do be good. I want you to go and see Mr. Jowers and inquire the reason of his absence. He may be ill."

"Oh, hang it, Loie! The man's a perfect sot."

"I asked you just to please you; I would much sooner go myself."

"That you certainly shall not; he's generally drunk."

"Who tyrannizes now? Well, but you must do it nicely. Say that I – that *we* take it very ill of him, and all that."

And strange to say he did it, and did it nicely too. But he had got into the way of humouring her years and years ago, when she was a tiny thing with hardly words enough to bespeak her commands, and I suppose he felt it hopeless to attempt a change now that she was a young lady with an accomplished tongue. He spoke to Josh on the threshold of his own cottage. Josh, who was as much sober as drunk, hung his head and looked at Posh, who lay in the path and scratched himself with perfect indifference to the visitor's presence.

"It's very 'andsome on yer to coom, sir," said Josh; "an' her, I do think she's the best-natur'd of all the ladies o' the land. But what can a man do? Yo mun talk to Posh. Theer! he's gone as soon as iver the subjeck's mentioned. It's that

what beäts me. I wish sometimes he'd bite me; it 'ud seem
more liker human natur. He wain't argy-bargy, he wain't let
fly, he will hae his own way. Yo see I've been mester on him
so long that he's mestered me. He's a 'eart-breaking dug.
But 'is judgment o' rots is nigh'and a meracle."

                    *   *   *

Arthur did not meet Nell again until near the end of March,
when the hunt gathered at Mansfield Wood. Their greeting
was a slight crook of the neck, a stiff touch of the hat. She
felt those blows still hot upon her back. He too was not well
pleased with her; but the why was something much more
obscure than a smart. It was not because she had trespassed
on his ground and broken his gates; it was not because she
had rapped him on the head; nor because her brother had
given him a black eye, nor because her hair was all but red.
I might fill this book with what it was not if time could be
bought and paper had for nothing, and yet be no nearer
what it was. Besides the huntsman is throwing in the
hounds; and I should hardly have mentioned a point of
mere metaphysics but for the curious form his anger took.

She was walking her horse backwards and forwards,
apart from the loud-voiced, snuff-sniffing, dram-sipping
crowd. He might have been listening to Mr. Rose, J.P., who
was painfully setting forth the injustice of the Blidworth
enclosure act to himself and its over-kindness to everybody
else. But all the while he was asking himself what those
bumpkins wanted. Was she not good enough and good
enough looking for them? For anybody indeed under the
degree of a well-to-do yeoman's son of Kent? He succeeded
in being offended with them because they did not pester
her with their attentions. One of them in particular, a tall
self-assured young man who seemed to be looked up to by
his comrades for his complacent laugh and the jaunty set of
his elbows, he unnecessarily and unreasonably singled out
to be angry with. Why wasn't he by her side with a humbler

simper? The conceited lout! Kicking with a pair of clean boots would have been too handsome a punishment for him. An unusual case that of Mr. Skrene's? Oh, dear no! Most times when we are angry we ought to be laughing.

But the hounds found; Arthur broke off his anger and the J.P. his grievance. The fox took them a merry round by way of Foul Evil Brook, Lindhurst and the lately re-planted Harlow Wood. Bustled thence he scampered through the adjacent Thieves Wood and despoiled Newstead, where he got to ground. While the hounds were being taken to the next covert Nell had a few words with the huntsman, a liberty few would have ventured on at such a time.

"I can't think what ails Hasty," she said. "He don't seem to take any interest in't."

"He does look a bit dull, miss. If yo'll ride 'im ower to the stables to-morrer our Bill Good'in shall hae a look at 'im. He's the best hoss-doctor I know on. It's the gift o' God; for 'e can't ride a ha'porth."

After which lengthy speech he left her at the covert side. She wondered whether she had not better return home. Would Hasty be offended if she did? The tooting of the horn, the cry of the hounds, the huntsman's loud encouragement, the crackling of dry wood, the voices of men, the disturbed scream of a jay, the baaing of some ewes and lambs which a shepherd and his dog were holding up not far off scarcely entered her thoughts. But when the fox had gone away, when a jubilant holloa proclaimed it, when the scattered hounds had been got together and acknowledged the scent, when they disappeared in full cry, every tongue vocal, and when every horse but hers was in eager motion, then old Hasty lifted his head, pricked up his ears and looked half-round wistfully, as if wondering what his mistress was thinking of. Still she hesitated, though her hesitation was giving way, so the old horse took the decision on himself and galloped off after his fellows. She neither reined him in nor urged him on.

The fox had broken away from Hagg Nook and crossing the turnpike had led them down Long Dale, where the sand holes are, through the gorse and bracken of Papplewick Forest and by Raven's Nest Oak. There he re-crossed the road, but there was no safety for him in a young plantation, whether named after Vincent or Nelson. By Stanker Hill he raced, he skirted Goosedale Bog, beyond which he turned abruptly and made the best of his way down the grassy valley of the Leen.

Nell followed at an easy pace, in company with many another, moderately horsed or moderate horsemen; she did not forget. But after they had again crossed the turnpike the crowd was scattered, some went down the road, some got among the hills and rough moor to the right of it, some rode straight for the Leen, beside which they knew that Papplewick lane ran level. Arthur Skrene had gone that way before them but more ignorantly and incautiously. He had not taken warning by the rushes, the persicaria and other coarse growths which betray a marshy spot, so first he got stuck in Congel Mires and then in Goosedale Bog; out of which he was floundering when the ruck swept by, high and dry, along the skirts of Congel Hill.

Nell was going steadily, choosing the easiest, never forgetting, round Race-ground Hill. All at once as she gained the ridge of a slight rise she saw Arthur just ahead of her, desperately urging on his roan mare, which was somewhat blown, in order to recover his lost place. The desire to get in front of him sprang into a sudden blaze within her and burnt up every other consideration. Before her lay the Leen valley, an almost level stretch of grass, though with a gentle transverse slope to the river. Six furlongs off, racing down the valley towards Bulwell, she could see the hounds with a dab of moving scarlet beside them, and the country between was green dotted with red and black. The old horse saw and mended his speed.

"Ay, push along, old boy," she said. "There's somebody

i' front wants taking down a peg; it'll do him good; and yo can do it if yo like."

He seemed to understand; he needed no further encouragement to put himself to his most emulous pace. Suddenly Arthur Skrene had the vision before him of a superb horsewoman on a gallant horse, her hair flying loose, her skirts fluttering in the wind she made. His own steed felt the steely prick two-fold behind the girth; she bounded forward in fierce rivalry and for a quarter of a mile it was a race between them. The younger animal, straining her utmost, did not gain an inch. Then all at once the vision failed; horse and horsewoman had dropped. Arthur looked back as he galloped. Nell had already risen, the old horse lay. With a right good will he tugged at the reins, but Nell waved her hand, either encouragingly to intimate that she was unhurt or impatiently to decline his assistance. Still he was loath to leave her. Down the wind came her shrill: "Yo'll miss the finish!" That and the hand and his mare's impetuosity might or might not have decided him; but the moment after a turfy hump hid horse and mistress from his backward glance; he was free to imagine the best, which he goodnaturedly did and galloped on.

They killed among the gorse between Bulwell spring and the sand-pit. Nell did not turn up even among the latest stragglers. The fat white-bearded miller of Edingley, who always got in last but always got in, had trotted up on his old white long-tailed mare with not a hair turned: but Nell did not come. Arthur grew a little uneasy. While the hounds were searching the warren hard by, he thought he would ride back a couple of fields. He rode all the way back. The old horse still lay as he had seen him lie. Nell sat on the ground at his head; she was very pale; one hand was round his neck, the other under her chin, and she never once looked either to the right or the left. Arthur saw that the old horse was dead. He got down.

"I'm very sorry for your misfortune, Miss Rideout."

She made no answer.

"Allow me to be of some service to you."

"I've killed him," she said with hoarse quietness; "I shall never hunt again."

"Indeed I hope you will."

"What's your hope to me? I suld feel as if I was riding on his ghost."

She rose to her feet.

"How shall you get home? Permit me to put your saddle on my mare."

He began to unbuckle the girth.

"No!" she said, "I shall walk; I'm a butcher, it's proper for me to walk."

They went a few yards, then she suddenly turned and went back. He did not look to see what might be the occasion of her so doing; he stood until presently she rejoined him. They walked together, he leading his mare, over the ground whereon they had raced so unfortunately.

"Did they kill?" she said after a while.

But her ear was full of the last word she had uttered and she did not hear the answer.

Presently the faint sound of a holloa reached their ears.

"They've fun' again," she said.

She stopped, but did not look back.

"Why are yo here?" she said.

"I've had enough for to-day."

"Then yo've no gret stomach."

He thought she was going to insist on his departure, he saw the tightening of her lips; but she did not insist; she only said:

"I suldn't ha' tho't yo'd ha' liked the Squire and the Colonel and Joe and Silly Walker to hae it all their own way."

Then they walked on again. At the top of the hill there is a gate; there she stopped and looked her last look at the little patch of dark brown on the green far away down the

slope. When they moved on the mare was between Arthur
and her.

One field in silence, two fields in silence, then she said:

"He was such a good oad horse! As true – oh, he was true
all through! He hadn't an atom o' vice; and no more temper
nor belongs two pair o' heels."

For a time there was no sound but the jink of the mare's
stirrups and the amorous "chicurr" of a pair of partridges in
a neighbouring field. At last Arthur said:

"I wonder whether you will ever think as much of any
human being."

"I shan't ever meet wi' one wi' such qualities. He was
such a good oad hoss!"

As soon as they were on the hard road she said:

"Get up and ride, Mr. Skrene."

She put aside his objections with a stern, "I've plenty o'
company, plenty o' company."

So he mounted and rode. But on reaching High House
he immediately dispatched two of his men with a wagon
and four horses to fetch the old horse home, giving them
such directions as he could for finding him. And seeing
Butcher Johnson's man on the premises – he had come for
a fat beast – he got him to accompany them, as being more
used to the handling and hoisting of dead weights. Then he
caused his sister's quiet-tempered pony to be saddled and
hastened back to meet Nell. She had come slowly and was
still three miles from home.

"Yo've gien yoursen needless trouble," she said; "I'd
sooner ha' walked." However she mounted the pony,
saying: "I shan't think it's him anyhow."

After going a little way she said: "Thisn's a nice-actioned
pretty little mouse for a young lady. She couldn't be safer if
she was at home."

A mile further and the wagon passed them. She
recognized Arthur's men and horses and looked at him
questioningly; the first direct look she had given him that

day. He nodded.

"Ride after 'em," she said, "and tell 'em to be gentle wee 'm. Tell 'em it's no knacker's job; he was a gentleman, tell 'em. They might call at the Burnt Stump and get a bat or two o' clean straw."

When Arthur came back from giving the directions she said:

"I'll sattle wi' Johnson for Sam Hosspool; he'll charge me a little less nor he would a furrener."

"I don't expect he'll charge at all."

"I'll see he does. Johnson ayther charges or charges double. I wain't pay for civility in wi' my meat, as if 'twere a higher-priced sort o' suet."

Arthur laughed.

"I will see," he said, "that it doesn't get into your meat bill."

Her glance and her words were impatient.

"Yo mun be satisfied if I don't insist on paying for your men and hosses."

A little further on she said:

"Yo've gotten here a kind-mouthed good-mannered little chap – for a lady. Anybody who could sit a sofy could sit him."

Then she sighed and her face set hard again and she spoke no more. They rode up to the Low Farmhouse together. She dismounted and delivered the reins into his hand. She pointed to the disputed way across the fields, saying:

"Yo'd better goo the gainest road." Then with a strange look which did not precisely hit the difference between a sob and a smile: "It is oppen, I believe."

"How did we come to dispute about it?"

"The aggravation of a padlock, the pleasure o' being contrairy wi' a contrairy chap."

"But I can't use the road unless you do," said Arthur.

She nodded; then turned and passed through the gate

into the yard. Arthur took a man's pleasure in her free and upright carriage as she trod the smooth water-worn boulders of the side-path. Then he rode off the field way, thinking how staunch such a girl would be to the man whom she took a fancy to; and at the same time disconnectedly regretting that she should say "yo" when she might have said "you."

Meanwhile she had passed the kitchen window, through which she knew Tish at the sound of her steps would peep and wonder why she was home so early and what had become of Hasty; but her own look was straight ahead. She entered the stable. The beautiful greyhound tripped daintily down to meet her. Nell stooped and gave her the expected caress, but her wistful eyes were not satisfied.

"He's coming, my pet," said Nell. "In a wagon."

The tense lines of her face were broken up; she burst into tears. The hound put a cold nose up to her hot cheek and whimpered.

CHAPTER X

HALLELUJAH!

THE sun's course waxed towards the larger circles of summer, the lambs thickened, the old sow farrowed, Whitefoot dropped her first foal, the turnips were sown, the cows came into full profit, the dull black buds of the ash-tree burst into a varnished russet and green, the high hedges looked as though they were snowed over, the sheep were washed and clipped, and Arthur Skrene met Nell Rideout again. He had indeed seen her once or twice at market in the meantime, had looked at her bags of samples, and while the grain dribbled through his fingers had passed a favourable judgment on her wheat and rye and not so favourable a one on her barley; but of course that is quite a different thing from meeting a person in a quiet lane on a Sunday evening.

She was on her way to the chapel at Blidworth; by the somewhat less direct way of a grassy forsaken lane which for a field or two was the western boundary of High Farm. Arthur Skrene was going to – but it is no matter where nor for what purpose, trivial or important, it was forgotten and never got done. He saw her as he was stepping over the stile off his own land into the lane. He stood half hidden by the elm which overhung the stile and watched her come up. She wore the usual costume for a summer's Sunday of rustic maidens of her time; a white muslin gown rather low-necked, blue sashed, with a white underskirt and white stockings peeping between it and the black bows of her sandals. Her white mittens reached as high as her elbows.

It was the first time that year of her wearing white, and she had on the new bonnet from Mansfield, a great coalscuttle thing with blue ribbons and a nodding white feather. But I do not think it was that entirely nor even the quiet of the road which had overspread her face with such placidity. Arthur had seen it in the excitement of hunting, the keenness of reckoning, the gravity of approval or disapproval, the concealment and the betrayal of emotion, but never before in repose. It was in some sort a new face to him. As she got abreast of the stile she turned her eyes from looking straight ahead and saw him. He at once went towards her.

"Good-evening, Miss Rideout. Whither are you bound, if I may ask?"

"To chapel."

He walked beside her up the hill. Short fine grass was their carpet, hedged with scented mayblossom and the differing yellows of gorse and broom. A long way off there was the brawling of men and the laughing of women, but the lane was quiet of everything but singing birds; and it was afternoon with them. The sun was warm to their backs and they walked slowly. A slight haze dreamt along the tops of the hills.

"The day I came," said Arthur, "I thought this was the dreariest country I had ever seen."

"I've never seed any other," said Nell; "and I don't want."

Her eyes watched a bumble-bee's way in and out of a bee-nettle.

Arthur took leave of her outside the Methodist chapel. Immediately he felt that the sunshine among houses is not as the sunshine among trees and hedges. He had walked no great distance up the street before he bethought himself that all that time he had been going out of his way. He turned back and again he passed the little Methodist chapel. The outer door was set wide open. His casual glance was arrested by a peeping hand's breadth of muslin skirt. He thought he knew it; he was taken by an impulse, he went straight up the steps; perhaps to make sure of it. He had a good eye apparently for a dress fabric; Nell was alone in the narrow lobby behind the door with her back to him. Perhaps Brother Lightfoot's watch was five minutes fast, perhaps though Arthur had said so little his company had been a drag upon her feet; anyhow she had arrived just after the brother had begun the opening prayer, and had had to stand out until it was concluded.

Having justified his eyesight Arthur might have withdrawn unperceived and gone upon his way. He did the unexpected thing, he walked in. She turned her head and saw him. There was a coming of colour under her cheek-bones; faint it is true and only noticeable because Nell was not one easily to change colour or courage. Still one may flush at almost anything, any sort of surprise, any sort of warmth. She made room that he might stand beside her.

Brother Lightfoot always spoke to the Almighty louder by far than to his earthly father, who was known to be hard of hearing. His voice, violently prayerful, went through the passage like a blast of wind; but they stood by in the corner and took no hurt. A ray of sunshine came through the chink between door and jamb; a row of children had settled on the bottom step and were chattering like sparrows.

But at length Brother Lightfoot had done uttering; Nell and Arthur passed in while the congregation were coughing their throats into tune.

"Let uz worship God by singing 'ymn number twelft, short measure:

> ' Come, ye that love the Lord,
> And let your joys be known.'"

So Brother Sam Jarvis lustily gave forth, a little big-voiced man whose white smock-frock elaborately needle-worked down the front contrasted strongly with his dusky red face;

and forthwith he struck up the appropriate tune.

The congregation, most of whom had no hymnbooks and could have got no profit by them if they had, sang the two lines with him. He then gave out two more:

> "Join in a song with sweet accord
> While ye surround the throne."

And so through the eight verses, nominally of short metre, but which with an added refrain of "Rollelujah for ever" loosely tacked on to the florid redundancies and repetitions of the tune proper became the longest of longs. But the most remarkable thing about the performance was that everybody sang, every man, every woman, every child, at the top of their voices; even the babies were not mute. We may have better psalmody now-a-days, irreproachably unemotional and empty, from our Mus.B.'s and D.'s, we have no such singers as those lusty enthusiasts who made the windows of that humble little meeting-house tremble. Folk tell us our wines are decadent, our poetry, our shoeleather, our vices; I sometimes think our voices must be too.

> "We're marching through Immanuel's ground
> To fairer worlds on high."

So they sang, often at variance in the words, never in the notes, doubling, trebling, quadrupling the refrain, forte, fortissimo, fortississimo, till the sound entered by storm the open windows of the Will Scarlett, silenced Dick Dunstan the pensioner, who was obliging the company with a scurvy song to a scurvy tune in a scurvy voice, and took the whole tap-room prisoners. Arthur did not know what to make of it. The only congregational singing he was acquainted with was a kind of mortified chant which had apparently replaced the obsolete penance of the old religion.

When they sat down to the reading of "the first portion of Holy Scripture" all Arthur learnt by it was, that Brother

Tom Jarvis, who was a larger edition of Brother Sam, thought it did not matter where he put his h's so long as he got in a fair average of them, and that he believed difficult passages could be explained out of a mere good-will to explain them. That was soon achieved, and he had leisure to feel somewhat uncomfortable in his unusual surroundings. It was the first time he had ever visited a dissenting meeting-house, and the unconsecrated ugliness of the room was as little to his taste as the free fervour of its worshippers. Nobody took the least notice of him but two or three peeping urchins, who got their heads audibly knuckled for so doing.

But Brother Sam Jarvis's jolly voice called on them again to sing hymn number 499, peculiar measure:

> "Come let us ascend,
> My companion and friend,
> To a taste of the banquet above."

He plunged at once into "Derby," not because he was sure it would fit, but because he was fond of "Derby," because its tied notes make it a squeezable sort of tune, because he trusted that its anapaestic swing would carry them over occasional rough places, and finally because he was incapable of hesitation. But the singing came to an end at "banquet," the last word being altogether unprovided for in the tune.

"She wain't goo," said Brother Sam.

"Yo mun humour 'er a bit, Samwell," said a voice in the congregation; "as if 'twere your Sarah."

Arthur cast a side-glance at Nell to see whether she were most amused or displeased. He could not see that she was either; it was the same still face which had seemed so at one with the quiet lane, and she had her finger in her hymn-book to keep the place.

They tried again, "humouring her," and by thrusting here and there two syllables upon notes only intended to accommodate one, and by repeating the last four words of the sixth line managed to get through, though with considerable jolting, which however nobody took amiss. Nevertheless the good brother was a little discouraged, not to say daunted; perhaps he felt it was not one of his days. After the second reading of Scripture, when he had given out next hymn (it was only trumpet metre), and all the congregation was waiting on his precentorship, he turned and looked up at the brother who had just mounted the pulpit in the place of the reader, and said:

"Yo may try her yoursen."

With a gently waggish smile in a pleasant elderly voice the new-comer immediately answered, "It appears to me it 'ud goo to 'Consolation,' Brother Samuel."

So "Consolation" they tried, and it did go.

"My text will be fun' in the second Samuel" – with again a sly glance at the first Samuel seated below – "the *second* Samuel, sixt chapter, fowerteent verse. 'And David danced before the Lord.'"

It was a clean-faced old man who now stood before the people; not meaning so much that his face was well washed and new-shaven, though it was that, as that it was clear of all pride, malice and guile. His hair was turning to white; his cheeks were of a transparent paleness, as though he had recently suffered a severe illness; he wore a decent black coat and white neck-cloth.

"I niver tho't, friends, to meet yer here again afore the mercy-seat and join with yer in congregational praise and thanksgiving. I looked afore this to be lifting up my voice in the New Jerusalem – wheer the tunes allus happens raight, Brother Samuel."

"Glory be to God for that!" shouted Brother Samuel.

"Howiver here I am in accordance with Divine dispensation among yer again to praise an' pray in God's house; to dance before the Lord, like David. I've hed a sore time on't, brothers an' sisters; what the pain an' what the anxiety, I were bein' nicked wi' a two-edged knife. But I've been bro't through; the deep watters has become shaller to my feet; the doctor was very good, bless 'im, and the Lord was mighty to save."

"Hollelujah!" shouted one and another of the congregation.

"How pleasant it is, friends, to feel free from pain of a fine summer's day!"

"It is, Lord; Thou knows it is," murmured a sallow-faced sister.

"To arise up from that weary bed, to know as the bottles are all emptied and chucked away, the doctor thanked and paid! I owe it to him to say as he dealt very generous wi' me."

"The Lord reward him fowerfold!" thundered Brother Lightfoot.

"But the Chief and the Captain of my deliverance, how shall I thank Him, how shall I pay Him?"

"I doubt it'll break yer, brother," said Brother Cuthbert.

"It will, brother; not only my purse but my sperrit also. But 'the sacrifices of God are a broken sperrit.' Pay Him I can't, pay Him I niver shall. Thank Him I can, imperfectly, wi' a stammering tongue, a bit at a time. 'O Lord, Thou presarvest man and beäst. How excellent is Thy loving-kindness, O God! therefore the children of men put trust under the shadder of Thy wings.' Brethren, my 'eart's brim-full; I shan't be easy whilst I've teemed a little on't out. Let uz pray."

But are you worthy to listen? At the most you would tolerate with a smile what Chris Nicholson poured forth with tears. We are a people who stand without in the street, and a friend's voice in the ear, greetings by the way, the hurry of care-shod feet, the tumult of our own thoughts, all the noises of the common road mix with the half-heard words of an unseen preacher. But when Chris Nicholson had prayed and had risen and wiped his eyes, he again proceeded:

"'And David danced before the Lord.' We're not to imagine that he danced one o' these 'ere wanton immodest morris dances or – or jigs or – or – Brother Charlesworth knows the names on 'em better nor me; if he hain't forgot."

"I'm on the way," said Brother Charlesworth, "wi' God's assistance."

"No, no! 'twere none that sort o' dance, no huggling an' pawming an' kissing, but just a plain h-honest hinnocent homely romp – *yo* know; hop up smiling, twizzle round and hop back again – such as the childern delight in towards Christmas-time, bless their happy faces! David danced before the Lord; and his dancing has this lesson for uz to-day, that religion een't intended to make our lives sorry. Oh no! Yo'd think to hear folk talk as Christians goo about with funeral clo'es on, because some on's wears black cooäts a Sundays. The black's nubbut o' th' outside, friends."

"Hollelujah!"

"Tailor Adams put it together."

"He did!"

"And I don't denies he gies fair vally for money; but the inside's cloth of a different colour and quallity."

"Glory to God!"

"' 'Tis religion that can give –'"

"Ay, ay!"

"' Sweetest pleasures while we live.'"

"'Tis so, 'tis so!"

"'In the Heavenly Lamb
Thrice happy I am,
And my 'eart it doth dance at the sound of His name.'"

"Praise the Lord! Hollelujah!"

"Look at my face, non-Christians – not at my cooät – do yo see any signs in't of regret or misgiving?"

"Not a bit on't," called out Simon Jackman.

"I weren't addressing yo just then, brother. Pike round, non-Christians; look if yo can see a sorry face among 's, ayther up-stairs or down. Purr about, don't be mealy-mouthed, gauze up an' down. Does Samuel Jarvis appear as if he repented o' his repentance?"

"Not him!" cried Brother Samuel.

"Brother Clifford tells me he's put on two stun sin' 'e becomed convarted. Look at Brother Charlesworth! Yo can count his teeth. This is better, brother, een't it, than when your shoe's sole was merry and your own soul in a desperate despair?"

"It's any odds," said Brother Charlesworth.

"What a sorry one-day-a-week merriment were that! Six days out o' the seven yo hed to goo ho'ding your mouth shut to keep the wynd off'n your stomach; now yo oppen it wi'out fear, in season and out of season, in commendation of Him who hath holpen you and comforted you."

"Hollelujah!" shouted the brothers and sisters in chorus.

"Do yo withcall them saving tears shed years and years agoo, Sister Morris? Do yo begin to be sorry for your 'oly sorrow?"

"It's now all my joy," said the sister in a thin aged voice.

"What, yo're all o' the same wadd? But mebbe yo, Brother Brown – the whittaw I meant, but yo can answer too, George, for I see yo've gotten your tongue ready twisted – Both on yer, are yo saying i' your hearts, 'Oh, gie's back the days we've messed away i' God's sarvice that we may spend 'em again profitably in drinking, gambling an' cock-faighting'?"

"No!" shouted both the Browns together.

"Nay, if yo're all of a tale –"

"We are," said the people.

"Then it's no good for to send my question round any more if it's allus to get the same answer. It's wunnerful too! There's little uns here an' gret big uns, strong uns an' poor wankling craturs, fair young maids an' down oad men, yet

your 'earts are all of a make. There's no misgiving, no
shame nor no fear in none on 'em. Yo dance afore the Lord.
Dance! not to the squeal of a bit o' cat-gut, but to the music
o' your own tho'ts."

"Glory!" they all cried together lifting up their hands.

"Drabbit them Methodisses!" said Seth Oldknow
wheezily in the tap-room of the Will Scarlett. "What loongs
they hev got, for sartain-lye."

"Loongs?" growled Sam Mosley. "They've as mooch
loongs as a blether, which is all wynd-room."

Arthur Skrene's prejudices were entirely on Sam
Mosley's side; sitting in the tap-room of the Will Scarlett he
would have passed the same judgment in less forcible
words; but he saw the sincerity of the men's faces; he could
not be so unfair as he would have been pleased to be.

As he passed down the scanty aisle at the end of the
service, many a rough hand was thrust forth to grasp his
and bid him welcome. He saw no reason why people who
had just worshipped together should not still be strangers.
He came away with Nell; he was glad when they had
escaped from the encumbered street into the quiet lane. Still
he laid part of the blame of his unamiable mood at her
door; he knew that if she had taken the service less seriously
he would have consented to be merely amused; so he was
teasing himself and would fain have been teasing her. I
think she understood something of his state of mind; she
said nothing to him; not a word. It was the hush of day; the
colours of earth and sky were still unmixed but softened.
The birds sang but sang of rest from singing.

"Wouldn't it be as easy for those people," he said, "to sing
hallelujah as rollelujah?"

"Ay, but when the heart's in a hurry it wain't wait to
spell."

There was a pleasant cooling stir in the air, but not
enough to ruffle the spreading heads of the cow-parsley by
the hedge-side.

"Do you suppose that man could be really so ignorant as to think David danced a Sir Roger de Coverley?"

"Why suldn't he? Yo see I've all Chris's ignorance and a good lump o' my own to boots." She gave a side-glance at his handsome discontented face. "It's a gret comfort sometimes not to be so knowing. 'Specially of a Sunday evening."

The last bee drew out of a broom flower yellow-thighed and flew away home.

"Still, I must wonder that anybody can prefer such ministration to that of an educated and properly ordained gentleman."

"I'll tell yer why; we know Chris Nicholson."

"No doubt he's a good fellow."

"Nay, the good fellows were across at the Will Scarlett. We know Chris. Can yo say as much o' your parson?"

"I see him most Sundays."

"Ay, he reads and he rides. Chris Nicholson stays amung-hand."

As they descended the hill the air became stiller, the quiet deepened. The lark which had been singing fluttered down to the earth.

"Well, it appears to me unseemly to interrupt a service – I suppose you would call it a religious service? – with either approval or disapproval."

Her serenity, hitherto perfect, was ruffled; she stopped and faced him.

"Man, I coom this-away becos o' the quiet; it seems to help me remember a good sarmon or forget a bad un. But I'd sooner pass through faighting men and brangling women than abide a continuance o' this picking small talk. So yo moan't be offended if I bid yer good-night and step forrard."

She was as good as her word; she hastened on and left him. He stood lost in indignation. She had openly preferred the loudest and rudest annoyance to the company of his condescension. But before she had gone many yards she returned. He did not await her coming but strode off in the contrary direction. She quickly pursued and overtook him.

"I can't bear to leave yer mad at me. Yo're such a franzy man, Mr. Skrene; yo're allus of hoss-back. Coom down a bit, do, there's a good un. Don't bear me no malice. I moot speak as I think or not at all; which een't civil when yo're axed a plain question. Coom, shake hands wi' me and part friends."

He could not resist the candour of her address; he turned and shook hands. The sky was still luminous but the discoloration of the earth had begun. He felt a change too in the values of his judgment.

"I perceive you think me a sorry coxcomb," he said.

"Sin yo ax me – I think yo've an ower good opinion o' yoursen. But let that be; and let Chris Nicholson be; he'll be judged by his works not by his grammar an' spelling; we all shall. And now goo your own way. Think o' summat quietening; the sweet haythorn bloom or the come-day-go-day whistle o' yon blackbird; the crops an' the price o' wheät, if yo can't fix your mind on noat better. And now, good-night once more."

She went down and he went up. The yellow of the gorse was indistinguishable from the yellow of the broom. A clump of white campions scented the air. Night had begun to fall.

CHAPTER XI

THE BADGER-BAITING

THE great-grandame of the Rideouts fell ill of her last illness;
a delusive tedious troublesome illness, a gradual sinking into
sleep liable to sudden awakenings or half-awakenings to
which clung much of the illusion of sleep. Among other of
the old woman's whims she would not endure the
ministrations or even the sight of Mrs. Spettigew, who had
hitherto served her; she demanded Nell's frequent, almost
constant attention. In the end she would hardly take bite or
sup but from Nell's hand. And that at a time when the
harvesting of grass, of white corn and black was demanding
all their energy. Fortunately Tant was a great stay to them;
he had kept sober ever since the rude shock of Miss Skrene's
disgust, and threw himself into the work of field and yard as
though it were something to be smitten and overcome. But
when the harvest-cart had come home decked with boughs
and laden with singing children, when the nights began to
eat up the days, when the stacks were all thatched, and the
farm-work after the late hurried fever settled again into its
autumnal routine of cleaning, ploughing and sowing, then
Tant broke out again violently for a week.

He could do with back-breaking labour from sunrise to
sunset; it dulled neither his body nor his spirits; he could
lie all day in the sun, listening to the bursting of the broom-
pods, watching the movements of a soldier-beetle, the
coming and going of butterflies, the antics of a blue-cap, get
up when the dew began to fall and go home quietly to bed;
but he was not disciplined to endure the hum-drum of daily

life. At the end of the week he was party to a desperate deed
of machine-breaking at Calverton. The next day the aguish
reaction came on after his hot fit of devilry. He tied himself
to the labour of the farm, but could not do enough between
dawn and dark to tire his remorse. The lady's face,
disgusted, horrified, was always before him.

Only ten days later there was another still more violent
and unfortunate collision between law and misrule at the
same place, but he had refused to take part in it. In this second
attempt the Luddites were interrupted by the arrival of a party
of Yeomanry under Sergeant Skrene's command. There was
a determined fight; three or four of his men were wounded
and a horse killed; on the side of the rioters there was greater
loss, one of them being shot dead, many said by the hand of
Skrene himself, before they were put to the retreat.

Thereafter Tant's doings perplexed his sisters. His shoes,
which were laid by the kitchen fire over night to dry, were
in the morning always freshly wet and muddied. The roof
of the long range of stabling which abutted on the house
sloped up within three feet of his bedroom window; so that
by removing two or three tiles purposely loosened he had
an easy passage between the rafters to a false floor under
the roof, and thence by means of a ladder to the ground.
This sly mode of exit he had sometimes used in his father's
lifetime and often since to conceal his night-wanderings
from the household. Tish and Nell knew well enough he
had been stealing forth by it night after night during those
first three weeks of October, departing as the latest stayers
were quitting the Barley Mow, and returning what time the
fox would be trotting back to his kennel. Yet his face showed
no signs in the morning of midnight riot or misdoing, and
his frame no lassitude; he did his share and more of the
farm-work with unremitting energy.

"I wunner what that lad's agate on now," said Tish one
morning.

She had to speak up, for she was on her knees before the

fire kneading bread and Nell was in the dairy churning out of sight. The grandmother sat in her accustomed seat knitting; Tish could just see her skimpy black gown hanging straight down from knee to red woollen slipper.

"I might ha' tho't," said Tish, "'twere nubbut a bit o' trout-fishing or rabbit-netting, but he –"

"Nay," answered Nell, shrill and unseen, "he goos out as reg'lar when it's dark as when it's moonlight."

"That's what I were saying, weren't it? D'yer think I'm hafe baked?"

She spoke at a higher pitch than need was, and therewith dabbed her large clenched fists more energetically into the stiff dough. Nell continued to turn the handle of her old barrel churn. Splash! splosh! went the cream. Click! click! went the grandmother's knitting needles.

"What cops me," said Tish after a while, "is that he don't drink wee't."

"So much the better," said Nell.

"May be. But if it's mischief he's after, dry mischief, let me tell yer, 's worse nor the drunkenest o' devilries. This last salt o' that Mansfield chap's no better nor rammel. I shall tell him."

The grandmother sat by the fire and no longer knitted.

"Two things works havoc wi' men folk, loove an' play," she said tremulously hoarse. "M'appen the lad's i' loove."

"Granmam!" cried Nell scornfully, almost angrily.

"Yo're working that churn too fast," shouted Tish. "It'll niver coom at that rate."

"I wouldn't say *that* on him," said Nell, "behint his back. He's none i' loove."

Tish lifted her hands from the dough.

"How do yo know?" she said. "What do yo know about it?"

Nell's answer was not quite ready.

"Now yo're working that thing as slow as yo did fast afore," shouted Tish.

"I tho't it was gethering."

"Gethering? Much. Yo'd seem to know as little about butter as yo do about loove."

At last Nell had her answer ready.

"He never laughs nor sings now-a-days, that's why I tho't; he's as sober-sad as rent day."

Tish rose from her knees.

"Yo gret sawny!" She was almost furious. "Yo babby know-noat! What do yo unnerstan' o' loove?"

Splash, splosh! went the cream, regularly rhythmic, neither hurried nor delayed, and Nell answered back out of the unseen coldly and calmly:

"Noat. I'm satisfied; I unnerstan' what I'm doing."

Tish answered not immediately, while she rubbed the dough from her fingers, and when she did answer her voice was a little softened.

"I let yer to know, gell, loove's a thing there's a deal more crying nor laughing in't."

She said no more and Nell said no more. Plip, plop! went the butter as it began to come. The grandmother stroked her knees and forgot her knitting.

In the evening when she had taken her staff and risen, and stood waiting for Nell's arm to lead her to bed she said to Tant:

"Gimme tha hand, lad."

He put his large muscular hand to her skinny tremulous one. The ends of the aged fingers fell naturally just where the young pulse strongly came and went.

"How does ta sleep, lad?" she said.

"Sleep, granmam? Like other folk; just goo to bed an' wakken up."

"Does ta dream?"

"Like other folk."

"Good dreams or bad uns?"

"How suld I know? Afore I've windered [winnowed] 'em they're gone."

"Does ta say tha prayers?"

"Nows an' thens."

"Thee can't dream to hurt thee after ' Jesus Christ's sake, Amen.' Will ta say 'em to-night?"

"Ay, granmam."

Nell's arm was ready, but the beldame stood, unusually garrulous.

"I mind me when thee were nubbut a little un, an' thee wouldn't niver say, 'forgie's our trespasses.' Say's I would thee wouldn't. Thee said God hedn't gotten no land at Blid'orth, an' the Colonel could look after hissen."

Tish attacked him more directly, not more successfully, in the morning, as he was going forth with a recent wetness on his boots.

"It don't look well, it looks bad," she said, "to start the mornin' wetchud."

"Would it ha' looked better," he answered, "if I'd slived down i' th' night an' changed shoes?"

Tish had a reply, she always had, but Tant had gone from the door and it went to waste.

Nell had a doubt of her own, which she kept to herself, so making a fear of it.

Towards the end of October a badger-baiting with Sam Mosley's badger was got up by Gill the landlord of the Lay Cross. This was the solitary wayside tavern at which on the day of his arrival Arthur, after long wandering, had got uncertain information of his whereabouts. It was a house with a reputation as mean as its appearance. It was situated on the outskirts of the forest, at the crossing of little-frequented pack-horse tracks to Mansfield and Ollerton, and had been notorious for generations as the nightly resort of foot-pads, burglars, poachers, deer-stealers, debtors eluding their creditors, topers eluding their wives, and indeed of all manner of characters from bad to doubtful. For which it was tardily condemned and pulled down shortly after the date of this story. But all that did not in the

least interfere with the attendance at the baiting of
respectable persons who were fond of a bit of sport. They
separated the ill-repute of house and landlord from the
unquestioned merit of the badger, as scrupulously as they
discriminated between the laxness of a parson's conduct
and the infallibility of his doctrine. So at the back of the inn
on a plot of ground cleared of gorse, broom and ling
gathered most of the farmers of the neighbourhood, a
sprinkling of their landlords, a good many sporting shop-
keepers from Mansfield and elsewhere, a couple of doctors,
an attorney in top-boots, licensed victuallers with and
without their wives, stockingers from Sutton and Arnold,
grimy colliers from the borders of Derbyshire. The parish
constable and the parish clerk were *ex officio* spectators. Of
course all the riff-raff of the country was there, including old
Squire Bellaby, who never missed prize-fight, cocking or
baiting within fifteen miles; but there were besides several
decent persons of the most serious aspect who seemed
surprised at meeting one another there. They were fellow-
worshippers at the Methodist chapel; but they did not come
in their Sunday coats. These hung on the outskirts of the
mob until a beginning of the sport was made with Jimmy
Strong's Irish terrier – it was five to three on the badger then
they pushed for the best places. Among these cannot be
reckoned Tant Rideout, who probably would come most
fairly under the heading "riff-raff and Squire Bellaby"; as
most certainly would Josh Jowers, as yet incompletely
drunk.

The badger's place of vantage was a wooden box about
three yards long, and but just high and wide enough to give
him and his persecutors room to battle in. Many a dog of
divers breeds or none at all was put in to him, but for the
most part the badger had the best of it. Great was the
hilarity – among the men – at the defeated howls of other
men's dogs. Only one of the latter species had the courage
wholly to refuse. That was Josh Jowers's cur, Posh; he

understood hares and rabbits perfectly; man from heel to ham, as well as need be, badgers not at all; but he was satisfied with his ignorance, and ever resolutely backward declined to enter for the study. Only the butcher's bull-dog and Sam's own Irish terrier bitch Sally were successful in drawing the animal; the bull-dog after much blood lost and the permanent disablement of one of his fore-paws, the latter with a great show of ferocity and plenty of barking, growling and rough tumbling, but without a hair's damage to either side of the contest. But Sally's victory over her grey comrade was an understood thing at Blidworth and brought Sam in no bets but from a few strangers, who as usual had to pay for being strangers.

Tant of course had nothing to do with him or her, but put his money for the most part on the bulldog. Among the rest he had a three to two wager in crowns with Ben Foat, who after all his other accounts were settled and he was ready to go kept him waiting, on the fair pretext that he himself had not yet squeezed his own winnings out of Josh Jowers and Medders's Tom, a work of difficulty. Ben was the only other active adherent to the Luddite cause at Blidworth. He was a longish, knock-kneed, grey-haired, rough-chinned man, and was in lessening degrees sot, thief, poacher, politician, sportsman and bricklayer's paddy; so Tant did quite right not to trust him five shillings till the morning.

It came on wet at the end of the grey afternoon, a straight-down noiseless discomforting rain, which had the property of damping more than it threatened. Premature night dripped from the clouds as it seemed with the rain; the company quickly dispersed, except such as chose patiently to await a change of weather at the inn. In the tap-room sat Tant with a pot of ale before him and a crowd of wet coats about him, some standing, some sitting, but all reeking malodorously, while their wearers talked together with an agreement so loud as to be disputatious of the scarcity of badger and the decadence of dog. Tant tired of this, still he waited until he had very deliberately finished his pint; then he rose to go. Ben met him at the door, it was more than he expected, with the money in his hand. They had to go into the kitchen to the landlord to get three shillings and a half crown changed into five-and-sixpence. It was pleasanter there; the sand had not been trampled to mire but cried crisply underfoot, and the warm pungent odour of the wood fire replaced the fetidness of wet clothing. The landlord gave the change; he was in his gala equipment – clean apron, face and hands as usual. There was nobody else present except a man who had sat facing the fire, but looked round before Tant could withdraw and said in friendly fashion:

"How d'yer do, mate?"

"First rate," answered Tant. "How's yoursen?"

At the same moment the landlord heard himself called for in the tap-room and went forth shutting the door behind him.

"I'm well enough," said the man, "if my fellermen was all well enough."

"If yo've got to wait while then," said Tant, chinking his money carelessly in his hand, "I reckon it'll be longer nor I've waited for this five shillings."

"I'll wait it out," said the man.

He stood five foot two in his shoes, but was of a sturdy build and about thirty years of age. His purplish nose and disorderly hair and dress gave him a pot-house look, which yet was not ordinary, for his crafty eye, his jaw terribly firm-set and his bull neck threatened a cold determination mated to reckless courage. Tant knew him well to be James Towle, a Basford man, the ringleader of the Nottingham conspirators. Apparently he had but just arrived for rain-drops glistened on his cap and coat. He filled a pint pot of ale from a big jug which stood by him on the table and proffered it to Tant. It would have been against his code of courtesy to refuse it.

"To yo," he said, and took a deep draught.

"And to our poor country," said Towle, drinking from his own pot.

"And our country. So far as the luck i'side one pot o' beer will goo."

"Sit down," said Towle, "the man as drinks standing gets no good and gives no good."

Tant sat and drank, but hurriedly.

"The luck's got to go all round yet, Tant Rideout, afore there's any luck for any of uz. We're all in the same boat, mind, uz working men; it's sink or swim for all of uz. By working man I signify any toiler, either at the forge or the loom, on the land or …"

"Or among the goss of a moonlight night," said Tant laughing.

"Or among the goss of a moonlight night," responded the other with perfect gravity; "or any other honest employment."

Tant's pot was empty. He rose.

"Well, I'm off to mine – it's middling honest – so I'll say thank yer and good-night."

"What's the hurry? The jug's hafe full yet. There's no sense in a man making himself a slave to his work."

"M'appen 'e wants to be off coortin'," said Ben Foat; "some says 'e's snuffin' after one o' the wenches at 'Igh 'Ouse."

"Do yo say so?" said Tant, reddening with quick anger.

"Not I," said Ben; "yo've been seed slivin' round theer a-nights; but I know noat."

"It's just as well for yo, for the man as says it i' my hearing will say it next time atween fewer teeth."

"Stop, I've summat to say to yer private," said Towle, for Tant was again going. With a beck of the head he motioned Ben Foat out of the room. "It wouldn't do to let knock-kneed lackeys like him hear everythink. Yo, Tant, we've hitherto considered to be as staunch as steel."

Tant's cheek was still red; he was not ordinarily quarrelsome.

"I'm staunch still; if any man says I ain't I'll chuck him out the winder. But I'll be staunch i' my own road, Jim Towle; I'll play butty to no man's opinions. To be plain wi' yer, I've partly changed my views."

Towle's countenance did not change; he kept his crafty eye on the speaker.

"Why?"

"Well, chiefly mebbe because I hain't been drunk but once sin the end o' Fcbuary. It's wunnerful what a difference that meks to the colour o' things."

Yet even while he spoke the colour of things was changing; the specious reasoning was drawing, the wild excitement was luring. There was bedevilment in the cups he had drunk.

"That's unfort'nate for we've discovered poor George's murderer, and we all thought 'twould be a treat to yer to help administer vengeance down on him according to Blid'orth law."

"What's Blid'orth law to yo?"

"As much as to yo; p'raps more. B stands for Basford as well as Blid'orth. And if Blid'orth law means short law I see no great diff'rence atween it and Ned Ludd's law."

"Who is it?"

Towle filled Tant's measure again, apparently without his noticing it.

"I called it murder, if yer noticed," said Towle.

Tant nodded, with the cup on the way to his lips.

"What d'yer suppose I meant by't?"

"Bit o' strong language; genteel sort o' 'd——n yer'"

"I thought y'ud think so, but I didn't; I meant it cool and calm and deliberate. Yo think he was shot indiscriminate, in the midst o' the scrummage?"

Tant nodded, and as it happened with the cup again on the way to his lips.

"He warn't; he was shot in the back, like a rat, tekken by supprise, with 'is hands in 'is pockets. It warn't no fair stan'-up faight."

Tant had finished his ale.

"I liked poor George. I gied him a lamming once; but there warn't noat disgraceful in't ayther to gie or to t-tek. 'Twere about a tarrier p-pup."

He stuttered; there was a stutter too in his reasoning. He pulled off his coat, as though about to step into the ring.

"Tant, man," said Towle, "it een't none o' yer hauly-mauly jobs, this een't. It requires summat sharp and short, this does."

He produced a pistol from under his coat and handed it to Tant, who received it, cocked it as it seemed mechanically, and holding it at arm's length took aim apparently at a vile print of Mendoza on the opposite wall.

"Who is't?" he said thickly.

"That cursed Yeomanry Sergeant, Arthur Skrene."

Tant crooked his arm again, uncocked the pistol and gave it back to Towle. The stutter was gone from his voice, the hitch from his mind.

"Put it out o' the road," he said; "it's a spiteful mischeevous little thing. As to the man I don't believe it on him."

"Why not?"

"He's a neighbour o' mine."

"So's the devil, so's the parson."

"I've fo't him. He's a straight faighter and a good-plucked un, though he's e'erything to larn pretty nigh that can be larnt. I'll never believe it on him; I'll never believe I'm mista'en in a man, once I've put my fisses up and looked into his eyes."

"Ax Jackson, ax Redditch, ax Dunsmore; they'll be up soon. They were theer."

"Jackson – Redditch – Dunsmore? I like 'em middling well; they're good chaps to goo on the spree wi'; they may be good stockingers for oat I know or care; but I wain't trust a man's life to a bridge o' their breath."

"Let it pass; we've plenty o' men to draw on wi'out pressing the back'ard or faint-'earted into wer ranks. But" – and as he spoke he fixed an eye of singular cunning upon Tant, watching his looks with far more heed than he listened to his words – "but that theer Mester Sergeant Skrene een't the immeejate business of to-night. We've a little job o' the General's at Rainworth. Are yer good for that?"

"No, not for that nayther, Jimmy Towle. For the future I'll leave them to smash machines as can mek 'em or use 'em. It moot be more int'resting to such."

"So yo've turned altogether chicken-'earted?"

Tant turned on him fiercely, seemed on the point of putting the threat of his eyes into deed; but on a sudden stayed his hand. Towle had not changed colour or demeanour.

"Yo're a plucky little bantam, I will say that, Towle, though yo're a deal too fause for the taste of uz Johnny Whop-straws. The match wouldn't be a fair un; on'y don't tempt me again; I don't often meddle wi' second thoughts."

"For once your second thoughts was best, Tant Rideout. If yer'd touched me I'd a jobbed yer in the vitals wi' this."

He drew a dagger from his coat-pocket, and as he did so a threat of murderous malice tore through the mask of cold cunning.

"It's as I'd begun to think," said Tant; "these here midnight meddlings wi' sword and pistol spoil a man for a faight. I'll hae no more truck wi' 'em. We part company, Towle, but let's part friends."

He held out his hand. Towle had already covered up his thoughts.

"Hoping for better times," said Tant.

"For the farmer?"

"For all men."

"So be it. For all men."

They shook hands; Tant went forth into the rain. But as soon as he breathed the cold night air his intoxication returned upon him doubly; he caught his foot in a rut as he reeled across the road. He stumbled and would have fallen, but that he was upheld by the hands of men whom he had not seen before and hardly saw then.

CHAPTER XII

THE MUSTER

As the great-grandmother's slow decay increased, Nell had taken to sleeping regularly at the Bottoms in the adjoining chamber. On the night of the badger-baiting she was uneasy about Tant. Twice she put off going to bed, threw a shawl over her head and shoulders, and went down to the farmhouse to see whether he had yet returned. The first time Tish berated her for her pains.

"If yo think a man 'll come the sooner becos a woman waits, yo've summat to larn, our Nell. M'appen yo're afeared he's gettin' wet? O' th' outside I mean. Get yo to bed! It's no night to be traipsin' back'ards and for'ards i' th' road lookin' for a bad sixpenny-bit."

The second time the house was cold and dark, but Tant was not in his room. She returned to the Bottoms, and after doing what she could for her exacting invalid went to bed. There was a period of complete stillness; for the ever-dropping rain, the ever-dripping eaves made a sound that was rather understood than heard. At last as she was dozing off she began to hear voices and footsteps. That lumbering tread which came and stopped she knew to be Spettigew's, who lived opposite. That step jerkily, jauntily unsteady was doubtless Sam Mosley's on his heigh-hos; the man singing the "British Grenadiers" in a throaty tenor could be no other than Dick Dunstan the pensioner.

Again there was silence; but Nell was roused and could not settle again. After a time, perhaps an hour, she again heard passers; three several pairs of feet she reckoned up walking together. She rose hastily and looked out of the window. There was a moon somewhere above the horizon, but its light came sparsely, dismally through the clouds and the rain. It was enough however to make a glimmering difference between the middle of the sandy road and its shadowy borders which underlay the houses. But the three passers walked on the farther and darker side, and with her eyes she could make nothing certain of them; though she was somehow convinced with that instinctive judgment which flies before seeing and hearing, that the midmost of the three, walking unsteadily and apparently supported by the others, was Tant. They were going in the opposite direction to Low Farm.

She hurried on her clothes meaning to follow; but while she did so two others passed the house in the same direction. She heard them though they trod more stealthily than the first three, and saw them though they too kept in the darkest of the shade. She went down, opened the door and looked forth. Overhead there was enough appearance of light indistinctly to part sky from earth. Spettigew's house of mud and stud whitewashed was masked in a darkness somewhat less dense than the Meadows's, which was of dull red brick. As she stepped out a man going the same way as the others almost walked into her. She drew back and bade him good-night. For a moment his answer hung, as though he were taken by surprise, then he returned her civility and went on; but stopped as at an after-thought, returned a step or two and said:

"Which is the road to Fishpool, missis?"

"Straight forrards."

Without another word he strode quickly out of sight. He was a little man and spoke more like a townsman than a countryman. She was disturbed. She wondered what it meant. It was full seldom folk were abroad at Blidworth so many and so late, even after the encouragement of a badger-baiting. She threw her dark shawl over her head and shoulders and hastened after him. He walked with a stealthy speed, but she was in time to see him presently instead of keeping straight on for Fishpool take the turn to the right for Blidworth. The deception in its pettiness had all the more sinister an appearance. She went back; she felt impelled to search out the meaning of that unusual movement; she was fearful lest Tant should be involved in any mischief which might be afoot. There was no light in Spettigew's cottage, but she entered by the unlocked door and spoke from the stair-foot.

"Are yo awake, Hannah?"

"Awake? Ah. Why not? I mostly am," was the answer in a sort of querulous patience.

"I've got to goo away for a bit. Suld yo mind sleeping i' my bed while I coom back? Gret-granmam een't very restless to-night."

"I'll do't to oblige yer; I'll set yer at liberty in a minute."

"As quick as yo can."

Mrs. Spettigew immediately arose.

"Yo shan't goo," growled the man, roused from his quick-come beery slumber.

The woman seemed to be huddling clothing on in the dark.

"Yo shan't goo," he reiterated.

She neither spoke nor desisted.

"I'll mug yer i' th' mouth."

Her heavier tread showed that she had her shoes on.

"I've warned yer."

She seemect to be fumbling for something that did not come to hand.

"Yo shan't play lackey to sich as her. Do yer hear?"

"I'm not deaf."

She seemed to have found what she wanted, and made a move for the door.

"Yo shan't, I say. Who do yer belong? Who's yer mester?"

She passed quietly forth, leaving him to mumble his drowsy threats to the open door.

"E'ery decent body ought to be abed i' their own beds." He had but just tumbled in himself. "What does she want trailin' about this time o' night? Noat good, I reckon. The d——d swine! B'leddy I shall hae to borrer that theer whip o' th' mester's afore I've done wee 'er, I'm sartain sure I shall."

But he had dropped back into his beery slumber before his wife was settled in her fresh bed or Nell fifty yards from the door. She had set off with her back to the direction of her thoughts. Just at the beginning of the houses the grassy lane turns off which has already been mentioned. It was a rougher and somewhat less direct route to Blidworth, but she meant by running all the way to arrive thither before the little man who had so big a start of her. But as she approached the mouth of the lane, she saw in front of her by the glimmering light a man who came up the road and turned into it before her. It might be Tom Tacon; he lived at Clifty Nook. She called a good-night after him in country fashion. He made no answer; he trudged on in surly silence. It was not Tom Tacon; he was always civil when he had been drinking. It might be yet a disappointed poacher. She hesitated a moment whether she should observe his movements at a distance, or race across Jackman's turnips and Ball's wheat so heading him, or else return the way she had come and follow in the little man's track. While she hesitated she heard a click down the road as of a stone kicked by a stumbling foot, and immediately afterwards she heard the foot. She went towards it and met the man.

"Good-night," said Nell.

"Good-night, my dear," said the man.

"Do yo know Tant Rideout?"

"Know 'irn? Ah; he's a mate o' mine."

"Hae yo seed 'im to-night?"

"Seed 'im? Mebbe I hev."

"Wheer did yer see him?"

"That's no matter, for he een't theer now. But I hain't said I did see 'im."

She stood, he came nearer. She did not know his voice; she thought he was probably a stockinger from Calverton or Arnold.

"Wheer is he now?"

"There's better men nor him. What's he to yo that yer mek sich a to-do about 'im?"

"He's a bit of a 'quaintance o' mine. Wheer has he gone?"

"The opposyte road to what I'm gooin'."

She could not of course see the knowing wink that accompanied the words, but there seemed to be a trace of it, perceptible to her ear, in the tone of his voice.

"And wheer are yo gooing?"

"If yo'll coom along wi' me I'll tell yer."

"I'll goo a little way."

He walked unsteadily and spoke thickly. He appeared to have been drinking, but she had brought a cudgel in her hand and was afraid of no single man. She walked abreast of him at a yard's distance, keeping a wary eye on his movements.

"I'm doing as yo wish, now tell me."

"Y'ar a wakken madam, yo are. There een't much as yo ain't up to."

As he sidled nearer she edged away. She thought she could hear footsteps behind them deadened the deep sand or the short grass.

"Yo hain't telled me wheer yo're gooing."

"How oad are yer? Atween yer fifteen an' fiftiet year? Why I ho'd that to be the prime o' life."

"Coom, yo mun be a man o' your word."

"I wish I could see yer; I'm that partic'lar I can't abide kissin' a dirty mug."

"Wheer are we gooin'?"

Still he sidled nearer and still she drew away.

"Don't be so stand-offish, Nanny dear."

The footsteps behind were plainly audible now.

"I wain't hae noat to say to yer while yo've answered my question."

"We're gooin' to Rain'orth. I mean Blid'orth. An' now –"

"Is that little man gooing with yer?"

"Ah. I said Blid'orth, yo unnerstan'? An' now yo've got to be as free wi' me as I've bin wi' yo."

"What are yer gooin' theer for?"

"Dang the huzzy's questions! I'm on strike now. Not anoother word while yo've gied me a kiss."

She had to be constantly alert to keep him at arm's length. When she looked back she thought she could see two shadowy forms appurtenant to the quickly approaching footsteps.

"Yo nedn't say, I know; yo're gooin' to Rain'orth to call of Sam Derry."

"D——n yer, I said Blid'orth! But if yer know, yer gallows besom, why the devil do yer ax? Now for that kiss! Yo can mek it a kiss an' a huggle."

His libertine hands were already upon her, but a smart smack in the face sent him staggering back. In a moment she was over the adjacent hedge and out of knowledge of his surprised faculties. She ran a little way through the wet stubble by the hedge side, then crouched and listened. The man made no pursuit, was capable of none. He stood and swore at random into the night until he was joined by two men from behind, who hearing the disturbance had hastened up. The three passed on close by Nell, who heard the fellow loudly commit her and all womankind to more than torrid regions.

"The brazen huzzy! She promised me a smack i' th' mouth an' gied me one i' th' eye. I don't call that jannocky."

But his comrades' laughter hardly sympathized with his complaint.

"It's just as well for thee, Davy," said the soberest of the three voices; "m'appen it'll caution thee to hae no truck wi' them sort o' cattle. An' what 'ud *he* say, if he knowed to't?"

"He don't know, and I shouldn't care a devil's hop if 'e did."

And so they passed on, he still swearing both particularly and at large. Then Nell rose from her ambush and followed them noiselessly in the shade of the hedge. But when they reached the two or three scattered houses at that end of the village, she turned from their direct pursuit and passing through a gate ran down the fields towards Clifty Nook. This is at the foot of the northern ascent to Blidworth, and was then a narrow passage overhung by red sandstone rocks. Close by is a meeting of lanes, leading to Farnsfield on the east, southwards to Oxton by way of High Farm and Lay Cross and northwards to Worksop and Mansfield. This last is also the route to Rainworth, a hamlet about two miles off.

Under the hill it was dark, and still darker beneath the hedge which at the foot of it divided the meadow from the road. It was a hedge high and bushy at the top, but with a thin bottom which let through a watery glimmer from the sandy middle of the track. In its black shadow Nell took her stand, stilled her breathing and listened; then walked a few yards further, stealthily, under the hedge, and again stopped, listened and looked. There was nothing but the natural night sounds and sights of that season. The rain dripped steadily down. Now and again she felt on her face the moist touch of a falling leaf, like some clammy night-thing. But she knew what it was; she knew that those patches of a faint whitish glint like little pools of moonless water were the backs of bullocks which had their lair beneath the hedge; she knew that those ghostly sighs were but their laborious breathing.

She moved on again, going more quickly in her anxious impatience. But in carefully avoiding one of the whitish patches she stumbled against the head of a darker-hued beast; black she always declared that it was; that it might have been merely a complete red she would not hear of. The beast, red or black, flung his head up and she fell over it to the ground.

"What's that?" said a voice not above two yards from her on the other side of the hedge.

The beast got up in heavy-footed surprise and moved off; she lay still where she had fallen all her length along the drenched herbage.

"It's only a d——d cow," said another voice, not so loud. "And here's them swinish loiterers coming up at last."

Nell thought the second voice was like the little man's who had asked her the way to Fishpool and had not gone thither. But there were approaching footsteps, and with strained eyes she could see through the hedge shadowy somethings go to meet them. There were muttered words of stern reproof and uncertain excuse; there was the approach from the rear of other men, shadowy, stealthy; there was the utterance of curt commands cautiously pitched. Nell again thought the little man was the chief speaker. She had ventured to rise from the ground, but could not get near enough to hear what was said. Once or twice she saw or fancied she saw a metallic gleam among the shapes that stood or stirred; once or twice she certainly heard a faint metallic chink, such as half-pence might make against the bunch of keys in a woman's pocket. Soon there was the squishy tread of passing feet on the sodden grass by the roadside, their numbers being as uncountable as shadows among shadows. Nell pushed through a gap in the hedge and moved noiselessly after them. They turned to the right and went briskly northwards, which was the direction of Rainworth. The rain fell on, the moon was near its setting and the night yet darker.

Was Tant among them? She must needs satisfy herself. At the foot of Brick-kiln Hill she again went aside by a path

which led to Thorny Abbey. When she had got a safe
distance from the road, she raced parallel to it up the watery
furrow of a stiff clay fallow. The wet flew about her legs; the
tenacious soil almost glued her feet to the ground; one of
her shoes was wrenched off and she had to step back and
grope for it. In spite of that delay she returned to the road
at the top of the hill well ahead of the band of conspirators.
She crouched behind a clump of wayside broom close by
the turn for Rainworth, and let them pass. She could have
touched them one by one as they passed and turned for
Rainworth. There were but seven or eight of them, and she
was convinced that there was none among them of Tant's
inches, hardly one taller than herself. Neither was there one
so short as the little man; her suspicions were disappointed.

In the inactive minute while they were getting beyond
hearing there was time for thought; time for pity of Sam
Derry whom she knew to be a hardworking man with a
family, for disapproval of an act of destructive violence,
both sentiments natural to a woman; time also to heat to a
glow her disposition actively to resist oppression, more a
man's quality than a woman's. And Tant was not there. She
lifted up her skirts as high as her knees and raced back along
the road.

All the mile and a half she ran to High Farm, where she
saw most hope of help. The house was locked up and dark;
it was midnight. She knocked loudly at the door but roused
no answer. She cast gravel from the drive at one or two of
the windows and was more successful. The first to awake
was Miss Skrene, who in much alarm called her brother up.
He put his head out and made inquiry. Nell told him shortly
how things stood. He was quickly down. She helped him to
saddle his charger by the light of the stable lantern, only
necessary speech passing between them. As she tightened
the girth she bethought herself of what she had hitherto
overlooked, that Tant and his comrades might have gone
on to Rainworth before the little band which she had

followed. She was half in a mind to undo the buckle again; she did not, she pulled it a little tighter.

"You'd make a gallant soldier's wife, Miss Rideout," said Arthur, meaning a compliment.

Apparently however it was not to her mind, whether as to the quality of it or as compliment *per se.*

"I've no opinion o' sojers," she said; "nayther play-sojers nor workaday-sojers."

"Thanks for the play-soldiers," said Arthur lightly, as he loaded his carbine, then slung it up in its case.

It looked very murderous to her. He mounted, but she still held his horse by the bridle.

No her pride would not let her utter the special request she had in thought, she merged it in general one.

"Don't be too ready wi' that thing, Sergeant Skrene," she said; "they're not Frenchies yo're gooing again. The lads hae their troubles too; don't be too hard on 'em."

"If I should give them a little less than their deserts, it will be because the priming's damp. Or for your request's sake, Miss Rideout."

"Do't for your own sake. 'Twill be a more human sort o' reason nor the one and a more accountable sort nor the tother." She held the gate open for him, "Above all ride wi' your eyes in your head. The roads are dark and the hedges high; there's good cover for varmin."

"Nay, I'll never calculate what I can't foresee. One more thing. Can I get you to rouse Selby up? His presence would add to my sister's sense of security."

She promised and he rode off. As he rode eyes watched him from behind his own hedge. A musket was levelled at him, might have ended his tale there and then; but the sudden sound hard by of Nell beating at Selby's door made the holder of it pause with his finger slackly on the trigger. The horse bore his rider and the opportunity swiftly off. Selby having been fetched sleepy and crusty out of bed proceeded to do the like by Wells, who lived in the adjoining cottage by the roadside, not because he thought there was any need but by way of indirect retaliation.

Meanwhile Nell returned to the house. Her quiet tap at the back door seemed something alarming to the disturbed women within, but by and by the assurance of her voice gained her a hesitating admission. Once entered, her courageous and unflurried presence seemed a real accession of strength to the inmates. These comprised besides the young lady the cook and the dairymaid, Harris the wagoner and Charley Strong the middleman, who slept in the house. Harris between the beginning and the end of a yawn had said, "A good night's rest's worth more nor health, wealth or a good supper," and then sank down on the first chair. The rest were huddled together in the kitchen without regard to precedence, Charley being most within the chimney and Miss Skrene by some inches nearest the door. She and Nell had never before met fairly face to face, and they each looked at the other with some curiosity. Nell saw a little daunted creature whose dark sleep-ravelled hair overhung a pale face, but with a pair of eyes that promised more courage than she showed. Lois saw a woman as tall as a man and with a man's frankness of outlook, yet a woman all over. She had a stout thornstick in her hand, was roughly dressed, and dripped rain from her drenched skirts and the fringes of her shawl; but her rude equipment and the injury of the elements did not in the least mar, rather enhanced her striking appearance.

While the cook began to kindle a fire in the wide grate, Nell put back her moist shawl from her head and tried to rouse the young lady's confidence.

"Yo mootn't be afeared; there's no danger hereabouts, not a scrap; all them dare-devils are at Rain'orth by this."

"How do you know?"

"I watched 'em tek the turn."

"How durst you?"

"I kep' a good lookout and my stick handy."

Harris yawned and yawned again.

"How far is Rainworth?"

"The best end o' three mile."

Lois shuddered; it seemed all too near.

"Besides my brother will be there, won't he?"

"Unless he misses his road. And if he does he'll be fine and mad at somebody or something, I reckon. But he has been out afore, yo suld be getting used to it."

"But I didn't know; he led me to believe that he was called out to – just to practise being called out."

"Suld yo like him on'y to practise? Just don his uniform on to air it, and doff it off to spare it? Not yo."

"You haven't got a brother there, I perceive."

Nell did not answer; she stood stock-still in the midst of the floor, which the drip from her garments had wetted round about. But presently she roused herself and looked towards the door.

"I moot be gooing," she said. "I'm making a pond i' th' middle o' th' floor, and if your Mary's like our Tish she'll hae summat to say. I'll goo and shift mysen."

"Don't go, Miss Rideout," cried Miss Skrene, Mary and the dairymaid simultaneously.

"I can't offer you a change," said Lois; "my things would seem like doll's rags on you, but Mary – she's broad, if she's not very long – and if you wouldn't mind allowing the too much at the waist to make up for the too little at the ankles, I'm sure she –"

"Oh, yes, Miss Rideout! and welcome!" cried Mary, who was still crouching over the half-kindled fire.

"I've summat to see to down yonner," said Nell. "If I can I'll come round again in a while."

Just then Selby opened the outer door, and between his entrance and Wells's she managed to slip out without further solicitation or excuse. She entered her own dark house and went up-stairs. Tant's bed was still empty of him. While she made a necessary change of clothing, she was

irresolute whether or not she should next return and see
how her great-grandmother fared. As soon as she was
dressed she again went forth. She walked indeed towards
the Bottoms, but her thoughts perhaps went other ways;
certainly her eyes sometimes did, up the hill for instance to
her right. The moon had set, relinquishing her feeble
controversy with the darkness.

The first time of her so looking up-hill she hardly saw,
the next time she fully perceived, a dull red glow hung up
on the black wall of night. It was small and about where she
would expect to see High House by day, yet it was too red
and too variable to be candle-shine from window or lantern.
But while she looked, and she did not look long, it grew and
grew, a dull red glow whose light was refused by the
obstinate darkness. Then suddenly a flame sprang up,
yellow mingled with red. It sank, only to spring up again
larger and brighter, not in the house though hard by, for
the glare reddened its white walls. Nell stood no longer; she
ran back to the house, got the lantern and entered the stable.
How she missed old Hasty at that moment! In Hasty's stall
there was a half-broken colt with a vile temper, which Tant
had bought at Retford Hop fair and given the name of
Ripper; a compact villainous-eyed animal, dark-chestnut as
to colour and standing an inch over fifteen. Him for want
of better Nell saddled and bridled, led forth, mounted, then
putting a gently resolute hand to either rein galloped off up-
hill in the direction of that increasing blaze; which now in
spite of the unceasing rain began to make a ring of light in
the dark low-hung sky.

CHAPTER XIII

THE WRONG HOUSE

A FEW minutes after Nell left, Miss Skrene, heartened a little by the presence of the men, went with a candle into her usual sitting-room for a book or something. It was a largish oblong room, the principal window being at the western end, a considerable book-case at the other and in the midst a round dining-table fronting the fire-place; near which was Lois's spinnet, so placed that the light of the setting sun would fall on it through a small window near the south-west angle. Lois as she entered gave a shiver, which was partly on account of the fireless chill of the room, partly perhaps in fear of its unlighted ends and corners and of the big black shadow under the table. She stood, but through the open doors the men's heavy voices rumbled in from the kitchen encouraging her. Candle in hand she crossed to the book-case; the shadows fled before her, but with a sort of timorous boldness, very like her own, kept at a little distance, never still. She stood holding the light above her head so as to examine the lettered backs of the books on an upper shelf.

All at once there was a fearful crash behind her at the other end of the room, the splintering of wood and the shriller shivering of glass. She turned; the large window had fallen in bodily as at some violent battering from without. Before her eyes out of the utter dark into the inner dimness a tall rough fellow staggered over the ruins of the window. She knew him; and the knowledge was worse than the most fanciful ignorance. Behind him the indistinct forms of other men were darkly visible, their faces somehow veiled as with a threat.

She did not cry, she did not fall, she did not even drop the candle; she continued holding it high as though frozen into immobility.

The first-comer came towards her with a heavy indirectness more terrible to her than a steadily-aimed hostility. Further in pushed his followers, a mass of moving dark only broken here and there by the furtive glitter, coming and going, of homicidal steel. What seemed more appalling was that their faces, which should have reflected somewhat however wanly of the candle gleam, were diabolically black; all but the first ruffian's, his was savagely human.

Then surely was the time for her to have attempted to fly, to have cried out, to have dropped, to have died of fright. She neither fled nor cried nor fell; she stood fixed and held the candle high. There was silence for a moment. Outside the shattered window she heard the soft ceaseless drip of the rain, as though it mattered whether it were fine weather or foul.

The others stopped on the farther side of the centre-table; their leader came so close to her that she could see and did the shiny rain-streaks on the bare arm of the hand which held a flail. She was frozenly expecting the blow. But she did not feel it. As soon as he came within striking distance he looked at her mazedly, he fell back from her, he turned to his men and cried out in a voice like horror:

"It's the wrong house!"

"No; it's the raight un!" answered a voice behind.

"Yo said – what did yo say? Rain'orth or summat."

"An' here's the rain; that's near enough."

And as voices behind were uttered, variously brutal, the speakers one by one seemed to come into distincter vision, a rain-soaked crew of masked desperadoes.

"Down with the murderer of George Ellis!"

"Down to hell wee 'm!"

"Burn 'im up stick an' stock!"

"And chuck hissen into the hottest o' the bunfire!"

"Clear out of here!" shouted the first speaker in a terrible voice more menacing than his uplifted flail. "This is no place for such as me and yo. Clear out, I say!"

"Not yet awhile, Tant Rideout," said his first answerer, coming forward in front of the table, a little man with a pistol in his hand. "If yer don't want to help the work yer may sit yer down an' watch uz perform it, but by God yer shan't stop it."

"It is stopped!"

Tant Rideout threw his arms about the little man, confining his hands also in their iron bands. The little man struggled furiously, during which his pistol went off, ineffectively shattering a vase on the chimneypiece, but the bands around him tightened, he was lifted up, carried to the window and flung forth into the dark. Immediately two strong masked fellows seized Tant each by an elbow. He violently wrenched himself loose from the one and in a twinkling had the other over his thigh. Up went the man's heels, down went his head, with great force striking a corner of Lois's spinnet. He lay and was in no haste to rise. The trembling chords of the poor little instrument raised a feeble wail and were still again.

"Yo're all afraid on 'im!" cried the little man out of the dark.

He himself rushed in again, tiger-like, with a murderous knife in his hand. He sprang at Tant, who with his flail dealt him a disabling blow across the arm. Lois heard the bone crack, heard the knife drop. She still stood looking on and holding the candle, unable to move, unable to faint and fall. The little man went aside, but sticks and steel and curses were raised against his antagonist. The passion of the masked faces could not be seen; it was the more terrible. Lois saw a ravel of blows; saw Tant's uncovered head flowing with blood, but how it came about did not distinctly see. It was a wonder against such an onslaught that he stood at all, with but that hinged stick in his hand.

He fought gallantly, with a deliberate fury; his desperation had none of despair's chill in it. He set his mark upon many, but could not give an eye to all his adversaries at once, and many a one marked him. Round him they swarmed, smiting with bludgeons, slashing with hedge-knives and old swords, thrusting with hay-forks, devil-visaged desperadoes; he with his face gory but uncraped seemed human in comparison. Lois had somehow been compelled to understand that he was fighting in her defence. But he was pushed further and further from the window by mere numbers.

And then, just as clearly as though her every faculty had been disengaged, she smelt the smell of burning, and first saw the blaze as of a conflagration without in the mid air. It lighted the leafless top of an old oak which faced that part of the house, but left its bulk in the gloom. The moment seemed at hand when she must drop the candle and see no more. But when despair was nearest, when there was hardly room between her and her defender for the backward swing of the flail, suddenly he cast from him his ineffectual weapon and stooped under the heavy oaken centre-table. They thought he was cowering from them, and they raised a kind of brute laugh. But he seized the table by its pedestal and uplifted it, presenting its round rim to his opponents shield-wise. Its use however was rather as a battering-ram. Forthwith he dashed upon them with astonishing force. One man who had been peeping under the table received it full on the crown of his head and fell senseless; over his body Tant rushed, and with irresistible impact drove two of his chief assailants back to the window.

"What are yo doin', comrades? We've set the villyand's barn all of a blaze."

It was the speech of an unapparent speaker outside; and

immediately on that the thud was heard of a horse's impatient hoofs on the soft ground.

"What the h——'s that?" said the man in the room nearest the window.

"It's the Yeomanry!" said the man furthest from it.

Two or three slipped out; the rest all wavered, all looked over their shoulders. The smoky blaze in upper air made the nether gloom all the obscurer; wherein nevertheless those next the window could descry the black outline of a horse and his rider, the horse madly rearing amid the group of outside rioters. They pushed forth; the room was emptied of all but Lois and Tant. Again the horse reared – was it a woman on his back? – and as his fore-feet touched ground there was a man's cry of pain. The rioters made a ring. A third time the horse reared – it was a woman on his back – reared and dropped. At the same moment there was the sounding smack of a whip; he bounded forward, overturning those who stood in his way. But his rider checked him on the instant, and with the cruel curb backed him again to the window; switching his tail and mightily resenting it, back he was forced.

"Strike me dead, if it een't his sister!"

So it was, if Tant's sister were meant. And while she was thrusting the angry colt in among them, she was thinking, "M'appen Tant's here;" and thinking, "But if he is, he'll be forrard where the faighting is;" and thinking, "If he een't, God help us! I can't."

One fellow hit the colt on the shoulder with a bludgeon, another tried to catch at his bridle, increasing his fury. Just then Harris, with a fowling-piece in his hand, and whisperingly encouraged by Selby and Wells from the rear, stole up to the door of the room and peeped in. He saw his mistress wide-eyed, still holding the candle; he saw one man with his back to him at the further end. Whereby much emboldened he went two steps in on tip-toe and lifted his fowling-piece. There were curses without and rough and angry exclamations.

"Shoot the four-legged devil!"

"And the two-legged un atop on 'im!"

"My priming's damp, else I'd a gen 'em both pepper afore this."

"This 'ere 'll tickle 'im up."

The speaker thrust with a pitchfork at the animal's quarters. Instantly, before his rider had cried "Look out!" the iron shod hoofs shot forth. There was the thud of hard against soft, mixed with the sharp crack of a fracture; there was the fall of a man; there was a sickening groan. At the same moment Tant had turned and Harris had made haste to fire. Tant dropped, Lois dropped, the candle was extinguished. Nell for the moment at the sound of the groan – it might have been Tant's – lost command of herself and her startled horse; he bolted off madly down the hill. Frightened by the sudden failure of light, Harris and his associates fled back into the kitchen.

For a minute there was a listening stillness, only broken by the groans of the injured and the rivalry of two crowing cocks, which took the riot of the flames for the generous haste of day. Then the little man, the leader of the gang, spoke.

"Now we have 'em, lads! Rideout's knocked o' the head by his own kind friends. In wi' yer! We'll not leave stick nor stun stanning in its place."

He had made a sling for his broken arm with his neckerchief and seemed full of a mischievous courage; but as he spoke a scout whom he had left upon the road came running in.

"The Yeomanry's out!" he said.

Not far off could be heard the galloping of horses on the stony road.

"Then we've on'y to get in and keep 'em out. Come on, lads!"

He stepped through the window, but the lads hung back.

"Fifteen's got 'is foot scrushed," said one.

"Ben's leg's broke, I doubt," said another, kneeling by the man who had received Ripper's kick; he lay on the wet turf and groaned.

"And wheer's oad Twenty-one?" said a third.

"In theer, feelin' badly," said a fourth.

The clatter of the cavalry drew nearer; there needed no listening.

"If I warn't sure i' my mind o' coming back another day wi' better fortune," said their leader, "I wouldn't stir a peg. Yo two, numbers Five and Fourteen, come in and help Twenty-one out. Not him, yo fools! that's the traitor."

"Should I nick 'im wi' this?" said a man with a hand-bill.

"Not for oat. Leave 'im to be hung by his friends. Eleven and Thirty-six, hoist Nineteen up as best yer can. Silence! stop that woman's noise; a brucken leg's better nor a brucken neck."

For the horsemen were heard riding in at the back of the premises. Towle went first without hurry; the others followed, carrying or supporting their injured comrades. He led them down the grassy slope away from the road. The mischievous light of their own kindling did not discover them; the ground fell away so rapidly that they were under the shoulder of the hill as soon as they had left the dark shadow of the house. The rain-drenched dispirited crew disappeared, things of the night into the night; while Arthur, hot with rage and the speed he had made, entered the house by the back door, he and the Yeomanry with him.

At his approach with the half-dozen hussars whom he had mustered, the first and smaller gang had desisted from their not very desperate attack upon Sam Derry's shop at Rainworth; probably it was more or less of a feint. And immediately on their retreat the conspicuous fire in the direction of High Farm had been noticed. Skrene had left a couple of troopers on guard over the threatened machinery, and himself with the rest had galloped back. As he rode down the long gentle slope to the house he had ample time, for all the reckless haste he made, to imagine with many differing degrees of fear the calamity that had befallen him.

In the sum he saw a great red blaze behind columns of smoke, which at first rising severally swelled out overhead until they formed one densely rolling mass, whose nodding head was lost in the clouds while its trailing skirts obscurely swept the ground. But what part of it lay directly between the eye and the fierce light it was seen by was visible in every detail, every twist and curl and puff and larger volume grandiosely extended; in every degree of transparency, from the purely diaphanous, a mere net to catch the reds and yellows of the fire, to the thick reek which completely intercepted them. And between the two extremes intermingled rarities and densenesses which variously transmitting and arresting colour gave also of their own; orange and amber, brown of every sombre shade inclining both to red and to yellow, uncertain greens, and here and there a fleece of woolly white.

Arthur understood that the smoke came from the stackyard, where the different attempts made to fire the stacks had been partly frustrated by the rain. The great barn however with its roofed-in mow of barley had been easily kindled, and now the flames were spreading from it on either side to the stabling and the implement-shed. He wondered what had become of Lois and whether the house were intact; he had time for that, madly galloping as he was, time and time to spare.

The flickering redness of the windows might be from the inside, might be a mere reflection. He hoped and he feared, and most he feared. As they rode past the back premises they heard the scream of a horse in pain or terror above a tumultuous lowing, squealing, neighing, bleating, crowing of newly-uproused fowl and beast.

Arthur detailed off two of the hussars to see what could be done for the poor animals, while he with the remaining two entered the house. In reply to his quick questions the men in the kitchen were almost as incoherent as the maids. The rioters had made forcible entry after such resistance as three or three and a bit could offer to a hundred – to five hundred. The house was then in their possession. And their mistress? They could not say; they thought – they were afraid – they hoped. Arthur snatched the candle up, and with sword in hand he and his two men went hotly to meet them. But the house was still, still and dark. Involuntarily they stopped in the hall and listened. Not a sound but what they brought with them. Not a sound? Yes, a little sound through the open door hard by, a little sound of much pain.

He entered, they entered; felt the moist night air, saw the ruin and disorder, saw a man lying all his length in a red death as it seemed, saw the young lady by the book-case not quite motionless, in the deadly anguish of returning life. She was carried to a neighbouring apartment, laid on a couch, and the cook and dairymaid summoned. There was no sign of injury on her; she seemed to have only the pain of sensibility. She opened eyes once, and once before she closed them again spoke, in a dying voice, incomprehensibly:

"It's the wrong house."

The men had for the present to leave the women to do the best they could for her with cold water and clamour; they themselves returned to the scene of disorder. Selby, Wells, Harris and Charley with reviving courage followed them in. Their first attention was directed to the man who lay like dead upon the floor.

Selby and Wells said, "That's the man we shot."

Harris said, "That's the man I shot."

All together with even closer agreement said, "It's Tant Rideout!"

Nell Rideout was almost in time to hear them; she rode up to the window the moment after.

"Who's there?" she said. "Friends or unfriends?"

"I believe, Miss Rideout," answered Arthur cold and

stern, "there is at least one of your friends here."

She slipped off her horse and looked in.

"Yo've druv 'em away, I see," she said.

"All but one," said Arthur.

The men who stood about the body moved aside that she might see it. And she did see it. All the illumination of the poor kitchen dip, which one of the yeomen held low, seemed to be concentrated on a white face and long hair, which in that light was almost of a colour with the blood it was dabbled in.

"Will somebody come and ho'd my hoss?" she said.

Selby bade Charley, but he shrank back from the dark window, so Harris went.

"Don't yek the bridle; he wain't stan' it. Be gentle wee 'im, and firm."

She went in; the men stood yet a little further off. She stooped and put a hand on his forehead away from the blood.

"Tant, lad," she said, "what hae yer been agate on now?"

"He een't dead," she said; "our side o' the family teks a frightful deal o' killing."

She went and took Arthur's hand and knelt to him.

"Yo wain't hang him, Mr. Skrene?" she said.

"That, Miss Rideout, isn't for me either to do or not to do," said Arthur.

"He might brek a winder – he's wild and ower wild, that I own – but he wouldn't set fire to a stack; never! He's a farmer hissen, and loves the sweet smell o' the straw and the grain."

"It's not only that; my sister lies in the next room unconscious. How far her injuries go I cannot at present say."

"Welladay! welladay! I'm sorry, sorry! the little lady! But he didn't do that. As if I'd been there, he didn't. He'd be the first to withstand it. Suld I kneel for him if I weren't sure on't?"

"Again I say, it is not in my hands, Miss Rideout; I can't interfere with the workings of justice."

She rose from her knees; a little paler but further from tears.

"M'appen yo'd let me tek and nurse him while he's better? I'd deal jonnocky."

"The constable must be sent for. You'd better ask him, Miss Rideout."

There was a gleam of fierce passion in her face and voice as she said:

"D'yer think I'd kneel to Tommy White?"

The look or the words found a weak place somewhere in his armour; he had nothing to reply. She turned again to her brother.

"Who'll help me," she said, "to carry him out into the kitchen? He's spoiling a fine carpet."

A stalwart yeoman proffered himself; but before they raised the wounded man she looked round and said:

"Who shot him?"

"Him and him and him," said the yeoman, pointing to Selby, to Wells and to the dark window.

"I niver did," said Selby," so no lies about it."

"No more did I," said Wells.

"I niver knew 'twar him," protested Harris through the window.

"I wish 't had bin a better shot nor yo, Jack; he'd a het him two inch to the raight, plump i' the throttle."

The rest of the men followed Arthur out into the burning yard. The yeoman lifted Tant by the feet; Nell who chose the head had the heavier burden. They carried him into the kitchen and laid him outstretched along the brick floor. As they did so he opened his eyes, muttered something about Number Thirty and closed them again. The yeoman went out; Nell was left alone to her sorry task of recovery. She went to work by a strange light; the red gleam from the conflagration coming through the window altogether predominated over the dim yellow of the candle. She could hear the voices of the men and the brutes as though she were among them; the roar also of the fire and the hiss of water tossed into it by ineffective bucketfuls. She tore off her own linen to make a compress for the wound, a wide red rent in his left shoulder, and bandaged it closely up with the drier half of the shawl she was wearing.

'Tant, lad," she said, "yo wain't thank me for this if yo coom to know."

Meanwhile Skrene had returned to his sister, who had made a further gain of consciousness, but was still pitiably faint. He sent the cook into the kitchen to give Miss Rideout what help she needed. She would accept nothing but a bowl of cold water, wherewith to wash a little of the gore from her brother's face and hair.

"I wouldn't hae him goo to jail," she said, "wi' a skin like a butcher's. But how's the young lady?" Having been answered she said again, "Goo out, Mary, wheer yo're needed. If yo nubbut carry watter in a cup, yo'll gie cupfuls o' help."

She was just finishing when Arthur came in.

"I have sent for the doctor, Miss Rideout," he said.

"And the constable?"

"Of course he will attend your brother equally with my sister."

"The doctor yo mean. Ay. If I hadn't knowed yo'd cure him yoursens to kill him, d'yer think I'd ha crooked my little finger to this? No!"

Tant turned a little and moaned, and her voice softened to the mother's coo.

"Lig still, lad, lig still. What does ta want? Thee'll shift tha bandages. And what then?"

She turned to Arthur.

"M'appen, sir, yo think him noat better nor a gret fow jail-bird, wi' that mucky coat on, and that white wheer it suld be red, that red wheer it suld be white? But if yo could

ha' seed him weshed and combed and respectably dressed,
and the sun shining on his face of a morning, yo'd – Coom,
let's goo and see what we can save of stick and stock."

Hour after hour they toiled, and with the help of the
weather were able to save the stackyard from complete
destruction, but the great barn and the outbuildings thereto
adjacent proved beyond recovery. There was some small
loss of cattle, much of valuable implements and other dead
stock. Nell herself at the risk of her own life saved a horse
of small value left forgotten in one of the stables. But amid
all that bustling to and fro she did not fail to hear the doctor
from Mansfield ride in. She knew well enough too when
Tom White the constable came, though he came afoot. Of
course she and Arthur crossed each other times and times
again, but did not speak a word, exchange a glance. Only
when nothing remained of the fire but the black ruin and
the all-pervading pungency of the smoke, he bowed to her
with a lift of the hat, as manners bade, and said:

"I have to thank you, Miss Rideout, for your extremely
useful exertions."

"There's no more to be done," she answered, "that I can
do. And I hae news to tek home, so I'll say good-night – or
I think it's good-morning."

For indeed over the ridge of the hill there was already a
grey infraction of the dark. By the lifting of the face it might
be perceived that it still rained, though but a rare drizzle. It
was colder too, as though there were loss of warmth in the
thinning of night's covering. The smoke hung, a cloud
beneath the clouds. The rooks croaked morose comments
from the tops of the leafless oaks. The roosters, who had
uttered their too vainglorious vaunts during the night, now
moped voiceless under brandriff and blackened wall.

Nell inquired not after her brother nor asked for one look
at him; she left him in the hands of the doctor and the
constable. She found the colt fastened up through Harris's
negligence by the front door without covering or shelter;

he was shivering and dispirited and seemed glad to see her. With a sudden weariness she was unable to mount him, and had to lead him across the heavy fields. Slowly, drearily, they plodded their way. On reaching the stable she punctiliously rubbed the colt down and saw to his comfort; then wearily, wearily mounted to her bedroom. Tish heard her heavy foot on stairs, and called to her:

"Why hae yer coomed back? Is gret-granmam worse?"

"No. Hannah's wi' her."

"What hae yo been doing?"

"Helping hang Tant. If yo've got your clo'es on yo might goo and see if I've gien Tant's colt his corn; I can't just mind me."

CHAPTER XIV

LOIS TAKES ACTION

Two days later the doctor, considering Tant's great strength, thought him able to bear conveyance to the county jail at Southwell. Having seen him off and attended on Miss Skrene he went to visit another patient in the neighbourhood, Ben Foat of Fishpool, who was suffering from a leg broken just below the knee. Ben claimed to have got it by a fall, his account of which was so unjointed that it was probably a drunken fall; not of itself an unlikely thing, though the doctor's own opinion was that it had been done by some terrible blow. Fortunately however in this case a knowledge of the cause was not necessary for the cure of the injury.

"Keep that beer jug out of his reach," said the doctor to Ben's wife, "and he'll do very well."

Lois's treatment was more difficult. She was slow in recovering from the shock; the pallor of fear did not pass from her face. She did not lie abed, but she did nothing when she was up. She did not speak of that dreadful night, but seemed to be always seeing it; every now and then a shudder would take her, hold her a minute, then let her go. The doctor advised that she should have a change of scene.

"And let it be," said he, "among people who don't know the cause of her illness, then you may rely on their discretion in not talking about it."

Arthur found her a comfortable residence at a farmhouse Retford way, took her thither and left her. While she was there she was apparently neither happy nor unhappy, though she took but a languid interest in what was before her eyes. But at three weeks' end the doctor rode over to see her, and his coming seemed to throw her mind backward and unsettle her. Next morning just after breakfast she said to the farmer:

"Mr. Stone, I'm very much obliged to you and Mrs. Stone for all the attentions you have shown me; I shall never forget your kindness."

"Law, miss," said the farmer, "why do yer say so?"

"Because this is my last opportunity of saying so."

And so she would have it. She refused to wait until her brother and her pony were sent for; there was nothing for it but that the farmer should leave the acres he wished to plough, take her up behind him on an ancient pillion and ride with her the twenty miles to Blidworth.

The motion and the fresh air seemed to revive her spirits. Along the way she talked with much of her customary lightness of this and that, and even made the heavy farmer talk. But when they had turned the ridge of the last hill and came into sight half a mile away of the aged oaks, of the house chimneys, of the black ruin of the farm-buildings, then she fell so silent that the farmer seemed a talker.

Mary the cook opened the door for them, while Charley led the horse round to the stables. Lois stopped her surprise with a cool "How do you do, Mary?"

"Middling, miss, thank yer. Sister Ann's to be married a month as yisterday. I'm sorry to see yo hain't got your colour back, miss."

"Colour, Mary? I never had any. Unless you call greeny-grey a colour'?"

"I dunno, miss; they've such diff rent names i' diff'rent plazen."

"Well, up in Kent we call red and yellow and blue colours, speaking of the complexion. This" – with glove to cheek – "is but a hue. If it's a trifle more greeny than usual, put it down to my not having dined. What have you for dinner, Mary?"

"I don't 'ardly know, miss. If I'd on'y been to'd – there's a tater-pie. And there's co'd beef."

"I'm hungrier than ever."

All that trifling was forced; she was shivering as with cold. She entered the room on the left hand of the hall. The window had been repaired, the disorder put right; it seemed to promise that the affair was ended.

"You've done very well, Mary," she said with some real satisfaction. Her eyes fell on the book-shelves. "When the *Decline and Fall* has been properly sorted from *Paradise Lost,* and Miss Clarissa Harlowe made a little less intimate with Mr. Tom Jones, I think it will do very – But why isn't there a fire? Perhaps you have put one into the east room?"

"No, miss. The mester's at Nottingham."

"Oh."

And she fell to shivering again; she did not know why. She roused herself sufficiently however to give orders for the best possible entertainment of her escort in the warm kitchen, then went up-stairs to change her dress.

When she came down again her thought was also to have gone into the kitchen, but as she passed the parlour door she heard the crackling of fresh-lighted firewood therein and entered. The dairymaid was kneeling on the hearth encouraging the new-born fire with the bellows.

"When did your master go to Nottingham, Elizabeth?" she asked.

"This mornin', miss."

There were some starlings hopping on the grass in front of the window and she moved towards it, chirruping to them. We are always going to meet outer trifles in the hope of getting at a little brief distance from what is in us.

"Pretty dickies! Swee–eet! Swee–eet! Did your master say when he should return?"

"Not while the 'sizes are ower, miss, I should think."

The next moment she saw a dark brown stain on the carpet in the best of the light. She knew the cause of it. She saw Tant fall again, and again she fell.

When she came to herself with a long drawn "Ah!" her face was wet with water, and the two maids were bending over her ejaculating oh's.

"What's the matter? Am I ill?" she asked, in temporary oblivion of the cause.

The maids gave the answer in duetto.

"Yo'll soon be better, miss."

"Poor thing!"

"It's very nat'ral."

"How d'yer feel now?"

"Could yer sit up a bit, d'yer think?"

She could and did. But as she sat on the floor the dark brown patch was just under her eyes. The maids saw it also.

"Shall I make a fire i' th' east room, miss?" said Mary.

"Well, he'll be hung for't, that's one comfort," said Elizabeth.

"How can yer!" said Mary.

"Well, he will. E'erybody says so; Tom White says so," insisted Elizabeth, obtuse to Mary's warning finger.

Lois was like to faint again at the mere thought of a hanging so nearly connected with her carpet. She but just gasped out:

"Who will be hung?"

"Tant Rideout, miss. There's nobody else took."

The name revived her more than the most pungent thrust of anything that can be smelt. She stood up.

"He? It can't be! Why?"

"Why?"

"Do yer ask, miss?"

"For house-breakin'."

"And stack-firin'."

"And machine-smashin'."

"And –"

"And –"

"And murder all but."

Lois's clear voice cut their volubility in two.

"No! for the prevention of murder! He saved my life."

They thought she was out of her mind.

"Poor thing!"

"Who iver heerd the like?"

"Oh, I've been ill too long!"

"Yo'll be better by 'n bye, miss," Said Mary.

"Yo'll feel more sattled like when he's out the road, miss," said Elizabeth. "I can't sleep mysen for dreamin' on't. The men talk o' noat else but the gallers now; I keep sayin', 'Do talk o' summat else,' but it's no use. I remember there was a murder at Farnsfield when I were ten year oad. The talk there was!"

You would not have thought Lois's cheeks could be paler, her voice fainter, but they were.

"When is it to be?"

"The hanging, miss?"

Her head drooped; it might be a sign, it might be a mere slackening of the central control.

"That een't fixed yet, miss, I should say, but the trial's to-morrer."

"To-morrow? Oh how cruel silence is!"

True; crueller than any activity, because so timid, so selfish.

"I must sit down."

They got her to a chair. The nearness of the danger seemed to crowd upon her, oppress her, almost suffocate her. The maids added something to her distress, assailing her, back and front, with pity and astonishment. But these she could waft away.

"I'm better now, thank you. I'm quite well. Elizabeth, you may take away your coal-scuttle. Mary, see if Mr. Stone wants any more pie."

She stood up for half a minute to prove that her legs were equal to the weight of her body, her brain to the pressure of her thoughts; but she sank again on her chair as soon as the maids' backs were turned.

It was so soon! She had done wrong to be ill. What should she do?

The figure of Tant came before her, as he stood over her brother in the snow, as he issued drunk from the Will Scarlett, as he stumbled in through the broken window. The three combined in one, not blurred as by the superposition of one picture over another, but with the edged precision of a triple terror. She shrank from such silent relation with him as a common accident gave, as her own thoughts admitted; she had an icy dread of keeping company with him on men's tongues.

Then came a thought filming over the sharp precision of her idea of him. She was convinced that she owed her life to him, that somehow for some reason that gallant struggle – it was acted before her again in every detail – had been for her. It obscured the outline of the picture, augmented the mystery, hardly lessened the terror.

"I think the fire'll do now, miss."

It was Elizabeth who looked in.

"Yes, Elizabeth, nicely, thank you. You may go."

Why hadn't he spoken? Or more likely he had spoken. Of course he had; it would be ridiculous to think otherwise. And had been disbelieved? Of course he would be disbelieved. Who would believe who had not seen?

Mary brought her in some dinner. To stay the maid's solicitations she went to the table and touched knife and fork, though the sight of food made her stomach revolt. But as soon as the cook went out of the room the plate and its contents went out of her thoughts; which receded from the present with a withdrawal like that of spent waves; until presently they were entirely lost in those five weeks of her illness, a time of indifference, indolence, oblivion, barely concluded, already dim to her. She was still in the midst of it when Mary came in to see if she wanted anything. To the good-natured maid's remonstrances she answered:

"I can't help it; I'm not so hungry as I was, Mary."

"After a twenty-mile ride, miss? It een't right; it een't nat'ral."

"I'd a very good breakfast."

"Breakfast! Yo'd ought to ha' clean forgot it two hour ago, miss. There niver was the breakfast as was worth remembering at dinner-time."

To escape further solicitation Lois said," I think I could drink a cup of tea."

While the cook prepared it she herself was harassed by the questionings of her practical inexperience. What could she do? What ought she to do? Whom should she go to? If her brother were but there to advise her! And yet she felt somehow an unowned unplaceable relief in his absence. The only thing clear to her was that she must act quickly; the very clearness of which only made the disenabling flutter of her thoughts the greater. She thought of consulting General Dene, the leading magistrate in the neighbourhood. But he lived between three and four miles off and would himself probably be absent at the assizes. The sun was already getting low, and time pressed. In her mind she ran through the different persons in the neighbourhood with whom she had acquired some slim acquaintance, but in the face of none of them did she see promise of aid or counsel.

Mary came in with the cup of tea and a slice or two of toast.

"Toast's no stay," she said, "but if a body feels tisicky she moot eat what she can eat."

To please Mary she fretted the toast into crumbs between her dainty fingers, to please herself she sipped the tea. Before she had finished it she got up and went slowly to the window, the smaller window facing west; through which shone the last rays of the setting sun blazing white in a clear sky; through which also were visible the chimneys of the Low Farm at the foot of the hill. As she stood there what had been a suggestion became a purpose. She must go down to Low Farm. She left her tea unfinished. It is impossible to give ordinary nerves any idea of the courage with which she reached down cloak and hat and opened the front door. She did not hesitate, she durst not. Once resolved she did it at once; although it was as if she, defenceless herbivorous thing that she was, were descending into the bonestrewn cave of one of the larger carnivora of legendary generosity, indisputable ferocity. She tripped along, she almost ran, over the cloddy fields, striving not to argue either for or against the probability of Tant's being at home, and yet all the while teasing herself with guesses at the bailability of arson and burglary. She almost forgot to be afraid of a herd of cows, though she wasn't sure that one of them wasn't a bull.

Nell was on a stack behind the house cutting hay. She saw Lois coming down the hill when she was yet a long way off. She turned her back on her and while she worked the knife in and out wondered, without any interest in her wonder, who it was and why she came. All at once without further looking she believed that it was Miss Skrene, and that she came about Tant. And she thought to herself:

"If she's wearing her red cloak it's a bad sign, if she's wearing her blue un it's a good sign."

She looked round, the white gleam of the dying sun was on Lois; she wore the blue. Nell accepted the omen, and immediately was wroth with herself for accepting it. She turned again to her work and looked no more. But yet she was coming from the stackyard with the hay-knife still in her hand, as Tish opened the door to the girl's timid knock. There was black trouble on the woman's face. Through the door Lois could see the grandmother seated by the fire, and her wheel was still.

"Who are yo?" she said.

"I am Lois Skrene."

"His sister!" The outward turn of her thumb indicated the High Farm and its tenant. "What does the sister of Mr.

Skrene want here?"

"Be't a good tale or a bad un," said Nell from behind, "the doorstep's none the place to tell it."

Tish glowered over Lois's head at Nell.

"Nell Rideout," she said, "when I oppen the door I ho'd the sneck on't."

In the woman's black face Lois saw another obstacle where she had hoped for furtherance.

"I thought you'd help me," she said and clasped her hands. "Oh I want help badly!"

She turned away and saw Nell's less repellent face behind.

"Oh, Miss Rideout!" she cried, "won't you?"

"I will," said Nell, "if it's my last deed."

At the kindness of the speech Lois burst into tears, and seized Nell's hand and said:

'We must be quick! They are going to – Oh, it's cruel! To-morrow! And he never did! Your brother is not guilty."

"Can yer prove your words?" said Tish,

"I can, I can!"

"Thank God!" said Nell.

"How comes it," said Tish still unwon, "if yo can prove so much that yo hain't proved it afore?"

"I didn't know; I've been away; I've been ill."

"Ill? What a poor cratur yo moot be to be ill when yo're so badly wanted! But yo stand, ma'am; please to walk in."

Nell led her in.

"Set her a chair," said Tish. "Not so nigh'and the fire. Can't yo see she's faint?"

Nell placed her in a chair set a little back from the fire, and as she did so whispered:

"Ne'er mind Tish; tek no offence; when we're put out we moot hae a slap at somebody. But tell's now, tell's quick!"

"What is't?" croaked the grandame bending forwards. "More bad news?"

"Nay, granmam, the contrairy o' that. But tell's quick!"

"Ay, tell's quick!" hoarsely echoed the grandame, and her blind eyes seemed to watch for the words.

Nell on one knee beside Lois fixed her seeing eyes upon her. Tish stood behind them all as upright as a drum-major. Lois was timid of beginning; she looked from face to face; she changed from one paleness to another.

"Pray tell me first," she said, "how he is. I've heard nothing. I saw him fall."

And she shuddered.

"He's as well," said Tish, "as a body can be wi' a helter tightening iv'ry day about his neck."

Again she shuddered.

"He hasn't been thanked! That distresses me. How can I thank him? Shall I thank you for him?"

Tish had doubts of her sanity. The obscure hope, barely kindled, was puffed out by a contrary wind; she answered bitterly:

"What thanks d'yer speak on, wench? Thanks for a bussen winder-frame, a burnt-out barn and a woman fritted out'n her wits?"

"Don't you know?"

"I know a many things; I don't know that."

"Hasn't he said?"

"He hain't oppened his mouth, so fur's we know, except to ax how yo were gooin' on."

"He left it to me!"

"Tell us; do!" cried Nell with her eyes fastened on her.

"He saved my life."

The sisters cried out.

"Hush!" said the old woman upright in her chair. "Let her say on. Nubbudy speak but me an' her."

"Oh, I am sorry! I have done wrong! I never thought but that it was known, and speaking of it seemed to me as bad as seeing it again."

"Speak up," said the old woman commandingly. "It's as if summat was hinged up atween your mouth an' my ears."

She gave a full and close narration of what had happened on that dreadful night, to the moment when her recollection was suddenly cut off. As she told her tale Nell ever kept her eyes upon her, though she had every now and then to wipe the mists from them. Tish still stood behind, but a little less stiffly. The old woman sat upright motionless and let the tears drip from her blind face into her lap, in a joy that was as hard to look on as any sorrow.

"Bless yer, ma child," she said at the end of it in broken tones, "bless yer! Yo've a voice as sounds like comfort out'n a good book."

"Gie granmam my handkerchief," said Tish to Nell; "yourn's as wet as a dish-clout."

Her own was not quite dry, but so she brazened it out.

"And now," said Lois, "I want you to tell me what to do. I have only just returned home after a three weeks' absence, and I find my brother away."

"He's gone to Nottingham betimes," said Tish.

"I'm very ignorant. My silence has been very cruel. I want you to tell me how I can put a stop to this dreadful injustice."

"Yo moot goo to Nottingham too," said Tish, "and say theer what yo've said here; say in a box what yo've said in a chair. Yo're a little scaddle thing, but yo mootn't let nubbudy daunt yer; brother nor nubbudy."

"My brother," said Lois, with some spirit, "is not the man to attempt that. He wouldn't willingly do anybody a wrong."

"That's well; nubbudy'll force him; it's a free country – so fur."

"Tish!" said Nell hotly, "Miss Skrene's coomed here to do uz a kindness, not to hear her brother miscalled."

"Who's miscalling him? Unless yo call mentioning him miscalling him?"

It had become dark in the house as they talked, and Lois was the more afraid of Tish's voice; for the flicker of the fire-light unsteadied the assurance of Nell's upturned face and distorted the blind beldame's immobility. She rose to take her leave.

"But how shall yer get to Nottingham?" said Nell.

"How shall I?" said Lois. "I hadn't thought of that."

"Can yer ride?" said Tish.

"Ay," answered Nell, "she has a nice well-behaved well-brucken little pony; an iron-grey wi' black points."

"Then yo may ride wi' uz if yo like. But yo mun get out o' bed early; we shall start at six o'clock time. Don't be late. And manage so yo're not ill."

"Thank you, I will come; you may rely upon me. And now I must go."

"Ay," said Nell, "yo're fain to be gooing. We can't offer yer any sort o' suitable thanks, but if we knowed how we'd welcome yer as if yo was an angel from Heaven; the angel that appeared unto Mary and said, 'Fear not.' Tish as much as any on's, for all her wry words. But we're a rough and humble sort o' folk, and we're not used to receiving angels except now and again in dreams like."

"Yo nedn't gie's away to that extent," said Tish. "One o' the Rideouts was once alderman o' Retford. But sit again, Miss Skrene, unless yo moot goo, and I'll light a candle."

"Yes, she moot goo," said Nell. "But afore yo goo, I suld like to thank yer for one thing mysen. Yo've made a Christian on me again."

"How so?"

"I'm a witness on the tother side, like your brother, Miss Skrene – again *my* brother. I've been sub peonied, they call it. Cruel, een't it? I went to a lawyer at Nottingham to ax if I couldn't get out on't, and for six-and-eightpence I larnt that it could on'y be by disbelieving the Bible and refusing the oath by't. Oh, many a time I've laid awake hafe the night trying to mind me o' what I'd heerd Shoemekker Morrish say again the miracles!"

"Yo wanted skelping," said Tish.

"But I couldn't remember oat except downraight blether, and I've cried because I couldn't, it seemed so hard to hae to witness again a brother and yo've nubbut one. But now, God bless yer, I shall say 'Our Father' to-night and not miss a word or a tho't, and I shall sleep all night and trust in Him for the morrer."

Tish was the last to shake hands with her, and her grip about the slender fingers was like a strong man's.

"I moan't speak," she said, "for yo're stanning, and 'twould be long."

Lois was afraid of her; still she looked up and by the just lighted candle saw the fierceness of the grey eyes filmed over with a glimmering moisture.

"Put your hood on," said Tish to Nell, "and see her by the cows i' th' Old Ley."

"Thank you," said Lois heartily.

She and Nell went. The sky was still white, but on the ground there was no difference between grey and green.

Said Tish to her grandmother: "There was a furren lady once at Lindhurst – do yo remember? – and *she* was afeared o' cows."

"Tell me what she looks like," said the old woman.

"She's little but not fow, and her eyes are dark but not dishonest."

"She's got kind hands and a sweet voice," said the old woman.

"I'm main glad I tho't o' them cows," said Tish.

CHAPTER XV

GALLOWS HILL

IT was a cold raw morning early in December when Nell and Lois set out together, the one to give evidence for King, the other for Rideout. There seemed to be but three gradations of obscurity in the sombre landscape; the starless sky, the sandy track before them, the land on either side of it, field and moor, hill and valley, all of a dim uniformity. No sooner had Tish mounted to saddle with the help of a cricket fetched from the house than she descended again. It appeared that she had been simultaneously struck with the rawness of the outside air and the slender fragility of Lois's make. She lifted Lois off her pony with her own strong arms, and so carried her into the house as one might a doll. She sent Nell up-stairs for one of her skirts, if not her best her second best, threw it over the girl's head and pinned it voluminously round her slim waist. If Lois made any sort of remonstrance she did not hear or heed it.

"Theer!" she said, surveying with more satisfaction the diminutive figure muffled out of all shape. "It warn't your mother's hand, anybody can see that, as dressed yer for a twelve-mile ride i' them foldidols. And it warn't a mother's deed, she'd say if she were here, to fetch yer out o' your warm bed this time o' day. It's truth we might ha' started an hour later and no harm gotten, no good lost. But it's better as 'tis for yo and everybody. I suld very like ha' been hafe cranky thinking m'appen he'd be hung afore we could get theer to stop it. 'The gret boafin!' yo're saying to yoursen. No, child, I'm no fool, accordin' to the run o' craturs i' this

part o' the world; but yo'll larn this wi' living, by an' by:
when the man's away the woman's nubbut hafe at home."

The last sentence confidentially, out of Nell's hearing, as
she was carrying the girl back to her saddle.

Nell was on the useful cob which she rode to market, but
for her sister there was no better mount than one of the cart-
horses. Tish, who was also an excellent horsewoman, fumed
at the sluggishness of her steed.

"I might as well be riding a load o' tunnips," she growled.
"I suldn't loase oat in action nor yet i' mettle."

"Yo may change with me if yo like," said Nell.

"Yo talk like a tailor. Wheer'd my seventeen stun be atop
o' that middling-sized rot? I'd as lieve be under it as on it."

And so the horse grievance usefully diverted her mind
from the larger trouble they were riding towards. Which
enforces reflection upon the value of the inconvenient as a
buffer to the inconsolable. If life were a plain-spun mixture
of pleasurable days seldom blotted but blackly, we should
faint, we should die under the first unmitigated shock. But
we are early and mercifully broken in to sorrow, as the colt
is to labour with the play-trouble of the longe.

It was a dreary morning, as I have said; there seemed to
be neither light nor shadow; there was no wind; there
seemed to be nothing alive but themselves and the animals
they rode. When Tish was not grumbling at her horse they
were silent. And so after a long colourless ride they reached
the borough boundaries. Tish at last had done grumbling.
To right and left of them was rough gorse-clad ground,
broken into hump and hollow, here and there fashioned by
the weather and men's hands into immemorial caves. Along
the brow of the slope in front of them were a dozen windmills all in a row; but their sails were motionless. The sun
had risen, but not shown himself. When they reached the
top of the hill, the town lay in sight below; or would have
done but for the vaporous screen which overhung it, less
the gift of the chimneys than of the vapour-exhaling

meadows and river beyond. Only the castle and the tower of St. Mary's rose above it.

Nell pushed as near as she could to Lois and leaning towards her said in a low voice, "Does what yo telled uz yesterday ho'd to-day?"

"Most certainly," said Lois.

"He saved your life?"

"Yes."

"I've been doubting all along the road. Trouble meks folk disbelievers of oat but trouble. Sometimes I wunnered if what yo said were a dream, and sometimes if these three hosses and uz three women a-top on 'em were a dream. But when we comed to this hill I felt the pain o' being awake. Do yer know the name on't?"

"No. What is it?"

"No, of course yo wouldn't."

Nell would have left it so; but Tish who had overheard said:

"It's no secret; they call it Gallers Hill."

Lois drank a cup of tea, the sisters a pot of ale each at the inn where they put their horses up. Then they went to see the attorney for the defence, a little unfresh up-all-night sort of man with a larger reputation for craft and drollery than for sobriety or scruple. He took notes of Lois's evidence, and foretold with much glee that it would upset Smetham K.C.'s temper.

"Not that it takes much to do that. It's a case of what we used at Dame Agnes Mellers's to call unstable equilibrium when it's at its best. I understand, young lady, that your brother don't know you're in Nottingham?"

"No," said Lois.

"We suld ha' liked her," said Nell, "to ha' seed him afore coming here – 'twould on'y ha' bin straight-forrard – but she don't know wheer he is nor wheer he's like to be."

"We're going to find him," said Lois, "as soon as you dismiss us."

The lawyer straightway determined that they should not find him in time to spoil his little surprise.

"Certainly, miss," he said, "you couldn't do better. But *tempus fugit;* I must have your evidence fair copied and read over to you before you go. This is what I suggest, ladies: I'll send Thompson to look Mr. Skrene up and let him know Miss Skrene's here. He's the youngest and the smartest of my clerks, and he'll smell him out in ten minutes; in ten minutes certain. Meanwhile you, ladies, can sit by my fire and warm your toes until the copying's completed."

"How long will that tek?" asked Tish.

"Oh, not long. If you want refreshments send Tom to the Crown and Cushion opposite. I can give my personal recommendation to both their eatables and drinkables. Don't suffer from cold, ladies; the coal-scuttle and the poker are at your discretion."

He popped out of the room in middle of "discretion." The fair copy was long in preparation; but it was very nicely written. Thompson returned just as the women were on the point of giving him up and leaving the office. In spite of his junior smartness he had been unsuccessful in finding Mr. Skrene.

"I shouldn't wonder if he's at the Court after all, miss," he said.

And so he was. They perceived him in the lobby as soon as they entered, in the midst of a moving throng of the wigged and unwigged, lawyers and clients, loungers and witnesses, some quite at home, others obviously at sea. Naturally he saw Nell and her tall sister first; he saluted them with a cold wordless gesture and turned away. He did not see Lois until she touched his elbow from behind. His surprise was great and loud; her reply brief and quiet.

"I thought I ought to give evidence, Arthur. I am quite well enough."

Arthur scanned her pale agitated face.

"I do not think so."

"I have been well enough to resolve to give evidence, to live through last night, to travel here."

"I see that you've survived, Lois. But it's so unnecessary! The doctor is prepared to certify that you're physically unfit to give evidence."

"No, Arthur; I'm unfit *not* to give evidence. It's a matter that can't be decided by looking at one's tongue."

"But the lawyers say that their case is perfect without your testimony, that they really don't need to take it."

"I can't dispute with lawyers, Arthur; I know I need to offer it. I can't say more here."

It was true; that loud bustling hall was no place for such communications as she had to make.

"How did you come?" he said.

"Mrs. Gillott and Miss Rideout kindly permitted me to travel with them."

Arthur was greatly dissatisfied.

"You came in strange company, Loie!"

"They were good enough not to allow me to feel the strangeness."

"Strange, I mean, under the circumstances. But I must tell the lawyers. I don't know how they will take your intrusion just at the last minute, while the trial is going on."

"Is he being tried, Arthur? Now?"

"Yes."

Her head went round; she was affected as bystanders are who witness a human life snatched miraculously from under a coach's wheels; she left the waft of death on her face. He had to support her. It got about that a lady had been taken ill. Bystanders crowded round. He was permitted to lead her apart into a quiet room; Nell Rideout reappearing supported her on the other side. A glass of water was fetched. Presently she recovered sight and hearing; just as Arthur Skrene's name was noisily echoed along the corridors, summoning him to the witness-box.

"Yo mun leave her wi' uz," said Nell. "We'll tend her as

if our lives depended on't."

And somewhat unsatisfactory though it appeared to him, so it had to be.

CHAPTER XVI

KING *v.* RIDEOUT

TANT'S trial had already made considerable progress. Counsel had opened; the first witnesses for the prosecution, the farm servants, had proved the firing of the stack-yard and outbuildings, the assault upon the house, their courageous encounter of the rioters and the shooting of Tant. At the mention of Miss Skrene the judge wanted to know whether she was not to be called as a witness; he had observed that her evidence did not figure in the depositions. The counsel for the prosecution said no. The judge said that it was unsatisfactory. The counsel replied that the lady was in a delicate condition, in fact very ill indeed, as the result of the shock and fright, and quite unable to appear, quite unable to bear questioning on the subject.

"Have you a medical certificate?" said the counsel for the defence, stifling a yawn.

"Her medical attendant will be called. We feel perfectly capable of proving our case without the poor lady's attendance."

The judge still thought it most unsatisfactory.

"So do I, m' lud, with y' ludship's permission," said the prisoner's counsel as he negligently examined his finger-nails. "It seems to me the prosecution is trying to make no case appear a bad one by leaving out the only witness they've got."

There was a laugh; the jury stirred on their seats and began to fancy the wagoner's evidence not so conclusive as it had appeared. The counsel for the prosecution, Smetham

K.C. by name, was a stumpy little man with restless little black eyes and a beaky nose. He was scrupulously attired and made an emphasis of everything, the ages of the witnesses, how they spelt or didn't spell their name – everything. Mr. Serjeant Manning, who appeared for the prisoner, with his wig awry, looked a tall man even as he lolled forwards over the table or backwards against the panneling. How tall he would have appeared had he stretched himself to his full possibility no man knew, for he never did; he was always lolling against something or somebody. A man stupendously indolent, his most by-the-way utterances had weight with the court, for it was felt by the most casual observer that he would not have said much even to save his own neck. He did, it is true, ask Harris a few questions after the King's Counsel had done with him, but his thoughts seemed to be as loosely attached as the half-crowns and keys which he was passing through his big hands in his big pockets.

"Was Miss Skrene armed?"

"No, sir."

"How long was it after you heard the smash before you entered the room?"

"Can't say, sir."

"T' oblige me."

"M'appen foive minutes."

"M'appen ten?"

"M'appen."

"M'appen fifteen?"

"M'appen; I can't exackly say."

"M'appen sixteen?"

"No, not sixteen."

"Positive?"

"As sure as sure."

"Then we'll say fifteen."

Smetham K.C. jumped up.

"He didn't say it was fifteen; he said it wasn't sixteen."

"Fifteen isn't sixteen, subject t' his ludship's c'rrection. Well" – he yawned tremendously and seemed dreadfully bored – "let's see – er – how many of the rioters were in the room when you first saw them?"

"On'y Tant, sir, properly in. The tothers was at the winder."

"He was leading them in?"

"Yis, sir."

"Back first?"

His "Yis, sir," was fairly out before the laughter of the court. The counsel took a pinch of snuff, but as if half in a mind not to oblige his nose at the expense of his finger and thumb.

"Well – oh – er – how far was the prisoner within the room when you saw him?"

"M'appen two or three yards."

"Four, m'appen?"

"No, sir, not fower."

"This Tant is a remarkably inactive man, isn't he? Like myself f'r instance."

And the counsel yawned illustratively.

"Not he, sir; he can run like a scoperell, can Tant; nubbudy can run wee 'm at Blid'orth."

"But he takes fifteen minutes to go two or three yards. Now I remember having gone as fast as that myself." Appearing to think the court would hardly accept the bare assertion he condescended to a detail carelessly jerked in: "Highwayman pacemaking, m' lud."

But the King's Counsel was furious.

"I object to words being put into the witness's mouth. He didn't say it was fifteen minutes."

"M' lud," said the Serjeant, "unless I've assurance of y' ludship's protection against m' learned brother's violence, I daren't proceed."

After the court had enjoyed that he added: "I acknowledge, m' lud, coming to the rescue of m' learned brother's desperate case, that the prisoner appears to have been advancing backwards. Well – er – oh – I think that's – there had been nobody but that young lady there to offer resistance?"

"No, sir."

"She was armed with a candlestick?"

"Yis, sir."

"Loaded with the usual candle?"

"Yis, sir."

"Tallow?"

"Yis, sir."

"Rush or cotton wick?"

"Cotton, sir."

The counsel for the prosecution got Selby to limit the interval from the fall of the window to Harris's entrance between a maximum of three minutes and a minimum of one; otherwise his evidence only differed from the first witness's in lessening the distance at which he and Wells gave the wagoner encouragement from a throw to a civil hand's reach. The Serjeant merely asked him solemnly to reswear, if he could, that it was Harris and not Miss Skrene who shot the prisoner. Which he did after some puzzle-headed, court-amusing hesitation.

"But she carried a candlestick?"

"Yes, sir, she did."

And the Serjeant had an air of still doubting whether it were not Miss Skrene.

After Wells had added his colourless confirmations Arthur Skrene detailed the coming of Nell, his ride and summoning of his comrades, his dispersal of the rioters at Rainworth, his seeing the warning fire, his return, the condition of the prisoner and his sister.

"And your sister has been very very ill ever since, I believe?"

"She has."

"And is still much too unwell to appear as a witness?"

"I think so, though to my great surprise she has followed me to Nottingham and is desirous of appearing."

The prisoner's attitude changed from that of hearing to listening.

"I wish we'd been informed earlier of her desire," said the King's Counsel.

"What a lady's man my brother is!" lazily ejaculated the Serjeant.

"Where is she?"

"In the precincts of the court."

"M' lud, I propose calling her."

"It's irregular, m' lud," said the Serjeant; "but I perceive the learned counsel's armed to the – er – tongue; so – er – at – the menace of his eloquence –"

And he offered no further objection to his chief witness being thus appropriated; he was indolently extended over half the table; his one care in the world, and that an unexciting one, seemed to be the balancing of his uninked quill on his big lazy fore-finger. He asked the witness but one question:

"You never had any personal quarrel with the prisoner, I believe, nor he with you?"

"We have had a quarrel."

There seemed to be some error in his instructions and he did not pursue the cross-examination. His learned brother however re-examined upon it, and received for answer that it began about a right of way.

"A very pretty subject too for a quarrel," his lordship condescended to say.

"M' lud, with y' ludship's permission," said the Serjeant, flicking half-heartedly at a fly on his sleeve, "it's a quarrel I can't understand; I can't understand anybody fighting to go anywhere – except perhaps to bed."

"May I be permitted to say, my lord," said Arthur, "with regard to that quarrel, that I don't think the prisoner has any reason to be ashamed; in fact he had the better of me throughout. Nor do I believe it left any rancour in his mind."

"It was a fair faight," said the prisoner, lifting his head.

Nell came next, and the little King's Counsel examined her as a hostile witness with a good deal of sharpness, which on the whole she bore with a decent self-restraint. Why had she gone to Mr. Skrene's house that night? How did she know an attack was meditated upon frames at Rainworth? So bit by bit he piggled out the story of her seeing so many passers that she had become suspicious.

"If it's considered so suspicious a thing to be out at eleven o'clock at night at Blidworth, how is it you were up and out, young woman? Are we to include you in the suspicion?"

"As yo please. My gret-gran'mother is ill and I was up nursing her."

She told how she went forth, saw more night-wanderers, followed them and so forth until they were fully on the road to Rainworth.

"And you tracked these desperate men so many miles, at midnight, in such weather, at the mere prompting of curiosity? Do you expect me to believe that?"

Nell drew herself to her height and answered:

"I'd as lief yo didn't."

"That is insolence, mistress."

"It's in a court o' justice I've larnt it."

"You must not use such language," said the judge severely. "You must not speak but to answer the learned counsel's questions."

She was not abashed, neither was she impudent.

"My lord, if anybody calls me insolent I tek that to be a question."

"Attend to me, madam," said the lawyer. "I may displease you worse yet. Why of all the people in Blidworth did you fly to Mr. Skrene with your news? Was he the nearest?"

"No."

"Are you very intimate?"

"I don't know him scarcely at all; he knows me still less."

"Then why?"

"Because I wanted Sam Derry's frames saving, and I knew he durst do't."

"When had you last seen your brother?"

"I saw him for sartain at one o'clock i' th' afternoon, afore he went to the badger-baiting."

"What do you mean by 'for sartain'?"

"I may ha' seed him later; I can't swear."

"When?"

Only the lowering of her voice showed the trouble it was to her to answer.

"About eleven o'clock time."

"The same time as you saw the others?"

"Ay."

"Going the same way?"

"Ay. But 'twere dark, and there are other tall men besides him. Whoever 'twere he was reeling drank and two men were dading him."

"What do you mean by 'dading'?"

"Leading and supporting."

"Then say leading and supporting."

"Did yo mother my tongue? Did yo larn it to talk?"

The judge interposed with the proper reproof.

"But it's hard, my lord, as he should do all the hammer-gagging; I wear a gown too."

"I respect yours," said the judge; "I shall require you to respect the learned gentleman's."

"My lord, if I mun I will."

The check she put upon herself was immediately manifest in her bearing, which was thenceforth more composed and greatly more dignified. Through her curbed lips the words came deliberately; only to her eyes she once and perhaps twice allowed their freedom. The first time was when the counsel after other inquiries which elicited nothing of importance said:

"Well, we will return to the time when Mr. Skrene rode off in the direction of Rainworth. What did you next do after you had seen him out of the way?"

Then her eyes blazed, and her countenance seemed to catch fire from her eyes; it ran up to the roots of her hair. She leant forward until she hung over the heads of the budding barristers seated beneath and over the paper-strewn table. The court expected an outburst, but none came. "Mr. Skrene thinks so and why suldn't he?" was in her thoughts; and lo! their eyes met, Mr. Skrene's and hers, for he had just returned to court and had taken his stand on the other side of the dock. Their eyes met and it was to her as if she had spoken. Perhaps to him too. She shrank back into her usual dimensions and patiently suffered her tormentor to draw from her how she had roused Selby and Wells, visited Miss Skrene and returned home.

"Did you find your brother at home?"

"No."

So quietly said, so sadly, that little word was to Tant the hardest to bear of any he had heard that day.

She then related how she had seen the burning stacks and returned on horseback; how she had viewed the fire and then ridden round the house to the front.

"What did you see there?"

"Men i' the dark faighting and cursing; heerd more than saw."

"What did you do?"

"Pushed towards 'em."

"With what purpose?"

"I've never reckoned that up. But there was the crack of a fowling-piece and my hoss bolted."

"Do your horses always bolt so conveniently?"

"Full seldom they bolt at all. He wouldn't ha' done then if my mind had been on him."

"What was it on?"

"On the trouble o' the women and the folly o' the men.

As soon as I'd mestered him I rode back,"

"As quick as you could?"

"Ay, and it warn't long."

"What had happened?"

"The men were gone from the winder, both the faighters and the swearers."

"Well?"

"I rode straight up to it."

"Well?"

"And looked in."

"What did you see?"

Step by step she was drawn, step by step, make them short and slow as she would, to the inevitable avowal.

"I saw men stanning up."

"What else?"

"I saw a man lying down."

"Who were the men standing up?"

They were Mr. Skrene, Tom This, John That, and so forth.

"Who was the man lying down?"

"Anthony Rideout."

Then as though she would not be seeming to disclaim the relationship, her part of the crime:

"My brother."

"What happened next?"

She turned in her distress to the bench.

"My lord, must I?"

"Answer the learned counsel."

"I went down on my knees."

"To whom?"

She could not utter the word, but involuntarily she lifted finger. Everybody in court looked as it pointed and saw Arthur Skrene; she was taken to have spoken.

"For your brother's life?"

"What else suld I kneel for?"

"For your own perhaps."

"Never!"

"What answer did Mr. Skrene make to that?"

"I'll never kneel no more, to man."

Again her eyes met Arthur Skrene's; that time not by hazard.

"You haven't answered my question," said the little nagger.

"I reckoned I had."

"Give me the exact words of Mr. Skrene's reply."

"I don't mind the words."

The Serjeant did not rise; he only put a little more of his weight on that elbow which rested on the table, as he said:

"I've really nothing – m' learned friend having been so kind as to cross-examine for me – still – When you rode round the corner of the house and saw the men at the window –"

"Yes, sir?"

"Did they appear to be marching in victoriously, unresisted, at the rate of one yard per five minutes, or was there a scuffle going on?"

"There was a great lumber next the winder and a good deal o' swearing round and about."

"Swearing? Hum – ah – as if at a young lady?"

"They swore like men who'd got ho'd o' the hot end o' summat."

"Of a candlestick?"

Nell shook her head.

"Of a fight perhaps?"

"Specially of a faight."

CHAPTER XVII

GENTLEMEN OF THE JURY

WE may pass the next witnesses over, one or two of Arthur's troopers, the constable who proved the arrest, the doctor who proved that he had earned his fees.

"Lois Skrene!"

At the sound of the name Tant's heart stood still. He had more fear of her verdict than the jury's. Involuntarily he stepped back a little from the front of the dock. But she did not see him, or not with recognition. Partly because she did not wish to see him, partly because she had never been in a court of justice before and did not understand the significance of that spiky enclosure; partly because she would hardly in any case have identified the pale grave man who stood apart in it with the desperate swashbuckler in her mind's eye. She saw the stately judge close to her right hand, the boxed-up jury on her left, the teasing King's Counsel in front of her with Arthur behind him; all the rest was a mere sum of listening ears, looking eyes. Still she was not confused though much disturbed. Her cheeks being so pale, her lips so white, all the life of her countenance seemed to be concentrated in her eyes. Tant hardly seeing saw it all; her nervous struggle with her glove before her right hand was bared for the oath, and then how the gloved fingers and the ungloved seized the edge of the box and held by it. She was more plainly and soberly clad than usual, for she loved gay fluttering attire. Being so slim and small she looked even younger than she was, and won the more pity for her evident distress.

"Arthur, I can't say it twice and I must say it then." So she had answered when some attempt was made to ascertain the character of her evidence, and her brother and her doctor, who was in attendance, had not permitted her to be troubled further. But Smetham K.C. did not feel his way as he should have done; he was too sure her story would be an echo of her brother's, as a good sister's ought to be. He went boldly at it with his customary snappish vehemence, only modified by a man's acknowledgment, inevitable however unconscious, of maidenly grace. She gave the first part of her testimony in full conformity with that of the other witnesses; until she came to the time when she had entered the dining-room alone and stood looking the book-case over; then she heard a great noise behind her.

"What kind of a noise?"

"Oh, a fearful noise!"

"What sort of a fearful noise?"

"I can't say; I'd never heard anything like it."

And the visible shudder that shook her told that she had no wish to hear the like again.

"But can't you give the jury some more notion of it?"

So he was insisting as those dully clever, heavily vehement men will, had not the judge interposed.

"I think we've had enough of the noise, Mr. Smetham. Let us pass on to what made it."

"I looked round."

"What did you see?"

"I saw something, something large, coming into the room, coming towards me, as I thought, and it fell down with a great crash."

"What was it?"

"I don't think I knew at the time that it was the window."

He stickled for the exact time when she came to know it was the window, but could get no satisfaction.

"And after the falling of the window?"

"A man came in."

Her voice shook as though she again saw the coming.

"Did you know him?"

"Yes."

"Who was it?"

"I've heard him called Tant Rideout."

"The prisoner at the bar?"

Lifting her eyes at that moment she saw Nell's pale anxious face in the gallery in front of her. She was not able to bear another fear added to her own. All at once she fell to be uncertain whether she were saving or hanging. Her eyes followed the lawyer's pointing finger. She beheld the spiky dock and instantly took in its significance. The prisoner she did not see; fear and pity made a mist before her eyes.

"Was it the prisoner at the bar?"

"I don't know, I can't see."

"Are you short sighted?" asked the judge.

"I don't think I am."

But the tears fell, one from each eye, betraying what ailed her vision. She looked again, but fresh tears had gathered and again she could not see. She turned a little aside and with a quick shamefacedness drew her handkerchief across her eyes. But still she could not see.

"Perhaps," said the judge gently, "the young lady had better be taken round to the front of the dock."

She was helped down and guided, scarcely understanding what was being done with her. She had just wiped her eyes again and she saw, not a yard off, a face and nothing else; a young face, pale, dejected, ashamed, yet gravely decent, and so different from her memory of him that at first she was ready to cry out, "It is not he!" Then she knew it was he. The tears fell again and shut him out. She was led back to the witness-box.

"You have recognized him?"

The drop of the head went for more than the faint "Yes."

"Tell me now what happened after the prisoner thus entered?"

"Several other men entered."

"Did you recognize any of them?"

"No, they all had black on their faces."

"And the prisoner also?"

"No, his face I could see. I was afraid of him. He came towards me. He shouted out, 'It's the wrong house!'"

Men seemed instinctively to know that the crisis had been reached. They stood a-tip-toes, they curved their hands behind their ears. She too seemed to remember again that her mission was to save not to condemn; she spoke more connectedly, in a louder voice.

"The wrong house? What did you understand by that?"

"I understood nothing; I understand nothing. He bade the others go. 'Clear out of here!' that was what he said. They were angry; he was very angry. A little man called him a traitor. He took the little man and threw him out of the window. The little man came back with a pistol in his hand. Mr. Rideout hit him on the arm and the pistol went off; then the little man went away as if he were hurt."

Each man there looked in his neighbour's eyes. A "little man" had been the town's talk for months. The King's Counsel was taken aback; this was not at all what he had expected.

"Was the prisoner drunk?" he asked.

"Oh, if he were, sir, I could understand men thinking they are the better for getting drunk."

After that he almost left her examination to the judge.

"What happened next?"

"There was a fight."

"Between whom?"

"The prisoner against all the others."

"Give us what details you can of it."

"Oh, my lord, it was so brave, it was so terrible! He struck two men down, then more and more came against him, some with swords and some with – I don't know what else. He had only a flail, my lord, a bit of stick. I prayed that he might win. But they were too many. They pushed further in, further in; their faces were all black; there seemed no help; I could not speak. All at once he stooped and lifted the table up as if it were nothing. He ran at them with it. A man fell down and groaned. The others were driven back to the window."

"How was that?"

"I can't say. It was only one man, my lord. I had my eyes on him all the while. I felt as if I were saved. Then a gun went off, close by; Mr. Rideout fell down. I saw no more."

The King's Counsel, immensely put out, asked her why she had delayed offering her highly-interesting evidence until the last moment.

"I did not know until yesterday of the trial. I have been ill; nobody spoke to me about it; and talking about it seemed worse to me than thinking about it."

Serjeant Manning rose in civility to the witness's sex, but as though he would sooner have sat. He said;

"I've no right to cross-examine my own witness. However – might – er – one thing matter of mere curiosity: You did not, Miss Skrene, with your own hands aid in the rout of the rioters?"

"Oh no!"

"You simply held the candle?"

"Just so."

"That's my case, m' lud," said the King's Counsel.

"And mine, m' lud," said the Serjeant; who addressed the jury to this effect:

"Well, gentlemen, no evidence whatever has been offered you to connect the prisoner with what went on at the back of the house, so just a word or two about what happened at the front. The prosecution has but one witness; m' learn'd friend will be obliged to ask you to disbelieve her; I ask you to believe her. Men like you could not but be touched by the manner in which she gave her testimony, which came almost with as much surprise to me as it did to my learn'd brother who essayed to examine her. For the man's noble modesty kept his deed a secret; his friends, his counsel knew nothing of it; until it was revealed so late yet so effectually by her. What does it amount to? There's the smashing of a window, by whom unknown. This young man with his face honest and uncovered enters by it in company with a masked mob. He cries out, 'It's the wrong house!' With unheard-of strength and courage he expels them from the room, saving it from further damage and that young lady from horrors the mention of which would be a horror. For thanks he gets that wound which the medical gentleman has described to you with a learning I admire but can't imitate. Well then, it appears the counsel for the prosecution has two counts to his indictment against the prisoner; his courage and his modesty. What can I say against them? If crimes be estimated by their rarity both are serious ones, and both have been proved against him. You'll be asked to hang him for them; or one of them. I shan't ask you not; but I don't think you will. Well, you'll say, but what was the prisoner doing in such company, and what did he mean by 'It's the wrong house'? Gentlemen, the prosecution can't tell you, the prisoner mayn't. After all it's only a matter of curiosity; but curiosity's a human craving, and I make this suggestion: It has been proved he was in a state of intoxication, and –"

"Nothing of the sort!" cried the King's Counsel.

"Miss Rideout's evidence," said the Serjeant.

"Fiddlesticks!"

"Miss Skrene's."

"Ditto."

"Be it so. I'm no hand at this sort of thing. After all, gentlemen; I am superfluous here, impertinently superfluous. That maiden, so young, so sweet, has already made the speech for the defence. You have heard her. Who am I that I should speak after her? Gentlemen, this lad's either a house-breaker or a hero. You've got to say which."

The King's Counsel spoke for an hour. He contended that Lois's brain must have been paralyzed by that first fearful noise, and that the remainder of her evidence was the gift of a disordered fancy. He certainly proved that Tant was keeping very bad company. But his length displeased the jury with his arguments, and contrasted ill with the Serjeant's brevity. The judge did not sum up altogether in Tant's favour either; there were many points in the evidence difficult, some impossible to wrest to a satisfactory interpretation; but by that time the jury had had enough of pros and cons, and gave him a respectful inattention. They sat for half-an-hour in a room with a view of nothing, until a lean man who had taken notes gave up his intention of forming an independent judgment, and then brought in a verdict of not guilty.

CHAPTER XVIII

THE INFORMATION

THE verdict was received by nobody with so much disappointment as by the Luddite leaders at Nottingham. The conspiracy had degenerated from that early austerity which lent its violences the mask of a judicial punishment; they were already made sometimes a means to private revenge or plunder, often a cloak to personal laxity. As the saying went, Ned Ludd had turned thief. He also turned informer. There was a standing reward of fifty pounds on offer by the government for such evidence as should convict any person of an act of machine-breaking within the proclaimed district. On the very night of the trial Ben Foat of Fishpool, who had begun to hobble about with a stick, received a secret intimation that he might earn the money if he would. He called on the nearest magistrate, General Dene of Spring Vale, as early as he might in the morning and declared his readiness and ability to prove that Tant Rideout, in company with others unknown, had a year before broken a frame which was being conveyed along the Rufford road. He himself was out bird-catching; he had lain among the gorse by the roadside and unseen had seen all. He gave the name of the Basford carrier who was conveying the machine, and added:

"What'll prove it's true, sir, 's this: It war the very day Mester Skrene fust coom'd to Blid'orth. The chaps stopped 'im on the roäd an' turned 'im back. He'd tell yer if yer-r axed 'im."

"How can you be sure it was Rideout," asked the General, "if he had a mask on?"

"A bit of a crape bluft is no concealment to a chap o' Tant's uncommon hair an' figure, i' broad daylight too. I'd guarantee to own 'im anywheer an' anywhen."

"But why didn't you lay your information sooner?"

Ben it appears was driven to his last resource for an excuse.

"Well, sir, it were this 'ow, my missis were again it."

After the General had properly insulted his cowardice he bade him call again in the evening and in the meantime not breathe a word about the matter to anybody. The General was a busy man that day. He himself rode over to Basford, saw the carrier and received confirmation of the story; put Foat's information into writing and swore him, wrote out the warrant and made the necessary arrangements for its execution. Tant's strength, activity and reckless daring being well known, two special constables were summoned to back Tom White up; besides which three or four troopers of the local Yeomanry were ordered to attend in case of emergency. These were instructed to rendezvous at High Farm. It was the side from which the arrest could be attempted with the least observation; besides it gave the General an opportunity both of requiring Arthur to take command of the Yeomanry, and also with the least loss of time of questioning him as to his alleged presence during the machine-breaking.

Night had fallen when the General called. Arthur was at home; it would have been a serious duty indeed which at that time would have persuaded him to leave his sister to other protection than his own. He was sitting at the table, which was overspread with account-books, and was trying to put some order into his affairs, which had been sadly disarranged by the disastrous fire; and yet his eyes did not always rest upon the ruled pages before him. Lois reclined beside the hearth pale and inert; she had not recovered from the injurious excitement of the trial. Her head ached, she could not read, she could not sew; apparently she found watching Arthur's puckered brow a sorry occupation, for at last she said with the affectionate peevishness of an invalid:

"For goodness' sake, Arthur dear, do lay aside that arithmetical countenance and give me one of your Kent looks."

Arthur was constrained to look up; and the constraint was mixed with the affection of his look, an equal ingredient.

"It's rent day, next week," he said.

He may have been thinking of the rent all the time; anyhow it accounted for puckers on the brow as well as anything else.

"Oh, I can't bother about anything so far away as next week. It seems as far off as Kent; so the one balances the other."

"I was wondering how much General Dene would give me for my roan mare."

He bent his head over his books again.

"Arthur!"

"Yes?"

Again he had to raise his head.

"You've seen her on horseback?"

"Yes. Who?"

His eyes dropped, but not his head.

"Didn't she look grand?"

"Who? Twelve – twenty – twenty-nine – thirty-five – forty-two. Two, four, two."

"I won't answer your question."

She lay back in her chair in a resolved silence, and broke it again in five-and-twenty seconds.

"If you know more than one person here to whom the question might apply, either your taste is more promiscuous than I thought, or Blidworth is favoured beyond the rest of the world."

"You didn't mention Blidworth, Loie; I thought your question was as broad as the universe."

In a minute or two she broke the addition of a long column by saying:

"Arthur, if I were a Haroun-al-Rashid autocrat, I'd sit in a lighted saloon hung round with the dark, and have her dash in and out on a wild Arab. I think the sight would shame my head into steadiness and my legs and back into strength,"

"Ninety-six at twenty-three and three –"

"Arthur!"

"Well?"

"When she came into the house on that night, wet, disorderly and great, a part and parcel of the elements, she made me dwindle into a rag-doll with ink-dots for eyes and saw-dust for soul."

"Three thirteens thirty-nine; and a half makes –"

"Arthur, what do you think? I didn't mention it at the trial; I wasn't asked. I heard a woman's voice outside among the men's just before – you know what."

"Hers!"

"But what would she be doing there?"

"She said in her examination that she didn't know. You can hardly expect me to be better informed than herself. Three at twenty-eight, seven, six –"

But five minutes thence and yet he had not completed the simple multiplication. His mind had gone off, as it had again and again that evening, on its erroneous ramblings. He would have liked to believe ill of Nell; and when for the momentary life-time of a thought he succeeded he was angry with his success. He would have liked not to believe ill of her, until he felt he was being compelled to be just; and then he was displeased with the compulsion. So believing or disbelieving, his feelings towards her were the same; bitter for the wrong she had done him, or bitter and more bitter for the wrong he was doing her. Of course it was all very absurd; his inmost judgment sitting in chamber exonerated her. Had he been in love now – the flushed epiderm of a lover is so irritably sensitive that it can feel the hot or cold of a thought. But Arthur Skrene's only excuse was that he had lost £500 by the fire, and was just then striking the balance of the year's profit or loss.

"But, Arthur!"

"Well, Loie?"

He was turning the leaves of a ready-reckoner.

"Has he been thanked?"

"Thanked?"

He pencilled a calculation on a margin.

"He has *not* been thanked! Yet! Come, Arthur!" She rose. "I'm quite well. Let us go, at once. Only think if his service had been as dilatory as our acknowledgment of it!" She sank down again into her chair. "I'm not quite well." Arthur renounced pen and book, got up from the table and went round to the hearth. "I'm afraid I'm more coward than invalid. The very thought of being in the same room again, of speaking to him –"

"You must not go, Loie; it is not fitting. What thanks are necessary I will convey. I acknowledge that he must be thanked since he has been acquitted."

"It was the question of our gratitude then that was put to the jury?"

"The judge summed up unfavourably."

"He saved me."

"Probably he was drunk and didn't know what he was doing. His desperate character is indisputable.

I believe he has long been a confederate with those scoundrels."

"Is there a moon to-night, Arthur?"

"No. Why? You remember my telling you how I had witnessed the smashing of some machinery by the roadside on the day of my arrival? This fellow was at the head of them. I jumped into recognition of him when – on that night; as he lay." A febrile shiver shot through her. "I wondered it had never occurred to me before."

He need not have wondered. What occurs to us (as we so funnily put it) is rarely what we are going to meet; as often as not it is what we are running away from.

In a minute she said:

"Are these machines very expensive?"

"Some of them are; they vary very much in cost."

"Like us." She rose again. "I'm a machine, Arthur, a little more delicate and intricate, though not so valuable. Still it's something to his credit that he prevented me from being smashed."

She was going from the room; he took her by the hand, led her back to her chair and with gentle force seated her in it again.

"You're not going, Loie; I'm going."

He went into the kitchen at once and pulled his top-boots on. But when he returned to the hall Loie was there reaching down her hooded cloak.

"It has occurred to me," she said, "that only the person can give thanks who feels them. I forget whether you said moon or no moon, and I don't care. Now only a thicker pair of shoes and I'm ready. I'm not afraid of Miss Rideout, nor half so much afraid as I ought to be of Mrs. Gillott."

As she pulled on her shoes in the parlour a rising thought seemed to give her stealthy comfort.

"And perhaps he won't be at home, Arthur."

"Most likely he'll be at the public-house." At which moment there was a knock at the door. Mary ushered in the General, who with absent-minded gallantry complimented the young lady upon her good looks, then asked to speak with Arthur alone. Lois withdrew. The two men's conversation did not turn, as Arthur half expected it would, upon the price of hunters. He gave additional support to Foat's information, and also undertook command of the squad of volunteer troopers. He could not do otherwise. He hardly wished to do otherwise. But he hoped Nell would be out of the way,

And yet, and yet, she was not quite out of the way even then. She had her eyes upon him, even as when she said:

"I will never kneel no more, to man."

CHAPTER XIX

THE WARRANT

AFTER leaving her brother and the General Lois went up-stairs to her own room, whence presently she heard the impatient crunching of the gravel outside by the hoofs of what seemed to be more than one horse. She could see nothing through the window; she ran down-stairs to the kitchen driven by new fears upon old ones.

"It's nubbut the Yeomanry, miss," said the cook.

"What have they come here for?"

"I dunno, miss – lackeying the Gen'ral about, I s'pose."

Lois remembered the last time Arthur had been summoned forth; she felt the fear of the past danger. She went to the front door, candle in hand, opened it on the chain and peeped out. By the strip of light issuing through the narrow aperture she had a glimpse five or six yards off of a horse's fore-quarters, his rider's legs and hands. She recognized the accoutrements of the Yeomanry Cavalry. From the room on her right the bass and tenor buzz of the General's and her brother's voices was heard.

"Who's there?" she said.

"On'y uz, miss; Archer, miss; waiting for the Gen'ral."

She undid the chain and opened the door. The whole of a horse and his rider was dimly visible, and she knew the latter very well.

"Oh dear, Mr. Archer!" she said, "are you called out again?"

"Nubbut a little bit of a jaunt this time, miss; don't be afeared. Next door as yer might say." He lowered his voice.

"We're not understood to know, so we didn't ought to tell; but" – still lower fell his voice – "Tant Rideout again, miss. Machine-smashin'. We've clawked 'im this time, sure-lye!"

So soon again? What an irreclaimable desperado! The nobler figure which through her tears she had seen in the dock was blotted out; she again beheld in its place the wild drunken swashbuckler who had at first affrighted her.

"As you can't leave your horses, Mr. Archer, I will send some refreshment out to you, if you'll allow me."

"Thank yer, miss, but we don't want to put yer to no trouble."

"No trouble at all, Mr. Archer."

She knew that the statutory punishment of machine-breaking by an act of the last session of Parliament was death "without benefit of clergy." In the short walk from the front door to the kitchen she saw all the hideous ceremony of a hanging; not in its own sordid daylight horror, but with the night-terrors of an ignorant imagination. She saw the agony of a black distorted face all the time she was speaking to the cook about a jug of ale. She put her gloves on. She had resolved on nothing.

Mary had gone for the ale, Elizabeth was out. She heard the handle of the parlour door turn, and the voices which had been a mere buzz immediately became loud and near. If she were to do what she had not resolved to do, there was no time to lose. She went out by the kitchen door, round crew-yard and stack-yard and across that first grass field. There she stopped afraid of the way before her, and when she looked back afraid of the return. The night was only lighted by the austerity of the stars. The early silence of winter was upon all things. She had never before been out alone by night in the open fields and it was awful to her. She saw nothing that she knew but the stars, and they were terrifically distant. Should she go back? She turned to go back; and there was the figure of one of the big oaks sombrely outlined against the sky; it suggested to her a black cap on the rigid head of an old, old judge, mercilessly just. Those two stars which looked through the boughs were his steely eyes. She turned the other way and sped across the dark fields, seeing as little as she could of the shadows that quivered in the still air like things dying, not yet dead. She had made no resolve. Many a time she started aside, many a time she would fain have gone back. At the bottom of the descent willow-trees lined the tiny mist-hung brook, making a thicker gloom where it had to be crossed by stepping-stones; and close by it was widened into a vaporous pool, inky black, at which the cattle drank. There she stood again, afraid to go forward, unable go back.

But she heard the steely chink of horses' accoutrements on the hill above; it spurred her, not to resolve but to move. Striving to make her eyes and ears deaf to her fancy, she felt her way across the dark stepping-stones. One stone she missed and went over-shoes; at the touch of the cold water she started as though something had gotten hold of her, and ran. In a minute she stood by the door breathless with haste and her fears, fear of the way she had come – that was passed – fear of the man, which now freshly sprang upon her like a new terror.

Through the uncurtained window she could peep into the kitchen. In comparison with the outer darkness the combined light of the fire and the one dip on the table seemed a bright and cheerful glow. The hearth was swept, the labourers had gone home, the day's toil was over; what remained was the work of pastime. The nearest figure was a man's, Tant's, as she knew with an unbelieving sureness. He sat by the table close to the candle, and with a knife was fashioning a piece of willowwood into the sole of a woman's clog, a kind of patten without the iron ring to raise it. Behind him was the fire and the three women; the grandmother and Tish on either side, while Nell basked in front of it in her favourite languorsome attitude. The old woman's wheel made a faint hum, as drowsily cheerful as a cat's purr. Of Tish she could only see the broad back and the industrious hands that knitted. Nell's was the face of one who had laughed and was ready to laugh again; her listening eyes were fixed on Tant. As if in response to them he looked up from his work and spoke with a soft-voiced mockery, which made the laughter ripple again on Nell's face. Tish answered him with her customary loud tartness; but as she turned her head to do so Lois saw that the severity of her profile was complacent.

The girl's hand hesitated at the knock in a wonder that made her for the moment forget her errand. What a strange man! Here was another of his moods. He seemed to have as many changes of personality as the better-to-do have of raiment. Who could have believed that pleasant high-pitched baritone was his, or those features fine for all their boldness, or the fireside mockery of his eyes, grey like Nell's, or – but she must knock. She hoped that Nell would open, or even Tish. But it was Tant's form that stood before her largely outlined; she shrank back a little into the dark, uncertain whether he were at the end of his metamorphoses.

"Who is it?" he asked.

It was the fireside voice; she came forward a little. His surprised recognition was immediate.

"Miss Skrene! Will you please to enter? It'll be a kindness to boots."

She went in, her physical and mental vision both dazed. The sisters had already risen and the grandmother's wheel was still. As soon as Nell saw her face she cried:

"Yo bring bad news!"

"It can't be bad news," said Tant.

He set a chair for her, and without his touching her or her willing it she found herself sitting in it.

"Speak, lass!" said Tish sharply. "Tongues need never ha' been invented if looks would ha' sarved."

"Let the lady tek her own time," said Tant quietly; "as is her raight."

He sat himself and with his hand motioned the others to be seated. It was a marvellous thing, but Tish obeyed the gesture as well as Nell.

"We can't hope to thank yer," he said, "but maybe yo'll let us try, at a time convenient? That'll be summat for fresh thanks."

"I too," she gasped, "I too – but –" She turned to the younger sister, as being the one of whom she was least afraid, and said in an awakened voice, "They're coming to take your brother! They're coming now!"

"For the same?"

"For machine-breaking."

Nell cried out in her anguish, "So soon again! Oh, Tant!"

"Welladay, welladay!" said the old woman and wrung her hands.

The sisters uprose; Tant sat beside Lois.

"It moot be an oad charge," said he. "I'm as clear sin then as if I'd been chained up. I don't consider mysen at liberty."

"They're coming now!" cried Lois. "They're on the hill!"

"They're i' the croft," said Tant quietly, not stirring.

"Mizzle out the road, lad," said Tish, "as quick's yo can."

"I could run without any on 'em," said Tant; "but they've hosses an' all."

"Yes," said Lois, nervous hand clasping hand, "there's the Yeomanry. And my brother."

"He'll hae a good hoss too," said Tant, and so saying he reached back and extinguished the candle. "It mootn't be knowed as I'm here." He rose. "Mek the door, Nell, quick and quiet; they're coming round the corner."

He himself took a large clothes-horse, which stood aside by the wall thickly hung with linen, and extended it in front of the fire so as to block its light.

"Where shall I go?" said Lois, starting up and seizing Nell by the arm. "They will know, they will know!" Which had not occurred to her before.

"They're all round the house now," said Tant at a

whisper. "I've a road out for mysen, but it's none for a lady."

"Oh take me, take me any way, so long as it is a way!"

"It's that or noat," said Nell; "they'll purr and pry into every corner."

Dearly came their whispers to the old woman behind the clothes-horse.

"Why do yer talk so low?" she cried. "Hae they ta'en him?"

"No, granmam, and wain't," said Tish. "Mek yer wheel hum."

With a trembling foot the grandmother pressed the treadle; the wheel span round, the wool ran between her trembling fingers; with her blind eyes she saw trouble. The others hurried up the narrow stairs, Tant leading. There was a knock at the door, and again a knock; at the third and loudest knocking the old woman's hoarse voice uprose:

"Who's theer?"

"Nubbut me."

"Eh? I can't hear. Yo moot stan' a while; they're up-stairs."

Meanwhile Tant had led on into his own chamber, opened the casement and cautiously removed the loose tiles from the roof of the shed, so gaining passage through to the false floor which underlay it at that end. He stood out shoulder high, and to make room for the young lady he took away two or three tiles more. The strong hands of Tish and Nell lowered the slight girl into his arms; he gently drew her down, and placed her on a heap of sack-covered potatoes on the floor. His whisper was agitated.

"Shall yo forgie me – sometime? I was fo'ced. There was no other road."

She could not answer. It was pitch dark. There was the sound of a horse pulling at his chain below; there was the sharp smell of the onions which overspread half the floor, and had been crushed by Tant's foot; there was a louder and yet louder beating at the kitchen door. She forgot under what aspect she had last beheld Tant; she was not sure of the permanency of any aspect; she was fearfully afraid of him again.

"Please to sit still," he whispered, "or yo might fall. I shall soon be back."

He appeared to go from her noiselessly; then she was afraid of his absence. And it was so dark!

But the darkness was broken by the glimmer of a lantern at the far end of the shed. The light increased as the lantern advanced, until it revealed a man carrying it and another walking behind him. Tant she could not see; he had dropped to the ground from the edge of the false floor. Then the light seemed to Lois a worse thing than the dark; but Tant gave it a halved blessing; it showed him the ladder for which he had been groping. He lay squat behind the colt which occupied the last stall, until the lanternbearer was on the point of passing round it; then by the same quick blow with the shaft of a fork he knocked the lantern out of the man's hand and smote the colt smartly across his quarters. The colt lunged out with the devil's own temper, so promptly that it seemed simultaneous with the fall of the lantern. The light was extinguished; the man cursed and swore.

"Drabbit it! The hoss kicked it out of my hand," he said, "and oad Nick knows wheer 'tis. It's well it warn't my brains. Woa! hoss, woa! and be damned to yer!"

Tant prodded the animal with the tines of the fork, and he kicked and plunged more furiously than before.

"I'm not a gooin' to risk my life for't. Yo'd better goo back for a light, Dan, whilst I stop here. What a vicious mortal it is!"

The second man departed. As quickly and quietly as he might Tant raised the ladder and again mounted to the false floor.

"Don't speak, don't fear," he whispered. "It moot be; though yo suld ne'er forgie me."

He took her up in one arm like a child; like a child she

instinctively put her arms round his neck. So he descended
the ladder. Their movements had been veiled by the colt's
continued plunging. There was a window in the wall
thereby opening into the field and closed by a wooden
shutter. That Tant undid. The creak of bolt and hinges, or
the sudden whiff of cold air and the glimmer therethrough
of something less than complete darkness called the man's
attention. The colt was quiet for the moment. He holloaed
to his comrades, than dashed after them. He was felled by
Tant's fist, and was lucky to escape falling under the colt's
hoofs. Tant lifted the lady out through the window and
lightly followed himself. But the man's outcries, standing
and falling, had roused his fellows. Tant espied two of them
running round the end of the building towards them; from
down the field he heard a hussar trotting up. There was no
time to lose; he took Lois's hand and fled with her round
the corner of the house. But where was the chance of escape
for both of them against such pursuit? With a sudden
desperate thought he stopped at the front door, opened it,
entered, drew Lois in after him and quickly closed it again.
The next moment their pursuers dashed by.

Tant's hope was that they might be able to pass through
the house to the back and so into safety, while attention was
concentrated on the front; at the worst he could give himself
up, when his fair would-be preserver could easily slip away
unnoticed. They had entered straight into the "room"; the
door on their right hand led directly to the kitchen. On this
Tant gently scraped with his finger-nail; such a noise as any
little gnawing animal might make. Immediately Nell on the
other side was heard to say:

"St, puss, st! There's a mouse."

Tant softly drew the bolt and secured the door. The
moment after they heard the General's well-known voice,
throatily authoritative:

"Are you troubled with mice?"

"Now and again," said Nell.

Tant returned to the front door and cautiously opened it a few inches.

"By gosh, so I tho't! We've hooked him this time! Sar tain-lye!"

It was Tom White who stood within two yards of the door and beside him one of the special constables.

"Is that you, White?" said Tant through the chink softly, but in exact imitation of the General, throatily authoritative.

"Yes, sir. Beg pardon, sir; I tho't …"

"We have captured the prisoner. Go round to the back of the house and await orders. Take the other men with you."

"Yes, sir."

"Have you the warrant?"

"Yes, sir."

"Give it to me."

The constable placed it in the hand held forth to him.

Two or three minutes later the General looked out of the kitchen door and saw the constables standing inactive in the yard; on the other side of the gate he also saw dim inactive shapes of the Yeomanry; all but their sergeant.

"What the deuce are you all doing here?" he asked.

"Waiting for orders, sir," said Tom White respectfully.

"Waiting for orders? You've got your orders. It's a thousand to one you've let your man slip through your fingers."

"Yo telled uz yo'd got 'im captured, sir."

"I told you, you infernal fool? When? Where?"

"Not a minute agoo, sir, round at the front door. And yo said –"

"I've never been there, you sublime jackass! You must be drunk."

"Well, sir, if it warn't yo, it war Tant his own sen."

The General's voice, throaty no longer, flew to its head-notes.

"Off with you! Sharp! Catch him! Fetch him! Or you

shall hear about it."

"I hain't got the warrant, sir."

"Where is it?"

"I gied yo it."

"You lie!"

"I mean 'im – Tant. Yo axed for't."

"I did, you Tom fool?"

"I mean 'im Tant."

The General cursed as fluently as though he had served in Flanders.

CHAPTER XX

LOIS'S PRISONER

As soon as the constables had disappeared Tant and Lois sped across the vaporous croft towards the crossing-place at the foot of the hill. But through the mist they were observed by one of the Yeomanry who was patrolling at the back of the out-buildings, and he came after them at a hand-gallop, calling on them to stop, threatening to fire. If they kept together it was impossible but that they should both be taken.

"Run, Miss Skrene, run," said Tant. "Cross the beck, lose yoursen among the shadders o' the trees and yo'll be safe. I mun stop and try what this saddle-bumper's worth."

Lois ran on scarcely understanding his meaning; he stood and was immediately overtaken. He had a desperate thought in his mind of unarmed resistance. Anyhow it would be better to be shot by night than hanged by day. But the carbine or something else daunted him; he made no attempt, but simply said:

"M'appen I'm the man yo want, Sergeant Skrene?"

"I'm sorry, but I must do my duty. What person was it who was with you?"

"I gie mysen up, I don't gie anybody else away."

"I must require you to walk before me to the house."

"I'd sooner goo first. But to be in order yo'll need this bit o' paper."

"What is it?"

"The warrant."

Arthur took it and Tant went before him towards the house.

Lois, scarcely understanding, had run to the verge of the

black shadows. Then she realized that she was alone, stopped running and looked back. She saw as she thought Tant and the horseman standing and talking some thirty yards off; the thin mist hardly rose higher than the horse's girth. She wondered and listened. The black shadows were dreadful. She went a little way back. She thought – approached a little nearer and knew – that the second voice was her brother's. She ran back. She was at Arthur's stirrup before he saw her. She was no longer the timorous maid.

"Arthur, this is my prisoner; you've no right to him."

Her brother's astonishment was great.

"Lois! What are you doing here?"

"Conducting my prisoner to prison. I beg you won't interfere with the course of justice."

"Ma'am," said Tant, "forgie me if I say yo're doing what yo've no raight to do."

"I can't argue against two men; but I can insist against a hundred. I do now."

"Lois," said Arthur, "you ask what is impossible."

"Fiddlesticks!" said Lois. "What I ask is never impossible."

"Would you have me fail in my duty, Lois, forswear my oath?"

"No, Arthur dear, I only want what I asked for."

"I can't, Lois."

"Well, if you take one you shall take both. There'll be the more credit."

Arthur sat his horse, undetermined.

"Put your head down. Lower; you forget what a midget I am." Then standing a-tip-toes she whispered in his ear: "Don't you understand that he might easily have escaped himself, but has given his life to save me from the twopenny disgrace of being caught in his company? The second time, Arthur. He must have a great many lives in his pocket; or else – or else what?"

He began to say that Rideout's offence was liable to nothing worse than transportation, having been committed before the passing of the act inflicting capital punishment, but he stopped at the first word, feeling that such a reply lacked force. Indeed in his opinion Botany Bay chiefly differed from hanging in its longer-lived horror. Seeing he had nothing to say, she turned again to Tant.

"Follow me, Mr. Rideout."

Tant did not stir. What his emotions were the night hid.

"Come with me, Mr. Rideout."

Still he did not move. She took him lightly by the cuff of the coat and led him off.

Equally displeased with his indecision and with any possible decision, Arthur sat his horse and worked the warrant into a pellet between his fingers, until the two were out of sight among the black shadows. Then he filliped the law-pellet from him into space and galloped back towards the house. Perhaps he hoped to shake something off in his gallop. On the other side of the croft he saw a shadowy man or men crossing towards the road to the Bottoms. He rode after them galloping furiously. When he was close upon them he reined in with a loud "Who goes there?" One of the men burst into a laugh, and said with Wells's voice:

"It's on'y huz, mester; it een't Tant Rideout. He's got clean off; he's fur enough by this."

"He war seen, an' he warn't seen, all of a moment," said the other, who was Spettigew. "There's been witchery in't, woman's witchery, tek my word for't."

And Arthur was much of his opinion. He rode back towards the house without haste, dissatisfied with himself and things in general. Half-way he met with Nell, who had come out on the grass just in order to avoid him and others. He passed her with a cool good-night, then reined his horse round at a kinder impulse and said:

"Your brother has succeeded in escaping."

"Yes," she answered; "yo hain't addled the fifty pound yet."

She turned from him and went away in search of a dark place; she felt the need of it. There was a white darkness where the grass sprang; it hid her feet; but to her head the starry sky was no cover, rather a discovery. She sought the brook-side. There were shady places there under the mingled overhanging of willows, crab-trees and stunted oaks, places where the instability of the water was indistinguishable from the firm ground; but yet there were escapings of light through the stirring leaves. She chose a spot under the blackness of a fir which domineered over the other trees; but even there, through the blackest of the black, she saw looking up a faint faint star like an eye peering down upon her. She returned towards the house; it was still, the intruders had departed from its precincts, Arthur and all; she entered the long stable. It had a darkness of its own, closed in, separate from the incomplete darkness of the open air. The invisible impatience of the colt, the loud champing of invisible cart-horses did not mar its solitude. She sat on a bat of straw in an empty stall, and gave way to the sweet bitterness of tears. For she too was a woman and subject to moods. She had been much tried of late by great troubles, great reliefs; she was overwearied too with an almost night-and-day nursing of her great-grandmother, on whom had fallen the last restlessness before the final rest. After a while she felt the light pressure of the greyhound's slender paw in her lap; she could not see the inquiry of her eyes but she answered it.

"There, there, my pet! we've cried a great plenty. Now let's sit and think why."

Meanwhile Tant and Lois went up the hill at as quick a pace as she could travel. The herbage, already stiff with gathering rime, rustled under their feet. Neither spoke; she was pondering actions, he words. He did not offer her the assistance which perhaps she needed but did not ask. She had released his cuff, and he kept at the severe distance which respect requires from such as him to such as her; and that, not reckoning fractions, whose lean misery I never could bear, is thirty-three inches by day and at least six more by night. If he could have had her once more in his arms, he would have flown and never felt the ground; if he might have led her but by the hand again, he could have run and never tired. But he let her spend her breath, and never offered the help which she did not ask. She only stopped, breathless, when they were under the shadow of the oak whose judge-like imminence had before affrighted her. But she did not know it was the same oak. Then he said:

"If 'twere for yoursen, ma'am, 'twas for summat; if 'twere anyhow for me 'twas for noat, and less than noat."

"I durstn't come slower," she panted.

Her quick breath made a little mist about her face. His voice was tremulous, as at a parting.

"One thanks for two lives seems too poor a market; and two thanks is nubbut two words more."

"You forget you saved mine, Mr. Rideout, and at a far greater risk."

"Being *there* was no merit o' mine; I'm ashamed on't, ashamed on't."

"But what you did being there, was there no merit in that?"

"No, for I couldn't ha' done different."

"It seems to me that is a merit."

"Ma'am, if yo're bent on being kind who can dispute it wi' yer?"

Lois felt herself being worsted in this debate of gratitudes, which she suddenly closed with a: "Please say no more; I don't."

"Yo've the raight to bid, ma'am, and I won't *say* no more."

"What are you going to do? Have you any plans?"

"Afore daybreak I ought to be thirty mile on the road to Boston."

"Have you money for your requirements?"

"Plenty, ma'am."

If so his requirements were few and small, for he had but

a shilling in his pockets. They proceeded until they were under the thick shadow of the house-end. Caution softened her voice to a whisper:

"Can't I do something more for you?"

"No, ma'am; there's no need."

"Good-bye then."

He bared his head. In that deep shade he must have understood by some other sense than sight that she was holding out her hand. He enfolded it for a moment or two in the large gentleness of his own. That their hands could not be seen, only felt, made more of an ordinary courtesy. She had never been so little afraid of him. Above them the stars gleamed frostily. Suddenly out of the apparently vacant firmament there sounded just overhead a strange wild cry, a hoarse scream. Lois was startled, she retained the hand she was releasing.

"What is that?" she said.

"It's wild geese gooing south."

She still retained his hand while she whispered:

"You're a brave man and to spare, Mr. Rideout; oh, if you were only a good one!"

"I've made a bad hand o' the first end o' my life, the rest on't's yourn, ma'am."

"No, your sisters' you mean."

"There's noat to divide. Poor Nell!"

Lois shivered; she had been heated by her haste and felt the cold the more.

"Well, I wish you farewell, and a safe – What's that?"

The sound of more than one horse could be heard coming up the field-way a little to the rear of them. The terror lest Tant should be taken returned upon her.

"Where shall you hide from them?" she said.

"I' the night. It's a large hiding-place and a good un."

The horses were evidently coming directly towards them. Tant did not move; but what she thought irresolution was merely reluctance.

"Oh fly! Fly somewhere! Fly quick!" she exclaimed, yet compressing her agitation to a whisper.

He had hardly bestirred himself when a bold clever thought came to her, half begotten of the frostiness of the night, half of the nearing chink of spur and bridle.

"Stop! Follow me!" she said.

Tant followed her. She led him to the smaller western window of the parlour.

"Stay, by this window," she said.

She flew round the house, and in a moment as it seemed opened the window from the inside.

"Come in," she whispered.

He held back.

"What does this mean, ma'am?"

"First come in."

He entered. She heard the rimy rustle of the grass under horses' hooves. She closed the window and fastened it with as much noise as she could make.

"Now you can't go back."

"Not while yo stan' i' th' road."

"I stand out of it, and still you can't. Come."

So peremptory was her whisper, he could not but obey. He followed her to the door of the room. From the back premises Arthur's voice was audible giving loud orders to the stable-boy. He followed her across the hall, and compelled by her up the carpeted stairs. For all his large frame and thick shoes he trod almost as softly as the lady did. Up the stairs and down a long dark passage she led him until she stopped by a door which she opened.

"I' God's name," he whispered, "what's your intention, ma'am?"

"That you should sleep in our spare bedroom tonight. It's the last place where you will be sought."

"I'm afeard this'll get yer into trouble."

"Can they" – with low reluctance came the word – "can they hang me for it?"

"I don't know as they can; but –"

"Well then!"

She transferred the key from the inside to the outside of the door. Arthur's passage from kitchen through hall to parlour could be heard, other feet and another voice accompanying his. All the more the fugitive had to bend head and speak low.

"Why will yer, why will yer?"

"Because I will. Isn't that reason enough?"

"Nobody has a better raight to reason a that how. And yet –"

"Don't be afraid; the bed's perfectly aired; I always keep it so – for such occasions as this."

"Many a time I've slept on ling and bracken."

"How could you?"

She gave a little shudder; she seemed to feel the starry lonesomeness of the night.

"I dunno, I dunno," he said with a pondering whisper. "Maybe becos the roof shuts the stars out and meks the moon gie more shadder than shine."

The just felt touch of a little hand irresistibly compelled him over the threshold of the room.

"You're my prisoner now. Good-night, Mr. Rideout."

"I wish a prayer – a prayer o' mine – but what manner o' good could it do yo?"

"Just try, Mr. Rideout."

She closed the door, and softly locking it withdrew the key. He thought of the key that but for her might have turned upon him that night, and instantly he was on his knees fulfilling her behest; while she went down to her brother. He had brought a guest with him, a farmer in a uniform, that Mr. Archer whom Lois had already addressed, honest, hearty and middle-aged. Lois smiled sweetly on him as she welcomed him, and asked how they had succeeded in their business.

"We've succeeded in letting a criminal escape," said Arthur, who did not seem in a very good humour.

"I'm glad we hae," said Mr. Archer; "I don't call this sort o' rot-hunting sport. Anyhow it een't a proper job for volunteer sojers. If sojers they want, let 'em call out the paid reg'lars; there's plenty on 'em at Nottingham doing noat for their living. And if there is anybody wants routing out o' this parish it's Ben Foat hissen. I shouldn't mind lendin' a hand to that."

"Who is Ben Foat?" asked Lois.

"The man as laid the information again Tant, miss. A man as hes a good many trades, and the honestest un is what 'e speaks most about an' practises least."

Tant was not again mentioned until the farmer had eaten and gone. Arthur's moodiness had been worn off by the necessity to play the hospitable host; he spoke to his sister quite kindly, though gravely.

"I wish, Lois, that this obligation of yours – of ours – was to a better man."

"It may be right, Arthur, for you to say so; I hardly think you'd like me to feel so."

"I hope at any rate it will be the last obligation of the kind, and this our last opportunity of making a similar return for it. I won't again violate my public duty for a private satisfaction."

"It would not have been like you to do otherwise, Arthur."

"For goodness' sake don't admire me for it," he said with a relapse into testiness. "Well, I hope he has had the sense to get clear off. The pursuit has been relinquished for the night, but in the morning it will be both keen and persistent."

"With your assistance?"

Arthur made a grimace.

"I think not. I like Archer prefer the ordinary kind of 'rot-hunting.' Still it would be just as well for Mr. Tant Rideout to keep out of my way."

"If he doesn't, you must keep out of his."

"I make no promise."

CHAPTER XXI

HIDE-AND-SEEK

AFTER Arthur had gone forth on the following morning to do his round of the farm, when the cook was busy cooking and the dairy-maid churning, then Lois took up her prisoner's breakfast in the concealment of her work-basket. As she handed it through the door the face she presented to him was pale and harassed, his on the contrary being brisk, fresh and confident.

"Are you ill, ma'am?" he asked anxiously.

"No, but I have not slept. I hope you have been more successful."

"I don't know what 'tis not to sleep when I want to sleep. It moot make a long dawling business o' th' dark. But one thing's sartain, ma'am, if yo can't sleep becos I'm i' th' house, I moan't keep yer awake another night."

"That's as I shall rule; you're my prisoner, you know."

And with a parting peep of fun from dark eyes which were seldom grave for long together, she drew the door between them and locked it.

About an hour later she seized an opportunity to steal upstairs bearing in a maund materials for making a coal fire.

"I have decided," she whispered to him as soon as he came to the door, "that you are to stay where you are for a few nights, unless you find your lodgings uncomfortable. They are making furious search for you in the neighbourhood and it won't be safe for you to travel."

"I shall be a deal o' trouble to you, ma'am."

"I've reckoned that up and it amounts to nothing like so

much as if I allowed you to be taken, I don't mean you to be nipped with cold." She produced the basket of coal and kindling. "This room has a common chimney-shaft with the one beneath it. We seldom use it, but I have had a fire made there on the pretext of airing it. That will prevent the smoke from being remarked by day, and you shall have dark curtains to screen the light by night. I've been thinking you perceive."

"I' th' night?"

"Yes."

"Thank yer, ma'am, though I'd liefer a deal yo'd slept. And there's no need for't, no need at all. I'm never co'd out o' doors, seldom i' the house."

"But it's cold, bitterly cold."

He held out his great hand. She understood he would have her touch it, so the tips of two of her fingers, cold though but fresh from the fire, rested for a moment on his warm palm and slipped away.

"I'm like to be a sore trouble to yer, ma'am. I can see Nell from the winder; she's i' Freeman's Cluss wi' Whitefoot and Tidy, rolling the land I ought to be rolling."

"I will let her know you're in safety."

"She'll thank yer."

So presently from the window he saw her trip scarlet-mantled across the rimy fields towards Low Farm. He saw her meet her brother on the nearer headland of the close of wheat, more white than green, but of course he could not hear what she said to him.

"Which is the way to Freeman's Cluss, Arthur?"

"How do you know that Miss Rideout is there?"

"How do you know, if I may ask instead of answering?"

"I have seen her."

"And I – I haven't. Don't our reasons balance beautifully like a brother's and a sister's? And now the way please to Freeman's Cluss."

"Who taught you to call it 'Freeman's Cluss'?"

"I'm afraid I'm in an unanswering mood this morning. Pray attribute it to this ungenerous contracting sort of weather, and ask me again when the thermometer rises."

"Yonder is Freeman's *Close* – you can hardly see it from here – on the left hand of that dead oak-tree."

"Are there any live cows?"

"There are some steers in the –"

"Steers? Don't tell me about steers, they're all cows." She clutched her brother by the arm. "Now do see me safe past them, there's a dear. And there's Paradise-pudding for dinner."

"The inducement is irresistible."

He escorted her safely past the steers in Three Furlongs, over the stepping-stones of the beck and through the grass-land on the other side, where some cows were grazing; but he stopped at the gate to Freeman's Close. Nell was not far off, sidefaced to them, plodding behind the cumbersome machine; her voice reached them as loud and shrill as a peewheep's curbing Tidy and stimulating Whitefoot. They stood awhile looking over the gate at her. Her dress was modified from that in which Arthur had first seen her. The old smock-frock had been exchanged for a plaid shawl, black and blue and green, crossed over her breast and pinned behind. She still kept the thick-soled shoes and gaiters, but on her head she wore a woman's calico hood, blue-sprigged, which only gave her mouth and eyes to those who exactly faced her.

"What do you suppose I'm thinking about?" said Lois.

Now Arthur had not been supposing anything but he immediately answered with pricked-up readiness:

"About frocks and bonnets."

"Remotely. I was thinking how ridiculous I should look behind those horses and that big thing."

"You would."

"But I couldn't imagine Miss Rideout looking inadequate anywhere. Could you?"

"In bulk do you mean?"

"I won't talk to you."

He opened the gate for her.

"Shan't you come to?"

"No, I decline to join your conspiracy."

"But you won't help to mar it, Arthur?"

"I make no promise."

"I do for you; that's half the labour; now you've only got to keep it. Wait for me. Those cows you know. And I've my red cloak on."

So she called back turning thrice as she tripped over the rough clods. Arthur having nothing better to do watched her until she came up with Nell on the far side of the close, and then he watched them both. When Lois was still twenty yards off, their eyes met and she called out eagerly:

"Don't be alarmed! All's well!"

Then she glanced up and down the adjacent road to see if anybody were within hearing. Nell left her horses and came to meet her.

"All's well, Miss Rideout," she said again as they got within speaking distance; "for the present. I promised to let you know. I can't stop; Arthur is waiting for me, and he's so fearfully impatient. And the Paradise-pudding would spoil."

Nell nodded in womanly tolerance of masculine frailty. Lois's eyes seemed only to see her; hers besides the little eager creature in front of her took in the cloddy rimy field – beneath every clod there was a little gleam of white – the bare trees and hedges, Arthur at the gate, and the long, low hill beyond, here brown, there dimly verdant. She looked wearily pale, whereas Lois's usually colourless face was flushed with excitement and the exercise.

"When did yo leave him?"

"About half-an-hour ago."

Nell looked surprised.

"Where is he?"

"I'll tell you. Can you see High House?"

"Yes."

"Can you see a bedroom window in the gable on the other side of the chimney-stack?"

"Easy." Then her paleness became a little paler and she said, "I think I can see somebody."

Lois gave a little laugh.

"Your eyes are better than mine," she said.

"Not to look at."

Nell's eyes fell to the eyes she spoke of and dwelt on them briefly in grateful admiration; then returned to the window.

"He can see uz too. I wish I could gie him a signal; but who knows who's on the watch? Yo mootn't bide here ayther, Miss Skrene; for that same reason."

Nell walked back with her across the field.

"Tell him to keep wide o' the winder. Other folk hae eyes besides me, folk as would mek their fortunes by seeing him; and the most I could gain's a suit o' black wi' my own money."

They had drawn near enough to Arthur to tell when his eyes were on their faces, when on the coming of their feet, and when on a kestrel which now hovered high in the air, now dropped plumb as a spider on its thread and hovered again.

"Does your brother know o' this?" asked Nell.

"Not yet. But if I don't tell him before he finds out –"

"Ay?"

"I shall soon after."

Nell stopped, though she had given no sign of being about to stop.

"I mun goo back to my hosses," she said. "Tell Tant nubbut this: so to manage as yo don't loase your labour."

Her grey eyes dwelt a little on the dark ones uplifted to hers before she added:

"A bad wish has just comed into my mind."

"What sort of a bad wish?"

"That yo might be in trouble yoursen. Good-mornin'."

She turned abruptly and strode back to Tidy's impatience and the unexpectant waiting of Whitefoot. Before Lois reached her brother she could hear her across the field:

"Gee then, Whitefoot! Steady, Tidy, steady!"

"Well, what had Miss Rideout to say to you?" said Arthur once the peril of the cows was passed and that of the steers yet a field off.

"She gave me a message to her brother."

"And how shall you deliver it?"

With upturned eyes, saucily sidelong, she answered:

"By post."

She wrote Nell's message on a sheet of paper as soon as might be after her return, and posted it by pushing it with a tiny rustling under Tant's door. She found no opportunity for again visiting him until it was dark. At the same time he took his basket of provisions and whispered:

"I suld think it a shame if I didn't."

"Is there anything more you need?"

"Six yards o' rope to equal the stress o' thirteen stun."

"What do you want it for?"

But even while she asked her too active imagination made a horrible suggestion. The floor seemed to open under her with the yawning suddenness of a hangman's drop. With an almost breathless "Oh!" she made a dizzy clutch at safety, and had the blind good fortune to lay hold of Tant's strong arm. His other strong arm brought round quickly to her waist thought nothing of her weight, but his fear was a staggering burden. It was his first acquaintance with nerves less steady at what they do not see than at what they see.

"What hae I said?" he cried too loudly. "What shall I do?"

"Sh!" she faintly hissed, not too far gone for caution.

There was a foot on the stairs, one of the maids'. The voice of real danger put out the suggestive whisper. She pushed his arm from her, quietly closed the door, and rustled by Mary on the landing. The dim passing candle-light told nothing of the fear which was present or the fear which had gone.

But at the tea-table Arthur could not but notice her pale face and want of appetite. He threatened her with the doctor and a return to Retford. She protested that there was no need, that she was decidedly better, that she ate so little at tea because she had eaten so much at dinner, that she was hungry even then; in proof whereof she proceeded to make a strenuous mouse's nibble at a bit of thin bread-and-butter.

"To put it in short," retorted Arthur, "it would be inconvenient to your plot to leave home at present."

"I don't know what plot you mean."

"Neither do I."

"I'm not in any plot."

"I'm glad to hear it."

"Should you like to know about it?"

She bent over the table, bringing her head within a plotting distance of his waistcoat.

"No."

"Then you just shan't."

She felt a real need to talk it over with somebody – probably it would have improved her appetite for bread-and-butter – and if Arthur had been willing to accept her relief as a favour to himself he should have had it at that price. But now she leant back in her chair and sulked good-naturedly and made no pretence of eating. Arthur finished his meal meditatively, and after he had swallowed his last mouthful put the sum of his cogitation into words.

"I wonder how it is a good woman always gets interested in a scamp."

"Are you asking me?"

"If you've an answer for me."

"I don't know about always. You see I'm seven years younger than you."

"Well, assuming that 'always' means just seventeen years and five months."

"If you mean me by a good woman –"

"I do, Loie."

"And if by a scamp you mean Mr. Rideout –"

"I do."

"And if by being interested you mean anything –"

"Again I do."

"I hadn't finished. Anything but a natural gratitude –"

"That or any other of the virtues, Loie."

She rose and went across to her spinnet; logically symbolic perhaps of a slight shifting of her position.

"Arthur, I'd only seen Mr. Rideout four times before yesterday."

"You don't say how many times since."

"You don't ask. Only four times before yesterday, and three out of the four I'm afraid he was more or less tipsy."

"On the fourth being locked up from the possibility of getting tipsy. A rare record!"

"For all that I don't allow he's a scamp, absolutely."

"Did all that strong liquor go to him or did he go to it?"

There was no answer to that, and Arthur showed by his rising that he expected none.

"Anyhow he's well known to be the most reckless dare-devil for ten miles round, and the country would be very well rid of him. So" – he was already at the door – "I hope your plot will be a short one."

"And a successful?"

The question barely overtook him between door and jamb, and he did not turn and answer it.

Later in the evening Lois took Tant the six yards of rope which he required. Giving it to him she said:

"But you remember you're my prisoner?"

"Ay."

And scamp as he might be, dare-devil as he was, she felt she could trust his monosyllabic sincerity.

CHAPTER XXII

OUT BY THE WINDOW

THE rope Tant knotted into nooses at intervals of about a yard, so contriving a rude ladder out of it. He made one end fast to his bedstead, and about midnight as nearly as he could judge by the long stillness and deep darkness, for there were no stars to reckon by, he quietly opened the window and let himself down by it. How sweet the outside of the house seemed to him! For an hour or two he could do nothing but exercise his legs and breathe the free air, raw wet night air though it was, full of a fine drizzle. Or perhaps the wide circuit he made was partly in caution, partly out of mere delight in motion and the ample darkness. Anyhow it was by way of Ear Baulker, Sansom Wood and the elm of Langton Arbour, that he got round nigh on two o'clock to his great-grandmother's cottage at the Bottoms.

It was a tiny dwelling with but one exit, that to the road, and but one room on the ground, though the floor above was divided into two sleeping-places. From the upper casement a light dimly peered at Spettigew's dark cottage opposite. Stealthily he opened the unlocked door, entered the house, crossed the room and looked up the crooked stairs. A faint broken light came through his grandmother's half-open door. He whispered Nell's name. If she were sleeping she was sleeping lightly for she answered immediately. Tant barred the outer door and went up to the little back compartment in which she lay. He stood beside the bed and held a low-voiced conversation with her. He had to stoop his head because of the slant ceiling in which the little sky-light was as a black blot. The only light struggled in by the door from the great-grandmother's room, and it was a light that showed nothing.

"Why did yo come?" asked Nell.

"To stretch my legs and tongue, maybe."

"Yo mootn't stop; both housen are being watched; I think they suspect yo hain't travelled far from home."

"How's gret-granmam?"

"She'll never rise no more. She'd been for ever getting out o' bed and falling down till yesterday. Then she fell and hurt hersen. I scolded her for't, and she said, 'It's the last time;' she lay down quietly and has hardly stirred sin."

"Do you know who spouted again me?"

"I wain't tell; yo'd be doing summat rash."

"No, lass; I've took lately to thinking afore I act. Not too soon nayther. I mind your message. But I've a suspicion, and a suspicion that een't fast tickles me like a loose hair."

"It were Ben Foat."

"I tho't as much; he's an unstayable chap. I could do wi' a clean shirt and stockings and my best clo'es."

"What for?"

He gave a little laugh.

"I'm visiting some o' the bettermost people, yo know, and to-morrer's Sunday. Yo could hide 'em in the oad haystack unner some loose hay. Put the knife on the top."

"All raight. To think as a teeny timorsome cratur like her suld dare to do't!"

"She's timorsome just as a high-mettled filly is timorsome, that'll scaddle away from a leaf and if need be scamper up to a cannon."

"I think Mr. Skrene ought to know."

"The lady'll do what's raight."

"I'm talking o' what yo ought to do."

"I'm afeard o' putting my hand in't; it's such a big un."

"The more shame if yo keep it i' your pocket. Now goo, yo've stayed long enough and to spare. But m'appen yo'd like to see the last o' your gret-granmam?"

Nell rose, slipped on a gown and led him to the adjoining
room. She snuffed the dim candle which had been burning
to waste on the table and held it above the bed. Partial lights
and shadows flickered over the patch-work coverlet, over
the fleshless hand that lay outside and pinched it, over the
white death-stricken face. The dame lay with half-shut eyes
breathing in slow pants. A wisp of white hair straggled
across the white forehead. Nell pushed it tenderly back
under the white night-cap. When Tant spoke to his
ancestress she blinked her white eyelids and mumbled
something, as one might through the close rifts of a dream.

"What's that?" whispered Tant.

"It's like somebody trying the door."

"I've made it."

"Then they'll know yo're here; I allus leave it so's
Hannah Spettigew can coom in i' th' mornin'."

"Yo'd better put the clo'es unner the second sheep-trough
on the tunnips. And my razor. Now goo down and look out.
If anybody's theer let 'em in, but mek a to-do as if yo were
fo'ced. Tek the candle wi' yer."

Nell descended and having set the candle down softly
opened the door like one who is cautious against surprise.
She stood inside the sill, and putting head and shoulders
forth looked up and down the road. On either side of the
door she saw a motionless something. She drew back and
banged it to with a haste that was not all feigned. But before
she could secure it she felt the rude strength of hands
applied outwardly.

"Thieves! Who are yo? Thieves! What d'yer want?" she
said, dividing her voice between a cry and the colloquial
pitch.

Her assailants did not waste breath in replying; they
continued to push their way in with a joint strength, gaining
admission of a toe, a whole shoe, a man's shoulder. Then
when their success was assured and they were cramming all

their force into a final shove, Nell suddenly withdrew her resistance. Two men, tripped up by the sill, sprawled inwards over the floor, upsetting the table in their fall; but it was Nell's foot that extinguished the candle. At that moment Tant dropped from the casement above into the road. He would have got clear away but a man had run across from Spettigew's house, very like the thick-set shadow of Spettigew himself, and at the instant of his fall put his arms about him.

"I've copped 'im! 'E's here!" he shouted.

The men within sprang to the issue. But Nell had pushed the door to again, the sneck was not handy to find in the dark. When it was groped for and found, it gave small purchase for a lusty pull, and Nell's shoe aided by an inequality in the rudely-paved floor made sufficient resistance. She received a heavy blow in the body together with a "Out the road, yo drotted cat!" but she held by a hook that was in the door and kept her ground.

"In the King's name!" said another voice. "I'm White the constable."

Up the road she heard Tant's whistle announcing escape.

"Yo might ha' said so afore," said Nell and let them through.

They found the shape like Spettigew sitting in the midst of the road half dazed from a heavy back-fall over Tant's thigh, and unable to tell them so much as the way the fugitive had taken. But he jerked forth:

"Why didn't yer coom whilst I had 'im?"

"Why didn't yo keep holt while we coom'd?" roughly retorted one of the two.

"Keep holt? I did keep holt as long as I could. What were yo a-doin' on?"

"She wouldn't let uz in," said the constable.

"Yo didn't want to be in."

"She wouldn't let uz out," said the other.

"Ben Foat, yo don't frame like addlin' no fifty pound, not yo."

"I'd liever hae truck wi' any man," said Ben, "nor wi' a huzzy like her."

"It wasn't hardly creditable how she fo't an' striv," said the constable.

"Damn the witch!" said Spettigew. "It's her again; it's allus her! But I'll be even wi' 'er yit, see if I don't."

While the men were thus coming round from mutual reproach to agreement in feminine dispraise, Tant was lurking hard by among the shadows of the road. He was still there when the constable and the informer came by, having taken short leave of Spettigew at his door. Tom White turned towards Blidworth, Foat kept on for Fishpool, and Tant chose to follow the latter. He did not always follow either; sometimes he walked abreast or a little ahead on one or the other side of the road; the marginal grass gave so soft a footing, and the air laden with a misty rain, that seemed rather to float than fall, was like a veil between what saw and what was seen. Once Foat, whose legs were none too steady, suddenly swerved so from the middle of the way as to bring himself within a yard of his shadower. Tant stood aside. He was mightily minded to strike an end-all blow. The dastardly accomplice-informer was at his mercy, as he himself might come to be at the pitiless mercy of the law. He clenched his fist till the muscles were strained tight; his face was invisible. But the blow was not struck, the man passed, the tension of mood and muscle was relaxed.

Still Tant attended his betrayer like his dog, sometimes a little before, sometimes a little behind. Further on where the road gives a sharp bend, there was then a spreading elder growing. Foat took the turn so abruptly that the men were again within arm's reach of each other, under the concealment of the tree's dripping boughs. Tant's former homicidal revengeful impulse was replaced – he was a being of quick changes – by a sudden Puckish freak, merely mischievous. With one hand he drew down a moist branch, bringing its twigs into dead-finger-like contact with Ben's face; and at the same moment with his other hand he directed from his own mouth full into Ben's ear such a "Wow!" as never issued from mortal tom-cat's throat under stress either of love or the duel.

Ben was shot to the other side of the way without volition, as by outside enginry. There sufficiently recovering to feel the need of courage, he gave vent to a round dozen of oaths, trivial perhaps in form but heart-felt in tone, against cats and that cat. He stooped moreover, groped for a stone, found one and hurled it at a futile venture; then walked on in the middle of the road. But his nerves were manifestly shaken; he walked faster, kicked more stones, often looked over his shoulder. Tant was delighted with his exploit, both as a piece of wild justice and as mere fun and mischief. He took the next chance of improving on it, but it was not until they were among the houses of the hamlet of Fishpool. The bulging wall of Remington's little cottage was supported by a disproportionate buttress. He lay in wait behind it, and when Ben passed again let him have it in the ear. One earsplitting "Wow!" Then silence. It was diabolic. Ben gave a gasp of terror that left him no breath to swear with, and started off at a run. His house was at a short distance, a hut of two rooms, standing detached in a garden. When Tant came up Ben was within-doors; he could hear him nervously chipping away at a flint trying to get a light and rapping his own knuckles as often as not. Tant put his mouth to the keyhole and uttered a low long-drawn "Wow-ow-ow" of feline disappointment. The man dropped steel and flint, bolted up-stairs, sprang upon his wife, who was sleeping, and roughly shook her.

"What the devil are yer sleeping for, woman?" he cried hoarsely.

"Why the devil suldn't I sleep?" said his wife. "Yo've pretty nigh scarred me out o' my wits, yo crack-pot."

The friendly insult seemed somewhat to restore his spirits; his next speech was less agitated in tone.

"Didn't yo hear that d——d cat?"

"What cat? I don't lig awake to listen to cats. Yo've bin muggin' too much at the Lay Cross; that's what yo've bin doin'. Coom into bed wi' yer, do. And mark my words; yo'll hae to stop at home to-morrer or yo'll be haein' a fit o' the blue devils; that's what yo'll be haein'."

These words gave Tant listening under the window a sudden thought, which like a crystallizing flutter immediately froze his whim into a purpose. He went softly away, and making a much smaller circuit than at his coming returned by the gorseclad slopes of the Assart in safety to his hiding-place.

We may suppose that his purpose grew in the night, for at his next seeing Lois he begged her to let him have a bowl of stiff wheaten paste, some strips of linen, and a dozen of the largest and stoutest sheets of paper she could procure. She took him up what he desired, including some tough brown paper which had been used for packing. Whereof he was occupied throughout the day in fashioning a strong tube about five yards long and an inch and a half in bore, but widening into a mouthpiece at the lower end, and so strengthened with cross bands of linen as to be able to bear more than its own weight; such a thing as he had made once before for some Christmas foolery. Lois stole up again in the evening and was curious to know what he had been at. Those occasional short-whispered communications through a half-opened door, his head down and hers up, had necessarily somewhat of the character of confidences. Tant put the small end of his tube out and invited her to take hold of it. It was so dark that she could not see what it was, besides speaking-tubes were not then so common nor so well understood as now. Immediately she heard a voice close by, low but distinct and pitched like a woman's:

"Ha, ha! I know where you've hidden him." She started and dropped the tube in fear of it. Then realizing that somehow or other she had been duped, she shut the door and went away, feeling a little hurt, a little angry.

CHAPTER XXIII

AN UNQUIET NIGHT

IN the dead of the night Tant again went forth by his rope-ladder taking the paper-tube with him. It was dark and cloudy, but the rain had spent its feeble will. He went across the fields between Blidworth and the Bottoms straight for Ben Foat's. All was dark at the Bottoms except for one spark of light, which he knew to be from his great-grandmother's chamber-window. Half-an-hour of his easy long-striding gait brought him to Fishpool. Ben was at home and asleep; the duetto snore of himself and wife was audible without. The bedroom casement was almost within touch of a man of Tant's stature. Thrusting with his tube against the tiny ill-leaded diamond-shaped panes, he found one which gave way with little resistance to the thrust, and fell with a tiny tinkle on the plaster floor within. Through the aperture he pushed the tube into the room until it touched the low ceiling, where he judged that its orifice would be over Ben's bed. Then he put his lips to the mouthpiece and let off a volley of high-pitched mews. Ben started up, the bed creaked under him; his wife awoke. Higher and higher swelled the infernal caterwauling, note linked to ascending note by shrieking appoggiatura, melody such as the maddest cat could only dream of, ending in a felo-satanic squeal. Ben cursed the cat's eyes, but only to keep his courage up; his wife cursed its liver, but with perfect sincerity. From the height of the ceiling just over their heads came a small-throated voice between cat's and woman's, low but horribly distinct:

"I'm not a cat."

Man and wife clutched one another.

"I'm a devil."

Man and wife dived under the bed-clothes fighting frantically for the blankets as the drowning fight for air.

"Wow, wow! Ss, ssss! Wow-ow!"

"Goo an' get a light," said the man in a blanket-stuffed, fear-throttled voice.

"Yo'd goo yersen if yo war a man," said the woman in tones unwomaned by terror.

"If you do I nab you. Wow-ow-ow!"

And so the diabolic voice again went off into a crescendo of cat-song. The couple, smothered under the blankets, prayed and swore and confessed their sins in the same breath.

"Devil tek it! Lord a marcy, Lord a marcy! I'll let Clark hae his hand-bill back to-morrer. Lord, I on'y borrered it."

"Our Fayther, chart in 'eaven. D——d the thing, it's awful, awful! I'll be good, I'll be good! For ever an' ever, Amen! Lord, what a unchristian beäst!"

"It'll be my death! this'll be my death! Lord, I confess I warn't jonnocky about that hafe-crown. Lord, Sam's bitch won. But, Lord, mine's as good as hisn. Oh, by gash, what a ran-tan! No, Lord, it een't; I tell no lig, I'd back hisn again mine any day."

"Stop the cratur, Lord, stop the cratur! do! It's coomin' nigher! I will be good, that I will. From to-morrer n' 'enceforth n' evermore. I'll not be nigly about pew-rent; I'll hae noat to say to Dick no more, niver! Amen, swelp me."

"Yo trolly! it's the fust word I've heerd o' that."

"Don't trolly me. Think o' yer own sins, yo swine. D'yer think I hain't heerd o' Fan an' who's 'er fancy? Mebbe others above uz knows too."

The voice, which had been dying away in thin long-drawn cat-pathos, suddenly flared up again into shrill menace.

"Oh law, oh law! Don't keep natterin' again me, man. Pike out summat o' yer own faults. Save yer own soul an' leave mine to heaven marcy, do! There were that scabby trick yo played oad Baxter."

"Stosh it, woman! shurr up! That were forgot. Lord, I'll own i'stead to what I did again them Wainwrights. If yer don't know what 'tis I've gien mysen away. Lord, but nubbudy thinks noat to them Wainwrights. An' Deb 'elped me."

"No, I didn't. Why need yo bring me in? Nubbudy knowed. Lord, I nubbut parted wi' the stuff. It on'y fetched seven-an'-six, Lord. Lord a massy, Lord a massy! Lord, what's seven-an'-six to sich as yo? For ever an' ever. Say amen, yo dalled sluggard."

"Amen. Ugh, how I do sweat!"

"I'm all of a moil!"

Suddenly the cat-music ceased when at its highest, cut through as at a slash. The twain lay with their heads under the blankets, panting, perspiring, afraid to stir hand or foot, hardly hoping yet that their prayers had been heard. For half-an-hour thus they lay, silent, motionless, wet with the ooze of their fear; until at last stillness and immobility became impossible. Ben had to stir hand and foot and mutter:

"I do believe it's gone."

Low but horribly distinct was the response from above their heads:

"I've not gone."

"Oh my gash!"

"I don't mean to go!"

"Law, law! it's too bad for oat."

"I'm waiting."

"Oh crimy!"

"Ax what's it waitin' for," growled the man.

"Ax yersen," snarled the woman.

"For Benjamin Foat," said the voice.

The man gasped under the blankets.

"Oh, Ben, yo've gone an' done summat wicked. An' I'm sufferin' for't."

"Sufferin'? Yo? What o' me? Yo're all raight; goo an' get a candle."

"You'd better not," said the voice, so gently that the menace was terrific.

"Is't along o' Tant?" asked the woman.

"He knows," answered the voice.

"It can't be," said Ben, half smothered by blanket, "it's a Guv'ment reward, and Gen'ral Ludd don't mek no bones."

"Don't talk so soft; much *they* care about your gen'ral."

"They care about the British Guv'ment – or had ought."

Said the voice, "The day Tant's fetched you're fetched. While then I'm here, waiting. Now go to sleep."

"I can't stan' it much longer," groaned Ben; "I'm fair smothercated, that's trewth, if iv'rythink else is a lig."

"Yo suld a letten folk alone," said his wife.

"It were yo, yo telled me to."

"Me? Niver, niver, mester; don't think it on me. I've noat again Tant, noat whativer."

"Nor noat again a fifty pound reward."

"Shut yer gawp!"

"Pugh! I'm as 'ot as 'ot."

"'Ot's no word for't; I'm just swimmin' in't."

"Hell's hotter," said the quiet felo-feminine voice; which reduced them to perspiring silence.

Tant showed the patience of a curbed impatience, the patience of a leopard lying in wait, of a Red Indian on the look-out, of a hawk on the hover, of a snake in the grass. Hour after hour he remained there through that damp dark night with nothing to occupy the intervals but anticipation. Every now and then exhausted nature would have its way with the Foats; on the rack men have been known to sleep, even under a wife's tongue; but so soon as he judged from their easier breathing or from the bed ceasing to creak with their constrained restlessness, that one or the other of them was dozing off, he again raised a loud unpreluded wail. Sometimes they started up, both or one of them, as though the agony were new, sometimes they groaned and moved not; but no refreshment got either of them that night until the anticipatory cocks at the farm began drowsily to crow. Then the woman lifted the blanket from her mouth and said faintly:

"I'm deäd if this lasts much longer. Say as yo'll proceed no furder again Tant."

"That I wain't," said Ben.

"I don't believe you," said the voice.

"Drot me if I do."

"You're such a liar."

"On'y by nows and thens."

"I can't trust you."

"Swear me on oat," said Ben with stifled eagerness; "swear me on summat as I *can't* break."

"Well, we'll see. I'll give you to-morrow. I shan't go but I'll go to sleep. Good-night; pleasant dreams. We-ow!"

CHAPTER XXIV

A QUIET DAY

As soon as Spettigew had finished his Sunday morning breakfast, which was not inconveniently early, he cleaned his shoes, put his best frock over his old jacket, and walked across the fields to High House. He was a six-day man and had no business there, but he had news in the telling and discussing of which he would have had many equals, many superiors, down in the Bottoms; whereas he was likely to have the advantage over Selby and Wells, over Mary and the dairymaid, who lived further from the source. Not that he went therefore in any sort of a hurry; he went as those go whose desires do not outrun their heels; at the pace which the local tongue was agreed to call "snaffling," with a heavyfooted slackness, that is to say, both of purpose and action. The morning was fresh and cold and clear, but Spettigew pushed his hands as far as they would go through the pocket-holes of his frock down into his breeches' pockets, and straightway forgot what kind of a morning it was.

There was the intermittent sound of a bell, which was distinct enough when the air was quiet, died away as the wind uprose, and anon became faintly audible again as the blast slackened; the slow tolling of one bell, which yet had many voices for different ears. For Spettigew its voice was as earthy as a clod, and having heard it once he hardly heard it again. His hands were warm in his pockets, his stomach was fairly filled. His eyes told him whether he trod upon unturned stubble or fresh wheat, short fine herbage or coarse old fog, which the cattle for the time being sniffed at but would tear up with their tongues as the winter hardened. Mr. Skrene was in the yard when he entered it, booted and spurred for riding.

"Fine mornin', mester," said Spettigew. "Th' oad witch is dead."

"What old witch?"

"Oad Granny Roideout. Died last night just as the clock strook twelve. Now she's wheer sich uns ought to be."

"And where's that, Spettigew?"

"In hell, mester."

It would seem that Mr. Skrene had a little leisure for such chatter while he was waiting for his horse. He said:

"Hell had need be a roomy place, Spettigew –"

"It is that, mester," said Spettigew in a tone of satisfaction.

"If it's to be the general waste-souls basket, the place to which we consign all whom we dislike or differ from."

"There's room for a good few yit."

Wells led forth the horse.

"Well, now the old lady's gone you'll be wanting somebody to father your side-aches, back-aches and poverty on."

"Nay, mester, nay," answered Spettigew impressively, "we shall ne'er be short of a witch at Blid'orth."

"You are determined on that?"

Skrene had gathered the reins in his left hand, but had not yet mounted.

"A witch can't die wi'out fust passing it on to somebody."

"That is so," said Wells.

"What is 'it'?"

"If I could tell yer," said Spettigew, "I should be a witch mysen. Leastways a wiseman."

"You're not that, Spettigew," said the master from the altitude of his saddle.

He rode off, but could hear Spettigew say in a voice pitched higher for his benefit:

"Folks'll be wantin' to know who's th' witch now."
"That they will," said Wells.
"I could gie a guess."
"Ah?"
"But we'll bide and see."

Lois was alone in the house. She had given Elizabeth and
the cook leave of absence to visit the parents of one of them
at Farnsfield, a neighbouring village. Arthur, not knowing
that, had ridden off to dine with a farmer friend of his at
Rufford. Harris and Charley accompanied the maids, who
started before noon, looking tall in the pattens which raised
their best shoes above the muddy road. Then Lois unlocked
Tant's door. He did not immediately come, softly open it and
show his face, as heretofore. She began to fear she had lost
her prisoner; she repented of her brief anger of the previous
evening. She knocked and waited; knocked louder, and
louder still. She felt sure the room was empty, she pushed
the door wide open. She beheld Tant in shirt and breeches,
looking as though but just startled out of sleep; he had the
rope-ladder in his hand and was in the act of unfastening the
casement. Hearing the door open he turned a desperate face
that way. Before he could see who confronted him, he had
put himself into a posture for all-venturing resistance. The
man again affrighted her. He had his fighting face on, his
eyes were dreadful, his hair unkempt, his arms prompt for a
blow, his whole body on the stretch; he looked terribly tall.
She shrank back from him repenting that she had let herself
be left alone. But instantly his aspect changed, as a man's
does when he beholds not what he expects but what he
desires. He seemed less as well as less fierce.

"I've frightened yer," he said remorsefully. "What a
glomax I am! But yo've allus knocked so soft afore."

She had recovered, but not entirely.

"How I must have startled you! But you didn't answer
my tap."

"I've been a sluggard this morning; I was asleep."

"I thought you'd gone."

"I'd gien my word."

There was a reproach in the gentleness and simplicity of it, and Lois felt it.

"I beg your pardon."

"I've first and most to beg yourn, ma'am."

He disappeared behind the door, and Lois went down again carrying his breakfast with her. The dish of grilled chops was already cold. She felt as she set it on the kitchen table, that she owed him amends both for her doubt and the spoiling of his meal. Her heart beat. She had got over her fear – at least that fear but still her heart beat. A thought had occurred to her coming down-stairs, so suddenly that we can note it precisely as happening while her left foot gave her weight to the tenth stair and her right yet toed the eleventh; that she would invite him to dine with her. And his sister Nell. The addition occurred to her on the seventh stair, was rejected for obvious reasons of caution before she had both feet on the mat at the bottom, but yet helped to familiarize her with the daring project. Probably however that buzz at her heart would not have allowed her to humour her desire – for desire it was – but for the work-a-day thought, or afterthought, that it would be a good opportunity for overhauling his bedroom, which must be in sore need of a woman's hand. There may have been curiosity in it too; but that and what else must remain for ever unresolved, the sight of those cold chops glued to that cold dish had so given the all-pervading undistinguishing flavour of pity to the impulse.

No reasonable being could ever withstand so many reasons, separable or inseparable, unless he or she wished; which Lois didn't. The yardman's loud whistle in the yard and the rattle of the well-bucket and chain were wonderfully sustaining. But something kept her from taking her invitation personally, which would have been the natural and least troublesome way; perhaps the fright she got at her last knocking was too fresh with her. So she wrote a polite little woman's note on her best note-paper, presenting compliments and requesting pleasure, pushed it under his door, gave a tiny tap with one little knuckle, and ran away. Then she was forthwith afraid of her own courage; again thought of Nell; went so far as to speak to one of the boys about a message to her; learned at once that the great-grandmother of the Rideouts had died in the night, and had to give up her intention, if intention it was.

The note said one o'clock. He was more punctual than she, for he set his foot on the first stair just as the old clock in the hall was preparing with much internal commotion to sound the hour, and she had to hasten from the kitchen to meet him. If she came from the kitchen fire, that was doubtless the red mark of it upon her cheeks. But she wondered at him; had it not been for the great stature and the abundant wavy hair that was not red, she would hardly have recognized him. The hair was combed back and tied with a black ribbon; he was scrupulously washed and brushed and shaven. His coat and breeches, decent though of rustic cut, were of the same dark-blue cloth; his waistcoat, which fell half down his thighs, was of black plush gaily beflowered; a voluminous black satin cravat confined his snowy linen; his stockings were of yellow silk and there were silver buckles to his shoes. Altogether he made a handsome appearance in his manly freshness. Lois doubted whether she had done well to consider her plain turkey-red merino good enough for the occasion, and whether it and her complexion showed any signs of her culinary occupation, as with the proper curtsey she made the proper greeting:

"Good-morning, sir."

"Good-morning, ma'am. I'm honoured, ma'am."

The bow, like the words which it accompanied, had an old-fashioned formality which savoured of the rustic, but not in the least degree of the clown.

"I must compliment you upon your punctuality."

He smiled very pleasantly. She thought it astonishing how pleasantly he could smile.

"The sun's a raight good time-keeper, ma'am. And so's hunger."

"Oh dear, yes! This is your breakfast as well as dinner. I wonder you were content to be merely punctual. But I mustn't feed you on compliments, standing. Will you please to come this way? We are quite alone. I ought to have told you before, so as to put you at your ease."

"There's no call to tell me oat, ma'am; I'm your prisoner."

She led him into the parlour. She had already drawn a screen before the window, cutting the room off from outside observation; the house-doors were bolted against surprise, back and front. Having seated him she excused herself, while she went and took up the couple of roast ducks and the dish of potatoes, and set them in the place of dignity above the apple-sauce, the cold sirloin of beef, the applepie and cheese, which were already on the table. In inviting him to be seated opposite to her, she made the customary formal apology for the scantiness of the fare. In reply he bowed and said, as our rustic great-grandfathers would have done:

"Ma'am, it's a famous good dinner. 'Twould be a famous good dinner without your presence."

It seemed to her he put more than the usual expression into the formula, and she could not help wondering what he meant by it and whether it were sincere. She could not help all through the meal taking more interest than she thought reasonable in his appearance, his sayings and doings. She had of course to keep a watch upon his plate in order to play the hostess with due hospitality; but even when her eyes were on her own, she seemed to see with the same distinctness how he bent his head to the words of her grace, how he used his knife more than was necessary, how he smiled and how he drank. He was much younger than she had supposed him to be; she now thought he could not be more than twenty. She took note that he liked much apple-sauce and gravy; that his teeth were white and strong and even; that he said "obleege" for oblige like her grand-uncle; that the slices of bread looked very small in his hand – she wished she had cut them larger; that when he smiled he always lifted his eyebrows a little, as though to make a larger window for the sparkle of his eyes; that the said eyebrows were a little darker than his hair; that he did not take much salt; that she had some silvergilt buttons which would look much prettier on his coat than those plain silver ones; that he did not seem to care for ale; that sometimes his North-country dialect had a pleasant flavour, but that hern instead of hers did not sound nice at all. She would have liked to tell him so.

He had not emptied his silver cup of ale until he had nearly finished his second helping of apple-pie. Then she wished to replenish it, for in those days it was the hostess's duty to press her guest to eat and drink more than the one thought desirable or the other judicious. He declined.

"With your permission, ma'am, I've fun' out that a little's better for me than a deal."

But he ate without any such limitation of his appetite. After they had bowed heads together in thanks "for what we have received," he rose and said:

"Next to that, ma'am, I hae to thank yo."

She laughed and said, "Your excellent appetite, sir, is the best and indeed sufficient thanks."

He would then have taken his leave, but she asked him to be seated while she cleared the table.

"I mootn't bide longer nor's convenient," he answered modestly; "but if I bide it's fitter for me to sarve."

"Let us both serve, then our state will be the greater by another servant."

She was within an ace of saying "sarve" in mocking

mimicry; she was not at all afraid of him just then. So they removed dish and platter together, he carrying not at all clumsily, like most men-folk, she doing little beyond directing where and how to place.

"Thank you, fellow-servant," she said with a little curtsey, when all was done. "Though if I considered the unequal division of our labour I might rather say, 'Thank you, servant.'"

"'Twould be raightly said; I am the servant and yo the mistress."

"Nay, I'm the jailer and you the prisoner."

"Yo're that an' all."

"How awful I must appear to you!"

She kept her laughing eyes upon him until he answered; but for which it appeared as if he would not have answered at all. First he paled, next he bowed his head, and so with slow reluctance he spoke.

"Yo do that."

Whereat she fell to be as ill at ease as he; or more so, for doubt and surprise were mixed with her disturbance, while he perhaps knew why and what he suffered. She recovered first, as was her right, sufficiently for a jest if not for earnest.

"If I am so awful," she said lightly, "you must do my command; which is, not to leave this room until my return. Do not go near the window; but my rigour does not debar you from amusing yourself meanwhile with the books or that portfolio of engravings according as your tastes are literary or artistic."

"I doubt they're nayther, ma'am; for what I like best man had little or no hand in."

"Oh, if your tastes are merely natural they're hardly to be called tastes at all, and certainly not taste. Well, there's an arm-chair and there's a settee, both excellent things in their way, although men did make them."

Lois was astonished to find Tant's bedroom in perfect order, the bed carefully made, the window open to the cold fresh wind. There were only the soiled clothes and muddy shoes which he had worn yesternight to point it out as the lodging of a rude intrusive clown. She examined with much curiosity the strange paper tube lying on the floor against the wall, and also the looped rope tied to the bed-post. She could guess at the use of the latter, but of the former not a whit. Out of his water-jug there stood a large sprig of gorse in full bloom.

What a strangely unequal man he was! She stood and mused at the open window, wherefrom she could see the roof and chimney-stack of the Low Farmhouse. The rude wild figure he made after he had fought with her brother; his yet more disreputable appearance later in the day, when he reeled before her in the open street drink-disgraced and shameless; the magnificent savagery of his defence of her against odds – again she admired and shuddered; his pale decency before the judge; the goodhumoured home-loving laugh in his eyes and on his lips as she peeped through the window at him; their recent meeting at the foot of the stairs, and the handsome respectability which his bodily gifts made only less than elegance and also more than elegance – she saw them all by turns exactly imaged. And that sprig of gorse was behind her on the wash-hand table.

She wished they had never met; but could not account for the wish. She wished he had fled from the stable alone and left her up in that dark roof to escape as she might, then she should have missed all the subsequent complications; nevertheless reproaching herself the while for willing such a rent in his courage and generosity. She felt again that fearful necessity of putting her maiden arm about his neck; again she felt the assurance of his strength as she hung in the dark neither seeing nor knowing. She wished she had never left Kent; there were no such men there. She tried to think what the Kent men were like, Mr. Smith's three sons, young Mr. Brown, young Mr. Robinson, but their figures were vague to her. She turned away from the window; she took the damp clothes and shoes and carried them down to dry by the kitchen fire.

She did not like returning to the parlour at all. She wished the house were not so still. The stable-boy had gone off whistling up the road to join his comrades; Selby and Wells had not yet come to make their four-legged charges comfortable for the night. She had been very imprudent in letting herself be left alone; she would be justly served if he considered her unmaidenly. Immediately she became really angry with him, red-angry, on the provocation of her own imaginings. Let him think so, it did not matter to her; after a few days she would probably never see him again; she should content herself – as the best and the worst of us have to do – with the consciousness of her good intentions. This new mood made her feel braver to meet him. Anyhow it had to be done. She went out into the yard and fetched Bob from his kennel, the surly old black and white retriever who sometimes accompanied her walks. In the kitchen she petted him with duck bones and caresses; then when he had eaten enough she resisted his obstinate wish to lie down by the fire for a digestive sleep, and coaxed him to go with her to the parlour. Even on the doormat she paused, balancing two contrary opinions and troubled by both. Would he think her bold? Or would he see that she was really timid? But Bob showed a tendency to slip back into the kitchen; she took him by the collar and both entered the room together. She would have liked Tant to think that Bob had been in the house all the time.

He came towards her immediately. He was standing ready to do so, making it appear that his action was a resolved thing. Yet resolution was less apparent on his face than diffidence. Bob growled and wriggled and hung back on his collar; the hand that held him was relaxed, he broke away and escaped from the room.

"Yo were angry wi' me yesterday," he said, with an intonation betwixt a question and an affirmation.

"Was I? I don't – for I've no right to be angry with you, Mr. Rideout. Besides it would be ridiculous."

"Yo've every raight, ma'am," he said gravely, "every raight that one like you can hae ower one like me."

His candour compelled hers.

"Well, I *did* think, considering all the circumstances –"

"The danger o' my neck, and what's more, your own inconvenience?"

"*All* the circumstances – I did think you might have been better employed than in inventing a silly toy to frighten a girl with."

"If it did frighten you I'm very sorry for't; 'twas far from my intention."

"It did frighten me. But I frightened you this morning, didn't I?"

The tone of their conversation, it seemed, was getting too serious for her, and she was glad to slip aside into flippancy.

"Sartainly yo did. First there was the loud knock that woke me. Bad consciences don't like loud knocks, ma'am. I never tho't but 'twere Tom White and the specials comed for me. Then when the door oppened afore I could hull the ladder out, it came to me like a flash I mun now ayther kill or be killed; and the choice was a stret un."

"It was thoughtless of me; it was cruel. I do beg your pardon."

"Such a word as pardon, ma'am, don't fit your mouth at all. Yo couldn't unnerstand; yo don't know what 'tis to hae a conscience that the constable's after."

Again she had to struggle to be trivial.

"Well, we'll reckon we're quits, my fright against yours, if you please. And now please sit and tell me the meaning of that funny brown-paper thing, if meaning it has."

He related to her his night-doings in miniature mimicry; she laughed and she shuddered.

"How could you?" she kept saying. "I should have died of fear. How could you? I should have died of laughing."

And she thought the strangely mixed story with its terror and its fun highly characteristic of the man himself. Then Tant fetched the tube down, and showed her how it brought removed sounds close to a listener's ear.

"So you had a purpose?" she said. "I see I was wrong, rude and wrong."

"No, no, ma'am; nobody else suld say so."

"Well, do you think that Foat will keep his word and retract his accusation?"

"He's a liar and he's a coward, I dunno which he is most. With your permission I'll goo to-night and larn."

"Arn't you afraid he may have told others, and that a watch may be set?"

"Not a bit. He's allus been a sore rascard to his neighbours. He knows they'd nubbut laugh and say, 'It sarves yo raight. I'm on'y sorry the devil's gien yer so much law.' He'll none tell. Now after I've thanked yer for this last o' your unexpected undesarved kindnesses, and afore I again set yer at liberty –"

He paused; she thought he needed encouragement; she said:

"What is it?"

"Yo'll think m'appen I've no call to ax."

"Pray tell me."

"I'm a rough-natur'd rude-bred man, ma'am."

"You haven't told me."

"Does Mr. Skrene know as he takes in?"

"What is that?"

"As he has a lodger, I suld say."

"No."

A full minute and he had not spoken.

"Do you wish him to know?"

"I'm your prisoner, ma'am."

"He shall know to-night."

He thanked her and rose to go. That time she did not attempt to detain him; she was bodily weary from so long a colloquy with a being so unlike her usual company; but she felt most of all the need of being alone that she might rest her thoughts upon silence, and put some order among her ravelled emotions. But before the maids came home about nightfall, she took up together with her prisoner's tea his clothes well aired and brushed and his boots nicely cleaned and blacked. He seemed shocked.

"I could never ha' letten this be," he said, "if I'd knowed."

It pleased her for the moment to humble herself.

"I'm a farmer's sister, sir, it can't misbeseem me to clean a farmer's shoes."

"Little o' the farmer I." He held the shoes in his hand. "If I donned 'em on I suld feel as if I were traddling on your fingers."

"Wear them to-night, sir, and if my fingers suffer you shall yourself judge to-morrow morning."

She held her delicate little hand out, as if inviting him to take an inventory of its present condition. He bent his head over it as if he were desirous of doing so. She wondered if he were short-sighted. A little final crook of his knees brought his eyes so near that she felt his breath warm upon it. Then she hurriedly withdrew it; and immediately afterwards was vexed with herself for the hurry. No doubt he was short-sighted. She would ask him another time.

CHAPTER XXV

CAT-AND-DOG LIFE

ARTHUR'S friend rode back with him and spent the evening at High House. Lois, who felt overdone with the day's changing excitements, was obliged to retire before he left; so of course she was unable to keep her promise to Tant. Promising, she knew and did not know it might be so. But we act as though the engagement were fateful, the fulfilment of our choice; knowing and not knowing that so long as we keep the bag of our promises clasped they are ours, once issued they belonged to the irresponsible unpromising future.

Knowing and not knowing which, Tant with his heart full of promises of his own shouldered his paper tube and crossed the fields in the dead of the night, making the short cut to Fishpool and Ben Foat. It was a clear still night; the little stars shone with as distinct a severalness as Aldabaran or Sirius; across the unutterable black stretched the white wonder of the Galaxy. On such a night the earth's dim differences of shade are but as a couch whereon to rest eyes weary of up-gazing.

Tant passed the Bottoms, and there was no light in his great-grandmother's bedroom. He thought to himself: "It was her bell I heard this morning; I doubted it." The thought made the earth seem the darker and the stars the better company. After he had crossed the road he stood on the hillside and looked back on the hamlet. He saw a speck of light among the dark. It could not be from his aged relative's casement, which fronted the other way. "M'appen," he said to himself, "Hannah Spettigew is taken worse."

There was a light too in Ben Foat's bedroom. Through the broken pane Tant could hear the secure breathing of man and wife. The man it seemed would fain be more liar than coward; at least like many a one before him he was trying to kill conscience with candle-light. Tant remembered that there was somewhere under the hedge an old barrel which had been used in the spring to protect Ben's rhubarb. He groped about and found it. It was bottomless and rickety, but he set it upright under the window, and cautiously planting each considerable foot on the thin edge of the chime so as to balance the other, ventured to trust his weight to it. His eyes were thus brought above the window-sill. Through the glass, vaporous with their breath he saw well enough the candle on a chair by the bedside, the two heads, one capped, the other with a red handkerchief round it, quietly reposing on the dingy bolster, the rest of their persons concealed by an old horse-rug. A lurcher lay curled up on the sole chair among Mrs. Foat's petticoats. Scratcher was his name and he usually slept out, but had been admitted that evening as an additional protection against ghostly cats. Tant reached the tube, which was leaning against the wall, and cautiously inserted it in the aperture which he had made the night before. First he aimed such a puff through it as blew out the candle. The two noses over the coverlet drew even unforeboding breaths; the dog stirred and sniffed. Then Tant pushed the tube a yard and a half further in, which he calculated would bring its mouth within an inch of the man's nearer ear. He did not study tone nor yet tune, he simply tried what his lungs were made of; such a blast he blew as either cat or devil might have admired. The sleeping couple and the dog upstarted together. The former affrighted at the exposure immediately fell back again, making a dark aim at the coverings. The dog sprang on the bed; his contact and his terror-stricken howls added to their terror. They curled their legs up in one intricate knot, and thought the devil had come for them in flesh and blood. Again Tant blared; a brazen squeal summoning to a cat's doomsday. The pair frantically hugged each other, and cursed each other for letting the light go out. The dog cowered between them and the wall and yelped, afraid with their affright and his own.

After the second blast there was nothing heard for ten minutes but Scratcher's hysterical howling, which was incessant. Man and woman lay and sweated terror under the blankets. At last the dog was mute. Then there was just one quiet little delicious devilish laugh high over the bed, and the dog began again; which was like the voice of their own horror speaking to them. After a long while Scratcher's yelp became a whine, his whine a dying whimper. There was quiet for a space but for the riotous beating of their hearts. Then Tant dipped the point of the tube as near as he might aim to Ben's ear and whispered cattishly:

"What a liar you are!"

"'Twere Sunday," Ben protested; "I couldn't do noat."

"Quite raight; you can't be too partic'lar about keeping the Sabbath holy. We are. We've one of our own in hell; every fift day."

There was no reply. They lay and felt the prickly horror from head to foot, like a physical pain. Tant was in no hurry, he had a long night before him. He allowed another ten minutes or so to pass, then tilting the tube so that the sound came from the foot of the bed said in the tone of cool leisurely mockery:

"You tho't I'd gone? Haha!"

It was a full minute before the second "Haha!" came, a fainter echo of the first. It was another five to the next utterance:

"I shan't never go. I've come to stop. Haha!"

And again just when their vexed ears had done expecting it, came the echoing "Haha!" thin, faint and devilish. The cur had begun again, a high-pitched whine, forlorn and continuous.

"If you don't stop that dog," said the cat-womanish voice, "I'll set mine on him."

Yet another weight to their *peine forte et dure!* The husband's and the wife's voices were uplifted together against the dog, calling him by his own name and others less seemly, cursing and blessing him, coaxing and threatening. They durst not put bare hand out to him, but as well as they could they stroked and buffeted, patted and kicked him through the blankets. But all in vain; they could never get him to be quiet a minute together; and every little movement seemed to make a breach in their coverings for the devil to get at them. They were cold and hot in the same breath.

"Why don't yer try an' beg off?" muttered the woman. "Down, Scratcher, down then!"

"Try yoursen," growled the man. "Scratcher, good dug! I'll split your heäd oppen."

"Gie 'm another trial, sir," whimpered the woman. "Good dug! Quiet then! He's a bad swine, I don't deny, but try 'm again. Please, mester. It's hard on me an' all, this is, as niver did noat."

"'Twere yo," said Ben, "as wouldn't lemme. Drot the yawping dug! Stosh it, will yer? 'Twere yo as said a farthing dip 'ud be as good as a Bos'ell's charm; it war. Quiet wi' yer, quiet, I say!"

"Yo're a ligger! An' a thundering big ligger!"

"So's yersen."

"Yo're fool! An' a gret soft fool!"

"Yo're another!"

"Be damned to yer!"

"Be damned yersen!"

"Hahaha!" cackled the thin fiendish voice; "you shall be, both on you. All in good time."

It froze their wrangling and even their malice. While the dog whined and whined.

"This is comfortable, this is!" said the voice. "We talk a

that how in hell. It's quite homelike. You only want the fire. I'll go and fetch you some. We've plenty and to spare."

"For Gord's marcy," roared the man hoarsely, "gie's one more chance! this one more chance! An' if I don't act jonnock this time, yer may squelch me flat, as flat as a gob."

"Do," said the woman shrilly, "do! An' if I don't keep him to't, hand an' foot, sir, yer may hae me too, sir. Let's off just this one night, just this one night. I'd gie oat for a night's rest."

"You're such liars," said the voice.

"Not me, not me," whined the woman.

"We hae bin, both on's," assented the man; "but if we don't speak the trew trewth this time, well, we *are* liars, sich un's yer don't often see."

"We've some very good uns with us. But we can't boast of 'em to you."

For a quarter, for half-an-hour there was silence; the dog lay still; the man and woman began to hope their prayer had been heard, and exhausted by their terrors prepared drowsily to resume their broken slumbers. All at once they heard the weird voice, cat's and woman's, shrilly at their ears:

"Should you like to see me?"

"No!" shrieked man and woman. "For Gord's pity, no!"

And the dog howled a long-drawn emphatic "No!"

"You can if you like. Open your eyes. Here I am!"

"Marcy! Hae some marcy!"

"Marcy? We never heard tell on't."

"Talk to's all night sooner nor that."

"Wow-wow-wo-o-w! Sss! sss! Wow-wow! Mew! Me-e-ew! Sss! ssssh!"

From the bed-foot, from the ceiling, from close by, from the other side of the room, from here, there and everywhere by turns, hissed and snarled and squealed and cackled the abominable non-vocables. The dog madly darted about the room, under the bed, over the bed, in every corner by turns, barking, howling, upsetting, afraid of his own tail.

"Why don't you look at me? Hahaha! Why don't you look? Hohoho! I'm nice to look at. Open your eyes. You shall open your eyes."

They did open their eyes, each of them, for a moment, as though charm-ridden, against their will; each saw what he or she would not have seen, and again they shut eyes tight with a feminine squeal, a masculine howl of terror.

"Why do you squeal? Ain't I good-looking? I'm better-looking than what you'll be, either on you. You are not keeping that dog quiet. Look again! look again! Or I'll touch you."

Tant dropped the tube across their legs. It was a wonder their minds held. Cold beads stood on their bodies, their skin pricked, each hair upheaved itself, stiffly separate; and again such a hellish caterwauling filled their ears and every corner of the room, that the dog's loud agony passed for mere accompaniment. He himself seemed to perceive its futility, even as an expression of terror. He suddenly ceased, again leapt on the bed and forced his way in between his master and mistress. They thought surely they were gotten at last. Up went the bed-clothes, out flew they straight for the door. They might have escaped, but Ben fell over the chair which Scratcher had upset, Deb fell over him; they felt the dog or the devil at them as they sprawled. They scrambled frantically back into bed, found some of the clothes, missed the rest, and so lay together, dog and all, one leg covered and another naked, hot and cold at once. At last they could do nothing but grip at the nearest thing for the shadow of safety, the bed-clothes, their own or one another's bodies, and keep on ejaculating between each short gasp, "Oh lor! oh lor! oh lor!" The air was fetid with their terror.

But the fiendish concert when it seemed to have no end ended. They did not know at first or could not believe; still they kept on panting and ejaculating, "Oh lor! oh lor!" their pants as loud as their ejaculation. But in time they appeared to perceive and believe, or perhaps they were merely exhausted into silence. They lay with their mouths open panting like dogs, but other sound was there none for a space by them immeasurable. Then the puss voice, thin and calm, half-way to the ceiling, said again at irregular intervals:

"It was too violent.

"I shan't do't again.

"I shall stop where I am."

"Thank Somebody for that!" cried the hearts of the two, but the only outward sound was a groan of relief.

"I shall stop where I am to-night."

How blessed the assurance!

"To-morrer I shall be an inch nearer you, Ben."

What fiend's meaning was there in that?

"The third day two inch nearer.

"The fourt day three inch.

"An inch nearer every day.

"Till I'm only an inch from you, Ben.

"The next day I nab you.

"The very day Tant appears at the 'Sizes.

"I'm just forty-one inches off, Ben.

"For forty-one days I keep my distance."

There was comfort even in that for Ben after the nearer horrors of voice and touch. The end of forty-one days seemed afar. Tant gave him five minutes or perhaps ten to be thankful in, then said:

"When I want to speak to you close or touch you I shall ask a friend."

"No more, for Lord's sake, no more!" groaned the man. "Two'd kill me deäd!"

"I've got one friend with me to-day.

"He's a devil, of course, but he's just like a retriever to look at. You'll fancy him, Ben, being a dog-dormer yourself. A well-bred black retriever.

"Except his teeth and his eyes. His eyes sipe hell-fire.

"If you'd like to see him, you've only to say."

"No, no!" groaned man and woman in concert. "Good lor, no! We're stawed wi' one."

"To-morrow there'll be three on's."

Gracious heavens! what new arithmetic was that?

"The third's a monkey.

"With a tail like a sarpent. It'll sarve to go all round the room, and a bit on't left to snuggle into your bed.

"The fourt's like a badger.

"You think *your* badgers can bite, maybe?

"Our badger's bite burns.

"On the forty-first day there'll be forty-two on's.

"Without yo, Ben."

The new goad pricked cruelly deep, but hardly raised a groan. The terror it spurred was not dead but simply exhausted. Perhaps Tant perceived as much.

"I'm tired; I can't be allus talking.

"I must think of myself.

"Even bogeys want a rest.

"Perhaps you'd like one too? Well, go to sleep.

"If you can.

"Haha!"

Devil never spoke so true as that. What with the constrained position, the prolonged vociferation, the inventive fatigue, Tant was in pressing need of a rest, or at least of a change. He quietly withdrew the tube, stepped down from his perch and went off for a quick leg-stretching ramble up by Barber's Wood and down by the Queen's Bower.

An hour later he returned to the house refreshed, again inserted the tube and barked like a dog sepulchrally deep. Man and woman started, they groaned, they could do no more. Perhaps they were on the verge of a haunted sleep, perhaps not. Scratcher barked back furiously.

"How do you like my dog's voice? Bow-wow-wow!"

He smote them across the body with the tube.

"That was his tail that tickled you.

"Haha!

"Bow-wow-wow-wow!

"Keep your dog still or mine'll fly at you."

Ben saw no way but to pinch Scratcher's throat until it could pass nothing but a throttled gurgle.

"Now go to sleep again, my dears; go to sleep, Ben and Deb.

"Sweet slumbers!

"Satan bless you.

"I'm watching over you.

"Hahaha!

"Bow-wow-wow!"

"Oh, Lord, when will't be mornin'?" groaned the woman. "Oh, Lord, mek it mornin' soon. Oh, Lord, mek it mornin' now. Oh, Lord, I'd gie oat."

CHAPTER XXVI

THE BROKEN DREAM

ARTHUR SKRENE woke in the dark, and what had awoke him he knew not. Soon he heard himself named, "Mr. Skrene, Mr. Skrene!" very distinctly, but by no means in a loud awakening manner. He heard it again. It seemed to come from under his window; he thought he recognized the voice, and wondered if he was really awake.

"Mr. Skrene, Mr. Skrene!"

The same voice, the same impression on himself. He rose, opened the window and looked forth. There was sufficient light to make out a figure robed in white on the ground beneath, from which again came the same utterance in the same tone at the same pitch.

"Mr. Skrene! Arthur Skrene!"

"I am coming," he answered.

If it were not Nell Rideout's voice there was no trusting sounds. Arthur dressed hastily, wondering what new thing had befallen. He lighted his candle at the night-light which burnt on the landing, ran down-stairs, unbarred the door and went out. Hard by, still under his chamber window, was the draped figure, expectant. He approached, candle in hand. The figure turned to the light. It was indeed Nell; she stood a little out of the concealment of the night in a long white bed-robe that trailed the ground. Her face was pale; there was no relief to the whiteness but the darkness of eyes and hair. Her hair fell about her shoulders. Arthur wondered greatly. At the sound of his approach she turned towards him.

"I've coomed to invite yer to our Tant's funeral; he was hanged to-day."

She spoke in a dream-drenched voice. Arthur advancing the candle a little saw that her eyes, though wide open, did not appear to take cognizance of him, of the light, nor indeed of anything. He concluded that she was putting a dream into real action.

"Coom; the bell is tolling. Hark!"

"Let us go then," he said.

He set the candle down inside the house, and immediately returning took her gently by the hand so as not to awaken her. As his hand touched hers, hers clasped his. She readily yielded to his leading, and hand in hand the two walked together towards Low Farm. Charles's wain shone over their heads; before them was the halved glory of Orion, soon wholly to set. The earth was still under darkness, but behind them on the eastern horizon the blackness of the sky and the brightness of the stars had suffered equal diminution; token that the waning dilatory moon was at last to rise. The air had become more frostily keen, and at the farm they were leaving a cock began prematurely to crow.

Across the grass the two paced together, at such a distance as might be and yet each retain the other's hand. The air-filling night was like a grey veil over Nell's long white robe. It trailed the ground, but at each step the toes of a bare foot or a white stocking showed glimmeringly beyond it for a moment and disappeared. She turned her head neither to the right nor to the left; her open eyes took no heed of anything; she seemed to feel neither cold nor discomfort; her hair fell about her face like the darkness of clouds about a cloudy moon Neither of them spoke.

The front door of the Low Farmhouse was wide open. Probably some dream-notion of a ceremonial toward had caused her to go out by that seldom-used exit. There was a light in the room overhead. Arthur gently led her into the house, himself going no further than the threshold; she was thus in the shadow, he in such grey light as there was. What then? It seemed he had come to the hardest part of his undertaking. He did not know what to do for the best. He shrank from rousing her sister, he durst not awaken herself, he was not willing to leave her to the guidance of chance. As he stood an unexpected gush of tenderness came over him, such as the self-reliant man-defiant day-seen Nell had never inspired; the tenderness of the strong towards the weak and dependent. As the first step to whatever action he began gently to withdraw his hand from hers. But hers was no puny grasp slackly retentive, and he had an increasing difficulty in freeing each successive finger; for as one and another was withdrawn she the more tightly clasped the remainder. At length he was only held by the ring finger. To release it he used no more force than was needful, but as the tie between them was completely broken she gave a little sigh. Then he was dimly aware through the darkness, less by sight than insight, of a change in the quality of her gaze; instead of being vacantly unattached it was fixed gravely, wonderingly upon him. She put her left hand upon the door-jamb, and resting on it leant her head forward until he could see a grey difference between the whites of her eyes and the pupils. Her long drapery flowing downwards from her remained almost lost in the shadows. He saw recognition swim into her eyes; saw or thought he saw surprise, fear, shame, accumulatively trouble their dark liquid depths. She fled into the house without a word. He listened, he heard a voice or voices; he quietly shut the door and withdrew.

It was Tish's light that burnt in the upper room. She had been awakened by Nell's going forth, had lighted a candle and lain listening ever since. She never doubted but that it had to do with Tant. At Nell's re-entrance she met her on the stairs and addressed her with matutinal acerbity.

"Where ever hae yer bin raunging all this night? Well, of

all! Yo moot be mad! To goo trailing about i' your nightgown. And in your stocking-feet! What fool's work hae yer bin agate on?"

"I don't know, I don't know!" cried Nell in sore distress, trying to push past.

"Yo might as well say and ha' done wee't, y'ave bin out getting your death o' co'd after that wezzlebrained good-for-noat lad of ourn."

"I hain't."

"No? What then? What sort o' gam's this, and your gret-granmam laid out for burial but not buried?"

"Lemme goo!" said Nell.

Tish held her fast.

"If 'tweren't our Tant who were't?"

"I can't tell yer, I wain't tell yer."

"Don't know? Can't tell? Wain't tell?" Tish's emphasis became more furious at each fresh negation. "Then I ax *him,* our Nell."

"No!" cried Nell, "no! not him!"

She endeavoured to detain Tish, but bewildered in mind, numbed with cold, encumbered by her drapery, she was no match for the man's strength, the fierce determination of her sister, who held besides the upper position on the stairs. Tish tore herself loose, rushed to her own room, flung open the casement. Arthur had lingered over his going; concern for Nell, perhaps some more personal feeling had made his feet slow. Tish saw him pretty well at about thirty yards' distance. It was not Tant, whoever it was. She took down from its hooks her father's fowling-piece, which she kept in her chamber loaded against burglary, returned to the window, cocked it and fired. Nell stood in the doorway.

"Hae yo hit him?" she said.

"I don't reckon to miss a man at thirty yards," answered Tish grimly.

Nell wasted no words; she went to her room, slipped on gown and shoes and came forth again. At the head of the stairs Tish confronted her largely obstructive.

Quietly, as one who has taken her last determination, she said:

"Yo wain't balk me o' this, our Tish, no more nor I balked yo o' that."

It was so; Tish let her pass, only saying with fierce mockery:

"Goo to him then, yo brazen madam. But he's gotten a wownd as need comfrey more nor comfort."

Nell overtook him not far away going slowly towards home. She had put aside her own perplexities; she said with much concern:

"Are yo hurt much?"

"Hurt? Is that you, Miss Rideout? Good-evening. Hurt? Why should I be? But I've always understood it isn't healthful to be out walking at this time of night or early morning, and if I *don't* suffer for it there's a good old saw spoilt. I don't suppose the climate of Blidworth's any more salubrious than the rest of the kingdom."

He walked more briskly, more erectly; had it not been for the bitter irony she might have thought him unhurt. The lessened moon had just risen clear of the long straight-chined hill; she gave not a fourth of her full light to the heavens and none at all as yet to the valley. There was an inkling of mockery in the way she lay on her back and turned up her toes.

Nell said, less resolutely by far than she had spoken to her sister: "I've a favour to ax, Mr. Skrene."

"It's a favour to be asked one by you, Miss Rideout."

"Let me do summat for yer. Lean a bit on my arm. Forget it's a woman's; if that's oat again it."

"You spoke of a favour to yourself, Miss Rideout; that is one to me. Of which I am unworthy."

Still he was going, though hardly so briskly, she by his side. She answered angrily, but of the anger that is near tears:

"Yo've a raight to say nay; yo've no raight to hap it i' so many fine words."

But almost immediately she added, less angrily:

"At least it's a raight as is better to keep nor to use."

Presently she spoke again, and the anger was gone.

"Mr. Skrene, I've bore a many sore mishaps o' late; and now another un strange and sore has befallen me this night. I've glegged the last end on't, but the first end and the middle's all of a raffle, all of a raffle: and the house I was born in looks skew at me. And yo wain't oppen your mouth."

To a nice ear it might have appeared that the tears which had before vexed the voice were now wetting the cheeks, but Arthur was hardly in a condition to weigh tones scrupulously. Probably he hardly heard the words; his eyes were on the shadow of a man in front of him with something like the shadow of a gun in his hand. As soon as Nell had spoken he cried, "That's the villain!" went forward a few paces and fell to the ground in a swoon. Immediately she was on her knees. The diagnosis was brief. There was mixture of triumph with the trouble when she said, still on her knees:

"Now, Arthur Skrene, there's nayther a long nay nor a short un again my doing summat for yer."

When she rose to her feet there was somebody by her side.

"What's the news, Nell?"

It was Tant.

"A man shot."

"Shot how?"

"Don't stan' axing fools' questions, but –"

"Why, it's Mr. Skrene!"

"I said noat to the contrairy. I was gooing for the barrer; but up wee him i' your arms – thank God, they are strong uns, Tant Rideout – and carry him for me to his house."

"Ourn's nigher."

"The oppen door's ever the nighest. Do as I tell yer."

Tant set down the strange long thing which he carried – Nell saw it but asked no question – and lifted the senseless body in his strong arms.

"Be gentle wee 'm, Tant."

"Why suldn't I be gentle?"

"Oh, but be very gentle."

She walked by his side giving tender support with her left arm to the hanging head. In her right she carried his hat. But once she held it for a few moments in her teeth while she stroked back the dark hair from the lifeless eyes; and again when she lifted the dead arm into an easier position across the chest.

"Put the hat on your own head, Nell," said Tant; "yo goo bare."

"It's a man's hat."

"If it be? Yo've wore men's hats many a time."

"How yo talk, Tant! Be quiet; it pithers him."

They walked in silence across the beck, past the shadowy trees, up the dark slope, until they emerged into the moonlight at the top of a little knoll. Then Nell exclaimed:

"How he bleeds! Welladay, how he bleeds! He'll ne'er last a this how. Yo mun goo faster, Tant, faster. But don't jot him."

A few more paces and she said:

"Set him down a minute."

Tant did so. She had one stocking on; she took the garter off, and wound it mid-thigh round Arthur's wounded leg.

"Catch ho'd o' t'other end," she said, "and pull it stret."

Tant did so. The garter it appeared was no modern flimsy thing, but home-spun, closely knitted, equal to the stress of a strong man's strength. Then the two again raised Arthur into Tant's arms.

"Yo mun manage alone," said Nell.

"Manage? It's like cadling a babby, this is."

"I shall ride to Mansfield for a doctor."

"Raight."

"Goo quick, Tant Rideout, quick; but gentle wee't. Don't meddle wi' the garter, but as soon's ever yo get him into the house – I think he bleeds less now – put a bandage about the wownd, and slear the bandage wi' some balsam, if any they hae, to sleck the bleeding; and put a cloth dipped i' vinegar the back of his neck."

She gently let the unconscious head droop until it found what pillowing it might on Tant's strong arm. The dark hair had again belike fallen across the closed eyes; with one gentle movement of her hand she smoothed it away. Then she turned and ran down the slope with her back to the slant moonlight, swiftly down into the dark. So and not so ran Dian's maids before the dawn; their haste was but their sport. So and not so ran Atalanta with the third apple in her hand; she feared, but for herself.

She makes her way straight to the stable. She fetches out the colt, that wild unbroken thing. She forces the roughened curb between his teeth; he flings back his head but has to lend his jaw to compulsion. She stays not for saddle; she leaps upon his back and rides him like a man, straddling. She forgets not her whip. Woe be to the colt if he obey not her will!

But the colt does obey her will. Rebelling in his heart, defying with his head, uttering mutiny with his heels, he yet flies under her the way that she would have him go. Through the dark Bottoms they rollup; there is a light but in one window. Did anybody look forth from it he would see a strange sight under the moon: a horse going wildly, a woman riding astride. Her uncovered hair trails in the wind; her ungartered stocking hangs at her heel; there is the flutter of a skirt, the glimmer of a white ankle. His hoofs are indistinguishably intermixed; they scatter fire and turmoil; it has passed.

Will he or nill he, the colt takes the left-hand turn for Fishpool and begins to go up-hill. Quicker, my nag, this is but play! Quicker, 'tis night yet and naked courage will not be seen. But before reaching the hamlet Nell bends the colt's rebellious neck and will and forces him to leave the road, as nobody durst do but one to whom every yard of land was known, every hedge, every ditch, every hump and hollow, every clump of gorse or broom. Across country he flies, a protesting conformist.

On with you, colt! though heart rebel and hell mutiny; keeping a little to the left, for on the right lies the steeper ascent. If you can't or won't jump that hedge, through it shall you press by mere weight. The moon glimmers on the grass but shines on the road.

It is down-hill now for a space; you may go more gently, breathe yourself a little if you will, for you pass by Fountain Dale, shrouded in trees and haunted still by Friar Tuck.

And now zig-zagging before you lies a rising track closely hedged by bramble, broom and gorse. The cruel whip descends upon your flank. Fly, colt, fly! up the long slope, down the short descent, grassy, sandy, stony, smooth and rough by turns. "Fly! Make it appear to be your own mutinous will to fly, not that of the stern she upon your back. Harlow Wood lowers dark upon your left for all the moon can do to lighten it, but shy not at it, it is dark but still.

On, on, in mad submission! Pound this rock, strike fire from these stones! If there be a waker at the Firs make him wonder at the fury of your hoofs, sit up in bed and wonder and fear. Hang the triumph of it on your neck, make an ornament of your compulsion, have a pride in your indignity. On!

Here is Berry Hill at last! Give your mind to it, good colt. Make your shoulders strong! Contend no longer. Now you need neither the whip nor the heel; tongue to palate gives you all the encouragement you require. The birch bark glistens in the increasing moonlight; but prick not up your ears and play at terror; there is stern work yet before you.

Press onward over the crest of the hill, colt. Fail not, although each breath be a pain. Yon two windmills which rise up ghost-like in front of you are landmarks, and a mile off down in that dark hollow to the left of them is Mansfield hidden away. It is a rude descent; the rocky surface, swept bare of sand by the winds, is strewn with loose stones; but your knees are young and strong, and the hand that has your guidance neither fears nor frets nor fusses. Down the rein from it to you passes a nerve-vivifying something electrical, and you too neither falter nor fume.

Steadily now, colt, steadily! Out of the moonlight into the dark street! And now you stop under the doctor's window, just twenty minutes from the start.

The rider slips down and bangs at the door; the colt stands reeking, panting, without a will. Quickly the doctor opens his window.

"What is it now?"

"A man shot at Blid'orth. It's a matter of haste, doctor, of life and death. Mr. Skrene of High Farm."

"Who shot him?"

"Is that oat to the curing on him? He *got* shot."

"And who are you, my outspoken messenger?"

"Shut your mouth, man, and your winder, and don your breeches on. While yo blether he bleeds."

"And if I don't choose to do your not over civil commands?"

"Your own heart wain't suffer yer."

"I only know the heart as a moderately-efficient blood-pump."

"I'll stan' an' thump at your door whilst all the righteous in this town come out and shout again yer."

"All their shouting wouldn't start a mouse."

He withdraws his head however.

There is a light in the dark house, the ringing of a bell, the sound of voices; and soon or late – according to the waiter's estimate or the actor's – the opening of a stable-door at the back of the house. Nell walks away, leading her now docile steed with a slack rein.

Good colt! for this you shall have pats and kind words now, and when you get home corn and warm gruel and the best of grooming.

Nell was too much of a horse-lover to task Ripper at the return, although her wishes flew back. But the doctor did not overtake her; he travelled of course along the better-frequented pack-horse road by Three Thorn Hollow and L Pond.

CHAPTER XXVII

NEDDY CLIFF'S CAPTURE

LOIS, whose nights at that time were almost sleepless, heard her brother go down and open the door. As he did not return to his room she became disturbed, her first fear being that the rioters had again set a trap for him, and her second that some new thing had befallen Tant. She rose and went to the stairhead, and seeing a light burning below she called Arthur by name but received no answer. Then under a sudden attack of courage she descended the stairs. She found the outer door unsecured and bolted it; whereupon her courage went as suddenly as it had come, she raced back to her own room and locked herself in. She sat on the bed awhile and frightened herself; then dressed vowing all the while that nothing should induce her to open door again but Arthur's voice bidding her. When she was dressed she sat again and frightened herself. During which she heard a gun go off. Straightway she snatched up her candle, unlocked and flew to Tant's door. Was it new courage or the old fear? to give or to receive protection? I do not know; I do not think she knew herself; perhaps it was a hash of the two. After knocking twice she opened the door. The room was unoccupied, the window open, and hanging from it the rope-ladder. She looked out, but could see nothing save the darkness of the earth, the dark-environed brightness of the stars. She remained there until she could make a living thing of any stirring bush or shadow; then she turned hastily away.

There is a time when a straw is a stay, and the sight of

another troubled face the consolation of our own. Lois was
going to call the maids up that their fear might encourage
hers, when there came a loud banging at the front door. She
stood still where she was; and while she stood still there was
again a loud banging, as of a foot, and a loud demand for a
speedy opening. She went down to the hall, stooped at the
keyhole trembling and said, "Who's there?" knowing who
was there.

"Tant Rideout, ma'am; and another wi' him – a friend o'
yourn."

She feared; his voice was strange to her though she knew
it; she feared.

"Don't be afeard; oppen quick; there's need on't."

She put a shaking hand to the key; her courage was
hardly a grain more than her fear, but that grain decided
the balance; she opened and held the candle forward. By
which she saw two white faces, men's; one of which was
alive and drew breath in short laborious pants, the other
appeared not to breathe at all. Tant saw a girl's white face
and the white hand that pushed the door back.

"Oh, what has happened?" she said.

"Mr. Skrene has gotten a hurt, ma'am. Noat dangerous,
I hope."

He spoke between gasps; he had come quickly.

"A hurt? Oh how?"

"I dunno." He entered. "Where shall I put him down?"

It was answered before she spoke. The tension of his
long-taxed muscles was slackened, his burden began to slip
from him; perforce he laid it on the floor just within the
door. In a moment Lois was down beside her brother,
almost as low as he, saying:

"Arthur dear, what is it?"

Then she looked up at Tant and said:

"Is he *only* hurt?"

"Just hurt. Don't look like that, ma'am; I lay him to
recover on't."

"Oh what shall we do?"

"Somebody has gone for the doctor," said Tant. "While he cooms, with your leave I'll do what I can for him."

He again took Arthur in his arms, carried him up-stairs, Lois going before with the candle, and laid him on his bed.

"If yo'd an oad sheet or blanket to put unner him," said Tant, "it 'ud save your bedding."

"Oh, never mind that," cried Lois. "If you can do anything do it quickly."

He unclothed the lower limbs and found that they had sustained a number of small shot wounds. Through one of them in particular much blood had already been lost, but the flow had been greatly lessened by the constriction of Nell's garter. It was further stayed by the linen bandages which Tant added. He did not forget the cloth dipped in vinegar. Lois stood at his elbow, afraid of the blood, afraid of the pale face and shut eyes, but ever intelligently ready to fetch or hold or do whatever was required of her. At the end of the operation Arthur opened his eyes, as sleeping children do when they are disturbed by their mother's candle in the dead of the night; they open their eyes, they give a puzzled look, mutter words without a beginning and sleep again. Lois took Tant's hand, both of hers to one of his, and wept and said:

"What do I owe you? Oh, what do I owe you?"

"Noat, ma'am; the balance o' debt's heavy on the tother side o' the paper. Now don't be at all uneasy about your brother; the shot hasn't touched any dangerous part."

"Oh! He has been shot?"

"It's nubbut as if he'd been freely bled wi'out any partic'lar need on't, as any doctor might do for him any day."

She thanked him, and gently withdrew her hand. But withdrawing it she seemed to withdraw from her comfort; she saw her brother's death-like face again and fell back into anguish. So those who drown at sea come up out of the salt death, snatch a taste of the sweet air and sink again. Tant may have seen the need of occupying her; at any rate he said:

"If yo could find some oad linen, ma'am, and be touzing it into lint, it 'ud be handy again the doctor comes. And if yo'll please to show me where the kindling is I'll light a fire i' th' grate."

So she did; and when the fire was lighted Tant sat down and helped her to pick the lint, which they dropped into the same basket. The same patch of candle-light flickered on her hands and his, his so rudely large and strong, hers so ladylike and frail. The crackle of the firewood seemed a noise. She could hardly believe under what circumstances they sat there so quietly, he and she, until she turned her head a little and saw in the shade her brother's face, grey on a grey pillow. He stirred a little and gave a faint moan. She rose and bent over him, but his eyes did not answer hers. She came back and said, like one who is about to lift the curtain of a mystery:

"You haven't told me yet how this dreadful misfortune happened."

He answered, like one who knows little and would fain know less:

"If yo'll allow me, ma'am, to put it off while we're not so throng, I'll tell all I know; which een't much."

They sat and picked linen to pieces, much more than was necessary, but it was as though the teasing of the fingers eased the teasing of the mind. The drowsy cocks began to crow and men to come forth to their work by the dim light of lanterns. There was a loud unlocking and unbarring down below; the maids had risen and gone down.

"You must retire to your room," said Lois.

"Ay," said Tant.

She had said so once before and he had made the same answer. He seemed loath to break the quiet of the room. A minute later he murmured:

"Coy's flail's agate. I made him the swipple to't."

The beasts lowed, expectant; the more impatient horses stamped and rattled their chains; man called to man through the frosty air.

"That's the doctor's horse at last," said Tant, "a little bit lame i' the hint-off."

Lois started up as at an unexpected touch.

"But you? Now indeed you must go."

"Ay, ma'am."

But he stopped to snuff the candle.

"Mr. Rideout, pray!"

"I'm none afeard o' the doctor. I know him well enough; I've sold him a hoss or two; not that wi' the lame hint-off. If he kills folk for a living it's another road nor Ben Foat's and a deal more respectable. It's a profession; say what yo will, Ben's is nubbut a trade; and that's all the difference atwixt a black cooat and a blue frock."

The humour of the disparagement was lost on Lois, who had gone to the door and was calling to the hesitating wondering maids to be quick and let the doctor in. Perhaps her voice broke the thin wall which had confined Arthur's senses. When she returned to the bedside he had his eyes open and they were fixed in a displeased surprise on Tant.

"Why did you do it?" he said very slowly and distinctly.

Lois hastened back to the bedside.

"Do what, dear?"

"That man shot me."

"But it was an accident, dear."

"No; I heard him open the window."

Then he dropped his eyelids again and neither saw nor spoke.

Lois turned her dark eyes on Tant. The grief that was in their anger only made it the more tumultuous, the more terrible. The doctor's heavy tread was already on the stairs.

"You wicked, you cruel man!" she said in a low accusatory voice.

"And yo think I could?"

There was no anger in the question; only the pain of a humbled humility.

"I believe my brother. If I had a man-servant at hand it would be my duty to send for a constable. As it is" – all at once the single-minded anger broke up into a mixture of emotions – "as it is – go free, and be, oh be a better man!"

"Ma'am, yo shall ne'er lack a man-sarvant the short while I've to live; I'll goo your arrand mysen."

"Come, young lady, what is this new mishap?"

The tall young figure with the troubled face had vanished from the doorway; pop! and in its place with the rehearsed instantaneousness of a show the doctor's short fat one stood, displaying professional concern and a case of instruments. Lois had to answer and point out and attend; to send for this and that, to give orders to the maids, to refuse to notice their obtrusive surprise and sympathy; and all while she was trying to puzzle out the meaning of Tant's words, unable to fix her mind either on the duty that was before her or the dread that was behind. It was behind, but only just; its shapeless shadow fell over her shoulders and took half the light from all she saw. She said yes when she should have said no, and could not even get the due satisfaction from the doctor's kindly assurance that there was no need for alarm on her brother's account.

"Whose happy thought was it to bind this garter round his thigh? In all probability it has saved his life, for one of the shots has pierced the popliteal artery. By the bye, that remarkably fine tall young fellow who passed me on the landing? He reminded me – of course it's impossible – but he reminded me – and by Guy nothing's impossible!"

But Lois was not there to answer him; she had slipped out of the room. The maids were on the landing, listening and whispering.

"Did you see anybody go out a while ago?" she asked.

"Yes, miss! Tant Rideout, miss!" they exclaimed together.

The brevity of their astonishment gave it an enhanced value, but the lady put it aside.

"Did you see which way he went?"

"No, miss," said Mary.

"We runned back into the kitchen," said Elizabeth," as sharp as we could."

"He'd a leather budget in's 'and," said Mary.

"I wunner what were in't," said Elizabeth.

"Did anybody iver!" said Mary.

"I shall niver feel safe nowheer no more," said Elizabeth.

The leakage of their surprise was widening into volubility, but Miss Skrene cut it short.

"Go both of you and see if the doctor needs anything," she said.

She herself went to Tant's room. She had a vague thought that he might perhaps have re-entered by the rope-ladder. She did not know it was hope until she was disappointed of it; it might have turned out to be apprehension if it had been realized. But the door was wide open, inviting inspection. She saw by a pale mixture of reflected moonlight and reflected candle-light, that the window was closed, the rope gone. She thought she saw that Tant's Sunday clothes had been removed from the chair in the corner and his best shoes from under it, that the bed-clothes had been smoothed over, and that the room bore no suspicious sign of recent occupation. He must have stolen in before leaving the house, and having made all straight as it were with one sweep of his quick dexterous hands, had carried away his own belongings in the budget which Mary had mentioned. She returned to her brother's room. The doctor was engaged in tying a ligature of the wounded artery; he had neither eyes nor ears for anything else. She bade Elizabeth remain in the room. Elizabeth durst not without Mary. She bade Mary remain also. She herself ran down-stairs, threw a knitted hood over her curls, opened the door and went out on to the gravel. The diminished moon was still the only

light in the sky; it peered at her through the bare upper
branches of an ancient oak like a wan distorted face looking
through prison bars. There was a little singing wind among
the trees and it was bitterly cold. She could see no shape of
man or woman. Her hope kept saying, "Surely he won't do
this or that," and her fear kept saying," Surely he will." She
ran to the gate and looked up and down the road. The
labourers had begun to gather to their work. There was the
rumble of a wheelbarrow in the yard, the bark of the sheep-
dog, the thud of a flail, and now and again a man's
chuntering winter-morning voice; but no human shape in
sight save one woman coming quickly down the road. Lois
started to meet her, stopped, started again, between an
impulse and a shame. It was Nell Rideout.

"Why hae yer sent my brother to his death?" she said
sternly.

"What do you mean? I never intended – But, oh, why
did he shoot my brother?"

"He none did."

"Arthur said he did."

"Can he see wee's back? For that's where he were shot."

"If he didn't do it, why, oh, why did he go?"

"Ax me what yo don't know."

"Fetch him again, Miss Rideout."

"I can't, I've tried; yo sent him."

"Come with me."

Nell took the proffered hand in her large grasp and both
sped up the road together. They would have overtaken him;
he had been delayed by his colloquy with Nell; they ran
and he but walked, though at the brisk pace at which a
zealous servant goes about his master's or mistress's
bidding; they would have overtaken him, but just as Nell
joined hands with Lois a thought had come into his head, a
treble twine of recklessness, mere whim and pure good-
nature. If he gave himself up to the sport of justice there
would be that reward of fifty pounds offered and nobody

the better for it, whereas if poor old Ned Cliff of the
Bottoms, decrepit, wifeless, childless, could claim it it would
add warmth to the cold kindness of the poor-law overseer.
He was not in the humour for nice balancing; he
immediately pushed through the high-topped hedge which
would so thoroughly hide him from view of the road,
crossed a fallow and a breadth of wheat, and so gained the
grassy lane which leads down to the Bottoms.

Nell and Lois ran until the younger and weaker of them
was out of breath; then they walked a little or went between
a walk and a run until she could run again. At the first such
break in their running Nell said:

"What does the doctor say?"

"That there's a something artery wounded but no need
for alarm."

But they saw nothing of Tant. They reached the town's
end and still had seen nothing of him.

"Do you think he would?" asked Lois.

"If he telled yer he would," answered Nell.

The heavy-shoed labourers were mustering with the
implements of their war, with sheep-hook and turnip-hack,
hedge-knife and bill, hatchet and spade and graving tool.
Each as he passed looked hard at them, then turned and
looked back at them. The moonlight and the pale trouble
on their faces were of the same quality; a man might doubt
and doubt, saying, "Is it trouble? Nay, it is the moon."

They met Josh Jowers; he had tied a sack over his smock
for warmth to his old shoulders. Now Josh Jowers lived hard
by the constable.

"Good-morning, Mr. Jowers," said Lois.

Josh touched his hat in passing with a gleam of light in
his bleared eyes. Nell whispered to Lois and the two turned
back after the old man. But Lois spoke. Josh stopped, but
Posh went on showing a contemptuous tail; for which Josh
apologized.

"'E's a dug wi'out any notion o' manners, miss. Nayther

good advice nor good example tells on 'im. Yo'd niver think as the back end of oat could look so contemptible at yer. 'E's a 'eart-breaking dug."

"Mr. Jowers, have you seen – anybody –" Lois dropped her voice. "It's between you and me.' Josh nodded and looked ignorantly knowing. "Have you seen *anybody* knock at White's door within the last few minutes?"

"No, miss."

"Yo'd know if anybody had, I suppose?" said Nell.

"Know? I couldn't help. My oad missis sits erklin' ower the fire wi' 'er face skew to the winder, an' if nubbut a cat goos by she meks a tale on't."

"Thank you, Mr. Jowers," said Lois heartily, relieved of part of her anxiety.

"Yo're welcome, miss, welcome."

Josh trudged stiffly off after Posh; Nell drew Lois aside into the churchyard. They could easily see over the low wall into the street, but were themselves almost invisible in the deep shade of the great over-hanging chestnut-trees.

"Let's bide here and watch," said Nell.

In the east the sky was preparing for the cold coming of the sun. Southwards between church and house appeared the grey semblance of hill behind hill, mile upon mile of phantom scenery. What could Tant be doing? Would he never come?

"The doctor will think it strange," said Lois, "that I am not by my brother's bed." She mused a little. "But he is not in danger of –"

She shivered. Nell took the warm shawl from her own shoulders and wrapped it round the girl's slighter form. Lois protested against the exchange; for all answer Nell drew it tighter about the slim neck and secured it there with a big pin.

"You make me ashamed," said Lois.

"I'm accountable to Tant," said Nell.

"Are you afraid of him too?" Lois whispered.

"I'm nubbut his sister."

Both Lois's little hands sought one of Nell's large ones and held it for the comfort and the warmth. And so huddled close together they whispered under the dark leafless chestnuts. The road was grey-white with the moonlight, but darkened every now and then at the passage of labouring folk, plough-boy in his frock, milkmaid with kit upon head.

"Should you be more afraid of him if you weren't his sister?"

"I suld if I were his sweetheart."

"Why?"

"I know I suld."

"How?"

"There's a deal more crying nor laughing about love."

"How do you know?"

"Tish told me."

"How does she know?"

"She's tried it."

There was a pause. Sparrows on the house-eaves uttered fussy proclamation of their being awake. Then Lois whispered lower still:

"One might be neither, you know; neither sister nor –"

"That 'ud be worst of all. M'appen Tant's not a very stayable lad to be in love wi', but he'd be a downraight terrible fellow to be hafe in love wi'."

There was a pause. In that sheltered spot the breeze did not stir the shadows, though it sang with a whispering shrillness in the higher branches of the trees.

"But – but" – Lois faltered, yet went on – "one might be neither wholly nor half, you know."

"Many a one, many a one," said Nell gravely; "but not here."

There was a soft sigh which only Nell heard, and a little trembling movement under the shawl which only Nell felt. Presently Lois bespoke attention by the additional pressure of her trembling hands. Otherwise Nell would not have bent her head and heard.

"Call me Lois."

"Lois."

"Nell."

The younger woman put her lips up child-like to be kissed. Both the grey eyes and the hazel were wet with tears. Thereupon they heard the shuffling of many feet, the sound of many voices. They looked over the wall and saw in the ghostly light of neither night nor day, first a number of children running, shouting and kicking up the dust; then a mob of men and women, and in the midst of them Tant, his arms tied behind him with a rope, the end of which was held by old Ned Cliff who hobbled eagerly after. One of the men tried to take the rope from Ned, but he held on and protested shrilly:

"He's mine! I copped him! The reward belongs oad Neddy Cliff!"

"If yo touch it again, Spettigew," said Tant, "I'll gie yer my foot."

Nell left Lois in the shade and went out to them.

Tant's face became troubled, but he spoke quite calmly, almost carelessly.

"Ho'd a bit, Ned, whilst I talk to my sister. I've run the rig, Nell."

"A sorry rig it is, Tant. She has sent me for you."

"It's too late, Nell. And I dunno as this could be mended anyhow. When we chuck rammel out the gainest way's the best."

She whispered: "Couldn't yo yet – For Lois?" His knees shook at the name. "I'll cut the rope and unnertake to ho'd Spettigew and Mosley off."

"I wain't be took in a scuffle, pully-hauly, like a tuppeny welsher on a race-course."

Spettigew tugged at her skirts.

"Yo shan't be whispering wee 'm no longer," he growled; "yo mean to witch 'im away as yo did it afore."

Tant sprang fiercely at him dragging the rope out of Ned's hands. With all his might and weight he butted his right shoulder in Spettigew's face, and at the same moment locking leg in leg hurled the man violently to the ground. The others looked on in wonder at such an exhibition of strength and dexterity.

"Here," said Tant, "take ho'd o' the helter, Neddy, and grip it tight; m'appen I shan't be so easy catched next time."

The constable and baker, warned by the uproar, came bustling out in his shirt-sleeves, holding his staff in his floury hand. But Tant did not see him, he had fixed his eyes in another direction. Had he caught an unsubstantial glimpse of a white face in the thick shade of the church, where nobody else saw anything? Anyhow Nell saw his face, both cheek and lip, go all at once as wan as the light, and he dropped on his knees in the midst of the road.

"Doff my hat off for me, Nell," he said; and Nell did so.

The crowd thought he was saying his death prayer under the consecrated shadow of the church, and stood quite still. One man took his hat off and another and another, until all had bared their heads but old Ned who held the rope, and Spettigew who had but just risen with a dusty back and a grim and bleeding mouth. But Tant's chin was not on his breast nor his eyes closed; he kept his head unbowed, his level gaze fixed on the same point of the thick shade. Presently he rose.

"Amen!" said Chris Nicholson the Methodist heartily.

"Now, Tom," said Tant, "yo may tek me in; but be sure and remember that 'twere Neddy here as captured me."

"Ah," said Neddy, "'twere me as captur'd 'im; oad Neddy Cliff. Wheer's that theer money?"

CHAPTER XXVIII

TISH MAKES A CALL

NELL said to Tish on returning to the house, and her face was white: "If yo don't do a hand's chare more, yo've done a big day's work a'ready, our Tish, and not eight o'clock yet. Yo've shot Mr. Skrene for no fault o' hisn –"

"So 'twere him?"

"And got Tant locked up for't."

"How d'yer mek that out?"

But Nell put kit on head and took piggin in hand and went off to her milking; for it was now broad daylight upon her trouble, and the moon was but as a puff of white vapour floating in the sky. The cows had long forsaken their cold dewy pasturage, and stood about the gate of the Old Ley lowing and poaching the ground with their heavy feet. Tish binged the peggy-tub for the day's wash, lighted a fire under the copper, put out the clothesline, gave the men their breakfast, but ate none herself. Then she changed her shoes and dressed scrupulously for out-of-doors in her best black silk dress, short-sleeved, low-bodiced, full in the skirt, with a black silk handkerchief over her ample bosom. Her own mourning bonnet had not yet come home, so she borrowed Nell's which had been hastily black-stringed and becraped for Sunday; a high-built bulgy structure as big as a quartern loaf, with a long gauzy border that half hid the face depending from the brim. Tish stood the proper time before the glass with pursed mouth tying the bow, then drew on her long black silk gloves up to her elbows, fastened the clasp of her long black mantle and went down-stairs. Nell had returned with her full kit.

"I've had to tek your bonnet," she said.

Nell nodded.

"It seems ridic'lous small; it scarce hafe covers my face. And I never did admire the style on't, even when 'twere fashionable. How does it look behint?"

"It'll do," said Nell.

"A poor 'do' too, I reckon. A cross o' velvet i' th' front 'ud improve it. We wain't wesh your sheets this week, being as we've such a heavy wesh."

Then she turned again to say: "If I don't coom back i' reasonable time, yo moot get Hannah to help."

"Sall Medders telled me she'd had one of her bad bouts i' th' night."

"M'appen Walker's Molly 'ud coom."

"I might send an' ax."

But once started it was not long before Tish stood at the door of the High House and asked for Miss Skrene. She was in the parlour, as far as she could get from an untouched breakfast. Tish strode three steps in, waited until the door was closed, and then said:

"I've coomed to gie mysen up. 'Twere me as shot your brother, not our Tant."

"Oh, Mrs. Gillott, how came you to do it?"

"Hae yo axed him?"

"No, he's so very weak."

"Ax him first. Mebbe hisn 'll be the handsomest side o' the tale."

"The doctor says that it's a serious wound, and if it had been higher it might have been very serious."

"I didn't aim higher."

"Then you really did it on purpose?"

"I'm not one o' them poor wezzling craturs who let firearms off by mishap."

"You shot my brother? on purpose?"

She said the words, conscious all the time that her anger was inadequate. But she was so tired, so tired!

"If I'd knowed it was your brother, maybe I might ha' lowered the muzzle a tinety bit more, but I didn't. Now do what yo will wi' me; I'm here."

"I don't want to do anything. But oh, Mrs. Gillott, what a heap of trouble you've caused!"

"If 'twere to do again I'd do't. But m'appen, as I said, an inch or two lower. That's all I've got to say. I'm here."

Lois slowly sadly shook her head. Her despairing face began to affect Tish.

"Yo tek on too much about this, lass. At that distance, i' that part, it couldn't be so very tickle. What does that nummy of a doctor say to't?"

"He speaks favourably."

"Yo look as white as a sheet; yo hain't eaten your breakfast."

Lois looked with horror at the food.

"Have you eaten yours?"

"Mine, lass?" Tish seemed almost disconcerted by the rejoinder. She stood a little before she continued. "What's thisn o' yourn against the sore wownd we ha' gotten? We've no call to eat. Our gret-granmam would ha' been a hundred coom spring, our Tant's nubbut twenty and a month, and this same black 'll do for 'em both. It's a saving, yo'll say; but we're not *so* keen."

It was more than Lois could bear; she sank back into the chair that she had risen from, covered her face up with her hands and broke into sobs, those dry and scanty sobs which give so little ease to pain. Tish stood her distance, surprised, perhaps a little resentful, as though her due of emotion had been given away to a stranger. But presently the girl's not appealing appealed to her; she went up to her, saying:

"A little cant like yo wants to hae it mother allus by."

But she laid her hand not at all roughly on the girl's head.

"I have no mother; I wish I had."

"Tant lost hisn afore he could do wi'out her. Co', co', it mootn't cry."

"It was I, Mrs. Gillott; I made him go."

"Who go wheer?"

"To prison. I told him and he went."

"Tant?"

"Yes! I!"

It was as though the passage of the words had opened a way through for tears; the cheeks that had been dry were wet.

"A little bit of a pale scaddle thing like yo? Who'd ha' tho't it?"

"It was wicked, it was wicked of me!"

"It was."

But the touch of the hand was still light on the head.

"A pair o' dark eyes an' a pretty Lunnon frock, and noat else as yo might say! It *was* wicked. Look at me! What are yo to me? But men ne'er scrooched down to me. They goo; as long's I shove 'em – I've a strong pair of arms, thank goodness – but when my back's turned, I'll tell yer how far I can trust 'em; as far as I can blow 'em. Co', co', yo're wetting that pretty bit o' ribbon. It's wesh-day to-day and the fun'ral to-morrer; and here stan' I. Nay, my little cant, for one to cry and the tother not to cry's no company at all. And I hain't the gift o' crying mysen. There's whiles I feel the lack on't."

Presently the tears flowed no faster than they could be wiped away. Lois lifted her red eyes and said:

"Do you think they'll let him off again?"

Tish's face hardened again, as though to put a case about her thoughts.

"There's locks to doors, God forbid we suld put locks to hope."

Then pitying the girl's pale face and the untouched breakfast, she did something heroic; she broke the laws of etiquette, which at Blidworth are more generally regarded than the laws of God.

"I'll own now I did mek but a skimpy breakfast on't;

we're allus so throng o' wesh-days. M'appen if yo were to ax me, I could just drink a cup o' tea."

"I beg your pardon, I ought to have asked before, but – pray do."

"Thank yer kindly, I will."

So Lois set about making fresh tea, and the trivial occupation did her more good than tomes of Boethius.

"I couldn't think o' taking your cup," said Tish.

"I will get myself another," said Lois. She did so, and also another plate. "We've only cold meats but I hope you'll partake of something with your tea."

"Yo're very good, but not unless yo're gooing to keep me company."

So they both ate a little, and the action of the jaws gave their perplexities something of an uneasy rest.

"Who says it's not a strange world?" said Tish presently. She was feeling the reaction of her boldness. "Yo hedn't so much as axed me to sit down!"

"I'm sure I beg your pardon."

"Nay, raight is raight; I'm not mealy-mouthed, but it's for me to beg yourn."

But when she accepted a second cup she seemed to suffer a return of the scruple. She gave a grim laugh and said:

"What would Sarah Wilkinson say?"

"I don't know," said Lois.

"M'appen yo don't know Sarah Wilkinson?"

"I don't."

"There's a deal i' that. But it gets me that the on'y day I've ever had bite or sup i' this house is the day I let blaze at the master on't."

Lois could not understand where her anger had gone; she made search for it, tried to account for its absence.

"You wouldn't have done if you'd known."

Tish swallowed down the dry morsel in her mouth.

"I suld. But maybe a tinety bit lower i' th' leg."

"I think you take sugar and cream, Mrs. Gillott?"

And so the needful question caulked the unnecessary sob.

"Yo'd think 'twere the end o' th' world," said Tish; "it's wesh-day to-day and to-morrow's the fun'ral, and me here!"

Again she said, "That's a pretty sleeve o' yourn; I've never seed oat like it i' th' Mansfield shops."

"It was sent me from London."

"Ah!"

Soon after Tish rose and said:

"Those two wenches o' yourn, lass, are like nobody else's i' this world or they're be slithering all this blessed morning away. Yo moot goo now and wakken 'em up. I'm for the wesh-tub."

She went, but seemed to suffer from an after-rush of pity for the disconsolate face she left behind; she came back a dozen yards and kissed it on the top of the steps. Lois kissed her back, and said betwixt old timidity and new confidence:

"Will you let me not be afraid of you next time?"

"If yo durst."

* * *

Tongues went faster than hands that morning in crew-yard and field as well as kitchen. Selby and Wells, Spettigew and the thrasher were gathered in the little barn, where the thrashing had to be done until the great barn was rebuilt. There was no work doing but each man held fast his token of it, Spettigew and his mate their flails, Wells the large coe with which he had been mucking out the stables; Selby being foreman had nothing but his authority. Spettigew had been giving them a pretty full description of Tant Rideout's capture by old Ned Cliff, passing by however the rebuff his own strength had received.

"Knelt i' th' middle o' th' road," he was repeating, "an' said 'is prayers."

"That's funny!" said Selby.

"It cops me," said Wells.

"I' the middle o' the road," said Spettigew. "If folk mun pray – I say noat agen't – let 'em pray in-doors. Nubbudy dresses hissen i' th' middle o' th' road. It een't nat'ral."

"I were at a camp-meetin' once o' th' Ranters," said Wells.

"This warn't no camp-meetin'. O' coorse a lot o' folk prayin' out o' doors is diff'rent to one man braungein' an' tekkin' it all on hissen."

"O' coorse," said Wells.

"Besides it een't the time o' year for camp-meetin's."

"God A'mighty," said Coy the thrasher, "can't be expected to stan' about i' the roäd these co'd dark mornin's on the off chance of a hafe-frozzen prayer or two; it een't reasonable."

With his lean arms he swung his flail over his head and banged the swipple down thud! on the oat-straw before him; then stood and listened again.

"What d'yer think to that?" said Spettigew, when he had finished his story.

"He mun a bin droonk," said Selby.

"M'appen," said the thrasher," he's made a bargain wi' Ned to divide the reward atween 'em." He smiled a dry lean toothless smile. "Five an' twenty pound! None on's would be cheäp at that market."

Again he struck one blow with his flail, then stood and listened.

"It's my opinion," said Spettigew, "it's a fetch o' hisn. He belongs a fam'ly that's as deep as deep."

"He does that," said Wells.

"What 'e means I don't say, but depend your life on't 'e reckons in that 'e's got a witch in his fam'ly to help 'im out."

"Nay, not now," said Selby; "she's deäd."

"She's deäd, an' she's alive."

"Coom, how d'yer mek that out?"

"Yo shall judge. My missis were sadly off last night, an' as she didn't sleep very well nayther didn't I. 'Owiver if I were awake I were awake, an' if I were asleep I were waked, an' I heerd a ran-tan outside like the gallop of a thousand hosses. I ups an' peeps out the winder, an' I sees a woman ridin' a hoss as looked an' galloped like no human cratur. They went by like a flash o' lightning. It were pitch-black, there warn't no light, but I seed 'em as plain as plain. I belders out, an' the missis joomps oop, an' she's took very badly, an' the devil of a time I hed wi' her. What d'yer think to that?"

"If yo can't ride a-days," said the lean thrasher, "it's summat to ride a-nights."

"Who were't?" said Selby.

"I know," said Spettigew, but did not say who.

"The mester were shot i' th' night an' all," said Wells ponderingly, like one who is trying to reduce odd numbers to a reckonable two and two.

"Nubbudy knows why or wherefore," said Selby. "I call that strangely odd."

"What d'yer think, surries?"

They all turned; it was Jack Harris the wagoner, who stood in the doorway and spoke. "I met a Fishpool chap t'other end o' the town, an' 'e told me as 'e'd heerd as Deb Foat's gone welly nigh off'n 'er 'ead. She ho'ds to't as 'er Ben were carried off i' th' night by the devil i' th' likeness of a tom-cat. This is trewth, Ben's nowheer to be fun'; up an' down they've searched."

"The devil were bound to hae him i' some shape or form," said the thrasher.

The others kept silence for a space. A prickly shudder ran down each back, not positively disagreeable in the half-day of the barn, for between Jack's shoulders and the lintel there was a glimpse of the unmistakable sunshine outside. After a while Selby, who was slow but pertinacious, addressed Spettigew.

"Who were't yo seed, Bill, of hoss-back?"

"I dunno as I shall tell yer; yit. But I'll be even wee 'er

afore I've done. It were for sich uns as Blid'orth laws were made."

He flung up his flail and began to thrash. The oat-straw crackled, the chaff flew. Jack went away, but the other men stood, seeming to take it for granted that Spettigew had not done speaking. Presently he stopped for a moment, while he said over his shoulder:

"I niver liked them fraunfreckles about 'er eyes; nor yit the colour of 'er 'air; there's a touch o' hell fire about it."

Again he thrashed with his back to them; the dust rose, the chaff flew, the men looked on. Suddenly he ceased, he turned, he came back to them, and leaning forwards on the hand-staff said in that tone in which a secret is uttered:

"'Twere Roideouts' Nell. But –"

With the unspoken menace in his eyes, of that dull obstinate dangerous sort which shows no light and little heat, he went back to his thrashing and smote as though he were smiting Nell to her death.

"We shall bang along wee't to-day, oh so gaily oh!" said the thrasher; and he too resumed his labour.

Wells shuffled off to his stable, Selby went down into the fields; not another word was said.

CHAPTER XXIX

FOAT'S MESSAGE

HALF-WAY between night-fall and bed-time Deb Foat knocked at the back door of High House and asked to see the master. Her nerves were still much shaken and she durst not have ventured out at night alone, so Dick Dunstan the pensioner had donned his cocked hat and gallantly escorted her thither. At that moment he was standing at ease against the gate-head awaiting her return. Lois had her brought into the parlour, and saw a dirty blowzy slatternly woman, slipshod at the heel, betowzled as to the head, and looking none the better about the eyes for her two broken nights. Of course Lois told her that it was impossible for her to see Mr. Skrene. What did she want with him? She hummed and haed and halted, and said it was summat very partic'lar, but if she couldn't see the mester – Lois again said it was quite impossible – she supposed it mun wait while she could. She sniffed and sniffed again, which may have been in repression of a tear or merely for want of a handkerchief, and she sat ill-poised on the edge of the chair which Lois had placed for her.

"Mr. Skrene is ill in bed," said Lois.

"Ah, so I've heerd tell, miss. Well" – sniff – "I promised Ben faithful" – sniff and sniff again – "but if the mester's so badly of coorse it wain't do for 'im to be put about for sich as me. So I'll be gooin', miss, an' thank yer."

She talked of going but did not look at the door.

"What is your business with Mr. Skrene? Couldn't you explain it to me?"

"No, miss, thank yer kindly all the same; I dussn't; Ben swore me ower and ower again to tell nub'dy but the mester. An' – an' – after two sich nights" – sniffing would not serve, she fairly blubbered – "oh, sich nights, miss! Nubbut two on 'em! an' I seem to can't mind noat else; they might be years an' years. No, I feel as I dussn't do noat wrong so soon. 'Twould be wrong; so soon. Why, miss, I feel a this 'ow, I feel as if I'd turn religious for one good night's rest, an' niver enjoy mysen no more."

But she stayed her sobs and smeared her tears over her face with her grimy hands. She looked up, and a ray of cunning hope shone foggily through her red eyelids.

"Would it be wrong, think yer, miss, for me to false-sweer mysen, if a lady like yo axed me to?"

"Certainly. I could not think of asking you to do that."

"If Ben niver knowed noat?"

"It would make no difference."

"But Ben's non sich a out-o'-th'-way good character hissen, miss."

"I'm sorry to hear that; but that makes no difference."

"I'll lay oat, miss, Ben in 'is 'eart niver expected me to fow-convenience mysen."

"Then I hope you'll do better than he expected. Won't you?"

"I leave it to yo, miss. Ah well!"

It was the beginning of a checked sob as she rose to go. But she had a new thought, a new hope, and did not go.

"There's diff'rent roads o' thinkin', miss; there's the chutch road an' there's the chapel road, and there's Ann Pybus the preachin' woman as has a road to hersen. I'm not sayin', miss, as yourn een't the best; but any on 'em's good enough for me. M'appen some on 'em thinks diff'rent about that?"

"God doesn't."

"And He's the gaffer. Ah well!" Her eyes were soiled springs of tears again. "I mun goo, miss; he's waitin' of me, an' he's got nubbut one chaw o' bacca left."

"Mr. Foat?"

"No, miss; I don't deceive yer; a friend o' hisn."

Lois had little doubt that she came about Tant; her heart was beating to know; yet the parting look she gave the poor woman's smudged and swollen face was mainly one of pity. Perhaps Deb saw it and pitied herself the more for seeing it; or perhaps the appearance through the open door of the starless night, seeming all the blacker from the lighted hall, reinforced her terror. She turned again and said:

"Miss, I'll tell yer. If it's wrong, I mun begin to be good to-morrer. It's niver too late, they say. But pass another sich night as them two I dussn't. Don't stop me, miss, please. I dussn't. Talk about cats! and talk about devils! After all it's nubbut a bit o' splauge for sich uns as me to talk about the raights an' the wrongs o' things. I'll tell yer. It's about Roideouts' Tant."

Lois turned pale and trembled.

" You'd better come into the room," she said.

"If yo wain't stop me, miss." And she rattled on as she went. "Ben's sorry he e'er hed oat to do wi' th' job. He weshes his hands on't. He withcalls all he's swore. Fifty poun's a lot of money, but a good night's rest's worth it all. He says *yo've* no call to be hard on Tant, miss; he says he acted proper by yo."

"Stop."

"I knowed yer'd stop me, miss," said Deb sorely aggrieved.

"I wonder if – I wish the doctor was here."

"Oh, he's not stret-laced at all, miss; he can talk according to his comp'ny, whativer that may be, I assure yer."

"I wasn't meaning that; I was wondering whether he would consider my brother strong enough for the interview."

"Now I've begun, miss, I mun keep on. Mebbe it's

wrong, but i' th' night I'm a deal more afeared o' th' devil nor o' God. That's trewth."

"You *shall* speak. Only wait a minute."

Lois went out of the room and up-stairs. She ran, but her heart went faster than her feet. In her eagerness she was above all tender of the woman's conscience. She entered her brother's room. He was stretched upon his bed; the pallor of his cheeks made the darkness of his eyes and hair the more noticeable.

"How do you feel now, dear?" she said.

But his eyes saw before his tongue answered.

"What is it?" he asked with a bloodless voice.

"Do you feel stronger, dear?"

"Yes. Tell me."

"Can you bear it?"

"I can bear anything but being put off."

"A messenger has come and she has promised to deliver her message only to you. I wondered, if you were to lie still and I were to do all the talking, whether you would be strong enough to hear what she has to say."

"Who is it?"

"Foat's wife."

Their eyes had met in the quick repartee of question and answer long before the sound was framed.

About –?"

"Mr. Rideout."

"Bring her up."

"You really, dear, consider yourself strong enough?"

"I mean to be, Loie."

"I wish I knew what the doctor would say."

"You shall ask him to-morrow."

"But you're not to speak, only to listen."

"Yes."

"And you're to keep your eyes quiet."

"Yes, yes."

Lois, still wondering what the doctor would say and

halting between ought and ought not, fetched Mrs. Foat up
and placed her in a chair at the bedside.

"Now please tell my brother, Mrs. Foat, what you have
to say; in as few words as possible."

Deb twisted her neck so that she spoke face to face with
Miss Skrene.

"Yo'd a tho't all the devils in – in the bad place were let
loose, miss, yo really would. Cats? I niver heerd no mortal
cats to touch 'em. Dogs? It really warn't human."

"You've something to say about Mr. Rideout?"

"Ay, miss. I'm not a-gooing to defend what Ben did. I've
no occasion; he een't here, an' it warn't me. Though fifty
poun's a heap o' money."

"It wasn't true, what he said against Mr. Rideout?"

"'Twere mixed like, miss; like hafe the tales that's telled;
mixed."

"But he had nothing to do with breaking that
machinery?"

"What's the use o' axing, miss? I wouldn't if I were yo.
'Tweren't your machinery; yo've noat again Tant Roideout.
He stood atween yo an' black mischief that night, that 'e
did. Besides I niver hed noat to do wi' sich carryings on, so
now Ben's mizzled theer's nub'dy to tell yer."

"Has Foat gone off?" asked Arthur.

"Hush, dear," said his sister.

"Ay, sir," said Deb.

"Where?" asked Arthur, even under his sister's eye.

"I dunno, sir. But it's wheer he'll niver coom back to
Blid'orth no more, that I do know."

Lois snatched the next question from his looks and
translated it to Deb.

"Tell Mr. Skrene why, please."

"So's 'e shouldn't hae to sweer Tant's life away; that's the
long an' the short on't. An' 'e made me promise to coom
'ere, afore bed-time, an' say this: say as 'ow Tant warn't no
willing party to the 'tack on your house; quite the contrairy,

Ben heerd; from a man as war theer; so 'e hed it from the firm end. He heerd as they put summat in's drink; 'e were mottled; 'e didn't know noat. But as soon as he got i' th' 'ouse 'e woke up, as sober as co'd watter, an' gollocky! didn't 'e lay it on! 'E didn't play butty; Ben heerd. There were six on 'em i' th' room besides Tant an' yoursen – tell me if I'm a liar, miss – an' 'e took the table up as if 'twere a wooden lader, an' scooped the hull hafe-dozen out at winder wee't. Ben heerd tell."

Lois's hand was on his arm, Lois's eye anxiously scanned his face.

"Are you no worse, dear?"

"Not in the least."

He had really borne it surprisingly well.

"An' while Tant were inside tow-rowing on 'em, his Nell were outside, of hoss-back – trewth's trewth – lashin' out again 'em like the mad madam she is."

Lois was quick to see the change in his face.

"It won't do, dear. It's doing you harm."

"Go on!" he said imperatively.

"She druv 'er hoss clean through an' through 'em, knockin' 'em silly, till they were glad to scaddle. There were brucken limbs too – Ben heerd tell."

"How did he get his own leg broken?"

"I niver heerd, sir; I'd no curiosity to ax; 'twere enough for me it were brucken. How she could I can't think. It warn' t like a woman; not if I'm a woman. But some upho'ds she's a witch."

"I think she must be," Arthur muttered to himself.

"Well, now I've made a clean breast on't. Yo may tell the Gen'ral it's no good expectin' Ben to coom back, for 'e niver will; if I know oat 'e niver will. 'E didn't run away, 'e flew. They might as well sit on a gate an' gawp for swallers. So they've no occasion to keep Tant i' jail not a minute longer."

Again Lois was quick to anticipate the question.

"I'll tell you presently, dear; in quiet."

"An' now, miss, please, theer's somebody awaitin' of me."

At the open door it seemed that the woman's fear came back again like a whiff of cold in-rushing night air.

"I've nubbut telled one lig – to speak on – in all I've spoken to-night, miss," she said anxiously; "nubbut one. D'yer think it 'ud be noticed?"

"Somebody has noticed it."

"Then I withcall it. 'Twere about Ben's leg. There'd be no sense i' gettin' mysen into a lumber about him, now 'e's gone. That's all. I trust *they'll* be jannock wi' me. But Dick's waitin', miss. And 'e's a bad waiter, like most men. Goodnight, miss."

Lois did not return at once to her brother's room. It would not be correct to say her hesitation was entirely in consideration of her brother's health. Still it was but a delay of a few minutes, so Arthur need not have said impatiently as soon as she entered:

"What a long time you've been!"

"Won't to-morrow do, dear?"

Her lips were white, her voice faint.

"You know it won't."

She went to his bed-head to smooth his pillow, and being there remained. He could not have seen her face without an uncomfortable twist of the neck.

"Arthur."

"Well?"

"You weren't shot by – the person you think."

"Who was it then?"

"You won't say, 'Vengeance is mine,' dear?"

"No; all that seems to have been bled out of me."

"It was Mrs. Gillott."

He lay as in a muse awhile; then said:

"But I want to know about that young man. I thought you and Miss Rideout were looking after him."

"Oh, Arthur, why did you say he did it?"

"I thought he did."

"I was angry." Arthur could but just in the stillness catch the words. "I said something about sending for the constable, if I'd had a servant at hand."

"Only of course you hadn't."

"I had. He said I should never-never – He went himself. Straight to the constable. And –"

Her eye caught something amiss in the arrangement of the bottles of liniment and lotion on the wash-hand table; she went aside and rectified it.

Arthur mused. He had feared lest his sister's generous gratitude should commit her too far in Tant's cause; but that was quite a new thought which had just struck him, with a suddenness which would have been a shock but for the brain-numbing debility that possessed him. The bottles made a little chink. He said just audibly to a fine ear:

"I could understand it, if –"

Lois knelt before the fire, and taking the little brush that hung by the chimney swept the hearth-stone clear of ashes. The uncertain glow of the fire was insufficient to colour her paleness. Arthur mused the languid musings of a sick man. At last he said as faintly as before:

"I can't understand it. Unless –"

Lois rose from her knees.

"I am going to fetch your supper now, dear.'

"Not yet. I couldn't eat yet. I heard the doctor say, 'It saved your brother's life; man's or woman's, it saved his life.' I've wondered, but I haven't asked. Now I do ask."

Lois fetched Nell's garter and laid it on the coverlet before him, a fabric of home-spun yarn plainly knitted and undyed. His eyes scanned it from end to end.

"It was tied round your leg, dear."

"What is that in the corner? I can't see."

"There's an H and an R, dear."

"You needn't move it; it's no weight. Put the candle out; the light tires me."

Lois extinguished the candle. She stood by the hearth;

the fickle fire-light was on her clasped hands but not on her face. The ticking of the old clock in the hall could be distinctly heard through the closed door; there was a low bee-like buzz of women's voices from some distant room.

"What are you doing, Loie?"

"Nothing."

"Come and sit by me."

She went and sat by him and held one of his hands. The flickering fire-light playing over the carpet with noiseless kitten-like tread seemed to be the only living thing; yet those two heads, one low on the pillow, the other only less than erect by a slight droop, were each a crowded city of thoughts. Lois's reverie was a maid's and inviolable; Arthur's was the ravel of a sick man's fancy. Yet amid all its inwoven intricacies certain scenes presented themselves to him again and again, without order but always with the same simple distinctness. A woman on her knees; her face besought, her words were few. A woman the centre of a sunset's magnificence. A woman in a lawless night-crowd, managing a plunging horse; the face was from him, but he knew the horsemanship. A woman in a white trailing bed-gown under the stars. A woman in a court of justice saying, "I will never kneel no more, to man." And again a woman on her knees. It was after many such recurrences that he said in a sick man's voice that but just pierced the vaporous walls of his muse:

"She knelt to me, Loie."

Lois made no answer, no answer seemed possible.

Through his passively busy brain the diorama moved intricately inconsecutive; until at last again he said:

"She'll never kneel to me again."

Lois made no answer, unless it were with the hand that was upon his hand. Time went on; the fire-light that had danced upon the floor now flew and frolicked on the walls and ceiling. Sometimes it touched, sometimes it left, the garter which still lay on the white coverlet. It would seem that the weakness which had relaxed Arthur's muscles had also loosened the strings of his reserve. He said:

"Do you believe in witches, Loie?"

"I thought I didn't. Do you, dear?

"I used not."

She stole her hand away and went down for his supper.

CHAPTER XXX

DEPARTURES

THE eldest of the Rideouts was carried up the long steep ascent to the churchyard on the stalwart shoulders of her neighbours, and buried with every decency. Tish and Nell and other relatives walked on either side of the coffin with heads bent, draped in scarves of black silk, in the one hand a wand, in the other a white linen handkerchief. Three generations were represented there; the sole survivor of the fourth and nearest wept at home, blind tears. The mourners stood around the open grave during the solemn ritual, and at the Amen to the final benediction dropped their handkerchiefs into it. It was an old custom in the family. The creeping of black and white up and down the hill could be seen afar. Spettigew saw it from High Farm and did not think the parish had gained much by the loss.

"We're shut of a blair-eyed oad witch," he grumbled to Wells, "as couldn't hardly hotchel across the floor, and we've gotten a young un, wi' eyes like a hawk's, as can run and ride wi' most. Yo'll heer summat. And afore long."

Ben Foat never came back to Blidworth to fulfil his obligations to legal justice. Nothing certain was ever known of his after history; there was all the more room for hearsay and conjecture, which then and for years after fluttered doubtfully between mouth and ear; that he had walked all the way to the Trent in order to drown himself commodiously; that he had given in by the way – Ben was always fierce to begin, slack at the finish – and hung himself in a hovel belonging to a man of the name of Smith; that he had gone into the cats'-meat trade at Manchester; had enlisted in the fifty-ninth or the ninety-fifth; had died of the small-pox; had emigrated to America at his own expense, to Botany Bay at the public; and so on and so on whenever and because gossip tired of the high prices of wheat and war.

Tant was remanded again and again and spent Christmas in jail; but Arthur Skrene refused to be certain enough to bear the full weight of a conviction; if anything he got less certain the more certainty was required of him; while the carrier would not swear to anything but what his wife said when he got home. Tant was sounded as to his willingness, if he were released, to fight for his country abroad; but he refused to discuss the matter. "I wain't 'list," he said, "wi' a helter round my neck." So in the end the magistrates were compelled to dismiss the information and discharge the prisoner. General Dene talked to him afterwards in the magistrate's room at Mansfield in language which was a blend of the judge, the squire, the soldier and the sportsman.

"You've had a very narrow escape, young man. I hope it will be a warning to you. I don't think it will. Probably you know better than I where this witness has gone, and why. But don't forget he may return. You can't square a man like Foat; he's too doughy to keep his corners. What are you going to do?"

"I might stop at home, sir, and work the farm."

"In short, do as you have done?"

"Do as I hain't done."

"A monstrous good resolution. Only remember we can't shift the Lay Cross and Will Scarlett out of walking distance. For one thing you're too good a walker. Besides Foat may come back. He's sure to come back. Unless you've put him out of the way? Well, which should you prefer, to be shot at at sixpence a day or hanged for nothing?"

"That's no great choice."

"Lucky for you it's not narrower."

"There are my sisters."

"They'll be infinitely better off without you than with you." To which, being unanswerable, Tant made no answer. "So would the parish. So would your country; whether you survive or don't. Think about it."

"I will. Though if there warn't a war on I'd as lief be hanged. I feel no call to be a barrack-booby, kicked here, cuffed there, goshawking on furlough, snuffing after kitchen-wenches, baugeing i' tap-rooms. But I'll think about it."

"If Foat should come back – and a man like him always comes back – if he should, out of sight, you know, out of mind. A brave soldier fighting for the King is out of reach of Tommy White. You're just the sort the country needs."

"The value set on us being sixpence a day, and find yoursen in pipe-clay."

The General was disappointed in the young man's spirit; he said coldly:

"A lad of mettle does not fight for that."

"He couldn't very well faight for less. However if I do 'list, sir, it'll nayther be for the sixpence nor to balk Tommy White of his fees."

"Whatever your motive I hope you'll encourage it; for a groat to a guinea that scoundrel comes back. And, by Gad, I should be sorry to see the Forest championship descend to yon Kirkby fellow."

If Tant desired reasons for stopping at home nobody helped him to find any. It is a sorry time for a man when he discovers that his presence is universally esteemed less profitable than his absence. Of course the good friends who were willing to part with him may have been thinking more of his welfare than their own convenience; but the fact remained that everybody, as soon as his possible departure was hinted at, began immediately to look resignation and to talk of it as a settled thing.

Arthur Skrene began to get about again just after Tant

was released. He rode down to Low Farm as soon as he was able, and most handsomely acknowledged his own injustice and Tant's services. Tant told him he had some thought of entering the army, but if he expected from him what he had not got from anybody else he was mistaken. Arthur cordially accepting the indecision as a resolve thought it excellent and said so. Tant's reply for once showed a trace of bitterness.

"For the parish? I've been told that so often I've no doubt on't; I'm trying to mek out how 'twould square wi' my own feelings. The sojer's jacket's a stret un; it wain't fit nobody without some humouring."

"I should have thought," said Arthur, meaning to be complimentary, "you were just cut out for a soldier."

"That's what they tell every blackguard thirty-four inch round the chest. Cut? I know I can be cut to fit the coat; I'd rayther the coat were cut to fit me."

Within twenty-four hours however he had enlisted in the forty-fifth. Nell expressed disappointment that he had not preferred a cavalry regiment. His reply showed that he had not acted without deliberation.

"For my own liking and the looks o' the thing," he said, "I suld ha' chosen to goo on four legs; but if a man puts his liking in his knapsack he moot throw summat out to mek room for't. And what matters looks? There'll be nobody there I care a hop about to see me. No, lass, I've considered this: the hoss-sojer comes on with a fullock an' goos off in a flusker; it's on'y the footman as can stan' an' faight. Now there's no true faighting wi'out stanning."

But he showed no sign of partaking in the hip-hip-hurraing patriotism of the day, either before or after he had taken the King's shilling; rather his eyes had a graver outlook, his mouth was drawn to a sterner line, and he avoided public notice. There was but one day, as it happened, and that was Sunday, between his attestation and the despatch of a draft of recruits from Mansfield to the regimental dépôt at Nottingham. Jack Whitehead and Nommer Brooks, who enlisted from Blidworth at the same time, spent it in flaunting their colours about the village, guzzling gratuitous beer and admiration and illustrating by turns each of the various valorous moods between half tipsy and dead drunk. Tant spent it quietly in-doors at the Mansfield inn where he was billeted; all but four hours and a half, two of which he gave to a going and a returning and the remainder to Blidworth. Of the latter he measured out but the odd half to his friends at home; and the greater part of that he spent in grooming and saddling Ripper the colt and in making a complete change in his own dress. He did indeed sit down awhile and talk gaily of the sergeant's red-hot nose and language and the peculiarities of his comrades; but as soon as the church bell on the hill began to toll he rose. Neither Tish nor Nell asked anything, but the grandmother said:

"Why are ta gooin' so soon, lad?"

"For a bit of a pike round, granny. Now forgie my gooin' so soon and all my other faults, and say 'God bless thee' as kindly as if 'twere the last time. On'y mind this: I coom again to-morrer if the red-beaked sergeant 'll let me."

The old dame spoke a tremulous "God bless thee, my child." Her tears wetted the cheeks she kissed; her mind misgave her. If that were not really her last blessing it was the very image of it and cast the same shadow. Between the loosening of her grandchild's clasp and the click of the door-sneck she saw a mob of noisy foreign deaths and one quite homely burial. Blind eyes are terribly far-sighted. The furrows on her face were moved as though it were a sea in little, leaden grey; the furrows on her face were fixed again, like the dark ridges of a sunless fallow. She sat with her hands upon her knees and saw.

Tish and Nell stood at the gate while he fetched his horse round. The sky was clear, the air still and frosty, the ground an inch deep in pure white snow, as even as a garment.

"Yo mun lend me your crop, Nell," he said.

Nell went in and fetched it. It was silvermounted; his own was plain.

"I'll send the colt back by Jackson's Jim or some other steady chap. He's yourn, Nell."

"I'll tek care on him," said Nell.

Not because she did not know, but because she would not seem to shirk knowing, Tish said:

"Yo goo to-morrer?"

"Ay."

"Tek this, lad; it'll be worth more to yer nor good words and wishes."

But he refused the purse with ten sovereigns in it which she offered him.

"What I hae to do I can do wi'out that; or not at all. I suldn't wunner if it 'ud buy Johnson's two-year-oad; she promises to turn out a useful nag."

"She's on the small side," said Tish.

"She's thick," said Tant.

"Well, we'll buy her for yer, if Johnson's oppen to a reasonable offer."

"And I'll break her in," said Nell, "against yo coom again."

So he kissed them at the gate and said good-bye, sternly ordered back Pitcher his terrier who was wild to follow him, mounted and rode away.

"He knows he looks well of hoss-back," said Nell.

At that moment a single funereal rook sailed slowly by over Tant's head. Tish saw Nell's eyes note it and turn away.

She said, "I hope Cherry-bloom wain't pick her cauf again."

But she was not thinking of Cherry-bloom any more than Nell was.

Tant unconscious of the black-winged omen, but his heart beating its own tumultuous prophecies, trotted on. When he gained the road he looked back without drawing rein and waved his right hand with the crop in it.

"He wouldn't for a thousand pound be late," said Tish.

"He'll none be late," said Nell; "he'll gallop as soon as he's by the housen."

"He wain't turn again," said Tish; "let's goo in to granny."

The three women sat by the hearth and comforted one another with their silence. The one-syllabled murmur of the distant church bell vibrated dimly through their thoughts.

It spoke a kinder summons to Lois Skrene, to whom it seemed the friendlier the nearer and louder it sounded. She was going to church alone for the last time as she hoped, for she expected that by next Sunday her brother would be strong enough in the leg to accompany her. Just where she turned off from the road to the bridle-path, by the oak saplings of Rooke's new plantation in that quietest part of the way where the snow was still untrodden, she met Tant. She had not seen him since his discharge. She knew the meaning of that bunch of gay ribbons pinned to his hat; she knew that he had enlisted; Nell had told her. He stopped his horse, bared his head and bowed; she curtseyed. She was very pale; she did not speak. She had never seen him in saddle before; she tried to make that account for the strangeness she felt. His decent great-coat was green, his top-boots brown, his breeches white, his broad-brimmed hat black, and his whip was silver-mounted. She thought he had never looked so tall and strong and handsome. His being on horse-back and so much the more withdrawn may have seemed to her the earnest of a parting. She felt very small herself and a little faint; she would have been glad of something to hold by. She tried to think it was the mettlesome horse she was afraid of; she remembered she had always been afraid of mettlesome horses. Tant leapt down and stood respectfully at the two yards' distance which separated them.

"I ax your pardon, ma'am, for the liberty," he said. "I've

said good-bye down yonner. It's the end o' your trouble. I'm gooing away."

She was in a strait. If she spoke she felt that she must also burst into tears. She was ashamed to do that; it would have been so absurd. She was ashamed to stand silent; it was so uncivil. Was ever maiden in a narrower strait? But as she was feeling more and more an inner push to be less ashamed of absurdity than of incivility, she was saved from both. Round the corner of Rooke's plantation trotted five children all in a row, a little girl of seven or eight in charge of brothers and sisters ranging down to the last toddler. They came along through the snow until they were within proper staring distance, four feet in our part of the country, then took their stand round Lois, a semi-circle of brown-holland pinafores, purple arms, red faces, bleached hair and blue eyes. They had not a pocket-handkerchief among them; their breaths hung about their mouths. A buzzing whisper, "A mester and a lady!" went round; then they remained expectantly silent with their eyes all fixed on Lois, whom they rightly regarded as the centre of interest. She wore a hat with bright-coloured bows and a feather nodding over the high crown; her long scarlet mantle, silver-clasped, black-braided, hid her hands, and her sable boa fell almost to the ground. They longed to take and stroke it and snuggle it to their cheeks. It had become impossible for Lois to cry, and at the same time easy for her to speak.

"There is still a little bloom," she said.

She pointed to the gorse bushes which flourish in that sandy soil, wherever there is a corner left unploughed or a margin untrodden. Rarely here and there among the white and the green peeped a yellow bud.

"Ay," said Tant, "it never quite goos out o' bloom; according to the by-word."

"What by-word?"

He had not expected the question; he had supposed that the old proverb was as well known to her as to all the countryside. Her eyes waited for his answer. The children shifted theirs from her to him, five pairs of china-blue.

"Quiet, Ripper, quiet!"

He took out his pocket-knife and cut a spray, the best he could find.

"Would yo accept a sprig, ma'am? It's prickly to handle but it keeps."

"Thank you. But the by-word?"

His eyes returned from the flowers to her face. He had made up his mind to it.

"They say, ma'am, it never goos out o' bloom but when kissing goos out o' fashion."

She looking at him and he at her inevitably their eyes met. There was a change in both of them; his ruddiness paled, her paleness flushed. He shook the snow off the flowers, removed the prickles from the lower part of the stem and gave it to her.

"Thank you."

Two poor little words; and a tremble in the voice.

"Posay!" chanted the youngest of the children.

"Prettay posay!" chanted the three above him.

"Say 'please, mester,' Georgeay," said the eldest

"Pease, mester," chanted the youngest.

"Please, mester," chanted the three above him.

So Tant had quickly to cut, trim and deliver a prickly sprig to each of the five. As soon as they had received them their interest in them ceased; they upturned their eyes again to Lois, the centre of attraction. Ripper chafing at inaction trampled the snow under his impatient hooves.

"Is your knife sharp?" she said.

"Pretty well. Would yo please to try it?"

She took the knife, cut a spray and trimmed it as he had done; then hesitated. She was afraid of the horse; but not so afraid as she seemed to be. She was conscious that the five pairs of blue eyes were fixed on her, wondering for which of them the flower was intended; but it was not that which made it so hard for her to lift her own. She was trying not to know whether a pair of grey eyes was on her and not to care; or rather not to seem to care. But she had the borrowed knife to return; of necessity, in mere honesty. She gave up the knife; and somehow with it in the same hand the sprig of gorse was left. That little lift of the eyes can hardly be counted; it was so timid, so uncertain, so momentary.

"Thank you."

Two meagre words; with only the emphasis of a strong man's gravity to make them weigh anything at all. He put the posy in his button-hole; she had hers in her hand under her mantle; the children had already forgotten theirs; they littered the snowy ground.

"The Frenchies shan't take it from me," he said, "whilst I live to defend it."

"We've got a baby under 'im," said the seven-or-eight-year-old. "'Er name's M'ria. She can say moo."

Lois looked down and smiled a quick smile; then looked up and the smile was gone.

"Oh, why did you?" she said in a low troubled voice.

"Will yo stan' still, colt? Ma'am, it behooved me to do it. It gies me a chance to coom back summat different. I ayther coom back different or I stay there."

The youngest but one had snuggled up against Lois's skirts, and was smoothing the pretty boa with a mottled hand. The seven-year-old slapped her arm and said:

"Bobaw, Sallay! Naughtay!"

In the moment of silence which ensued the persistent church-bell succeeded in capturing Lois's ear.

"I'd forgotten," she said. "I shall be late for church. Were you going, Mr. Rideout?"

No bell that was ever cast, of pure silver or the most cunning admixture, ever sounded so sweet an invitation.

"I *am* going, ma'am. I doubt where I'm bound there'll not be much plenty o' churches, but I'll never miss of a

Sunday afternoon if one's anyhow come-at-able. It'll mind me o' summat. I'd no intention, ma'am, of spoiling your walk, but this was the on'y road by which I *could* goo away. Now I've my hoss to dispose on. And it's not for such as me to be seen wi' such as yo. I hae been seen wi' yer of a Sunday afternoon i' yond street once." Pain stared from his face. His voice fell to the tone in which men question of life and death. "Ma'am, can watter wesh it away?"

"No."

"Can fire burn it out?"

She shook her head.

"The daub mun stick? Ay, it mun stick."

Again she shook her head.

"There is summat?"

She nodded her head. There was a tear in each of her eyes. She saw him through them. He seemed farther off, and yet nearer. As if at the invitation of her tears his own eyes filled and ran over. She must have seen so much, for she whispered:

"Yes, it is even so."

Five pairs of amazed blue eyes could not fix themselves either upon her or him but flitted from one to the other; and a busy buzz went to and fro among them, compounded of the loud twittering of their whispers and the low hissing of their eldest sister's hushes.

"She's cryin'."

"Sh! Sh!"

"An' 'e's cryin' an all."

"Sh! Sh!"

"She's 'urted 'ersen."

"Sh! Sh!"

"'E's lost 'is knife."

"Sh! Sh!"

Lois scattered one little smile over their flaxen polls – there was a good deal of April wet about it – and a sprinkling of the moist brightness fell on Tant.

"Tata, children," she said, and was answered by a chorus of tatas. She turned away; only then did Tant put foot in stirrup.

If there had been only the children she would have looked back once. She only looked back once as it was; at the same time that Tant looked back. There passed no sign between them; only the look. Next moment the colt dashed round Rooke's plantation; she could see nothing but the snowy road and the children pointing and looking after the vanished horseman. There was a passing touch of vanity in her next thought. She wished that he had enlisted in the Horse-Guards; she had seen their bravery in London. She carried the sprig of gorse under her mantle. The bell ceased tolling.

The colt romped round Clifty Nook, and Tant was so fortunate as to find Jackson's Jim dozing on his own hearthstone. So without more delay than the taking off of his greatcoat, and the delivering of it and the reins with the shortest of explanations into Jim's hands, he could hasten to church close upon Miss Skrene's steps. She was in the porch waiting until the clerk's squeaky "Lord's name be praised" should give signal to the congregation to shuffle to their feet. They stood there together for a minute in company with two or three more laggards. He wore his sprig of gorse in his coat, she carried hers under her cloak. On their entry into the church he would have turned humbly aside to where folk of no account sit in bare unbought seats, but one little finger of the hand that did not hold the gorse bade him follow her, and he had to follow. She made way at the pew door and let him pass in first. Everybody saw. Nobody was surprised. After Josh Jowers nobody could be surprised; not even Miss Wilkinson the independent lady, who had nothing to do except be surprised and account for it.

Yes, one was surprised, and that was Tant himself. He was in a sweet amaze, such as troubles a soul new-entered into Paradise and strange to its own self. He stood and he sat, and did not so much as know whether he stood or sat; only he knew that something was going on in the way of heavenly thanksgiving and his heart joined in with great pulsations.

> "All people that on earth do dwell,
> Sing to the Lord with cheerful voice;
> Him serve with fear, His praise forth tell,
> Come ye before Him and rejoice."

It was the second hymn. The familiar words and the familiar tune, the "Old Hundredth," and the sweet unfamiliarity of the voice – he heard but one voice – pierced the mist that obscured his happiness. He added his baritone to her tremulous treble, at first softly, tentatively, soon resolutely, strongly, now in unison, now in harmony, sustaining it, embellishing it.

> "The Lord ye know is God indeed,
> Without our aid He did us make;
> We are His flock, He doth us feed,
> And for His sheep He doth us take."

So they sang. The walls widened out, the people and the surpliced man disappeared; there was no roof between them and the sky.

It was only four verses. If it had been forty she would not have tired, so much did that other voice uphold hers. But the song ceased. The walls came back; the people reappeared, if mistily; the surpliced man mumbled a text. There was again a roof, but it had a skylight in it, through which came a glimpse of the outer sunshine.

The preacher's voice was like that of a man calling to another man on the distant hill-side. She was passionately fond of music; and that Tant could sing so tunefully gave a new delight to her, a fresh hope. She sat like one who has a strangely interesting book in his lap with many pages yet unturned. He has lifted his eyes, he has folded his hands and is musing of what he has read and what is yet to read.

By and by the preacher's voice came down from the hillside. She knew he was talking about Abraham and Isaac, which is all she ever knew about it. But she calmed down; the flutter of her hopes and fears ceased. I believe that for the time being, that short time being she was quite happy. She saw through the window in the roof; she regarded neither the past nor the future; she was as God is, who has only a present.

"Now unto God the Father, God the Son and God the Holy Ghost –" and so forth.

The transition, the bustle of uprising disturbed her as though she had been hustled out of the sanctuary into the street.

> "O God, our help in ages past."

It was now Tant's voice that called on hers, which made but a feeble response. The tune was "St. Ann," majestically major, with but that hint of the minor in it which human singing shall hardly escape; but her notes quavered, her thoughts wailed throughout. The time was so short. He heard her voice falter, and at the fifth verse fail altogether.

> "Time, like an ever-rolling stream,
> Bears all its sons away."

But he sang manfully on, unisonally, encouragingly, singing what he could not say, thinking what he could not sing.

> "O God, our help in ages past,
> Our hope for years to come."

And so to the last loud Amen! She was glad to drop on her knees. She seemed to lose herself there; she did not rise when the others did. Tant, feeling rather than seeing it, continued to kneel beside her. The other worshippers dribbled out; they remained hidden away in the high pew.

Only Miss Wilkinson scanned them over the door, as she went by, in thin-lipped displeasure. As she understood it, when the parson had pronounced the benediction God's audience was closed.

At last they were alone; preacher and preached-to, all had gone. Or perhaps there was the shuffling of some unseen clerk in some obscure corner. Then she rose and let him pass. The last rays of the setting sun whitened the memorial tablets on the wall in front of them. She put the prayer-book she had been using in his hand. She did not look at him, but her cloak opened and showed that she still held the little sprig of gorse. As soon as he had passed she sank to her knees again. He went forth softly, so that if it were possible she should not hear him going. He did not look back; he was a soldier already.

In the road the snow had already been trodden and denied by many feet. He saw Jack Whitehead and Nommer Brooks being led about brutally drunk, propped by a man at each elbow, with a half-mocking half-applausive rabble at their heels. His heart fled back to the still church and knelt beside Lois.

CHAPTER XXXI

VOX POPULI

ALL through February men were shut in between white earth and grey sky. Towards the end of the month Spettigew's wife died; the doctor said because of the extreme cold acting on a weak heart and low vitality; Spettigew said because the young witch was stronger than the old one. He had never shown his wife any tenderness while she lived; that did not hinder the gush of a tear or two at the grave, nor the proper funeral feeling, as of an interpolated and duller Sunday, for the rest of the day; until in the evening he went out and got drunk. During the whole of the ensuing week he was more or less drunk, "drownding his trouble," his easy-judging neighbours said and encouraged him to think. The neglected children, pinched with cold and hunger, cried for their mammy; for which he cuffed and cursed them at home, and betwixt pot and pot at the alehouse pitied them.

But his superstitious hate was much more persistent and deeper rooted than his pity, ranking next to thirst among the emotions of his mind. Like his thirst he felt it as much dry-lipped, hot-mouthed, red-eyed in the morning as when he oozed beer in the evening; a dull obscurely grounded passion, ineradicable, which might lie for years and years under the surface of action or might any day emerge at the up-push of opportunity. As well as his wife's death he laid his own debauchery, his children's famine at the door of Nell's witchcraft. His sluggish persistence made it the common topic of conversation, more even than conjecture upon the coming campaign, at the alehouses most frequented by him. These were the Barley Mow at the Bottoms and the Lay Cross inn already known to us. He preferred the former for drinking, the latter for getting drunk in. That is to say the Barley Mow sold better ale and lay near at hand, but had a sour landlord who reproved bad language and expected his guests to walk at ten o'clock. The Lay Cross hours were as loose as its morals; it refused nothing to purchase and found clean straw for the consummated customer. If Spettigew went straight thither from his supper at High Farm it was but a down-hill mile, and he had eluded the cry and the recollection of his children's wants; so thither of late he had chiefly resorted.

The ground was sealed up; there was little work doing; the resources and the tempers of the overseers of the poor were strained. And besides the general misery there was Timmy Jones, who had sprained his ankle so badly that for three whole weeks he had been able to crawl just so far as the Lay Cross and no further. He blamed Nell for it in preference to blaming his wife, who would have answered him. Jesse Limm had lost his best-loved little girl a while aback, and had always attributed it to unblamable diphtheria, until he was helped to see a woman's devilry in it; so he blunted his sorrow against his anger. Luke Meadows had been unlucky before Nell was born, he was unlucky still; that did not hinder; he could not have been madder against Nell if he had only last week chopped a finger off upon the block, like Sam Horsepool, the butcher's journeyman. But there came a time of night, nearer eleven than ten, when it appeared more and more probable that even the weather and the idleness of the plough were the work of hell-craft. Two or three old topers, Spettigew being one, never separated before it was not merely probable but proved. Every night and two or three times a night, Spettigew would tell in almost the same words, how he saw Nell gallop past his house in the dead of the night on a witch-horse, and how his wife worsened immediately.

"I warn't deceived; I gied 'er up from that very moment. But to mek sure safe I went to the wiseman at Suth'ell, an' he told me as she were witched. But 'e couldn't do noat for 'er, 'e said, 'twere too late, 'e said, 'twere growed too strong. I axed 'im who 'twere. "Twere the person as yo think it is,' 'e said. That's law-coort evidence, if I know oat about law. And now them poor little kids is left motherless." What with beer, what with pity, the man's eyes were wet. But immediately he hardened again into a threat. "See to't, mates; some o' yo'll be missin' 'ere coom next Febuary."

Each man looked uneasily round, as though perchance he might discover the fated by their faces.

"They say," said David Hardstaff, "as there's a unfailable sign of a witch. There were three witch-children at Bods'orth born of a birth; they smothered 'em i' th' bed-clo'es an' buried 'em together i' Bods'orth chutchyard. I've seed their graves; anybody can see 'em. They'd each on 'em a pap unner the left arm."

"What 'ud that be for?" asked Timmy.

"For the devil to soock at."

"Damn her!" said Luke, as much disgusted as if he beheld there and then the criminal meal.

"I'd fair warnin'," said Spettigew, "I will say that for 'er. She told me welly nigh two year agoo as she'd do me one. An' she hes. She's a truthteller."

"Hark at me, mates," said Jesse, and his face was white. "The Scriptur says, 'Thou shalt not suffer a witch to live.'"

"That's good Scriptur," said Spettigew; "it's the best Scriptur iver I heerd; it's just what I say mysen. Well, oad Moll Roideout were a proved witch, warn't she?"

"Ah," said a scattering of voices.

"Well, then, all we want to larn is, who did she pass it on to? Would she gie't away from the famly? Not likely."

"But," said Josh Jowers, "yo don't niver 'ardly heer tell o' sich a yoong witch."

"That's the wust on't. Most plazen looks to hae a down oad witch; that's noat out o' th' way, that een't. But when it cooms to haein' a yoong un like thisn, as can run an' ride an' raunge about, why, surries, yo might as well hae oad Nick hissen i' yer midst!"

Each man looked uneasily round to see if old Nick were in their midst.

"Rabbit 'er!" said Luke Meadows.

"I should like to gie 'er a taste o' Blid'orth laws," said Jesse Limm.

Said old Jimmy Squires, the whittaw's journeyman, very quietly from the corner where he was playing at cribbage with old Wilson:

"If so be she is sich as yo say – I've no opinion this-away or that-away mysen – but if so be she is I wouldn't let on as I knowed – if I did know. M, u, m, spells the same backwards as forrards, I'm to'd. M'appen she's a-listenin' now; m'appen not."

Each looked round on his companions collecting their fears from their faces.

"We shall know to-morrer," said Spettigew, but at a whisper. "Mark my words. We shall know to-morrer."

There was little more said that night; but they drank the more, and presumably thought the more. And the next day sure enough they heard that the farmer at Lindhurst had lost a cow of milk fever. Timmy Jones worked on his farm; the connection was obvious; especially after ten o'clock. And so night by night beer and talk heated their imaginations until the threat of "Blid'orth laws," a local name for the rough justice of Judge Lynch, began to take somewhat the shape of a purpose. Neddy Cliff, the oldest standard in the parish, remembered with an aged intermittent memory the trying of a witch in L pond. As she failed to drown she was burnt; her dying shriek drove Sal Swanwick out of her mind; but that was her last ill deed.

The weather was bitterly cold; the landlord's blazing fire

scorched their knees and left their backs out of doors; but such talk heated them through and through, and gave their ale a more fiery zest than anything the brewer put into it. And so they talked, kindling fear against fear, courage against courage, malice against malice, as men do. And the recent machine-breaking disorders seemed to bring violence nearer to their intentions than otherwise it would have been.

With a shift of the wind to south-west the six weeks' frost came to an end at last. The white vanished from the hillsides, the brown and dirty green appeared. Every furrow was brimming full, every ditch running over; the scanty dribble which divided the Low Farm from the High became a small river and threatened for a few hours to flood the house. And in that muggy drizzly vaporous unhealthy season old Wilson fell down dead of fatty degeneration of the heart. Old Wilson had sat and drunk night by night at the Lay Cross inn, sat and drunk and played cribbage, and just nodded perhaps twice in a long night when a safe thing was said. It was plain to the company at the Lay Cross, that if he were taken there was no security for anybody being left. It was not only thought it was said again and again.

The following evening Arthur Skrene came through the front gate into the road just as Coy and Spettigew issued at the back. The thrasher stood, Spettigew turned down in the direction of Lay Cross. Now the more he drank and talked by night the less he ate and talked by day, and the farmer suspected that all was not well with his odd-man. He was for shuffling past with the gruffest of good-nights, but his master stopped him by saying:

"You seem to be going a long way round, my man, to your home and children."

"I've got to call at the Cross for a hatchet as Gill promised to len'me."

"Mind you don't cut yourself with it."

"Ah."

And Spettigew shuffled off. The old thrasher stood at the back gate looking down the road after him. Skrene went up to him and said:

"What makes you shake your head so solemnly, Father Coy?"

"The little there's in't, mester; just what makes a blether waggle so i' th' wynd."

"But your head isn't always shaking."

"An' a blether's sometimes still. Mester, when a man o' my fine leanness can't tek the measure of a man o' his brede o' belly" – his finger pointed down the road after Spettigew's broad back – "I mun gie up vauntin' mysen to be a witty man."

"You think there's something unaccountable in Spettigew's behaviour?"

"Mester, I've ne'er been friendly wi' another man's wife, I'm not likely to meddle wi's important consarns. Good-night."

He hobbled a few steps on his thin bandy legs, stopped and turned.

"Accordin' to Scriptur God made man an' then makled woman up out'n the waste. One more or one less i' th' world o' her sect's noat ayther to be glad at or mad at."

He again made as if going, again turned, measured the distance with his eye and seemed to think it too great, came half-way back, and again opened his narrow slit of a mouth and pitched his pipy voice.

"If I were any kin to Rideouts' Nell, I suld want to know if I were down in 'er will."

"Why?"

"So's I could set my face according-lye."

"What do you mean?"

"Ax me to-morrer, mester."

"To-morrow may be too late."

"If a man says oat an's fun' out his own meanin' by to-morrer, it's rayther soon nor late."

The dry toothless slit of his mouth closed again as if for the night, he turned finally and hobbled off up the road. What he had said seemed to Arthur like that mockery of a light which suggests snares and pitfalls to the night-walker, but without the precision which would enable him to avoid them.

"How restless you are, dear, to-night!" said Lois anxiously. "Does your leg feel worse?"

"Quite the contrary, Loie. I think the exercise is doing it good."

For every now and then he would be going to the door and peering forth into the dark drizzly night; or he would draw aside the curtain of that little westerly window which looked towards Low Farm; as though any danger which might be impending over it could by strain of eyesight be read in the black page spread out before him.

"To-morrow!" he kept saying to himself. "To-morrow I'll either know more or care less."

That same night nearer eleven than ten by the clock a band of men whose identity the night muffled, five or it might be six of them, for they were not distinctly countable, issued soaked in alcoholic courage from the Lay Cross inn, determined to put a stop to sudden death and cow-ailments in Blidworth at all events. There was a dog too but he was sober, and unheard as well as unseen; not so much as a sniff telling whether he led or followed. One of the men carried an iron crow; he felt rather than thought – felt as though the cold iron spoke to his hot hand – that it would be useful either to weight a drowning or forestall one. But they schemed no contrivance; drunk or sober they were not capable of any; what part of their intention was not mere bludgeonry was mere memory.

They followed their thoughts, which made straight for a small piece of water hard by called Archer's Water. It was ordinarily a mere shallow widening-out of the upper beck, there augmented by fresh springs, but it had been swollen by the thaw to something more than a horse-pond. The low ground adjacent was marshy in wet weather with its oozings, and was called the Bogs. It was a cloudy night and the air was full of a soft drizzle; but there was just enough light to make a sullen difference between wet and dry and to divide the men that moved from the bushes that stood. Down-stream there was the harsh clamour now and again of water-fowl. Splash! splosh! The man with the crow-bar seemed to be sounding the depth of the water. There were muttered speeches, the utterers undistinguishable.

"It een't above two foot an' a hafe."

"It's three."

"It's fower furder in."

"Two an' a hafe 'll sarve – wi' a bit o' humouring."

"I once pulled one o' their ship out o' the Bugs for 'em. Gash me if I'd a done it if I'd knowed!"

It was a recollection which served them better than their collective imagination could have done.

CHAPTER XXXII

BY ARCHER'S WATER

IN the stillness of the night a man stood under Nell Rideout's window, and with a long wand wrenched from one of the willows by the brook tapped at it until she awoke.

"What's the matter?"

"One of your yowes hes got bugged i' the Bugs."

"Why didn't yo fetch her out?"

"The watter's too deep an' I hedn't no lantern."

"How d'yer know it's ourn?"

"There een't non others nigh'and. Skrene's is all on tunnips t'other side the roäd."

"Anyhow it's somebody's ship. David, een't it?"

The answer was slow and sullen.

"What's that to yo or the yowe?"

"I know it is."

The retort was quicker, but still sullen:

"Then why d'y' ax?"

She did not attempt to say; she closed the casement and hurriedly dressed, thinking only of a poor sheep's distress. The proper place for suspicion, parasitical spy that it is, is behind a man's shoulder. Those who look back often see it often; to the true, the brave, the straight-looking it appears seldom and late. In a few minutes she came forth with a lighted lantern in one hand and a sheep-hook in the other,

"Gi' me the lantern to carry," said the man. She delivered it to him. He held it so that as little light as possible fell upon his own person. Being discovered he made a sham security out of not being seen. The grass squished beneath their feet like a full sponge. In each hollow was a pool, which Nell leapt resting on her sheep-hook; the man splashed stolidly through them and filled his shoes with cold water. A peewheep, disturbed by the sound of their passing, uttered his loud wail, which was answered by others of his restless kind. The lantern cast a sprinkling of light on the colourless grass, gnawn turnips or glimmering water just before their feet. Once and again a ewe got up out of their way and baaed for her lamb. A sheep-bell tinkled intermittently, warning off the fox.

"Yo were at Lay Cross, I suppose?" said Nell, as they trudged down-hill to the Bogs.

"Ah. I heerd 'er blart an' I went."

"I don't hear noat."

"Nayther don't I, now."

"Well, David, be't our ship or no, we're beho'den to yer."

The man grunted; it might be taken either for modesty or surliness.

"It's dark," said Nell.

"Ah," said the man.

"The weather's very slack."

"Ah."

They were pushing their way among the dank ling and bracken that bordered the Bogs. Nell stood, and screening her eyes with her hands vainly strove to pierce the hedge of darkness.

"I don't see no ship," she said.

"Nayther don't I," said the man.

"Where is she?"

"This-away."

They almost trod on a partridge which whirred blindly off into the dark.

"I can't hear noat on 'er," said Nell.

"Nayther can't I."

They had got round to the pool. For a yard or two before them and beside them the lantern showed the bleached feathers of the tall reeds, the black treachery of the water.

Nell did not see that shapeless shadows were closing in upon her, back and sides; but presently she did hear the stumbling of a heavy foot against a tussock.

"That's no ship," she said, and stopped to listen.

Her conductor opened the lantern and with horny forefinger and thumb nipped out the flame.

"Why hae yer done that?" she said, and instinctively put herself apart.

Then all at once the shadows became obscurely visible to her as moving bushes. She started away, but as she did so the man David snatched at her hook. She wrenched it free, with the iron end dealt him a stunning blow over the head, then darted off again. But the moving bushes, now appearing limbed something like the ghosts of men, were behind and on either hand of her, the water was in the front. She doubled back – David had not yet recovered his wits – and as she ran between two of the pursuing shapes, she brandished her weapon to keep them off. One of them was slow and out of reach; the other more active was hit, but idly above the elbow, and the blow delayed herself more than him. He pressed on, he stretched his hand out, he all but had her; but reaching forward too eagerly he slipped on the slimy ground, struggled to keep his footing, caught his toe in the roots of a gorse bush and fell all his length. She seemed to have escaped. Hitherto there had been no sound but of the runners' running muffled by the coarse herbage and of the quick labour of their breathing.

But as she made for the higher ground she heard a low whistle behind her, and almost immediately felt a weight upon her activity, something that clung to her gown, heavy, voiceless, tenacious, that would not be shaken off. She reasoned rather than saw that it was a dog. She could not tear herself loose. Her pursuers were coming up. She leant back over her right shoulder – it was no time for compunction – she shortened her hold of the hook, she smote once, she smote twice, she smote thrice. At the third smiting instead of a dull thud something cried crack! the weight fell from her gown, and the air was filled with the squeals of a dog-agony. But again pursuit was closing in on her, and the ground before her was much encumbered with the wild growths of the moor. She hurled the sheep-hook with all her might at the nearest of her besetters; it hit him full in the body and checked him for the moment. She gathered her skirts in both her hands and flew obliquely down towards the smoother but moister margin of the Bogs.

She was the master of any of them at running; she increased her distance; a voice in the background, much like Spettigew's, was heard cursing her for a doubly-qualified witch. The dog's shrieks did not cease. But in the darkness she ran into the upper and narrower end of the Bogs. Being in she had to keep on and make the best of her way across it. It was only some thirty yards, but her shoes sank deep in the slimy bottom, the icy water was about her knees and her progress was slow. Meanwhile her assailants had hastened round the head of the marsh, and just as she regained the firm ground, one of them dashed forward and with the sheephook hooked her by the leg as a sheep is hooked. She fell helplessly to the ground. When she rose she was held by each arm in a substantial grasp, and moreover two substantial shapes confronted her, men, not flying soulless bits of the night; bad men it was to be feared.

"What d'yer want wi' me?" she said.

"A damned witch like yo," said one of those in front, whom she immediately knew to be Spettigew, "suld know wi'out tellin'."

She feared then what she feared most, and cried out:

"Kill me, men, kill me! Hae some marcy! Kill me!"

"Why don't nubbudy shut yon yawpin' mongrel up," said one at her elbow; "we shall hae the keepers down on's."

"He's gone hissen," said another man.

And indeed just at that moment the fearful dog-shrieks gave way to mere self-pitying discontinuous yelps; while

Nell was still protesting:

"Kill me, kill me! For God's sake kill me! And I'll thank yer."

"That's just what we're agate on, yo black-hearted varmin," said Spettigew.

Then when death was the fear before her she feared death.

"Why would yer kill me?"

"Becos yo're nubbut a damned witch; that's why."

"I'm no such thing."

"Yo're a damned ligger."

"I ain't that nayther. I'm no witch, men; I never tho't o' such a thing; believe me, men, I ain't."

"Yo witched my Hannah, yo she-devil," said Spettigew; "that's what she died on."

"I never did; she'd been swaling as long's I can remember."

"Yo witched our little lass," said a more passionate, less brutal voice; "an' she's dead."

"I never did – is't yo, Jesse Limm? – I liked the little lass."

"Yo've witched a many a'ready," said he at her elbow whom she had called David, "and yo'd a witched uz if we hedn't gotten aforehand on yer."

"No, no, I never did and I never suld! I never did, believe me, and I never suld!"

"Yo're a rotten devil!" said Jesse.

"How much longer shall's stop 'ere argy-bargyin'?" said David. "It's as long as a fun'ral sarvice, this is."

He pulled at her arm; his head was still sore with the knock it had gotten; the others closed in and hustled her along to the water-side. The dog's yelps had diminished to a whimper. The water seemed more devilishly terrible for the blackness that hid it, making of the inconsiderable pool a bottomless pit.

"Are yo gooing to drownd me?" she said.

"If so be yo can drownd."

"And if I can't drownd?"

"Then I'll cauve yer heäd in wi' this," said a fifth man who had just come up and carried the crowbar.

She turned her face hillwards, she drove her voice forth at its extremest pitch and force; it cleft the air like the far-reaching scream of a sea-gull.

"Help! Arthur! Arthur Skrene! Help! They're killing me!"

One man struck her over the lips; blood filled her mouth. Another clutched her by the throat.

"We'll shall hae to founder along, mates," said Spettigew. "She's summonsed 'im an' he'll coom; sure as fate he'll coom."

They dragged her a few yards further; their usage was of the roughest.

"It's deepest here," said one.

And there they stopped. Hurriedly they threw her down and began to tie her legs together and her arms. The hand that compressed her windpipe must have been relaxed for a moment, for she managed to say in a hoarse whisper close to the ear of one of them:

"Suld yo like your Peg, Olf Roberts, to be i' my place?"

The man let go his hold. The naming of him seemed to bring daylight to his deed. He uttered a low hoarse laugh. Then he fumbled again at the cord he was binding about her wrists. Nell's throttle was again gripped; she gasped for breath close to his ear.

"This is a damned long co'd way o' dyin'," said the same man with the same sort of ashamed laugh. "Een't there no other road o' judgin' on 'er? quicker? an' warmer?"

"Rip 'er smock off," said Spettigew – he was at her feet – "an' see if there een't a pap unner 'er arm. If there een't yer may drownd me."

The man at her wrists rent away the kerchief that was about her neck. The action jogged the hand that throttled her speech and loosened its hold.

"Let me be, man!" said Nell fiercely. "Yo're free to drownd

me, on'y drownd me decent. I'll die quiet; I'll nayther say nor do."

"She's axed uz to drownd 'er," said Spettigew; "yo're all witnesses. It een't manslaughter howsumdever, for she's axed uz. That's the law. All ready? Now then! Ketch ho'd of 'er shou'ders, yo two. Heave 'er up. Now, lads!"

The hand was off her throat, but she uttered no cry. There was a great quiet, even the dog's whine had died away. The water was black on her right hand.

"One!"

By leg and arm they swung her to and fro to give impetus to the cast.

"Two!"

To and fro they swung her.

"Three!"

Their muscles were already as train for the effort.

"What are you doing?"

The cords of their muscles were relaxed; for another voice put the question, another shape stood beside them, within touch, as though it had suddenly taken form there condensed from the black air, or had sprung out of the ground.

"What are you doing?"

"Hooray for Blid'orth law!" said one of the ruffians at her head. "Who are yo? Play slingy wi' 'er, lads. Doin' what yo wain't balk uz on; so ayther gie's a hand or stan' aside out o' the gate."

"Is that you, Nell? Why don't you speak?"

But the promise was on her tongue.

"Is she dead? Have you murdered her? You shall account for this."

"Yo talk big for a little un," said the same man – it was David, and his head was sore – "but she een't murdered – yit – if yo call lawing murder. She don't speak becos she's owned to being a witch, an' furder speech 'ull nayther save nor sauve 'er."

"Yo lie!" cried Nell; "I'd gied my word. I'm no witch, Mr. Skrene; though that's why they're drownding me. I'm no witch."

"Sling 'er off, lads. Finish what we've begun on."

"Stop!" said Arthur. "If you murder this woman" – he was so near that he could put his hand on her – "you must also murder me, or else you put a halter round your own necks."

"Stay!" cried Nell. "Hae some pity! I'm a dying woman; don't dishearten me. Why suld yo too die afore your time?"

But he had found one of her hands and did not let it go. "Spettigew!"

At his sudden naming, as though it had been a blow, Spettigew dropped his share of the burden and fell back.

"If this woman dies I witness against you; against all of you. Beware of me, I've a good memory; I shall make an excellent witness."

"B'leddy, but yo shan't witness again me!" said David.

He let go his hold, and the girl's body slipped through the other two men's hands to the ground.

"Damn thee, wheer beesta?"

He was groping about among the rank grass for something. Arthur had dropped on one knee so as not to lose his possession of Nell's hand.

"I'm a dying woman, Arthur Skrene," said Nell; "this is my death-ruttle; gie me my dying comfort; save yoursen."

"I know no other way. If it fails I've done my best."

"Tek care o' yoursen!" she cried, and at the same time struggled violently to lift herself up; but her bonds mastered her, she fell back panting.

For David had found what he was searching for, and now stood over Arthur with the iron bar poised for a deadly blow.

"I lay this to cure any blab-tongue," he said.

But his aim was balked, for Spettigew hung on to his right arm hampering it.

"I wain't hae't," said Spettigew; "the man's none to blame. She's witched 'im an' all; which I've misdoubted it this long while."

"It's false, Mr. Skrene!" protested Nell. "Yo've noat again me. I never witched nobody; yo least of all, least of all yo."

"Stop your chap!" said Spettigew. "D'yer think I'm your day-man still? But he's not i' fault; I wain't stan' by an' see 'im touched."

The other men seemed to waver.

"We moan't goo too fur," muttered one of them.

"Yo hain't the heart in yer of a fuzz-ball," said David, and wrenched his striking arm loose. "Stan' by then an' let me do."

"Posh is deäd."

It was only Josh Jowers who had tottered down to them, but his unnoticed coming and funereal words seemed to shake to the ground what still remained of their criminal courage. David dropped the crow-bar.

"Posh is deäd. See! An' I'm sober." It could be seen that he carried a dim lifeless something in his arms. His tongue stuttered and his knees shook under him.

"Downraight sober! What hae we been agate on? Dal me if I remember oat. Summat i' th' nettin' line? But it's too cloudy for oat o' that. I get sore mixed up when I'm sober."

"Good-evening, Mr. Jowers," said Arthur, still on one knee.

"Good-evenin', sir," said Josh, more mixed up than ever. "Posh is a corp; I'm dead sober."

"Here are some of your friends, who are also I believe soberer than they were; but perhaps none the worse for that. Men, as far as I'm concerned I promise that this night's work shall rest, if you carry it no further. I've as good a memory for forgetting as for remembering; I've begun to forget already. I hope you won't disturb the process. Has one of you a knife on him?"

A knife was put into his hand. He carefully cut the cords

that bound Nell; then helped her to her feet. At a little distance was a huddled cluster of shadows, guessably other than the dark background of the hill; but it vanished before it was certainly distinguishable. They were alone. They walked by the dark water-side together. "This een't your way," said Nell.

"No, but it's yours."

A little further and Arthur kicked against a fallen lantern and picked it up.

"Thank yer," said Nell; "it's mine."

"Take care of it, Nell; don't let the men singe its horn with candles fitted awry, nor batter its frame out of shape against the stable door. Its light first made me suspect mischief; and afterwards the fearful howling of that dog. I should like to beg it for myself."

"Take it, Mr. Skrene. Any thanks I could gie, any reward I could offer, would seem as poor by this sarvice; so take it."

Her voice was troubled, which would have been remarkable in so strong-nerved a person but for the terrible experience she had just undergone. It had recovered however when she added:

"Your gainest road would yet be by the Cross."

"I'm a little lame yet, Nell, as you perceive, and I lost my stick jumping the beck; should you mind lending me your arm as far as your door?"

"Furder if need be."

They walked on together, his right arm in her left, so that he could feel her heart thumping against her side. The drizzly darkness was as a wall between them and the world; of which the intermittent tinkle of a sheep-bell, the cough of one asthmatic old ewe was the only rumour. They walked slowly, and spoke no word.

But when they were going down to the house, then Arthur said:

"One thing surprises me, Nell, and only one."

"Ay?"

"That you should let yourself be caught at such a disadvantage by such pitiful contrivers."

"I were never one to pike round a busk for bogies."

"For you are a witch, Nell Rideout, say what you will."

"How can yer say so, Mr. Skrene? Oh, how can yer? Yo know it's not so. It's anything but so."

"Spettigew says you are."

"Spettigew! It behooves such as yo to be above quoting such as him. His name's not proper company for your mouth, Mr. Skrene."

"Then you deny that you have witched me?"

"How can yer? Of course I deny't. I never witched nobody, never nobody. Indeed, indeed I'm not a witch! Could a woman be a witch wi'out knowing on't?"

"It would almost appear so. For there's proof besides that unmentionable brute's affirmation; you called me and I came."

"But I'm not a witch."

"In the very nick of time too."

"I'm not a witch."

"But why did you call and I come? Why did you call, Nell? call me, Arthur Skrene? I wasn't even aware you knew my name was Arthur."

"E'erybody has a Christian name."

"Christian names being so common why did you favour mine? High House was further off than Low Farm."

The answer was slow a-coming.

"I tho't m'appen yo weren't such a heavy sleeper as our Tish."

"Was that your only reason?"

Nell stopped in the middle of a puddle and said fiercely:

"If yo call me that again I'll –" But all at once her bold tone failed her. "I suld never ha' tho't that yo – yo least of all, least of all!"

She went on again. Dark was the night, endless the drizzle.

"I wunner yo walk wi' me, thinking as yo do on me."

"Well, letting that go, there's the second query: Why did I come?" In that low-lying part the ground squished underfoot like a full sponge. "You neither ask nor answer; it does not interest you."

"There's a ship-hook of ourn left by the side o' the Bugs."

"I'll send Charley for it in the morning. But perhaps you already know why?"

Nell neither assented nor denied.

"In that there would again be a suspicion of black art."

"It's too bad on yer!"

"Well, *I* haven't told you."

"Tell me."

For Nell the request was remarkably timid and low-voiced. And yet her heart beat more strongly than ever against his hand.

"It is late and you are tired and here's the door, and the answer is one of some length and difficulty; it must be until we meet again. But I won't forget that you've asked me."

They stood and his arm was drawn from hers.

"I hope," said Nell, "yo wain't suffer for this. Let me goo all the way with yer – just a little o' the way with yer; I'm none tired."

"Thank you, Nell Rideout, but until your character is cleared I mustn't use your company more than I am obliged."

"Oh what a man, what a man! What a hard man!"

"If you will lend me a hooked stick and put a candle in my lantern I shall manage well enough; and not suffer in reputation."

Nell brought him a stick and put a light in the lantern.

"There's a plank across the beck now," she said.

"For Lois's convenience? Yes, I know. By the bye what shall you do about those miscreants?"

"Yo've gien your promise."

"My promise doesn't bind you."

"Don't it? Then I choose to be bound."

"I half repent of my undertaking; they may make another attempt, the villains."

"Happen they may."

"You're a brave girl, Nell!"

"Me? Nay; I was sore afeard down by yon watter. While yo came. But it seems as if noat could frighten yo, it really does."

"If it seems so to you, Nell, it only shows how well I can cover up."

They stood silent awhile, she on the doorstep, he on the doorstone; which gave her a great advantage in height. The candle illuminated a pair of miry shoes and a drab woollen skirt from its bedraggled hem to where one strong hand hung against it. It was disordered and besoiled, and had a wide rent at the knee which showed something of a dark-blue knitted petticoat beneath. Behind her the interior of the house was impenetrably black. Her other hand rested on the doorjamb high up. She had reason to believe that her thoughts and features were as secret as though they were locked in. Suddenly, unfairly, he lifted the lantern, taking her face by surprise, capturing the expression of her eyes; there were tears in them, tears on her cheeks. The red rushed to her face; she fled within doors.

CHAPTER XXXIII

SPILT MILK

SPETTIGEW came to work next morning in good time but with a hang-dog demeanour.

"A word with you, Spettigew," said his master to him.

He led him out of the yard to the grass close beyond, where he could put, besides the bole of a giant oak, what the fire had left of two rows of great stacks, white corn, black corn and hay, between themselves and Well's curiosity. First he returned him the knife which he had borrowed the night before, saying:

"Do you expect any thanks for it?" Spettigew did not answer; his downcast eyes vaguely searched the grass at his feet, as for something which he did not look to find. "Well, thank you. And while I'm thanking you, there's an iron crow in the barn which Charley found this morning by the Bogs; I'll thank you to return it to its owner."

Said Spettigew gruffly, with difficulty, "Yo've allus bin a man o' yer word, mester. So I telled *them.*"

"Much obliged for the testimonial."

"David said –"

"No names, if you please."

"'E said as a man's promise wouldn't bear the stress of a man's weight; a helter would. 'E's off full-drive to Nottingham to 'list i' th' King's army. 'E reckons they wain't waste hemp on a hable-bodied sojer so long's there's so much plenty o' lead."

Spettigew's eyes were fixed for the time being on the hassock of coarse grass which he was pecking at with his toes. "That's all very well for a come-day-go-day chap like him, but when a man's sattled 'e'd as lieve hang as flit. I've my kids, fower on 'em; Jesse's hisn, five or six; an' Olf –"

"No names, I say."

"He married Slater's Peg last back-end. We ho'd by yer promise, mester."

"And what of Miss Rideout?"

Spettigew at length lifted his lowering brows.

"If she swears we mun swear again 'er; we're five to one."

"Five to two, Spettigew. You forget that if she chooses to subpoena me the law will compel me to give evidence, willy-nilly."

"Then we're done!"

"Neither done nor undone, unless so you will. Miss Rideout is mercifully inclined to let by-gones be by-gones. I expect you to trust her and show yourselves sensible of her high generosity."

Spettigew's evasive eyes were on the ground again.

"If she means to she will, and if she don't mean to she wain't; there een't a woman i' the hull world more of 'er own way o' thinkin'."

"About the future then; she and I require of you that you never enter the Lay Cross again. It is too distant for you to get conveniently drunk there."

"I don't want to, if that's all; Gill's beer een't worth belly-room."

"Moreover you must understand that in these degenerate times witches have their rights just as much as farmers and labourers. It's the same murder to kill one of them as to kill a sempstress. It may be wrong; but that's the law. I don't mean Blidworth law."

"A fool's law an' all," muttered Spettigew.

"Perhaps; it is true that the law is made for fools; anyhow it's a law, Spettigew, that must be obeyed. You quite understand?"

"Ah! I've gien it up. She's too strong for's, I see that; we shall hae to play butty. She's witched yer, mester, true as I'm 'ere. Wish yo may niver repent on't."

"You speak like yourself, Spettigew – as usual."

"Yo'll tek yer own roäd, I know."

"Well, Spettigew, to take one's own road and repent, there's something exhilarating about that, exhilarating at the commencement and not despicable at the close; but to repent of taking somebody else's road, Spettigew, is satisfactory neither at this end nor that, but altogether weak, flat, empty and contemptible."

Spettigew went away as much impressed as if he had understood all that had been said to him. He had never seen Mr. Skrene look quite so alertly confident in himself or differ with quite so overmastering an indifference to the difference.

"What did 'e want wi' yer?" said Wells to him.

"To tell me as 'e'd a mind to do as 'e'd a mind, an' be danged to me."

"Ah?"

"An' be danged to him, so I think 'e will."

"I suldn't wunner," said Wells; "'e's allus bin very mooch that way o' thinkin'."

"He is this mornin' more nor ever; I think he'd turn the wynd round to his likin'; so y'ad better ger on wi' muckin' out yer hosses."

And yet Arthur Skrene had suffered a sore disappointment that very morning. From a knoll on his own land out of which there grew one stunted oak, he could get a view of the greater part of the pasturage which the Low Farm milch cows were then grazing, and particularly of the gate to which they were driven to be milked. He had taken his stand there as soon as it was light enough to tell a white cow from a red. They had ceased to feed and stood about the gate lowing for the milker. The milker came and set her stool and piggin under a black and white Welsher. But it was not Nell; he turned away before she had put head to flank and hand to teat.

For six days he did the like and still Nell did not appear. He might have gone down to the house and seen her to the prosaic accompaniment of pot and pan, chair and table, but he would not. It she had been kept in by anything serious he would have heard from Lois, who often visited the Rideouts. On the seventh morning she came. For all his impatience he waited until she had done milking; he would not have her attention divided between himself and a red smooth-skinned Leicestershire or a black rough-coated Welsher. A cold dry east wind had been blowing for the last three or four days, driving the mists from the air, licking up the superabundant moisture from the ground; now it had veered to the south and its gentle wafture beckoned spring along. The crescent moon and her attendant planet still shone in the sky but their influence had paled before the coming sun. The hills in front of him and the woods that crowned them, dense larch, bare oak and beech were clearly defined. The smoke from the house chimneys was gently dispersed without rout. The grass at his feet showed the green through the brown; the purple osiers along the brook were bursting into bud; a blue-cap was singing, "zitter-zitter zee-zee," in the tree over-head; the rooks were incessant, coming and going.

But at last he could see that Nell had finished milking; one by one the three cows had returned to their pasture, she was starting for home and he went down the slope to meet her. But he did not gulp his delight; he was epicure rather than glutton. It was for this he had waited, putting so stringent a restraint upon himself the night of the rescue. He was not content to hear and touch and know unless he should also see. He stopped on the hither side of the close next the meadow, stopped and sat down on the crooked bole of an old thorn-tree and waited. The sun was just flashing over the brow of the hill before him. Stars and planet had disappeared; the moon, shorn of her attendance, was a mere ornament in the sky, little more luminous than the fleecy clouds that here and there dappled the blue-grey. He had the delight of seeing her before she saw him. Her path for the time being lay obliquely to him and her eyes were directed straight forwards. The smock-frock and men's gaiters in which he had first seen her come from the milking had been exchanged for a primrose-coloured bodice and panniers above a short russet skirt, which left at least half a foot of dark blue stocking showing. She had a hood on her head of a lighter blue, and additional warmth was given to her robust shoulders by a woollen kerchief, red checked with black. Her shoes were raised above the dewy grass by pattens, which like ancient cothurni gave imposing height to her else unusual stature. Her gait was weighted a little by her burden, but was still too youthfully strong and free for comparison with the tragic tread of the Athenian stage. In one hand she bore her stool, in the other the one-eared piggin into which she had milked. The large wooden kit upon her head, magnificently poised, swayed with her body as though it were part of it.

But that sideways partial view of her soon came to an end. When her path met the brook she had to swerve a little to the right, which brought her face to face with him at some fifty yards' distance. The radiant sun was exactly over her head; she was in the shadow of the hill, but shielding his eyes with his hands he saw her perfectly well, backed by the sunless brown of a ploughed field. And she saw him. Immediately her face was one trouble of reds. Still she came on at an unvarying pace, but her cheeks showed red upon red, accumulatively red, and her eyes were as though they were wet with brightness.

Soon she advanced out of the shadow and into the shine. The polished hoops of the kit on her head, the piggin in her hand shone like silver. And still as she approached she came more and more into line with the sun, and he found it increasingly difficult to separate her many-coloured excellence from the white glory of the luminary behind her.

Until at last the two were merged; milk-pail, blue hood, crimson cheeks, bright eyes, floating hair were wrapped up in the indistinguishable blaze. He was dazzled and awed, but continued to gaze. So perhaps, in such a concealing light, a dread enwrapping a love, appeared the angel to Hagar by the fountain in the wilderness, by the fountain in the way to Shur; so perhaps to Manoah and his wife by the rock in the field, or to Gideon under the oak of Ophrah. But why talk we of angels? They do not visit us now by day, only by night, hardly in a cloudy dream; before we can say lo! we are awake.

Nell was close at hand. She did not swerve from her going nor lessen her stride, but the fixity of Arthur's gaze confused her understanding, troubled her eyesight. At last she cried out:

"Don't look at me so! Yo balk me."

But before the words were complete she had struck the iron ring of her patten against a tuft of grass; the check threw her head forward and marred her balance; she could not drop what her hands held in time to steady the tottering pail. Down it fell splash! Arthur's thoughts and eyes fell from a great height to the ground. He could see nothing at first, but by degrees amid the lessening number of little black clouds that swam in the air he saw the overturned kit, the milk whitening the browngreen grass, Nell's dismay.

"Never mind," he said; "we've plenty of milk at High Farm to replace it."

"Do yo think Tish wouldn't tell the difference? She would at a gleg."

"Is yours better?"

"It's different."

"Are you afraid of Tish?"

"No more nor yo'd be."

"Well, I'll go with you; it's only fair."

He picked up the empty kit.

"Gie't to me," said Nell.

"Allow me."

"I couldn't think on't."

"Well, we'll both carry it."

So it was; they put into it piggin, stool and the roll which Nell had worn to ease her head of its pressure, then went towards the house bearing it between them, each holding one of its upright ears with finger and thumb. The soft breeze blew directly in their faces cooling them deliciously. The short grass along their path was emerald hoary with the shimmer of the dew, although on either side the coarser wintry herbage was still brown and yellow. From the willows by the brook a throstle began to sing that was not singing before. The sun was now sovereign both of sky and earth. The mixing of crimsons which had left Nell's face at the disaster to the milk returned; but Arthur could not see whether her eyes were still as bright. What their lids and long lashes did not hide was seen only by the grass and the rare daisies that flecked it. She might have been counting them. So they walked gently swinging the kit between them rhythmically with their stepping; and the breeze was as coolly sweet to their hot brows as the difference between love and friendship.

Half-way to the house Arthur said, "Do you very much mind?"

"Not so very."

"Neither do I."

That was all that was said; only under the corner of the house, before they should turn it and pass through the gate into the yard, Arthur hung back. The gentle check to Nell's right hand naturally brought her left round a little towards him. He seized it. They were face to face. Slowly the curtains lifted and showed the full orbs of her eyes to his. Her lips were cherry red.

"Nay," she said; "somebody's looking."

But he had received her look, and it went through him with the stab of a poignant sweetness. They turned together into the yard.

"Don't be far behint," Nell whispered, as she opened the door.

There was in her countenance that self-consciousness which always attracts the attention it shuns. Tish was on her knees doing the hearth up, but her eyes were instantly on Nell.

"What ever's gotten the milk?" she cried. "It's not tithe mornin'."

She looked unusually large-bodied, loud-voiced, fierce-tempered, as she rose and went towards Nell, brush in hand.

"I've spilt it," said Nell.

"Spilt it? Yo gret – All on't?"

"Ay, all."

"Yo left-handed lommox! Who ever heerd tell? Spilt it? Yo thing! All the milk? What next I wunner?"

She did not or would not see Arthur, who had already slipped into line with Nell.

"I beg your pardon, Mrs. Gillott," he said; "it was my fault entirely."

"Then yo shall pay for't."

"I will, with pleasure."

"Then yo shan't, with pleasure."

Her keen eyes were taking them both in; she advanced two paces upon Nell, a movement that in itself had the appearance of a menace.

"A hull meal o' milk might be a trifle, Nell Rideout!" she said, but nothing like so fiercely as she had threatened.

She looked from Nell to Arthur, from Arthur to Nell, keenly. They bore the scrutiny with some fortitude.

"Tell me, our Nell," she said; "hae yo spilt noat beside the milk this mornin'?"

Nell gave Arthur a half-look but did not answer; Arthur gave Nell a whole look, but said not a word.

"What's all this arley-parleying about?" said the grandam from the chimney-nook. "I ain't very light o' hearin' this mornin'; yo mun speak up."

Nell crossed the floor, Arthur by her side. Tish stood looking on, still with the brush in her hand.

"I've spilt the milk, granmam," she said.

"Welladay! What a sour mishap!" cried the old dame, lifting each skinny hand.

Nell went nearer, so that she needed not to speak so loud, Arthur still by her side.

"And I've gotten a sweetheart," she said, no louder than she needed to speak, her face like a rose.

"Well, that's amends, that's amends indeed. If so be it's the raight quallity o' sweetheart."

Arthur's right hand was by Nell's left, just touching it; she took and laid it in her grandmother's. The old woman's skinny fingers closed about it,

"But thisn's a gentleman's hand," she cried, "not a farmer's!"

"Indeed I am a farmer, grandmother," said Arthur; "and with your consent I would make Nell a farmer's wife."

"And a good farmer too," said Nell; "though he has summat to larn about the management of our light forest land."

"You'll teach me, Nell," said Arthur.

"Skegs'll grow where noat else will," said Nell, "and they're unaccountable good for cows i' th' straw." Again she addressed the old woman. "Still he's a main good farmer. I never seed a better crop o' tunnips nor that on Three Oak Cluss; and he has a wunnerful fine-woolled breed o' sheep. They don't scale as much as ourn for the butcher, but a wunnerful fine wool. And he knows a hoss, granmam; and can ride one too. Though I wain't praise him for that; he's too venturesome." That in the tone of reproach with face half Arthur's, half her grandame's. "A sight too venturesome, too venturesome by hafe."

"I shall be careful now, Nell," said Arthur.

"Yo wain't," she insisted in tender contradiction; "not till some day yo mek me a sorry woman; or till, please God, yo're an oad man and mount at the block." She turned again to the dame and her speech was less fluent. "But he can be venturesome off'n hoss-back, granmam, an' all. He'll venture his life"

"Tut-tut, Nell," said Arthur.

"For a lass –"

"What of you, Nell?" said Arthur.

"For me, granmam."

"That's a good property," said the dame.

"And I will say this for him," said Tish from the rear, still holding an idle brush, "he's a lad as can stan' a sprinklin' o' small shot in's legs and theerabouts wi'out malice."

"That's another good property," said the dame; "them's all good properties. Still I like a rough hand mysen; it seems more clingy."

"And to my mind," said Tish, "he's four inch short o' being a fair match for our Nell,"

"Nay," said Nell quite eagerly, "Arthur's more nor my match a'ready. And he's a very good height-th, a very good height-th indeed; it's me that's a deal too lanky for a woman."

"Five sooner nor four. However if I'd meant to say oat again it, lass, I should ha' outed wee't first off. After all there may be little spunk in a big body and plenty on't in a little un."

"Be that as't may," said the grandmother, "he's gotten our Nell and she's not a wench to be gotten lightly."

The aged woman resting one skinny hand on each arm of her chair uprose to her feet. Her face was that of one near the term of life, one who has seen more sorrow than joy, so takes even the joy apprehensively.

"Sir, a many men ha' coom to me wi' th' same soft tale, coortin' one or another o' my gells."

She stood silent. Perhaps she was adding up the performance of those same gallant wooers and arithmetically subtracting it from their larger promises. She continued:

"Thisn's the last, the youngest, the best; the last I hae to give or to refuse."

Her sightless hand sought something; Nell guided it to what it sought, the comfort and support of her own arm.

"She can bake an' she can brew, she can plough an' she can milk; she's been to school. That sampler i' th' room she worked wi' her own hand. She ne'er gied me a wry word in 'er life. We spell her name wee a haitch." She turned again to Nell. "Did yo say his name were William?"

"No, granmam, Arthur, Arthur Skrene."

"It's none the worse. 'Twere a William as married Susan. Ah well! Do yo promise me, Arthur Skrene, as yo'll behave well to my little lass?"

"So help me God," said Arthur fervently.

With the touch of his right hand on the hand which Nell still cherished he enforced his oath on the blind understanding. Whereat a wan pleasure, as it were a shadow of light, passed across the aged face; passed and left nothing but the former ashen pallor. So on a day of shifting shadows something a little more of the sun, a little less of the clouds may flit athwart the wintry furrows, scarcely seen, straightway unseen.

"Maybe," she said, "yo'll behave bad to her after all. Then yo'll say God didn't help yer, and so back out on't."

"No," answered Arthur, "I should make no such excuse, for it would be a devilish lie."

The old woman sat down again silent and sightless. Tish put by her idleness and her brush, took a simmering iron pot from the hob, and pouring linseed pottage therefrom into a bucket began to mix it with last night's milk. Nell expected her to recur to the loss of the warm new milk which should have gone to the mess, good for the fattening calf, but she said not a word. A chair was placed for Arthur in the chimney. Nell stood by.

CHAPTER XXXIV

THE LITTLE QUEE CALF

"Yo don't know," said Nell, "how 'tis I've been kep' in all the week wi' a sprained knee."

"You didn't tell me that," said Arthur.

"I never knowed mysen while mornin'."

She then in spite of Arthur's dissuasions related how she had been rescued from the lynchers. Tish strode up with a hand all mealy and offered it to Arthur.

"Arthur Skrene," she said, "it's high time uz two shook hand and was friends."

"Nothing," said Arthur, "could please me better."

They shook hands, and if the grip of Tish's friendship was as strong as that of her hand it was something inestimable.

"I was only paying a little back," said Arthur, "of what I owed."

"Dal me," said Tish, "if this don't mek one ashamed o' being so big. It's as I said; sperrit may be spreed thick on a little bit or thin ower a gret hunch."

The grandmother's face was like a rain-dashed window-pane when the sun is promising to get the better of the clouds.

"What didsta say he were called?" she asked.

"Arthur, granmam," said Nell.

"I get strangely mixed up, haein' hed so many. Arthur." Her blind face was turned towards him. "Yo wain't vally an oad woman's blessing at the same market as a young woman's fancy."

"I should value it highly, grandmother."

"Yo hae it." She stretched out each skinny hand and her voice put on a new emotion consonant with the tear-splashed face. "My blessing on thee, my son. Nay, nay, who am I? *God's* blessing rest on thee, night and day."

Her hands dropped down on her knees. Arthur durst not answer.

"'Twill mek my daily prayer that much longer," she said in a voice less upraised. "Next hern."

The life which had momentarily disturbed the withered face receded inwards to the more vital parts. The wrinkled skin again hung flaccid about the toothless mouth.

"What mun I larn to say i'stead o' Nell Rideout?"

The rose on Nell's cheeks deepened, but she did not answer.

"Tell her, Nell," whispered Arthur.

But the rose only deepened yet the more.

"Tell her yoursen, lad," said Tish from the other side of the room. "It's a cowardice that a maid suffers from. I hae felt it mysen."

Then Nell, not to be charged with cowardice, did a bold thing, but shamefacedly.

"Say Nell Skrene, granmam," she said. "But not yet."

"Nell Skrene," said the old woman.

She mused awhile on the strangeness of it; then murmured:

"A change o' names is a terrible thing!"

Thereafter she sat silent and sightless. Nell thought of her for a moment, then Arthur's hand touched hers and she forgot her. The lovers went aside to the window; the old woman was left to her thoughts. She sat by the fire and stroked her knees with her trembling hands, as though she were smoothing her emotions into satisfaction, or at least into quiet. Tish filled the kettle from the water bucket in the dairy and set it on the fire, flung a white cloth over the centre table, made a rattle of knives and forks and plates.

The lovers stood by the window, hand not clasping hand for shame's sake, but just in contact. They stood enjoying the delicious uncertainty of that hand's-touch never quite withdrawn, never more than just perceptible. They could not see the sun – the pigs routing among the muck and straw of the yard were still in the shadow of the house and stabling – but they could perceive its pleasant effects in the flushed tiles of the outbuildings, in the uplighting of the soft weather-stained browns of the barn thatch, in the silvery glistening of the stacks, in the shiny greyness of the one leafless aspen visible between, in the hoary emerald shimmer of the strip of dewy herbage beyond the gate, in the graduated haziness of the hills, the dappled whity-blue of the sky. The moon being searched for was still visible, beautiful still in her serene acceptance of eclipse. It is abominable being out of doors to hear a bird sing in a house; being in a house it is sweet to hear a bird sing out of doors. It chants of what is not actual to the eye and is therefore the more inward to the mind.

After a while Nell started into recollection, withdrew her hand from Arthur's with quick ashamed reluctance, and began to assist Tish in the preparation of breakfast. Arthur from the window watched with pleased eye her movements, quick, certain, wellrounded, with an untamed naturalness which made them in all their haste never once angular or ungraceful. Now and again she caught his eye and was stayed for a minute, lost, as though she were saying to herself, "Is it true?" Then she remembered shamefacedly and put down what she was carrying or sped the faster after what she was fetching. The grandmother was but as one of the darker shadows in the corners; Tish though so large was only noticeable for her opacity when she intercepted his view of Nell, making brief eclipse.

After a while Tish said to Arthur in her abrupt way, "Mebbe yo'd like to stop to breakfast wee's? Yo can if yo like. We've nubbut bacon."

Arthur said that was what he liked best and thanked her gratefully. Nell skimmed across the floor to the dairy. As she returned bearing the bread on its snow-white platter she whispered to Tish, with her eyes on Arthur to see if he were listening:

"Let's hae the blue plates, Tish, and the best knives and forks."

"When I want your interference, child," said Tish sharply but not sourly, "I'll ax for't."

She cut rashers from a well-streaked flitch of bacon and covered the frying-pan with them; not the hasty merchandise of the shop but bacon deliberately bred, fed, killed and cured. Soon a pleasant sizzle made concert with the kettle's song, and a rich unctuous odour filled the room putting the last edge upon hungry appetites. Nell passed close by Arthur on occasion or in mere need of it. For an instant the tips of her fingers touched the tips of his and the pleasure of the contact changed their faces. They thought they had done it secretly, but Tish saw and it vexed her recollections.

"Eh, lass, eh, lad," she said, "it's all very well so long as it ho'ds, this looking and longing, this gawping and gawming; but what'll come on't all, d'ye think, after twelve month o' matrimony?"

"The same or better, Mrs. Gillott," said Arthur boldly.

"I hain't fun' it so. Look at me; I ain't amiss to look at e'en now, when I'm dressed up; the lad I chose stood six foot two in's stocking-feet and spoke me fair. Twelve month on't were enough for me, and more nor enough."

"I'm sorry your experience has been so unhappy," replied Arthur with remarkable moderation as he thought, "but that ever incompatibility of temper should cause such a division between Nell and me –"

"Man alive! Incompatibility o' temper? 'Twarn't that as parted Ted Gillott and me; it were our tempers being so wunnerfully alike."

"Our tempers aren't alike," said Nell. "Arthur's is worse nor mine – much worse. So there's no fear o' that."

"Have I the worse temper?" said Arthur, a little surprised at bottom. "Well, we'll try it with a curb."

Perhaps the prick of Tish's remembrance had stirred her to a quicker perception of those languorous meetings of the lovers' eyes; she said to Nell in that sharp authoritative way of hers:

"Put your hat on and goo and show him the little quee cauf."

Nell's eyes modestly consulted Arthur's.

"I should very much like to see it," he said.

She did not throw on again the hood she had just taken off, nor reach down the sunburnt harvest-hat which hung on the wall, she ran across the kitchen and up the stairs, opened a door, put her head into a room, and in a moment of incredible shortness came down again with a deepened blush on her cheeks and a fresh white-strawed blue-ribboned thing crowning her head. It was her second-best, good enough almost to go to Sunday meeting in, almost too good for a week-night service. It might reasonably have been expected that Tish would have said something, but she did not; proof that there is no temper in the world which can be called certain. Nell tripped back from the threshold to whisper in her sister's ear:

"Don't forget the best knives and forks and the blue plates."

Tish's temper was only dormant; it was roused by the provocation.

"Is this breakfast," she said back, "your consarn or mine? It it's yourn clam ho'd o' this frying-pan and I'll goo and show the man the little quee cauf."

The little quee calf was in the long range of stabling on the other side of the yard. Thither the lovers went, and we may suppose if we like that they gave her due attention and admiration; stroked her silky hide and let her mumble their hands between her toothless gums; but they must have found time for something else, for only a few minutes and Arthur was saying:

"Darling, there's this advantage in my being a little under-sized for you."

To make sure however he again compared their respective heights by the readiest and surest of methods, juxtaposition. We may believe he made the most of his inches, we may surmise that she did not of hers; or if she did it happened that she stood in the gutter. Anyhow as they were then chins and noses and the lips between them were perfectly on a level. To confirm it the acutal contact that ensued was hardly necessary.

"I don't have to stoop for this as most men do." The greyhound bitch came down to greet her mistress, delicately treading the uneven pavement with ladylike composure, but finding her presence unheeded lay down under the nearest manger too proud to court notice or show jealousy.

"Yes, yo do stoop to kiss me," said Nell gravely; "I'm an ignorant person to pretend to be the wife o' such as yo."

"You're talking about dress, Nell, frippery which anybody's money may buy, with something inside to walk them about. There's a woman in this;" he touched Nell's country-made bodice with a caress, "and that's unpurchasable. Do you know who taught me that?"

"No."

"You did, Nell. How long have I been – a year and a half? Not so much as that – at Blidworth? You must be a rare school-mistress, Nell. I went to school in Kent for nine years and learnt nothing in comparison."

The lovers sat on a heap of straw in the nearest corner of the stable. The half-closed doors secured them from outward observation; the chain-jangling horses champed their provender and minded their own business. The rapid gradation of gloom down the long shed was such that Captain's dark brown seemed a lighter hue than Tidy's bay.

All along the roof there was a timid flutter of light under the tiles. Arthur took possession of Nell's waist; and the time went by unheeded, while Tish patiently kept breakfast waiting and the grandmother sat by the fire stroking her knees.

Said Nell, "I hain't thanked yer yet."

"What for? Oh, if you talk of that, here are five months gone and you yet unthanked; you must think me dreadfully remiss."

"There's no need, love."

"Neither for you nor me?"

"No, not now."

"It would be as if we thanked ourselves. Or if we must be thanked –"

How the time sped! The minutes had not the winged duration of clock-measured seconds.

Said Arthur, "You asked me a question – do you remember? – the other night, which I promised to answer and haven't done."

Said Nell, "There's no need; I know."

"Perhaps you knew then."

"Maybe; but knowing now and knowing then are such different things."

Nell espied the soft liquidity of the bitch's eyes under the manger. At her beck the animal with a dog's forgiveness immediately rose, with a delicate shiver flung from her fine coat the particles of chaff which adhered to it, and stepped daintily forth as though it were the first opportunity she had given her mistress of greeting her.

"Good-morning, Treasure, my pretty," said Nell laying hot cheek against cold moist muzzle, a pleasant difference.

"Een't she a beauty?" she said to Arthur. "Her head's like a snake's, her feet's like a cat's, her back's like a beam – but her tail's like no rat's that ever I seed."

So she chatted, finding also a cool pleasure in the brief drop to a trivial topic, in the restful return to what she had said yesterday. But what was chief in her mind would not consent to be secondary on her tongue for more than a minute or two.

"This is my sweetheart, pet," she said. "Love, this is Treasure, my grew."

"Oh, she is your treasure, is she?" said Arthur affecting to sniff.

"Tsh! love," whispered Nell, "it's nubbut a name." Then to the hound who held back from the introduction. "Nay, if yo love me yo moot love him. Your hand, my cant; like a lady."

The bitch made no clamorous protest, displayed no shallow-hearted fussiness as the human female might have done, but just submitted to the introduction with polite formality; then lay down the other side of Nell, out of sight of the male supplanter, and closing her eyes with proud delicacy gave her mistress an excuse for forgetting her.

But at length and at last the lovers had risen, at last they were going. No, Arthur held her back from the open door and strained her in his arms and called her witch.

"For witch you are," he said.

"Ay, just as much as yo're a wiseman."

"Do you still deny that you have witched me?"

"I deny noat; yo suld know. But if I can witch I can unwitch. Shall I? Yo've nubbut to say the word."

"Nay, that is impossible. Witch though you be you cannot do that."

Tish confronted them, at the door.

"Yo've bin a strange while," she said. "I meant yo to hae your bite and sup i' quiet. Now the men's coomed in, and Lambert's got a bad co'd in's head – the man's allus got summat – and Dick's barking like a dog, and Perry such a –" She stopped abruptly; perhaps she perceived that her reproof did not stay on the faces of the reproved; she added less tartly: "But yo did as yo'd a mind." Then with completed magnanimity: "And yo'd the raight on't."

However she had laid the round table for them separately by the fire with the best knives and forks and the blue plates. The two men and the boy ate by themselves at the oblong table under the window; with more constraint than usual in the shuffling of their feet and their continual demands for "A bit more, please." As they chewed they furtively eyed the separated couple. Lambert sniffed, the boy coughed, Perry smacked his lips as loud as a pistol; but Arthur made an excellent breakfast, talked with Tish about the curing of bacon and the value of sulphur to pigs; with the men about the fall of lambs, the top-dressing of wheat, the treatment of land that is tired of clover; with the grandmother about the great cheese riot at Nottingham Goose Fair in '66. To Nell he said scarcely anything. She hardly spoke, but did not appear to eat the more for that.

The meal was ended, the men shuffled off. Dick however was detained by Tish, who in a voice as loud as insult said:

"Afore yo goo to-night, lad, yo've got to coom to me an' say, 'Missis, yo're to gi'me summat to do my cough good.' Just like that. Can yo remember it?"

"Ay," said the lad timidly, looking for the door.

"Then mind yo do."

The lad hurried off glad it was no worse. Nell accompanied Arthur to the door. The musy languor of her eyes was giving place to their usual work-a-day outlook, seriously business-like.

"What are you going to do now?" said Arthur lingeringly, perhaps hoping for some prolongation of their love-idling.

"I've gotten a brede of woats to sow in the New Piece."

Arthur's quick imagination pictured her to him with the sunlight among her hair, the wide shallow hopper bound in front of her and her skirts shortened. He saw her boldly stride across the well-cleaned land; with a strong free action she swayed her body and tossed her giving hands to right, to left, more truly than any poet's rhythm. He would fain have stood and watched her corporeally, near enough to see the grey of her eyes as she turned them on him and the change of her cheeks.

"And what are yo agate on this morning?"

He was roused out of his dream.

"First of all I've got to pick out a hog for killing; then I shall go down and judge if that lowlying end of Hollow Close is in fettle yet for the plough; then I must ride to Johnson the butcher's to witness the weighing of a bullock, and call at the whittaw's and order a new collar."

"Yo might ax him to let uz hae our pad back as soon's he can. What shall yo ride?"

"Nancy."

"She's a quiet mare," said Nell with obvious satisfaction. "I like a bit o' mettle my sen when I'm out for the day; but I don't believe i' doing business on a hurricane."

She went round the corner with him, qualified her plain "good-morning" with the addition "love," watched him to the first gate, where he turned and waved his hand for the fourth time, then went back purposeful of the day's work. The sunlight possessed already one half of the yard, dividing it diagonally with the shade. The pigs basked in it with well-fed indolence. Nell felt its warmth even under the shadow of the house.

"An uncommon fine day, miss, for the time o' year," said Lambert from the barn-door.

Nell surprised him with the heartiness of her assent.

"I think it's the finest day that ever I seed."

CHAPTER XXXV

THE FULL STOP

ON the foregoing Sunday Josh Jowers had appeared at church with a shred of crumpled crape tagged to his hat. Left a free man by Posh's violent death he regularly occupied a seat in Lois's pew, and was ever after less drunk and more washed on Sundays than other days. In the fall of the year Arthur Skrene married Nell Rideout. In the early spring they heard that Tant had sailed for Portugal among the numerous drafts dispatched to recruit Wellington's army for the impending campaign. But now that this book is wearying to a close is not the time to enlarge on military adventures. He shared the toils and dangers of his regiment in that famous march by the rugged margin of the Douro, among the tremendous Pyrenees and the swift rivers of France. He wrote his first letter, hopeful and ill-spelt, from Tarouca soon after his arrival.

"DEAR FRENDS AT HOME,

"By God's favour we have landed safe on this furren shoar. We had a tremendus storm by the way in the bay of Bisky witch all but riv the ship a-two. At witch being night I boath trembled and admired. Next morning we gave the dry land a harty cheer though it was nubbut a fow barren rock. Now I long to be on the moove. The hills here are bigger than at home and the men smaller. How soon we are to march and wheer every drummer boy in the army knows, better may be nor the Duke himself. Well, the sooner the better. They say the generals of the French army hafe of them were as low or lower nor what I am at the start. If you should come across Mr. Skrene or Miss Skrene pray mind them that Ime there obeedant sarvent. I am granman and sisters,

"Yr. dutyfull granson and affex. brother,
"A. RIDEOUT.

"P.S. But doan't shew this the spelling neads mending and I've a very bad pen."

Nothing more was heard from him until the receipt of a letter dated from Ookray (possibly Urcuray) the 2nd of February of the following year, shortly before the Duke made his final thrust at his famous antagonist.

"DEAR NELL,

"So far I am alive by God's will though in the midst of death. I wunner wether you bought Johnson's filly. If the war's so nigh an end as they say horse flesh will drop in vallew. Our ridgment had some sharp work at Vitoria I thought I had much to write but my thoughts seem far from my pen. The mountains and rivers in this country are a sight to see. It's a strange thing as a free man should be so ready to hopple himself. A hoss would have more sense if he had the freedom. I have been made sergeant on the field of battle and reduced to the ranks again for a hasty word. I care not a hop for that. A sergeant here Ime most frendly with and he is a man has enjoyed that honnour this twenty year without losing it or adding to it. The officers all but one look skew at me. It began with my refusing to faight Tom Wild of the 96th for ten pounds, which they genrously offered to subscribe. Don't think but what I continue to be prouder of being an English private nor a french anything. These Spanyards too are a come day go day people. I think that is all. The enclosed is for Miss Skrene if you should chance on an opportunity to give it to her without offense.

Your affex. brother,
"A. RIDEOUT."

The following was enclosed:

"MADAM,

"I entreet pardon for this great libberty. We are very short of comfort in this furren land. The weather also continews very bad. Thank God I am not in the cavelry else I think these roads (so they call them) would break my heart. We have fought often and never been bet. There is a young leftnent in my company very much my frend. Others officers less frendly. I pray every night but only (I trust) for what it behooves me to pray. I have so far been fortunat that I have not been wownded save a few trifles. Soon we shall be at it again. God is our help and hope. The wimmen of this country are not so fair as our English wimmen by much. But the goss grows here too. At oppertunity I go and look at it. War is a dredfull trade to anybody not born and bred a butcher. I have writ more and less than I meant but this is a very bad pen. They use cheefly mules which same have sure feet but unsure tempers. Now I must conclude or be wearysome."

    Madam,

       "Your obedient servant to command

          "and prisoner at large,

            "A. RIDEOUT."

Over which letters there needs no pause, save perhaps for a momentary wonder how it was that the "obeedant sarvent" of the first should have been so perfectly corrected in the last.

Two months later the final unnecessary battle of Toulouse was fought. There by the bridge of Jumeaux headstrong Picton threw away four hundred men of the third division including the colonel of the 45th. In course of time Nommer Brooks and Jack Whitehead returned home, but Tant Rideout did not return; he had stayed there. When the laggard certainty of it arrived Nell kept her own tears back and took her husband aside and said:

"I moot tell Loie alone."

Arthur made a look do for many words.

"Ay, 'tis so."

"I feared it."

"I've often wunnered how 'twould end. And now 'tis ended."

And Sarah Wilkinson had something to say because Lois Skrene wore crape of the same depth as the sisters of the deceased.

THE END

GLOSSARY

Chapter II
Wetchud   Wet-shod

Chapter III
Ep'n   Handy
Gos-hawking   Idly gaping or staring
Heder or sheder   Male or female
Fast   Engaged, busy
Grew   Greyhound
Stret   Tight, narrow
In ("in wee 'm")   Be intimate with
Lumber   Bother

Chapter IV
Stawed   Stalled, satiated

Chapter VI
Gainer   Nearer, more direct

Chapter VII
Dallicked   Spoilt with rough wear
While   Until
Napern   Apron
Fowest   Ugliest
Cluss   Close (i.e. a close)

Chapter VIII
Hutt   Hurt

Chapter IX
Argy-bargy   Dispute

Chapter X

Whilst	Until
Pike	Spy
Purr	Peer
Gauze	Gaze
The same wadd	The same sort
Whittaw	Saddler
Wankling	Weakly
Blether	Bladder
Franzy	Hot-tempered

Chapter XI

Windered	Winnowed
Wetchud	Wet-shod
Fause	Crafty

Chapter XII

Wakken	Wide-awake, knowing
Jannocky	Fair

Chapter XIII

Yek	To jerk

Chapter XIV

Tisicky	Queasy
Fow	Ugly

Chapter XV

Boafin	Simpleton

Chapter XXI

Dawling	Tedious

Chapter XXV

Bos'ell's	Gypsy's
Dog-dorum	Dog-fancier
Sipe	Ooze
Stawed	Satiated

Chapter XXVI

Hap	Wrap
Glegged	Glimpsed
Raffle	Ravel
Pithers	Pesters
Jot	Jolt
Stret	Tight
Cadling	Dandling

Chapter XXVII

While	Until
Throng	Busy
Erklin'	Cowering shiveringly
Gainest	Nearest, most direct

Chapter XXVIII

Wezzling	Harum-scarum
Cant	Pet, indulged child
Scaddle	Timorous
Scrooched	Crouched
Slithering	Working slackly
Braungein'	Swaggering
Fetch	A crafty scheme
Belders	Bellows

Chapter XXIX

Fow-convenience	Inconvenience
Splauge	Ostentation
Mottled	Muddled
Scaddle	Skedaddle
Gawp	Gape
Jannock	Fair

Chapter XXX

Hotchel	Hobble
Fullock	Great impetus

Flusker	Fluster
Pick	Slip

Chapter XXXI

Bods'orth	Bottesford
Brede	Breadth

Chapter XXXII

Swaling	Wasting away
Argy-bargy-in'	Disputing
Founder	Hurry
Out o' the gate	Out of the way
Pike	Peer
Busk	Bush

Chapter XXXIII

Gleg	Glance
Lommox	Clumsy person

Chapter XXXIV

Gawping and gawming	Gaping and gazing
Clam	Seize
Cant	Pet
Brede	Breadth

Compiled from The Nelson Library edition

AFTERWORD
Tony Simpson

'When the dead go unread ... there's gonna be trouble!'

Margaret Cavendish and Geoffrey Trease, Mary Howitt and William Booth stalk the pages of *Dawn of the Unread,* a collection of graphic stories printed and published in Nottingham in 2016 to mark the city's new status as a UNESCO City of Literature.

These four diverse Nottingham writers rub shoulders with Lord Byron, D H Lawrence, Stanley Middleton and Alan Sillitoe, who are probably better known outside the Trent Valley. Alma Reville (Lady Hitchcock), born in St Ann's, inspires the comic 'Psychos', in which she meets Kerrie-Ann Hill, a little the worse for wear, at a rave in a disused library in the north of Nottingham. They share experiences of being in relationships with 'challenging partners'. Kerrie-Ann features in Nicola Monaghan's acclaimed novel, *The Killing Jar.* 'Psychos' is written by Nicola and drawn by Judit Ferencz.

Dawn of the Unread started life as an online serial, as James Walker explains in his Introduction. Nottingham Trent University nurtured the project, which won *The Guardian* University Award in 2015. But before it became an online serial, *Dawn* broke as an idea in James's head, 'initially created as a reaction to libraries being closed down'. He points out that the UK is 'the twenty-second most illiterate country out of twenty-four industrialised nations'. Notwithstanding its fine Library Service, Nottingham has a deep literacy problem across the age range. Its emphasis on addressing this challenge underpinned the city's successful bid for UNESCO Creative City status.

If the idea and inspiration for *Dawn of the Unread* came from James Walker, the digital production is the work of Paul Fillingham and his company, Thinkamigo. As

Christmas 2016 approached, Paul visited Russell House in Old Basford to pick up some copies of *Dawn* as presents. Whilst chatting, he mentioned *Forest Folk*, a novel by James Prior, and its Luddite/Napoleonic Wars context. As a native of Blidworth, Paul's head teacher at primary school made sure her charges knew of the novel and why the local public house came to be called 'Forest Folk'. I recall seeing the pub on occasional visits to Blidworth, prior to its demolition in 2005 to make way for Tesco Express. Some of the stained glass from the pub, depicting scenes in the novel, is preserved in Blidworth Village Hall. But I had never heard of the book.

We quickly tracked down a copy of the original Heinemann edition of *Forest Folk*, published in London in 1901. Instantly, I was drawn in, particularly by the vernacular, which echoes down the generations, still to be heard in some mouths. The story is pacy and the characters surprising and interesting. The backdrop of the Napoleonic Wars and Ned Ludd (who doesn't get sympathetic treatment) give the novel a grand sweep which suggests wider forces at work in people's lives.

So it is that the dead no longer go unread, in the spirit of *Dawn of the Unread*. Nicole Morris joins me in this endeavour, giving the project the thumbs-up and compiling the partial glossary based on a later edition. Bromley House Library, Nottingham's 200-year-old subscription library, published its own edition in 1946, preceded in 1925 by the Mansfield & Kirby Chronicle Edition (double column, economy price), 'A Fine Copyright North Notts Novel'.

Prior ended his days in the village of Bingham, in the Notts countryside on the road to Grantham. I well remember Lushai Cottage in Fisher Lane, up the road from the Wheatsheaf pub with its friendly back room. Prior hadn't moved far from his early home in Mapperley Road, Nottingham. 'For these are streets of stories. This is a city of writing,' as James Walker reminds us.